I0599357

The World Above the World
and Other French Scientific Romances

also by Brian Stableford:
The Empire of the Necromancers (1: The Shadow of Frankenstein; 2: Frankenstein and the Vampire Countess; 3: Frankenstein in London); The New Faust at the Tragicomique; Sherlock Holmes and the Vampires of Eternity; The Stones of Camelot; The Wayward Muse.

also translated and introduced by Brian Stableford:
Anonymous: Sâr Dubnotal vs. Jack the Ripper; *Anthologies*: News from the Moon; The Germans on Venus; The Supreme Progress; The World Above the World; *Cyprien Bérard*: The Vampire Lord Ruthwen; *Richard Bessière*: The Gardens of the Apocalypse; *Félix Bodin*: The Novel of the Future; *André Caroff*: The Terror of Madame Atomos; *Charles Derennes*: The People of the Pole; *Henri Duvernois*: The Man Who Found Himself; *Achille Eyraud*: Voyage to Venus; *Henri Falk*: The Age of Lead; *Paul Féval*: Anne of the Isles; The Black Coats (1: 'Salem Street; 2: The Invisible Weapon; 3: The Parisian Jungle; 4: The Companions of the Treasure; 5: Heart of Steel; 6: The Cadet Gang); John Devil; Knightshade; Revenants; Vampire City; The Vampire Countess; The Wandering Jew's Daughter; *Paul Féval, fils*: Felifax, the Tiger-Man; *Octave Joncquel & Théo Varlet*: The Martian Epic; *Jean de La Hire*: The Nyctalope vs. Lucifer; The Nyctalope on Mars; Enter the Nyctalope; *Gabriel de Lautrec*: The Vengeance of the Oval Portrait; *Georges Le Faure & Henri de Graffigny*: The Extraordinary Adventures of a Russian Scientist Across the Solar System (2 vols.); *Gustave Le Rouge*: The Vampires of Mars; *Jules Lermina*: Panic in Paris; Mysteryville; The Secret of Zippelius; *Marie Nizet*: Captain Vampire; *Henri de Parville*: An Inhabitant of the Planet Mars; *Gaston de Pawlowski*: Journey to the Land of the 4th Dimension; *P.-A. Ponson du Terrail*: The Vampire and the Devil's Son; *Maurice Renard*: The Blue Peril; Doctor Lerne; The Doctored Man; A Man Among the Microbes; The Master of Light; *Albert Robida*: The Clock of the Centuries; The Adventures of Saturnin Farandoul; Chalet in the Sky; *J.-H. Rosny Aîné*: The Givreuse Enigma; The Mysterious Force; The Navigators of Space; Vamireh; The World of the Variants; The Young Vampire; *Han Ryner*: The Superhumans; *Jacques Spitz:* The Eye of Purgatory; *Kurt Steiner*: Ortog; *Villiers de l'Isle-Adam*: The Scaffold; The Vampire Soul; *Philippe Ward & S. Miller*: The Song of Montségur.

The World Above the World
and Other French Scientific Romances

translated, annotated and introduced by
Brian Stableford

A Black Coat Press Book

English adaptation and introduction Copyright © 2011 by
Brian Stableford.
Cover illustration Copyright © 2011 by Mandy.

Visit our website at www.blackcoatpress.com

ISBN 978-1-61227-002-9. First Printing. May 2011. Published
by Black Coat Press, an imprint of Hollywood Comics.com,
LLC, P.O. Box 17270, Encino, CA 91416. All rights reserved.
Except for review purposes, no part of this book may be reproduced or transmitted in any form or by any means, electronic or mechanical, including photocopying, recording, or by
any information storage and retrieval system, without permis-
sion in writing from the publisher. The stories and characters
depicted in this novel are entirely fictional. Printed in the
United States of America.

TABLE OF CONTENTS

Introduction 7
S. Henry Berthoud: *A Heavenward Voyage*...........................27
S. Henry Berthoud: *The Second Sun*.....................................40
René de Pont-Jest: *Mimer's Head*..70
Alphonse Daudet: *Wood'sTown* 112
Camille Flammarion: *Love Among the Stars* 117
Charles Recolin: *The X-Ray*...126
Michel Corday: *The Mysterious Dajan-Phinn*.....................134
Jules Perrin & H. Lanos: *The World Above the World*........171
André Mas: *Drymea, World of Virgins*................................258

Illustration by H. Lanos for *The Word Above the World*

Introduction

This is the fourth anthology of stories relevant to the early development of French speculative fiction that I have assembled for Black Coat Press, following *News from the Moon* (ISBN 9781932983890, 2007), *The Germans on Venus* (ISBN 9781935543566, 2009) and *The Supreme Progress* (ISBN 9781935558828, 2011).

I was prompted to compile another volume so quickly on the heels of the last because the opportunities for gaining access to relevant material have greatly improved over the last few years, thanks to the prolific addition of electronic versions of books and periodicals to the Bibliothèque Nationale's website *gallica*, which has made many texts readily available that are virtually impossible to locate in physical form. Although the last two texts come from reprint editions issued by the small press Apex International, which has also rescued numerous interesting texts from undeserved oblivion, the rest all come from *gallica*, and would have been very difficult to locate otherwise.

As with the earlier volumes, the present selection attempts to present a cross-section of relevant works, this time extending from the 1860s to the 1920s, but any limited sample of texts is bound to include a few duplicated themes and stances, and this one is no exception, in that several of the stories reproduced herein take a critical view of scientific and technological progress, often leveling similar skeptical charges against the notion the moral and scientific progress go hand in hand. Although the acute disenchantment of the final item is readily explicable in the fact that it was written in the immediate aftermath of the Great War, it is surprising how many premonitory echoes of its tacit lugubriousness can be found in the earlier stories, going all the way back to the earliest one of all. The latter is, admittedly, somewhat atypical of its period, but not so very atypical that no common threads extend therefrom through the darker aspects of the other stories bridging the parenthetical items, although their content is quite various.

The first story in the anthology, "Voyage au Ciel," here translated as "A Heavenward Voyage," was initially published in 1840 in *La Presse* and reprinted in 1841 in the *Revue des Feuilletons*. It was futuristic at the time, in that it features the invention of a dirigible balloon long before any such feat was actually achieved, and was probably inspired by the recent setting of a new altitude record for human ascent, which the device in the story is intended to smash. Its interest from the modern viewpoint, however, is not reliant on its modest and long-superseded innovations, but derives from the imaginative context in which it presents them, in which science and religion are juxtaposed in such a way as to draw comparisons and contrasts.

The protagonist of the story is introduced as a nephew of the religious poet Friederich Klopstock, the self-appointed "Christian Homer" who spent much of his adult life producing the Messianic epic *Messias*. His fictitious nephew also conceived messianic ambitions of a sort, which reach their critical moment when he makes a balloon ascent to what seem to him to be the limits of the physical world, beyond which lies a tacit barrier imposed of God to separate the Earth from "the Heavens"—not quite the innermost crystal sphere of Ptolemaic cosmology, or the realm of the quintessential aether, but something imaginatively and symbolically akin to it. For the hero, as a scientist, that barrier exists only to be crossed, and his inventive genius will give him the means to cross it: a determination that his neighbors—represented in the story by the local pastor—consider to be evidence of madness.

The symbolic scheme extends a little further than that, as the reader will discover, but its intricacies are perhaps less fascinating than its ambiguity. The history of 19th century French literature is, of course, littered with works of the "madman's manuscript" variety in which ambiguity is the privilege of unreliable narrators, but "Voyage au Ciel" is not a first-person narrative and its ambiguity is more objective. The question it raises is not so much whether Ludwig Klopstock is mad—of course he is—but the whether his madness might not, in some respect, be finer than sanity, and that question is not seriously affected, let alone undermined, buy the evasiveness of the ending. It is a question that recurs constantly, if sometimes mutedly, in most of the other stories making up the collection. That science is blasphemous is taken for granted; that scientific genius is intrinsically insane—in modern parlance, a variety of Obsessive-Compulsive Disorder—is also taken for granted. The key question remains, however, as to whether that blasphemous insanity, no matter how destructive it might be, has not something within it that is worth more than mundane aspirations and moribund delusions. Only a minority of the stories reproduced here, as in the entire spectrum of speculative fiction, come down firmly on one side or the other, but the real point of asking the question is not to supply a ready-made answer, but merely to wonder, anxiously.

The same nexus of ideas provides the narrative background to the second story by Berthoud reproduced here, "Le Second Soleil," translated as "The Second Sun," which juxtaposes a conventional sentimental romance with a chronicle of scientific madness, again leading to a conclusion whose ambiguity is deliberately complicated. I have not been able to trace the periodical publication of the story, but it was reprinted in book form in 1862 and the internal evidence—which is, admittedly, not entirely consistent—suggests that it was probably not written very long before that date. The consistency of attitude revealed by the two stories does, however, result from their selection as stories on the margins of speculative fiction; the author was remarkably versatile and prolific.

The author of "Voyage au Ciel" and "Le Second Soleil," S. Henry Berthoud, is not widely cited nowadays as a significant pioneer of speculative fiction, mainly because those of his works that contain a speculative component are, almost without exception, very tentative. By the time anyone was able to

9

conceive the idea of a history of speculative fiction, most of Berthoud's hypothetical inventions, like the dirigible balloon in the present story, had been actualized after a fashion, and his more ambitious guesses as to the fundamental nature of reality seemed naïve as well as obsolete. He does, however, remain a writer of some significance in the development of French scientific romance, especially in terms of its relationship to the popularization of science

Berthoud was born in Cambrai in 1804 and educated in medicine; some eulogistic accounts of his life and career identify him as a "medical pioneer" although there does not seem to be much evidence that his keen interest in science led to any significant discoveries in his own field. The only relevant publication listed in the catalogue of the Bibliothèque Nationale is an account of a cure supposedly effected by music, unless one counts his various endeavors in "marriage guidance." His medical career always had to compete with his literary interests; he published his first volume of poetry in 1822 and his first collection of short stories, *Contes misanthropiques* [Misanthropic Tales] in 1831. His first novel appeared in 1832. Much of his early work was set in Flanders, and his most significant work of the first phase of his career was a three-volume collection of *Chroniques et traditions surnaturelles de la Flandre* (1831-34). His interest in folklore and the supernatural is reflected in several of his early novels as well as many of his short stories.

Although did not give up on his literary endeavors there is something of a hiatus in the record of Berthoud's publications in volume form from the mid-1840s to 1860, doubtless assisted by the disruption of the marketplace caused by the revolution of 1848 and Louis Napoléon's subsequent *coup d'état*. He was presumably concentrating on his medical career for the interim. Whether or not he retired permanently from that career in 1860 I have not been able to ascertain, but the trickle of his publications turned abruptly into a flood in 1861, when he must have devoted himself full-time to writing for a decade. His interest in the supernatural was still strong—three of the numerous books he published in 1861 were *Le Dragon rouge, ou l'art de commander au demon et aux esprits infernaux* [The Red Dragon; or, The Art of Summoning the Devil and Infernal Spirits], *Le Grand Albert et ses secrets magiques et merveilleux* [Albertus Magnus and his Magical and Marvelous Secrets] and *Le Baiser du diable* [The Devil's Kiss]—but it was his interest in science that really came to the fore in the second phase of his career.

In 1861, Berthoud began an annual series of *Les Petites chroniques de la science* [Little Chronicles of Science] which extended until 1872, and also published the first two of four volumes of *Fantaisies scientifiques de Sam* [Sam's Scientific Fantasies], the latter volumes of which followed in 1862. Each volume of the set runs to more than 400 pages; the whole assembly totals more than half a million words; the project must have been moderately successful, because the four volumes were reprinted in 1866-67. The two stories translated here were both included in the set, although they are not typical of what Berthoud meant by "scientific fantasies." Most of his science-based stories are not speculative fiction at all, but merely accounts of contemporary life whose characters have occasion to discuss recent scientific discoveries or to encounter some of the bizarre phenomena recently revealed by the rapidly-expanding database of scientific discovery.

The "Sam" named in the title of the four-volume collection is Berthoud himself, whose first name was Samuel, although it is worth noting that he had published *Les Histoires de mon oncle Samuel* [Uncle Samuel's Stories] in 1845. He followed up the four-volume set with *Contes du Dr. Sam* [Dr. Sam's Tales] (1862), whose inclusions are modeled on folktales, although not entirely innocent of scientific input, and he also reproduced selections from their contents, along with some new material, in *Le Monde des insectes* [The World of Insects] (1864), *Les Féeries de la science* [The Enchantments of Science] (1866) and *L'Esprit des oiseaux* [The Spirit of the Birds] (1867). Each of the four volumes of *Fantaisies scientifiques* had been carefully categorized; the first volume containing sections headed "Entomologie" (7 stories), "Botanique" (15) and "Inventeurs et Savants" (4), the second "Reptiles" (4), "Mammifères et Oiseaux" (10), "Physique et Chimie" (5) and "Industrie" (3), the third "Négoce et métiers" (4), "Médecine" (6), "Minéralogie" (4) and "Ethnologie" (4) and the fourth "Archéologie" (4), "Voyageurs" (2), "Martyrs" (9) and "Histoire" (3).

Berthoud might well have planned to expand the contents of several more of the categories identified in the *Fantaisies scientifiques* into entire volumes, but this prolific period of endeavor only lasted a little over ten years; after *Soirées du Dr. Sam* [Dr. Sam's Soirées] (1871) and the final volumes of the *Petites chroniques*, he published very little that was new, although *Histoires et romans de Vegétaux* [Stories and Romances of Vegetals] appeared in 1882. The probability is that his health had deteriorated, although he did not die until 1891.

Berthoud's prolific period coincided with a more general boom in the popularization of science, which had a considerable impact on the early development of French scientific romance. This was the decade in which Camille Flammarion first began to publish prolifically, experimenting with quasi-fictional frameworks in a spirit not dissimilar to Berthoud's, and the similarly prolific scientific journalist Henri de Parville undertook an experiment of his own in *Un Habitant de la planète Mars* (1865; tr. in a Black Coat Press edition as *An Inhabitant of the Planet Mars*, ISBN 9781934543470). Jules Verne's first novel, *Cinq semaines en ballon* (1863; tr. as *Five Weeks in a Balloon*) began life as a series of articles on the techniques of ballooning, before he was persuaded to turn it into an adventure story, and his second, *Voyage au Centre de la Terre* (1864; tr. as *Journey to the Center of the Earth*) drew so heavily on Louis Figuier's recent popularization of geology and paleontology, *La Terre avant le Déluge* (1863; tr. as *The World Before the Deluge*), that when Figuier issued a new edition of his book in 1867, Verne felt compelled to modify his text in order to keep abreast. The version of *Voyage au Centre de la Terre* that everyone reads today is the revised edition published in 1867, which differs significantly from the original; the original was never translated, so no English version exists.

Berthoud was acquainted with Figuier, who provided a preface to the final volume of the *Petites chroniques*, and was similarly enthused by the paleontological discoveries of the decade, including the unearthing by Jacques Boucher de Perthes of a human jawbone that supposedly, but controversially, provided the final proof that the antiquity of the human species extended far beyond Biblical chronology (it was ultimately revealed to have been a hoax, but not until genuine finds had been made). Berthoud produced two books dramatizing these discoveries, *L'Os d'un géant, histoire familière du globe terrestre avant l'homme* [A Giant's Bones: An Intimate History of the World Before Humankind] (1862) and *L'Homme depuis cinq mille ans* [Five Thousand Years of Humankind] (1865), the latter of which extends into the future, in the most adventurous of the author's speculative endeavors. Had Figuier reprinted any of Berthoud's work under the heading of *romans scientifiques*, which he attached to all the *feuilletons* reprinted in his popularization of science magazine, *Le Science illustrée*, founded in the late 1880s, Berthoud might have received a little more credit for his early endeavors in the field, but they probably seemed a trifle outdated by then. I hope to repair the omission by compiling a more extensive collection of his work, representing the whole spectrum of his relevant endeavors, next year.

The third story in the present volume, "La Tête de Mimer" by René de Pont-Jest, here translated as "Mimer's Head," first appeared in the September 1863 issue of the *Revue Contemporaine*. It also has some connection with the boom in the popularization of science and its extension into scientific romance, in that its author began legal action against Jules Verne, alleging that *Voyage au Centre de la Terre* had plagiarized it. The legal action was eventually dropped, presumably because Pont-Jest was advised that he had no chance of winning the case, but it does seem probable, on comparing the opening sequences of the two stories, that Verne *had* read the Pont-Jest story and decided to borrow its central narrative device: a cryptogram written in runes that directs the solver to go to a particular Scandinavian mountain on a particular day and follow the direction given by a shadow at a specific time of day.

Beyond that initiating device, Pont-Jest's and Verne's stories are completely different—diametrically opposed, in ideological terms—but what adds an extra dimension of irony to the aborted lawsuit is that the continuations of both stories lend themselves just as readily to accusations of copycat behavior than the part they have in common. Louis Figuier did not seem to mind in the least, however, that Verne had paraphrased whole chunks of *La Terre avant le Déluge* while taking his characters through the Earth's geological strata to a fictional reproduction of the antediluvian world, and Pont-Jest was safe from any accusation that he had illicitly plundered the *Faustbuch* (1587), not so much because the latter's author, Johann Spies, was long dead, as because so many others had preceded him, from Christopher Marlowe to J. W. Goethe, that the game had become an honorable tradition. Pont-Jest would doubtless have claimed that his narrative transfiguration was more extreme than most—not least because of the remarkable way in which the Devil sets temptation before the central character—but the fact remains that his story is, in its essence and its ideology, a more straightforward ideological repetition of the original than its more famous predecessors.

Pont-Jest's full name was Louis-René Delmas de Pont-Jest (1830-1904) and in private life he preferred to be known as Léon Delmas. His first career was as a naval officer, and his early writings were mostly books on naval affairs and explorations, but once he had retired from the sea to become a full-time writer he dabbled in several kinds of popular fiction, including detective fiction. Scientific romance was, however, one genre of which he steered well clear, for reasons that "La Tête de Mimer" presumably spells out. Here, as in the original

Faustbuch and all of its previous transfigurations, the lure that the Devil lays down for the protagonist is that of curiosity, the promise of being able to know all the secrets of the natural world, but Pont-Jest inevitably has a sharper consciousness of the progress that science is making in pursuit of that quest, and a proportionately sharper sense of the danger it supposedly poses. Unlike S. Henry Berthoud, he knew almost nothing about the content of modern science, and was therefore content to be very vague about what there might be to be learned by means of study and experimentation, but that only made him more strident in shaping the moral and symbolism of his story.

What is interesting about "La Tête de Mimer" in the context of the present collection is how closely it echoes Berthoud's stories in its analysis of the social and psychological demands of scientific endeavor, and the crucial opposition that supposedly exists between the abstract intellectualism of the dedicated scientist and the requirements of intimate family life. There is a sense in which Pont-Jest's case has already been conceded in advance by such supposed champions of science as Berthoud, who accepts the judgment that scientists are, *ipso facto*, not merely tacitly Faustian in their hopes and dreams but quite insane in their obsessive antisocial proclivities. Berthoud—who, it will be remembered, titled the first collection of his own works *Contes misanthropiques*—is perfectly prepared to start from a defensive situation with a siege mentality, being content to wonder whether there might just be a glory in scientific madness unknown to sentimental Christian doctrine.

Pont-Jest was, of course, in the majority within the literary community, where suspicion of and hostility to science ran rife. *Conteurs* in general tended to favor homely morals, and wherever modern apologues strayed into the realms of fantasy and speculation, they tended to take the side of Berthoud's Stierna or Pont-Jest's Marguerite against the masculine dreamers who reject placid domesticity in favor of a higher dream. Disenchantment with the direction in which tech-

15

nological civilization seemed to be heading became common-place among its beneficiaries, and parables in the vein of "Wood'stown" by Alphonse Daudet (1840-1897) became in-creasingly common. I do not know whether it was the first appearance of the story, but it was included in the collection *Études et paysages* [Studies and Landscapes] (1873).

Daudet went on to become famous as a Naturalist writer in a milder and more nostalgic vein than the Goncourt brothers or Émile Zola, but did retain an interest in more imaginative work; the young writers he welcomed into the salon he hosted in his later years included Joseph-Henri Boëx, alias J. H. Ros-ny Aîné and Henri Ner, alias Han Ryner, both of whom made significant contributions to French speculative fiction,[1] and his son Léon wrote several fantastic novels. He remained poles apart, however, from such visionary writers as Camille Flam-marion, who used fiction almost exclusively as a vehicle for popularizing scientific ideas, especially in the field of astron-omy. Astronomy was one of the few fields omitted from Ber-thoud's list of category headings, although the central charac-ter off "Voyage au Ciel" is first and foremost an astronomer. Berthoud knew how difficult it was to incorporate the discove-ries of astronomy into a fictional framework if one were un-prepared to take the crucial step of trying to devise a plausible means of space travel. Flammarion was, however, unfazed by that difficulty, and quite prepared to lend the visionary jour-neys undertaken by his characters a supportive logic derived from spiritualism.

The Flammarion story reproduced here, "Un Amour des astres"—translated as "Love Among the Stars"—first ap-peared in the February 15 1896 issue of the *Nouvelle Revue*, and represents something of an afterthought to his earlier works in the same vein, most notably *Lumen*, the first version of which appeared in *Récits de l'Infini* (tr. as *Stories of Infini-*

---

[1] Han Ryner's *The Superhumans* (ISBN 9781935558774) and six volumes of the works of J.-H. Rosny Aîné are available in Black Coat Press editions.

ty) in 1872 before an expanded edition appeared separately in 1887, and the best-selling *Uranie* (1889; tr. as *Urania*). An earlier English translation of the present story appeared in the December 1896 edition of *The Arena* as "A Celestial Love," but I thought it worthwhile to produce a new one because the earlier one is so difficult to find.

Flammarion is, of course, at the opposite end of the ideological spectrum from René de Pont-Jest, but if Pont-Jest ever read this story it would not have upset his prejudices regarding the Faustian tendencies of scientists, and would only have confirmed his convictions regarding their insanity. Even Ludwig Klopstock might have regarded the hero's voyage into the Heavens as a step too far in terms of plausibility. With opposition so weak and exotic, it is hardly surprising to find far more verve, if not plausibility or moral integrity, in contemporary anti-scientific fantasies like Charles Recolin's "Le Rayon X," here translated as "The X-Ray" and initially published in the March 7, 1896 issue of the *Revue Bleue*, formerly known as the *Revue Littéraire et Politique*.

"Le Rayon X" is perhaps most interesting historically for the rapidity of its reaction to the discovery of X-rays by Wilhelm Roentgen in 1895—a discovery so sensational that it wrought a virtual revolution in the horizons of possibility envisaged by scientific romance, ushering in a new era of quasi-magical rays capable working of all kinds of miracles. Recolin's story is, however the first to imagine a human equipped with "X-ray vision" and to begin the exploration of the possible utilitarian and psychological consequences of such a faculty. Recolin was a Protestant minister, so it is not entirely surprising that he takes a dim view of the relevant potential, echoing Pont-Jest rather than Berthoud—and it is impossible to imagine that Berthoud could ever have weighed up the imaginative account-books is the same highly unbalanced way. Recolin wrote several novels, all now forgotten (some are missing even from the Bibliothèque Nationale's collection) and is remembered, if at all, only for a book of essays, *L'Anarchie littéraire* [Literary Anarchy] (1898), which complained bitterly about the supposedly anarchic condition of contemporary letters and predicted that Edouard Rod would one day be recognized as the greatest literary genius of the day.

The next story included in the anthology, "Le Mystérieux Dajan-Phinn,"—translated as "The Mysterious Dajan-Phinn"—first appeared in two parts in the April 14 and May 15, 1908 issues of *Je Sais Tout*, one of a new generation of French "middlebrow" magazines, which was specifically modeled on the English periodical *The Strand*. Like *The Strand, Je Sais Tout* gladly played host to several flourishing genres of popular fiction, giving pride of place to detective fiction, including stories featuring Maurice Leblanc's famous Arsène Lupin,[2] but by no means scorning scientific romance— although, as with *The Strand*, its editors soon decided that scientific romance was insufficiently popular and gradually de-emphasized it. The author of the present story, Michel Corday, was a prolific contributor to periodicals of that sort, but he soon learned that it was more profitable to concentrate on more popular genres, although he retained an interest in the genre in spite of the difficulty in marketing it, producing an offbeat thriller in collaboration with André Couvreur, *Le Lynx* (1911; tr. as *The Lynx*) and two quasi-Utopian futuristic fantasies.

There is a sense in which "Le Mystérieux Dajan-Phinn" harks back to the 1860s boom in the popularization of science, in that it refers to one of the great controversies of that decade, brought to a head by a presentation made to the Académie des Sciences in 1864 by Louis Pasteur, who claimed to have demolished Frédéric Pouchet's alleged experimental demonstration of the spontaneous generation of life by a process of "fermentation." Although it was a spectacular coup in terms of

---

[2] Several Arsène Lupin stories pitting the gentleman-burglar against Sherlock Holmes and Countess Cagliostro are available from Black Coat Press.

public relations, and is still held up today as a triumphant victory securing the "germ theory" against its inept competitor, the precise extent of the consequences of Pasteur's demonstration remained questionable, and modern commentators tend to forget that his primary motivation was his hatred of Darwinism, which he supposed to be dependent on spontaneous generation and which, therefore, he thought he had demolished along with the latter.

Corday's story is interested in the way in which "orthodox science" rejected the theory of spontaneous generation so conclusively that it began to dismiss any argument in favor of it *a priori*, regardless of any experimental support that such arguments might claim. In developing this theme, however, it is very noticeable that Corday is still working with the same assumptions that underlie Berthoud's stories, regarding the psychology of scientists and the incompatibility of scientific obsession with the joys of domestic life, and using those assumptions to generate the narrative tension of his melodrama.

The next story in the anthology, "Un Monde sur le monde"—translated as "A World Above the World"—was also announced for publication in *Je Sais Tout*, in 1907, which implies that a version of it might have been written before "Le Mystérieux Dajan-Phinn." It is not clear why it never appeared there—one of its authors, Jules Perrin, contributed a similarly cataclysmic fantasy, which began serialization later that same year, "L'Hallucination de Monsieur Forbe"—but it might have seemed a little too controversial, or a little too implausible, for the editor's taste. It is, at any rate, more reminiscent of garish pulp fiction than the slightly more sophisticated fare favored by *Je Sais Tout*. It eventually appeared in a more downmarket periodical, *Nos Loisirs*, in 12 parts, from November 13, 1910 to February 5, 1911.

It seems probably that Perrin was primarily responsible for the writing, as Lanos was a professional illustrator, although the latter did receive a joint by-line with E. M. Laumann for a subsequent futuristic novel and wrote his own text for two illustrated scientific romances for children. Biographical information on Jules Perrin is difficult to locate, partly because it is such a common name, but he appears to have been born in 1862 and published nothing more after the 1920s, most of his work consisting of pulpish adventure fiction.

"Un Monde sur le monde" carries forward the pattern of disenchantment with technological civilization and scientific discovery, but moves it into a more modern industrial context. It features the construction of what might have been a Utopian city, and puts the blame for its eventual ruination on the mad scientists whose work is primarily devoted to the development of sophisticated weaponry, which they yearn sadistically to see in use, but its misanthropy extends much further than that, seemingly considering human nature to be essentially vile and treacherous. It has to be admitted, however, that Aeria is surely the most ineptly-planned Utopia ever envisaged, as well as the most undiplomatic and aggressive—and when a belated attempt is made to repair its most obvious deficit, the strategy adopted is as monumentally idiotic as it is morally reprehensible. The design and fate of the hypothetical society surely reveals more about the psychology of the author than the supposed psychology of his anti-hero, and calls into question the continual suggestion that there might, after all, be something magnificent in the protagonist's patent insanity.

Despite its manifest logical flaws, however, "Un Monde sur le monde" is interesting as a early example of a subgenre that became surprisingly popular in the early decades of the twentieth century, in which scientific geniuses extrapolate their obsessive antisocial tendencies into the threat of violent opposition to the world that refuses understand them, for motives they consider virtuous, or at least justifiable. As usual throughout the early history of scientific romance, the image held up in contrast to the obsessive objectives of mad science is a preternaturally beautiful girl; the reader who starts at the beginning of the anthology will not be at all surprised, by the time the conclusion of its ultimate story is reached, to discover that, in spite of the extraordinary efforts made to shield her, the dream-girl in question eventually falls victim to the fate usually reserved for characters of her type in fiction of this sort.

Read with the benefit of hindsight, it is difficult not to find all kinds of premonitions of the Great War in "Un Monde sur le monde," as there are in the entire subgenre of future war stories that gradually became the hard core of the broader genre between 1870 and 1914. Long before the actual war mounted a spectacular demonstration of the manner in which technology had modified conflict and promised go modify it further, countless fictional Jeremiads had been produced in anticipation of that quasi-apocalyptic misery. It is hardly surprising, given this circumstance, that the actual war had such a devastating effect on the ideological and economic development of the genre, seemingly underlining all the anxieties that writers like Berthoud had broached in the early part of the 19th century, which none of their successors had ever shaken off or successfully countered. Scientific romance became almost unmarketable in France the 1920s, those works that did appear being driven to the margins of the genre as well as the marketplace. In slight compensation, however, some of the works that did contrive to appear were possessed of a truly bizarre eccentricity, and the final item in the present collection, *Drymea, monde de vierges*, first published in volume form in 1923, here translated as "Drymea, World of Virgins," is surely one of the most bizarre of all.

There is a sense in which the Utopian vision presented in Drymea stands in complete contrast to the image of the world presented in "Un Monde sur le monde," but in ideological terms, the two stories are in complete harmony, exhibiting a very similar and all-consuming misanthropy that bundles human science, industry and technology together in the same hateful package. Like his predecessors,[3] however, Mas sees the things he hates as quintessentially masculine, and, like them, he holds up as an opposing image a woman of preterna-

---

[3] I am assuming that André Mas was a man, although the person behind the pseudonym has never been identified.

tural beauty and virtue: his heroine, Hertha Helgar. Rather than leaving Hertha to suffer the slings and arrows of outrageous fortune that send most of her literary peers to the grave, however, Mas improvises a miracle by which, when she swallow poison after being consigned to a shell and fired from a huge gun, she is allowed to remain dormant during a long interstellar voyage. She finally ends up on the counterpart world of Drymea, in which sex has never been developed as an evolutionary strategy and masculinity, with all its hideous corollaries, is therefore absent.

Mas was by no means unfamiliar with the masculine aspects of scientific romance; before the war, when he was a member of a early rocket society, he had written *Les Allemands sur Vénus* (1913; tr. as the title story of the Black Coat Press anthology *The Germans on Venus*), a pulpish adventure story in which obsessive male scientists lead the conquest and colonization of a not-quite-virgin world whose evolution has run more or-less parallel to Earth's. The war must have chastened him considerably, however (although it is not entirely possible that the post-war works signed with the pseudonym are by a different hand) for his next work was a visionary poem, *Sous leur Double Soleil des Dryméens chantent* [Beneath their Double Sun the Drymeans sing] (1921), of which *Drymea* is an expansion of sorts. At least some of the conspicuous lack of narrative drive and coherency exhibited by *Drymea* is attributable to its origin as an adaptation to a poem, although Utopian fictions in general do tend to be undramatic and rambling. Its transition into prose demanded that more attention be paid to matters of explanation and rational underpinning, but it must be admitted that the author's attempts in that regard are distinctly weak-kneed, partly because of the logical difficulties involved and partly because of diplomatic difficulties.

The important difference between Drymea and previous account of parthenogenetic human societies, such as *Mizora* (1890) by the pseudonymous "Princess Vera Zaronovitch" and *Herland* (1915) by Charlotte Perkins Gilman, is that the earlier texts describe societies whose ancestors had two sexes, and whose parthenogenetic faculty is a relatively recent modification, while the entire sequence of Drymean animal evolution has been sexless. (Like most Utopias, Drymea is rich in flowers, so its plants presumably still have sex.) How this has happened is not clear, especially as Mas takes the trouble to stress that the general results of Drymean evolution have been milder than the effects of Earthly evolution because its species do not produce the surplus of offspring that gives rise to natural selection. What motor has led to the evolution of a quasi-human species thus remains unclear, although no suggestion is offered that it might have been the result of an arbitrary act of creation by the Drymean deity.

Presumably, Mas could, if he wished, have given more details of Drymean ecology and evolution, and his failure to do so is therefore one of his own imagination or inclination, but he was not in a position, in 1923, to go into much detail about certain other corollaries of his central hypothesis. Fiction still had strict standards of decency to observe; even back in the mid-19th century, S. Henry Berthoud had been able to publish marriage manuals tentatively describing the details of sexual intercourse, but he would never have been allowed to put the same details into his fiction, and things had not changed much in the subsequent decades. The whole point of Mas's story is the absence of the details in question, but it is an absence of which he cannot speak directly, even though it is the heart and soul of his narrative.

Drymeans, unlike the women of Mizora or Herland, are entirely innocent of sexual passion. No anatomical details can be provided, but we can probably take it for granted that one thing with which Drymean evolution did not equip them is a clitoris. The feelings they have for one another cannot be sexual; they cannot be lesbians, in the sense that the inhabitants of Mizora and Herland are able or condemned to be; nor, in spite of the language of the text, can they be "virgins" in the way that word is commonly defined, since it can have no counterpart in terms of their existence. By contrast, Hertha Helgar, in spite of being the most virtuous woman who ever lived on Earth, apparently not a lesbian by inclination, and very definitely a virgin, cannot escape the fact that she is innately equipped with sexual feelings. She might be able to rechannel those feelings in response to circumstance, redirecting them toward her own sex rather than the opposite one, but she cannot escape them. On Drymea, therefore, she is faced with a rather peculiar moral dilemma; she is capable of feeling passion for the Drymeans, but any such passion would be implicitly misdirected, because it cannot be reciprocated. How, then, can she conduct herself toward them, and what would be the consequences of her contact with them, if she permitted herself to express her innate passion?

As a personal problem that would be acute enough— although some readers might feel that, given the seeming amenability of Drymeans like Drythea, the problem is not as acute as she makes it out to be—but it is not just a personal problem. Indeed, it is a messianic problem, for the superior scientific and technological knowledge that Hertha brings to Drymea has the potential to transform Drymean society drastically. Can that transformation possibly be anything other than corrupting? Is there any way that the corollaries of masculinity still incarnate in Hertha—which supposedly include both the capacity to feel sexual passion and to develop scientific knowledge—can enhance Drymean perfection rather than undermining it? And if they cannot enhance it and make it stronger, what will happen to Drymean society if and when, however distantly in the future, the Drymeans encounter a human race that is akin to Hertha's rather than their own, or shaped in some other way by the urgency of natural selection?

The ideological conundrums lurking in the background of "Voyage au Ciel" still remain in *Drymea*, drastically recast and reformulated, but still, in essence, the same. Is science implicitly insane and/or unholy? If it is, is there any way that the sane and the holy can nevertheless share in its benefits? And if, at the end of the day, the sacrifice of intimate personal fulfillment is the price one has to pay for sowing and reaping the rewards of science, is that a martyrdom worth enduring?

Scientific romance cannot tell us the answers to those questions, no matter how convinced some of its practitioners have been that they know what the answers are, but there is no other way that the questions can be meaningfully dramatized and clarified. That is justification enough for the genre's existence, and the careful comparative study of its most interesting inclusions.

Brian Stableford

Illustration by H. Lanos for *The Word Above the World*

S. Henry Berthoud: *A Heavenward Voyage*

(*An Anecdotal Story of the Nineteenth Century*)
(1840)

In 1803, in the city of Altona, the capital of Holstein, there was a scientist named Ludwig Klopstock. When I say scientist, I am not expressing the general opinion of his co-citizens in that regard, for they generally claimed that the poor fellow possessed no other merit and no other ability than bearing the great name of Klopstock. His sole entitlement to interest, according to them, consisted of being the nephew of the author of the *Messias*.[4]

In appearance, at least, Ludwig justified the low esteem in which he was held. Always distracted and dreamy, he sought out solitary places, spent hours with his eyes raised toward the heavens, had no fixed meal-times, and had no idea how to earn an *écu* by means of his labor. He lived as best he could on the modest returns of a farm that he owned in the village of Oltenzen, and an annual income of about 800 livres, produced by capital invested with a merchant in Pallmail-strasse. At any rate, neither his meditations in the open air nor his uninterrupted 12-hour sessions in the study in which he locked himself away had ever produced the slightest known result. Whenever he was asked what he was doing among his scientific instruments, or what he saw through the large tele-scope installed on the roof of his house, he became discon-certed, blushing and stammering, and the questioner went

---

[4] The German poet Friedrich Gottlieb Klopstock (1724-1803), who considered that his vocation was to be "the Christian Homer," spent 25 years writing and publishing his epic *Mes-sias* (1748-1773; tr. as *The Messiah*); he produced other Bibli-cal epics thereafter, but they never attained a similar prestige.

away shrugging his shoulders, convinced that Ludwig was nothing but an imbecile.

This conviction became even more unanimous in Altona when it was learned that Ludwig Klopstock was going to marry. His marriage must, indeed, have seems very singular, for the young woman that the poor scientist was marrying was an orphan of 16; the death of her father had left her abandoned and destitute.

In spite of the mockery of all those who knew about his plan, Ludwig led his bride to the altar. Ebba took over the management of the scientist's household; order and propriety—which had been banished from the residence for some time, if they had ever entered it—flourished therein, and gave the desolate dwelling a cheerful and celebratory appearance.

Ludwig himself appeared in the city in clean linen, stocking without holes and garment that did not disappear in myriads of stains of all colors. His pallid complexion and livid thinness gradually gave way to a plumpness at gave his appearance a freshness and gaiety. He was still seen, every evening and well into the night, taking long walks in the country, but, instead of wandering at hazard, he was guided—or rather led—by Ebba. With her gaze directed at the ground, while her husband kept hers raised toward the Heavens, she sustained him, after a fashion, like the angels of which the psalm speaks, in order that his feet should not be injured by the pebbles of the path.

Gradually, Ebba's figure rounded out, and one morning, Ludwig, sitting by his life's bed with his eyes full of tears, heard a little child utter that first cry, which causes so much emotion in a paternal heart. From then on, the scientist devoted himself less exclusively to science; he even forgot his telescope in order to dandle the new-born on his knees; he looked out with greater patience and greater happiness for the little creature's smile than he had ever done in discovering the mysterious conjunction of two stars.

The child grew; he was as beautiful as his mother, and his broad forehead indicated to Ludwig the promise of a powerful intelligence. Simply to say that concern was manifest around the crib in which the pale angel slept would be an understatement. Ebba gazed at him incessantly and Ludwig's calculations were confused by the slightest cry emitted by the infant's rosy little mouth. Alas, one night, the child's respiration became halting, his gaze lit up with a strange flame, and his cheeks became red. He had the croup! When day dawned, there was no longer anything but a cadaver on Ebba's bosom.

The poor mother thought of dying herself. It would surely have been better if God had reunited her body with that of her baby son in the same grave, as he had reunited their souls in Heaven. Ebba's soul never came back down to Earth. Her body acted at hazard; her voice no longer proffered any but inconsequential words. She was an idiot.

Ludwig's friends advised him to send his wife to a lunatic asylum, by which means, in consideration of a modest boarding-fee, he would be rid of the annoyance and the sad spectacle that the presence of a madwoman in his house occasioned. Ludwig became indignant at this suggestion, and persisted in caring for the insane woman with the tenderness and devotion that she had shown him when she had enjoyed her reason. There was no more studying for the scientist; he lavished his intelligence, his time, his days and nights, in humoring the bizarre caprices of the maniac. People ended up believing that he was going mad himself.

Nothing discouraged Ludwig for five years; nothing diminished his devotion to Ebba. At the end of that time, he fell victim to a further misfortune. The merchant in Pallmailstrasse, with whom he had invested the capital that yielded an income of 800 livres, went bankrupt and fled. That event left Klopstock with no other resource than the meager returns of his farm in Oltenzen. That would still have been sufficient for the scientist, who would not have minded being subject to privations, but the privations in question would affect poor Ebba. He decided to apply for a chair in astronomy that had just fallen vacant at the College of Altona.

Imagine what anguish, annoyance and distaste a poor timid man who never went out, and who only maintained rare and distant relationships with two or three friends, must have experienced when he had to solicit employment, explain his request to the burgomeister and submit to the disdain of the councilors. No one took his request seriously, and a professor was summoned from Drontheim. When Ludwig learned that, he sold his little house in Altona and set out for his farm in Oltenzen, taking nothing with him by his scientific instruments and his telescope. Ebba followed him mechanically, without knowing what she was doing. Her soul, as you know, was in Heaven, with her child.

Ludwig's farm was near Oltenzen church. From the window, he could see his uncle's tomb, shaded by a linden tree that the great poet had once planted. Ludwig sent his tenant farmer away and set about cultivating the land, with more intelligence, and even more strength, than anyone could have expected of him. The peasants began by laughing at his experiments and innovations, but they ended up copying him. The time that Klopstock did not spend harrowing and laboring, he devoted to study. The telescope took possession of the roof of Ludwig's farm; he hardly slept—for sleep is like friendship; it only lavishes its favors on the fortunate—and spent his nights studying the stars. During these vigils, consecrated to the admiration of celestial marvels, Ebba lay her head on the scientist's knees and descended into a dreamless torpor that resembled death.

One morning, on descending from his observatory, Ludwig, who was ordinarily sad and absent-minded, manifested an unusual and heedless joy. The scientist's manifestations of happiness could not have been more energetic if Ebba had recovered her reason. He spent six nights writing a long letter, with which he was never satisfied; he began it over, annotated it, consulted his telescope again...

Finally, the important work complete, he placed his memoir carefully in an envelope and posted it in Altona, after taking the precaution of franking it and obtaining a receipt from the Post Office. The package was addressed to the director of Hamburg Observatory, and contained the discovery of the axial rotation of Saturn in 10 hours 32 minutes.

This is the reply he received:

If your letter is not a hoax, Monsieur, you are a little too late to claim a discovery made and published a fortnight ago by Frederick William Herschel.[5]

In response to this cruel disappointment, which stole all the glory of which he had dreamed for his name, Ludwig only manifested his chagrin by his habitual sad smile.

Let us admit, however, that in the meantime, that obscure and timid man had been devoured by a thirst for celebrity. He dreamed night and day of making a name for himself. He sensed a mysterious force within himself that elevated him above vulgarity and only required to manifest itself to be resplendent forever. Poverty and misfortune, however, rendered that manifestation impossible.

When, two years later, he announced that it was possible to solidify carbon dioxide, no one even wanted to read his memoir, nor examine the diagrams he had attached thereto for the construction of the machine necessary to carry out the experiment. The Hamburg Academy remembered the belated discovery of the rotation of Saturn, and treated as fantasy the great operation that was to be reinvented a few years later, by our illustrious scientist Monsieur Thilorier.[6]

---

[5] Frederick William Herschel (1738-1822) published his discovery of Saturn's period of rotation in 1790, which seems inconsistent with the date in the following note—and neither sits well with the date of 1803 given at the beginning of the story—so Berthoud is evidently employing a certain poetic license here.

[6] Adrien Thilorier (1790-1844) first produced "dry ice" (accidentally) in 1834. Berthoud knew Thilorier personally and wrote a eulogy after his death, categorizing him as a "martyr" because he was a casualty of one of his own experiments.

Several years went by without Ludwig leaving the village of Oltenzen or making any further attempts to publish the results of his studies.

One day, when the aeronaut Bitorff, in the midst of an immense crowd of spectators, was getting ready to depart from Hamburg and make an aerial voyage, he saw a little man in a large threadbare black coat coming towards him. Without any preamble, the man proposed that he should accompany him on the excursion that he was about to make by balloon. At first, Bitorff thought that he was dealing with a madman, but as the unknown man insisted and even offered the aeronaut several handfuls of gold to obtain what he desired, he ended up giving his consent, all the more willingly because the strangeness of the proposition and the discussion keenly excited the general curiosity. Like a good speculator wanting a double return, however, he told Ludwig that his ascent would only take place two weeks hence, because the balloon—he alleged—was not yet powerful enough to carry two travelers. Ludwig consented to this delay, and calmly went back to Oltenzen, from which he returned on the appointed day.

During the two weeks, Ludwig Klopstock's project had been the only topic of conversation in Hamburg. The old story of the axial rotation of Saturn, discovered a month after Herschel's publication, was exhumed, and a thousand jokes were told. Bitorff had never attracted as many spectators as he did on the day when the ascension of his travelling companion was to take place. Ludwig, intimidated by the crowd, the eyes of which were fixed on him, approached the gondola awkwardly and almost tore the balloon by bumping into the scientific instruments with which it as laden, in order to carry out experiments during the voyage. To his great regret, the aeronaut obliged him to leave part of his luggage on the ground. They both took their places, the ropes were released and the balloon rose up rapidly like a bird.

Ludwig's first sensation, when he felt himself borne away by the frail machine, was terror. The immense abyss gaping beneath his feet furrowed the scientist's brow and surrounded him with swirling dizziness. Each commotion was succeeded by a sort of perfidious satisfaction. He leaned over the earth, attracted by a mysterious force, and was about to launch himself forth when his companion seized his arm and held him back. Once extracted from this peril, Ludwig recovered all his composure, armed himself with resolution and set about looking down with a freedom of spirit by which the aeronaut could only be astonished.

There is no way to describe the sensations that the scientist experienced. As they drew further away from the Earth, one might have thought that his soul separated itself, disengaging itself from its original clay and freeing itself from the bonds of his body. An indescribable well-being penetrated every part of him; a gentle warmth enlivened him; his mind worked powerfully; he forgot all his misery, all his suffering, all his mundane humiliations. He was finally himself!

Around him sparkled a kind of light that resembled an opaline gleam. Above his head extended the immensity of the azure of the Heavens. Beneath his feet the Earth was retreating and the horizon slowly became more distinct. The rivers presented all their sinuosities simultaneously; the houses and villas seemed to spring from the bosom of the Earth; the sea extended in the distance like a vast sheet of silk, stirred by the wind; the fields displayed their golden escutcheons, quartered in green and purple; the forests covered vast expanses with their somber mantle; people were no more than little dots moving hither and yon, vain and imperceptible dust! Then again, there was no sound and no movement around the aerial voyagers. A profound, absolute silence! Not the bleak and somber silence of human solitudes but a silence that was, so to speak, melodious. It seemed to them that the distant harmonies of the celestial worlds were about to reach their terrestrial ears.

While Ludwig concentrated on these new and sublime impressions, Bitorff, to whom they were familiar, managed the aerostat and devoted himself to various experiments whose program he had organized with his companion before leaving the earth. When his calculations informed him that they were at an altitude of 600 meters, he told Ludwig; the latter shivered, for the aeronaut's voice burst forth with supernatural force, and had nothing human about it. Meanwhile, the atmosphere was beginning to get chilly. The ineffable wellbeing that Klopstock had experienced was succeeded by a period of icy cold. Bitorff's voice lost its marvelous vibration. A hum began to deafen their ears. They were at 1200 meters.

Ten minutes later, Ludwig thought he could make out an almost-unintelligible murmur. He tried to ask Bitorff whether it might originate from speech addressed to him. To his great surprise, he could not hear his own voice at all, and he had to make great efforts that wearied his lungs and throat to proffer his question.

"We're 2000 meters above the Earth," Bitorff finally managed to make him understand. "The expansion of the hydrogen gas contained in the balloon, which has been increasing since we left the ground, has now reached such an extent that I'm obliged to open the valve. Otherwise, the envelope of our vehicle would burst under the strain."

Meanwhile, a thick veil, similar to one of the heavy mists that sometimes expand over the Earth during a thaw, obscuring darkening entire cities with these noxious shroud, spread over the earth and ended up concealing everything from the voyagers' eyes. Soon, dull roaring sounds rumbled in the distance below the balloon. Terrible noises burst forth. Broad lighting-flashes hurled their fiery wings through the chaos. Flamboyant serpents of lightning launched forth in all directions. There was something terrifying about that revolution of the elements, seen and heard by two men who were only sustained in mid-air by a frail piece of taffeta inflated by a little hydrogen. Bitorff felt fear grip his heart, but Ludwig experienced a sort of savage joy. He laughed strangely; he clapped his hands; he jumped up and down. One might have thought him the spirit of tempests, in the midst of his accursed triumph.

The balloon was still rising, by virtue of a regular movement completely imperceptible to those it as lifting. The storm ended up by no longer being anything more than a mute black dot beneath their feet. That dot gradually dissipated and disappeared. The earth showed itself again, but confused. One could still distinguish, with great attention, roads like black threads and rivers like tresses of silver and gold. Above the aeronauts, the sky was resplendent with a serenity of which the earthbound can have no inkling, even on the highest mountains. Its azure took on a deep blue tint, which declined towards the lower regions into a greenish hue.

"Four thousand meters!" shouted Bitorff's voice, beginning to recover its strength, to his companion, who was numbed by a violent cold.

That voice burst forth in deafening vibrations a quarter of an hour later, when it announced: "Six thousand meters!"

Nothing was any longer visible on the Earth but large masses. Bitorff threw into the air two birds that he had brought on the balloon. The poor creatures extended their wings to take flight, but they fell like leaden masses; their air, too rarefied, could no longer lend them support. Ludwig's respiration became more difficult; his chest was oppressed, chilled by the cold—and yet he felt excited by a feverish agitation. His heart was beating rapidly, his breathing accelerated. Two birds and a rabbit that still remained in the gondola began to choke, and were not long in dying for lack of viable air.

"Eight thousand meters," said Bitorff.[7]

His voice had become dull again, and with a gesture he showed Ludwig that nothing any longer remained beneath their feet. The Earth and the clouds had disappeared; the im-

---

[7] Berthoud was probably inspired to write this story by the fact that Charles Green and Spencer Rush had set a new altitude record of 7.9 kilometers in 1839, which was to remain unsurpassed until 1862. The description of Ludwig's experiences is presumably based on those reported by Green and Rush. The previous altitude record of 7.28 kilometers had been set in 1803, which might help to explain the date cited in the story's opening.

mensity of space surrounded the balloon in every direction. As for the cold, it was intolerable. Their shallow breath was scarcely sufficient for the conservation of animal warmth. Blood leaked from the eyes, nostrils and ears of the audacious duo; their words were inaudible. The balloon, the only object they could see, seemed about to expire, so impetuously was the hydrogen gas escaping. Beneath them, the blue of the sky; above, strange and unknown darkness, through which the stars projected a light deprived of scintillation, which had something funereal about it. There ended physical nature. There were located the impenetrable barriers imposed by God on human audacity.

The gas condensed, and the balloon ceased climbing.

"Master," said Bitorff to Klopstock, "if we don't want to die, let's make haste to descend to Earth! You can see it: the divine hand has written in terrible letters: 'Thou shalt go no further.' But what are you doing? Have you lost our mind? What! You're throwing out our ballast! You're taking off your clothes!"

"Because I want to go further!" cried Ludwig, enthusiastically. "Yes, I want to cross the barriers imposed on humankind. Look! The balloon, free of all ballast, is still rising; let's break the gondola, hang on to the cords and reach the Heavens!"

He began to put this plan into operation. Bitorff launched himself toward the valve and opened it, in spite of the despairing efforts of his companion. The balloon descended; the air gradually became less cold as they arrived in less elevated atmospheric layers. The Earth reappeared beneath them, initially as an indistinct grey mass; then it gradually took on a more precise form. Its rivers and roads became visible, details reappeared, people and animals increased in size…and the balloon finally touched down about two leagues from Hamburg.

Bitorff exploded in transports of joy.

Ludwig Klopstock wept with rage and disappointment. "We could have gone into the darkness of infinity!" he repeated to his companion.

"We would have perished!" the latter replied.

Without paying the slightest attention to the delight of the crowd that surrounded the two courageous voyagers and lavished applause upon them, without replying to members of the Hamburg Academy, who were imploring him to write a memoir on what he had observed and experienced, without even shaking the hand of his companion in peril, Ludwig drew away silently, climbed back on his horse, and rode back to Altona without stopping.

There, he bought large quantities of gummed fabric, loaded his purchases on to the rump of his horse, and shut himself up in his little house in Oltenzen, from which he did not emerge for an entire month. No one was able to see him during that retreat—not the farm laborers, nor a deputation from the Academy of Hamburg, nor even the village pastor. He did not even deign to reply to them though the door, which he refused to open. Were it not for the walk he took with his wife toward nightfall, and a few purchases of food, he might have been thought to be lying dead in his house.

Needless to say, this mysterious retreat gave rise to many strange suppositions. Some favored the hypothesis that Ludwig had lost his reason during his aerial excursion, others that he was devoting himself to a work of magic. The latter belief was not entirely implausible, for it was eventually discovered that Klopstock was building a strangely-shaped machine, which resembled a fish armed with large oars similar to fins; they were moved by means of a mechanism of cogwheels that was both simple and admirable.

That judgment became possible one morning when the inhabitants of Oltenzen saw Ludwig in mid-air, seated on his huge fish, maneuvering it more easily than a horseman guides a docile horse. In spite of the violence of contrary winds, he steered it to the right and the left, forwards and backwards, up and down. He finished by descending into his courtyard, so tightly that the two ends of the machine almost touched the sides.

The pastor, a learned man, in his admiration and at the risk of being indiscreet, went to knock on Klopstock's door , and begged him so insistently to open it that the scientists gave in. He took the pastor into his courtyard. At the first glace it was easy to see that Ludwig had found the secret of steering balloons.

"Your name is immortal, my friend!" cried the minister. "The entire universe will repeat it with enthusiasm! What glory will be yours!"

"Earth! Glory!" Ludwig repeated, disdainfully. "What does that matter to me? It's the Heavens I want! No one has been able to go higher than 8000 meters; I shall go to 20,000! I shall go to 200,000! I shall go into the realm of other worlds! I shall go to other worlds! I shall go beyond! I shall study nature! The immensity and the unknown will belong to me. I've found the means of steering my aerostat. That was an easy problem to resolve. But I've done better. The hydrogen gas that my machine contains expands or contracts as I dictate, without loss. These canisters contain the means of procuring me vital air, even in places where it is impossible to breathe. Cold itself, I have vanquished; it will be unable to hurt me!"

The pastor stood there, astounded by so much genius and madness at the same time.

"Farewell," said Ludwig. "Here is my will. If I fail in my enterprise, or if I no longer deign to return to the Earth, I leave it to you to look after that poor woman. Farewell!"

Without paying any heed to the remonstrations of the worthy churchman, he climbed into his balloon. He was about to take off when Ebba suddenly ran toward him, gazing at him with haggard eyes, clung on to the machine and shouted: "Don't go! Don't go!"

"You're right," said the scientist, after a moment's reflection. "Come! You shall share my fortune and my joy."

He picked her up. He seated her next to him. He waved to the pastor, and flew off into the sky.

The minister watched him for some time, maneuvering his machine easily, which ended up rising rapidly, soon appearing as nothing more than a black dot that gradually melted away into the azure of the Heavens.

The worthy cleric awaited Ludwig Klopstock's return with great anxiety.

Ludwig Klopstock never returned.

S. Henry Berthoud: *The Second Sun*
(1862)

If there is a charming place in the world to take the waters, it is surely Spa. One finds in combination there all the picturesque qualities of wild nature and all the comforts of the most exquisite research. One can be a poet in the morning and an epicure in the evening—and only a few hours on the railway separates Spa from Paris.

Here is the approximate genre of hygienic treatment followed by one of the so-called invalids who found himself at Spa 15 years ago. A poor writer, pursued during the winter by balls, dramatic spectacles, study and the social whirlwind, in order to cure himself he needed pure air, verdant countryside, undemanding distractions and perhaps, strictly speaking, a little water extracted from a mineral spring.

Thus, waking up late in the morning, he roamed the countryside, visited the magnificent manor of Justenville, sat down in the shade of the ruins of the old Château de Franchement, and always came back from these artistic excursions fairly early, so as not to miss the pleasures of the evening.

Among the brilliant and joyful host that gathered at Spa, an old phantom of sorts was seen wandering, whose status as an invalid no one could conscientiously contest. Lazarus emerged from the tomb could surely not have displayed a more livid and emaciated face. Sometimes he followed fervently the prescriptions of the doctor who presides over the waters and seemed to be clinging to life with all his strength. At other times he threw himself into the most dangerous excesses, drinking like four Englishmen—not water, but wine—consuming his nights gambling, and passing disdainfully by the fuming waves of the fountain of Pouchon.

The irregularity of the hygienic habits of the stranger was reproduced in his social habits. Sometimes he stayed alone and apart, and scarcely replied to the servants who asked for his instructions. At other times he was gracious, assiduous, amiable and witty with everyone, and caused the strangeness of his appearance to be forgotten by means of the section of his speech and the melodious softness of his voice.

One day, when the Parisian feuilletonist was walking past the spring of Sauvenière, preoccupied by some novel or other whose idea he was developing, the stranger suddenly accosted him.

"Monsieur," he said, without any other preamble, "If you're looking for a subject to write about, I'll give you one that would, I think, lend itself to dramatic development in a singular fashion. Sit down here, if you please, and lend me your ear.

"The story opens in Copenhagen…"

The man of letters found the opening sufficiently original and unexpected for it to be worth the trouble of listening to the story. The old invalid, who expressed himself quite fluently in French, collected his thoughts for a few moments, placed his hands on his knees, and fixed the strange gaze of his large green-tinted eyes upon his auditor.

The story, as I have just told you, Monsieur, begins in Copenhagen. No city in Europe, especially if one considers its population, has a greater number of colleges than Copenhagen. In 1479, Christian I founded an *alma universitas* with statutes drawn up by the Archbishop of Uppsala, endowments of land and various privileges. Christian II enriched it with wealth confiscated from the clergy. Christian VII increased the number of professors and modified the statutes in such a way as to rejuvenate them and render them useful and practicable. Today, numerous royal or private foundations give bursaries to two hundred pupils; a cloister serves as lodging for a hundred others, who also receive free books and food.

The university of Copenhagen has a dozen extraordinary professors and 16 ordinary ones; the rank and salary of the former correspond to the rank and salary of a major, without counting the four *écus* paid annually and personally by the majority of the pupils that they instruct.

Doctor Magnussen had been the Extraordinary Professor of Philosophy at the University of Copenhagen for 19 years, 11 months and two days when he fell gravely ill and died.

The death of that man, one of the most knowledgeable in Denmark, whose modest and laborious life had been as honorable and pure before God as before men, left is widow and his daughter Stierna in a state verging on poverty. He bequeathed them nothing for a heritage by his library, a few scientific instruments, a little house in the suburbs and a sum of 300 or 400 *écus*, which would give them an income of 100 livres at the very most. In order to live, the two women had been counting on the pension to which the widows of professors were entitled after 20 years service on the part of their husbands. Alas, those 20 years were 28 days short of accomplishment, and the rector, after consulting the other professors and the minister himself, declared to Madame Magnussen with tears in his eyes that the letter of the law had to be rigorously observed, and that she would not be inscribed on the pension list.

The widow received this sad response to her application with more resignation that she had expected of herself. She accepted her fate courageously and resolved to live on her industry and handiwork.

This proved more difficult to do than she thought. In vain she asked everyone she knew for embroidery work, or even dressmaking, but no one wanted to entrust a lady with work that professional seamstresses would inevitably do better and at a lower price. The resource on which the widow and her daughter were counting was therefore lacking; they decided, as a last resort, to take advantage of their house, and to let the dead man's bedroom and library to two boarders.

It cost Madame Magnussen a great deal to introduce strangers into her home in this way, and to become, in a way, their servant, but she was able to put so much dignity and noble simplicity into the manner in which she carried out her humble duties, that she only seemed more worthy of consideration and respect. Her first guests were, in any case, persons attached to the University and thus, so to speak friends.

One of them was an old Extraordinary Professor who taught Theology, the other a young man appointed, by virtue of the modifications caused by the death of Dr. Magnussen, to the Ordinary chair of Medicine. His name was Bertel Granh, and did not take long to obtain pardon from the widow for his 26 years, thanks to his correct conduct, the mildness of his mores and his passionate love of study. He only came down from his room at meal-times, said a few kind words to Madame Magnussen, bowed timidly to Stierna, and, on leaving the table, returned to his scientific labor—unless it was a holiday, and he was invited to take tea in company with his old colleague and two or three friends of the professor's widow.

A year after her husband's death, Madame Magnussen fell dangerously ill. Dr. Bertel Granh lavished his care upon her, so devotedly and so expertly that he succeeded in warding off the fever that had put the poor woman's life in jeopardy. The recovery of the convalescent was celebrated by a family feast. Stierna embroidered a tobacco-pouch for Dr. Granh, and the latter resumed his solitary and laborious life as before.

In the meantime, the old Extraordinary Professor completed the 20 years that gave him the right to retire from the University, and he resolved to spend the days that remained to him in the village where he had been born. The loss of the boarder was a significant matter in Madame Magnussen's household, raising the serious question of how he might be replaced. Bertel, when consulted, proposed a new professor, a childhood friend, who had come to teach medicine in one of the University's three Ordinary Chairs. Ole Matthiesen thus came to occupy the room that had fallen vacant, and was not long delayed, like his friend, in gaining the affection of their hostess.

Good fortune seemed to have returned in full to the widow's house, and her prayers thanked God every day for the consolations he deigned to accord her; a mother would not have been happier and more contented in the midst of her children than she was in the company of the two young men. Stierna lived alongside them as if she were their sister; she supervised the bleaching of their linen, put her care and pride into keeping it in good condition, and the last thing in the world she would have wanted was to leave them the least concern regarding their material life. You should have seen her in the morning, in her little corset and a short skirt, with her lovely arms bare, putting the cravats and vests she had just bleached out to dry on the washing-line in the courtyard, and hastening to make breakfast as soon as the cathedral clock struck 7:30. The two professors never had to wait a minute for their first meal, and they set off for the University afterwards with their arms fraternally linked, not without having received a maternal greeting from Madame Magnussen and a smile from Stierna's rosy lips that said: "Au revoir!"

When they came back at midday, the young woman had replaced her pretty morning garb with a dress that was simple, but did justice to the suppleness of her figure and left the smooth contour of her swan-like neck all its grace and purity. Ordinarily, she knotted her blonde hair with ashy gleams on top of her head, which thus left uncovered a forehead as white as ivory, on which an angelic serenity was ensconced. The large near-black lashes that veiled her blue eyes gave her naïve and noble physiognomy an expression of ineffable candor that had nothing terrestrial about it. That glint of another world, moreover, was evident in her entire person; her feet did not seem to be made for trampling earthly dust; her hands, before which Thorvaldsen[8] would have knelt, retained a divine whiteness in spite of her domestic chores; finally, one could not hear her vibrant and melodious voice without being moved. Everything—including her name, Stierna, which means *star* in Danish—concurred in rendering that harmony of grace and celestial virginity more complete and irresistible.

---

[8] The Danish sculptor Bertel Thorvaldsen (1779-1844).

To see the two young professors going to the University, arm in arm, knowing that they had been childhood friends and were living under the same roof, one would naturally have believed them to be united by the most tender amity and the most absolute confidence. That was not the case, however. Under the appearances of a cordial fraternity, they lived more isolated from one another than if they had been separated by a great distance. Always ready to exchange the little services of which they might mutually have need, to settle a bill, to lend a book or to explain the obscure meaning of a difficult passage, they had never felt the need to say an affectionate word or to deposit in one another's hearts the slightest intimate thought. Grave and melancholy during meals, scarcely raising their eyes toward Stierna, they only spoke to her in order to reply to her questions; Matthiesen never showed her more intimacy than Granh, and Granh made every effort never to cross the respectful limits at which Matthiesen stopped.

Madame Magnussen and Stierna put no difference into their affection and their conduct with regard to the two lodgers—but in each of them, that fashion of acting was natural, while in the two young men it resulted from real calculation, tacit convention and a set purpose that would have been evident to souls less naïve and confident than those of the professors widow and her daughter.

For two entire years, nothing changed, at least in appearance, in the relationships between these four individuals—except that Ole and Bertel became increasingly somber, and an amicable reproach from Madame Magnussen or an affectionate reprimand from Stierna could not always succeed in restoring a little serenity to their brows.

The young woman and her mother attributed this sadness to the fatigue of study. As for the two professors, neither of them was unaware of the true cause of their mutual and somber depression. Each of them had read his comrade's heart. However careful they were not to meet one another's eyes, hazard occasionally brought the glances of hatred that they darted at one another into collision.

One night, Ole Matthiesen, who could not sleep, had got out of bed and tried to distract himself with study, that opium which, perhaps better than any other, can numb the passions, suspend thought and daze the mind by means of intoxicating vertigo. Absorbed in his reading, he suddenly shivered, for the door opened abruptly and Bertel's pale and somber face appeared.

"We can't go on living like this," said the latter. "Don't you agree, Ole Matthiesen?"

"Yes, Bertel Granh," Ole replied, getting to his feet to take down two pistols that were hanging on the wall. What you've just said, I've been thinking for a long time. When you came in, I was wondering whether I ought to go find you. The death of one of us, that's what's required."

"Listen to me, Ole—a duel would put the whole city in turmoil. The survivor would be lost forever, forced to renounce his title of professor, obliged to flee Demark or submit to the rigor of the law. He would only be satisfied in his hatred—and we want more than that, don't we. Ole?"

"I understand you, Bertel. Yes, let the hazards of chance decide between us. The one who is not favored must die, but die in secret, without anyone knowing his fate, without anyone in the world being able to discover what has become of him."

"That's what I wanted to propose to you. Very well, pick up that Bible and that dagger I see in your belt. Here's mine, for we've been wearing daggers for a year. In a few seconds, the cathedral bells will chime midnight. At the moment when the last chime begins to sound, we'll each bury our blade in the pages of the book. The one who picks out the letter closest to the beginning of the alphabet will dispose of the destiny of the other."

They waited for a few moments in silence, their eyes lowered and their hearts pounding; then midnight began to chime. At the final stroke, they slid the daggers between the pages of the holy volume, profaned by their sanguinary pact. Each one search avidly for the letter picked out by his adversary.

"A D!" cried Bertel.

"You have a B," Ole replied.

A mortal silence fell between the two enemies. Ole was the first to break it. "So be it," he murmured, in a low hoarse voice. "I will keep my word, and you shall never hear mention of me again. How much time will you give me?"

"Three days."

"That's more than I'll need." Ole added, with bitter irony: "You're generous, Bertel—let me be."

Bertel went back to his room, his heart gripped by an iron hand. He felt a thousand times more miserable hand before. Far from soothing the distress he was suffering, the loss of Ole added to its harsh violence. He wanted to go back to his old friend and release him from his fatal promise, but he found the other's door locked, and when he knocked and begged him to open it, not only did he receive no response, but Madame Magnussen, woken up by the unaccustomed noise came running, hastily clad in a dressing-gown, to ask anxiously whether Bertel felt ill. The latter, disconcerted, admitted an indisposition, and was obliged to resign himself to drinking strong herbal tea and submitting to the care of the worthy and obstinate woman until the moment when he could, without implausibility, assure her that he was no longer feeling poorly and that his illness had dissipated. Only then did Madame Magnussen go back to bed, congratulating herself on the success of her cure, and not without admiring more than ever the marvelous virtue of centaury[9] tea for curing stomach cramps and nervous spasms.

The next day, Ole and Bertel went to the University arm in arm, as usual. They did not exchange a single word, but that often happened, especially when one of them had an important lesson to prepare.

When Ole came back at midday, he found a letter; it had arrived during his absence. He opened it, and as soon as he

---

[9] *Centaurium erythraea*, a herb of the gentian family.

had cast his eyes over is contents, he manifested an excessive joy.

"Good news!" he cried. "I'm rich now! A distant relative has left me a considerable fortune: 100,000 *écus*. I have to leave tomorrow morning for Holstein, where my new domains are located. I swear that I shall only have one regret in leaving Copenhagen—the pain of leaving friends like you, Madame Magnussen and Mademoiselle Stierna; you too, my dear Bertel—give me the pleasure of employing with you, before leaving, the language of a brother.

"I will write my resignation as professor, Bertel; you shall hand it to the Rector yourself, begging him to excuse me for the precipitation of my abrupt departure. You will inform him of the necessity that obliges me to leave Copenhagen immediately. I shall not take any luggage; that will permit me to go more quickly. Then I shall exchange a poor life for another—a life brilliant with pleasures, no doubt. I want to make legacies and write the testament of my agonizing poverty. Madame Magnussen will inherit my two sets of silver cutlery; Mademoiselle Stierna will accept this ring that my mother gave me; and Bertel shall have all my books, for which I shall henceforth have no further use!"

He said this with so much gaiety and frank folly, that even Bertel wondered whether Ole's supposed fortune might be real.

"To table!" Ole went on. "To table! Let Mademoiselle Stierna serve us her best preserves; let French wine be brought out of the cellar, as on high holidays! Is not the great news of my fortune and my liberty a celebration for us, my friends?"

They sat down at the table, and when the meal was over, and the two women had clinked glasses with the traveler, the latter offered a large glass of brandy to Bertel.

"How pale you are, friend," he said. "What? The one who is staying is sad, while the one who is going away rejoices? Away with tears and grief! Let us embrace, brother, and say farewell."

As he said that, he kissed Bertel on the cheeks, then hugged Madame Magnussen. Stierna, who was emotional, came forward and presented her forehead to Ole's lips. All the young man's false gaiety collapsed then; tears filled his eyes, sobs punctuated his voice and he almost fainted. He struggled visibly against that cruel emotion, but he soon mastered it, brushed the beautiful child's hair with his lips, and went away precipitately.

Having arrived at the extremity of the suburb of Copenhagen, he stopped, waved his handkerchief in a gesture of farewell, and disappeared.

He had been out of sight for a long time, but Bertel was still standing on the doorstep, motionless, pale and exhausted.

"What a nice young man!" murmured Madame Magnussen. "And to think that we'll never see him again!"

"We'll see him again!" cried Bertel. "I'll run after him; I want to stop him from carrying his fatal journey to its conclusion."

He had already set forth when he heard Stierna sobbing, and saw that the young woman's cheeks were streaming with tears.

"It's too late!" he said, stopping. "The carriage is carrying him away along the Holstein road."

Either by virtue of fatigue or emotion, the old man interrupted his narrative momentarily, but he resumed it in these terms.

After Ole's departure, Madame Magnussen's house was overtaken by a profound sadness. Be it understood that the house did not lose its gaiety, for it had been very rare for the four people previously inhabiting it to have emerged from the melancholy habits that two of them owed to the loss of a father and a husband, and the others to the passions that were tormenting them, but it lost its movement and its life. Bertel proposed to the widow that he should take over, for his own use, the room left empty by Matthiesen's absence; he offered as a pretext the impossibility of devoting himself, in his small cell, to the studies in physics that he intended to undertake. In reality, his sole objective was to prevent any other person from coming to live under the same roof as Stierna.

By virtue of a seemingly-inexplicable contradiction, however, he had never been less inclined to seek the young woman's company. He even seemed to be avoiding her, and let entire days go by without addressing a word to her. Sometimes, nevertheless, the naïve young woman would catch sight of Granh's gaze furtively attached to her, without her being able to explain or understand what motives brightened that gaze with a dark and almost sinister fire. At times she wondered anxiously whether the departure of his friend might have disturbed the young man's mind, for he was subject to strange fits that seemed not far from madness. At table, he forgot to put the food into his mouth; he let his pale head slump on to his breast, and it was necessary for Madame Magnussen to call him by name three or four times before extracting him from that waking sleep. At night, he was heard wandering around his room, and opening the window to spend entire hours gazing at the sky. He often wept, yielding to fits of despair, and Ole's name escaped his lips convulsively.

One morning, he came down so pale and disfigured that Stierna's heart was moved to profound compassion. She went straight up to the young man, and stopped him when he tried to go around her and go outside.

"Don't run away from me like that, Dr. Bertel," the gentle creature said, in her ineffable voice. "I need to talk to you. For a long time now, you no longer talk to me; you seem to be avoiding me. Have I offended you unwittingly? If so, tell me, in order that I can avoid committing the same fault again. Above all, forgive me, for I deeply regret having injured you."

"You haven't offended me at all, Stierna. If I no longer speak to you, if I avoid you, it's because I feel unworthy to address you, ashamed to soil you with my presence."

"What do you mean, Monsieur Bertel? For the sake of the friendship that my mother and I have for you, put an end to this sad mystery—explain it."

"When you know, Stierna, it will be you who turns away from my presence, you who will no longer want to see or hear me."

"Me, Bertel? The person who has lived close to you for so many years? The person who loves you like a brother?"

"Like a brother, you say? Well, if that brother had committed a crime, would you not expel him from your presence forever?"

"A crime! Oh, that's not possible!"

"And yet I have committed a crime! Blood soils my hands! I'm a murderer."

"Oh, be quiet" Be quiet! I'm afraid. Let me go away."

"You shall hear me out now, Stierna. Now that you've forced me to open the abyss, your gaze shall penetrated its depths. Listen, then! I loved a young woman; another also loved her…I staked my life against that of my rival. I won; he has killed himself."

"Horror! Horror!"

"Don't you want to know who that young woman is, Stierna?"

"Oh no! Don't tell me. Let me go!"

"That young woman is named Stierna Magnussen."

"Take back those fatal words, Bertel—take them back, I beg you on my knees. See my anxiety, my despair! Tell me that you're playing with me, that all this is nothing but a cruel game! I'll be your accomplice. For me, someone would shed blood! For me, someone would commit murder! Oh, something more frightful still! An unfortunate has been reduced to suicide! He has lost his body and soul at the same time! Tell me that it isn't true!"

"It's true."

"It's true, and you haven't yet fled this place? Father, in the Heaven where you reside, your gaze must be turned away from me that such shame should afflict your house and soil your child! Back, Bertel! Back, murderer! Can't you see that you horrify me?"

Obstinately, Bertel remained standing before the poor desperate girl. "Before repeating the order to go away and never see you again, before telling me again that you're horrified, Stierna, listen to what I have I say: if I leave this house, it will be to die."

"To die?"

"Yes. You've already damned one soul; you will damn another."

"My God! My God! What have I done that you should subject me to such cruel ordeals?"

"Can you believe that I have struggled against my remorse, that I have repelled the thoughts of suicide that pursue me, for any other motive than the love I feel for you? In the midst of the inferno of my heart, a joy sometimes gleams that suspends its suffering. That joy is seeing you, hearing your soft voice. You're sending me away; perhaps you're doing the right thing, and being charitable—I shall now have the courage to die."

"You're right, Monsieur—stay. You must. Since I am the involuntary cause of your crime, I must submit to its expiation, and accept my share of your remorse. Stay, and may God grant you repentance, as he has given me eternal despair."

"Repentance! Remorse! Oh, God did not wait for our prayer to give me that. You don't know, then, that the nights are sleepless for me, that a slow fever is devouring me incessantly, that a name sounds incessantly in my ears? That that name is constantly on my lips, ready to escape with the confession of my crime? Remorse! If you could understand the remorse that I suffer, instead of the horror I inspire in you, you would take pity on me; you would hold out your hand to console me, and you would mingle my name in the prayers you address to God. You would cry out, saying: 'Lord, have mercy on him!'"

Compassion was indeed the sentiment that Stierna did not take long to experience for Bertel. After the initial moments of horror and fright, she reflected that he was unhappy, and unhappy because of her. From then on, a dangerous pity preoccupied her keenly, and kept her thoughts relentlessly fixed on the young man, day and night—for sleep had quit the maiden's room henceforth. She was distressed by Bertel's sin and remorse, asked God for forgiveness on his behalf, and sought by a thousand affectionate means to give the guilty man some hope in divine mercy. She lavished interest and indulgence upon him. To render his sin less burdensome, she generously took half of it upon herself, and tried to bear it with him.

That community of secrecy and repentance, the sublime and voluntary complicity, did not take long to become a sentiment more tender than Stierna herself believed, against which she did not protect herself. No tender word ever emerged from their lips, but whenever Stierna saw Bertel paler than usual and prey to spasms of despair, she furtively took his hand and fixed her large blue eyes upon him, shining with celestial compassion.

In the meantime, Bertel's mother fell dangerously ill. He was obliged to leave abruptly in order to see her one last time before death separated her from her son forever. He wept so bitterly, and suffered so keenly, that Stierna promised of her own accord to write to him for as long as his absence lasted, and kept her promise. She only talked, in her letters about the dying woman, God, hope and Heaven's forgiveness, but she nevertheless wrote every day, and, so to speak, devoted the entirety of every day to Bertel.

When the professor returned, his mother was dead; there was no longer a single wretched person in this world to love him. Stierna tried to render that isolation less cruel—so successfully that one day, sitting next to the large fireplace in which a fire of pine-logs was blazing, forgetful of the past and their clasped hands, they found themselves talking hopefully of happiness and the future.

Many trials and years separated them, alas, from the day when they would be able to realize the beautiful dreams they forged. They were both too poor to be able to marry for some time to come. Bertel possessed no other fortune than his professorial salary, and he still had to pay off, with the same revenue, the rather considerable debts that his mother had left in dying. But what did time and trials matter to those in whose hearts hope had succeeded despair, and who could at least glimpse, however distantly, future felicity? The memory of Ole sometimes returned to trouble them, like a reproach, but it seemed to them nevertheless that forgiveness descended on them from the heavens, drop by drop. Before the magnificent splendor of love, the somber glow of remorse faded away.

A year went by in that fashion, for Stierna and for Bertel, in the ecstasy of a powerful and chaste tenderness. Madame Magnussen knew and approved of the secret engagement of the two young people, although they had never taken her into their confidence. It was thus that she had loved her husband for a long time before marriage became possible. Such mystical unions are common in the North, where poverty reigns so harshly. With a noble pact of love in the heart, a young man struggles courageously against the difficulties of life, and conquers, if not a fortune, at least a measure of ease. Then he comes to kneel at the feet of the one who is waiting for him without mistrust, even when time and distance separate them.

Uncomplainingly, Stierna and Bertel lived under the same roof, beside one another, and although they never exchanged a kiss, they looked forward desirously, but not impatiently, to the distant epoch that would bring about their marriage.

This situation, which would seem impossible and perilous in our French *mores*, became quite simple and full of charm in Copenhagen. The two lovers spent their life in a sweet and mild intoxication; the body slept, only the soul lived.

In any case, they saw one another only a little more frequently than in that past. Only meal times and the occasional family occasion brought them together.

Bertel devoted a large part of his evenings to studies in physics—an interest inspired in him by the instruments left behind by Stierna's father and long forgotten in a little room where things the family did not use were stored. He loved to talk about the phenomena of the science to which he was passionately devoted, and he initiated the young woman into the mysteries of that fantastic new world and that unknown nature.

All of that was marvelous to Stierna, whom her father's prudence had wisely left in a charming ignorance, and who only went out of the house twice a year, and even then with her mother. The past, the present, the future—real life, in sum—consisted for her of Bertel, her mother, her little house and the memory of Ole, the last of which became vaguer and more distant every day.

The sweeter such an existence is, the more painfully the blow that overturns it strikes. Madame Magnussen fell gravely ill, and there was soon no more hope of a recovery. According to the Gospel, a strong woman who has long been prepared for a holy death by a life of virtue only feels anxiety, in that redoubtable moment, for the child she leaves behind on Earth. That anxiety was consoled by the thought of the love she knew Bertel to have for Stierna. One morning, she summoned them to the bed in which she would soon die, and took them both by the hand.

"Bertel Granh," she said, in a faint but distinct voice, "you love Stierna, and Stierna loves you. I therefore leave her a protector down here, and can quit the Earth without dread. I know that you have tried to conceal many mysteries from me, my children, but I know that secrets, even the most innocent, love to remain in the darkness. May God bless you as I bless you, my son...Stierna!"

They fell to their knees, for it was before a cadaver that they were praying and weeping.

The day after the day on which Madame Magnussen's mortal remains were buried in the cemetery, Stierna, leaning on Bertel's arm, went in tears to the house of an aged female relative, to spend the period of her mourning there and await the moment when she might marry her fiancé. That moment need not be far away, for Bertel hoped to pay off all his mother's debts within the year, and it would then only remain for him to amass the small sum necessary for him to establish a household. The lovers therefore separated on the old aunt's threshold.

It was agreed, before the separation, that the professor could make occasional visits to his intended. Admittedly, Bertel also promised to pass beneath Stierna's window every day, while travelling to and from the University, and that Stierna added that she would always be at the window.

The fiancés, therefore, saw one another twice a day, at 11 a.m., when the professor came back from the University, and at 2 p.m., when he returned for the afternoon classes. During his first departure and his second return, darkness pitilessly deprived them of that happiness.

Stierna was able to invent ingenious pretexts to be leaning on her windowsill when one of these sweet moments of the day, so keenly anticipated, drew near. From some way off she watched Bertel approaching, only walking slowly in order to allow is eyes to linger on the young woman for longer. When he arrived before her, they exchanged a long, tender gaze; then, hearts beating, one of them continued his route while the other, smiling and excited, pretended to work fervently at some dressmaking project, while actually following the sound of footsteps drawing away with her ears.

For six months, the life of the lovers was entirely encapsulated in these two daily rendezvous and in the visits that Bertel made about once a fortnight. They liked their rapid but free encounters at the window much better than the solemn visits, during which it was necessary carefully to lock their love away in the depths of their hearts, in order that the secret of their souls did not fall into the power of a bourgeois and meddlesome curiosity. Sierna therefore counted down with the charming anguish of expectation to the moment when Bertel would bring her happiness all day long. Bertel forgot the fatigue and annoyances of his laborious profession beneath the consoling and tender gaze that he received in passing beneath the balcony.

Monsieur Magnussen's widow had died in the autumn. At the end of summer, Stierna felt herself becoming vaguely anxious and sad, for several times, Bertel, in going to the university, had arrived several minutes late, and had passed under his fiancée's window almost at a run, in order not to arrive after the beginning of classes that was being signaled by the last strokes of the bell. Another day, she felt her eyes fill with tears on remarking the preoccupation of the young man, who only remembered to look up at her window after leaving it five or six paces behind him.

These evidences of distraction and lack of enthusiasm were repeated several times. The guilty party seemed only to be carrying out a duty or following a habit in coming to receive the tender greeting of his fiancée. Stierna struggled for a long time against her own conviction before accepting that painful thought, but in the end, she could not mistake the fatal reality, for Bertel passed by without raising his head on two consecutive days.

While she sought despairingly to explain the cause of this deadly change, a few friends of the aged relative came to dinner in the old lady's home at Christmas. The majority of the guests were at the University.

In the evening, when they had left the table to surround the fireplace, the conversation turned to an Extraordinary Professor's chair that had become vacant. They talked about the competitors who had applied for it, but no one mentioned Bertel's name. Now, if he had acquired that position, the young man's honoraria would have been doubled, and nothing would any longer have opposed their marriage.

"I thought that Dr. Bertel Granh had more right than any other to apply for that chair?" objected the blushing Stierna, who could not master her emotions, and could not bear the crushing weight of doubt any longer.

"You're quite right, my pretty maid," replied one of the old professors, "but since Dr. Granh has come into a considerable inheritance, he is not longer concerned to occupy a chair that would necessitate new and laborious studies. He is even disposed to enjoy his fortune more freely, for he came to ask for an unlimited leave of absence yesterday, while I was with the rector. It's my nephew Christian who will take over Dr. Granh's chair in medicine in the interim."

"Doctor Granh has only received news of this inheritance in the last few days, then?" asked Stierna, who could not yet believe in such ingratitude and treason.

"All of Copenhagen has been talking about it for four months. It's not at all astonishing that you don't know anything about the news. You live in such a profound and reclusive solitude."

Pale, beside herself and bewildered, the young woman hurtled out of the apartment and ran, mad with despair, to the house where she had once spent so many happy moments, and where Bertel now lived alone.

She knocked, but no one opened the door. She called out, but no one replied.

In the end, a neighbor put her head out of a widow and shouted: "There's no longer anyone in the house. Dr. Bertel Granh left a little while ago by mail coach, for a long journey."

Sierna collapsed in a faint.

The old man interrupted himself, but did not notice that he had stopped speaking. His gaze wandered vaguely through empty space, and seemed to be pursuing memories full of bitterness and despair. Sweat was streaming down his forehead, laden with profound wrinkles; his green-tinted pupils burned with the sinister flame that the accursed angel emanates. Several minutes went by. Suddenly, he woke with a start from that sleepless dream, and looked around in astonishment, as if he were surprised to find himself in Spa, beside a stranger. He needed some further time to get his ideas in order and reconnect the present with the past that had earlier come to live before him. A smile, full of sarcasm for the weakness of the human organism and for himself, creased his lips, while an impulse of shame and anger made him shrug his shoulders.

"Do you know Stockholm?" he asked the Frenchman, abruptly, with the evident intention of extracting himself, by means of a violent effort, from the dolorous thoughts that were assailing him.

"No," replied the man to whom the question was addressed.

If I were a poet, like you, I could make a brilliant description of the Capital of Sweden. I'm not a poet, and I shall only tell you that there is, on a hill in Stockholm, a quarter inhabited by the city's poorest inhabitants, named Mosebacke. Steep, muddy, narrow, plunging paths, sometimes mere wooden stairways—such are the roads of Mosebacke. I leave you to imagine the houses. In particular, there was one there more wretched and hideous than the rest, but in exchange, it had the advantage of standing in the most isolated spot, and the only inhabitants it sheltered were workmen who go out at daybreak and return after nightfall. At the summit of the hovel, like black eyes, were two round windows. They served to provide air and light—my God! what air and what light!—to two miserable lofts. No one in the quarter knew who lived there, and no one wanted to know.

An old woman, a kind of cretin, half-sorceress and half-idiot, was the only living creature who had any relations with the tenants of the mansards. Every morning, she deposited food at the thresholds of their doors and received a coin in exchange.

One evening, a terrible explosion burst forth in one of the lofts, and a huge flame escaped through the window, in a manner that threw the entire Mosebacke quarter into alarm. People came running, broke down the door, and found a young man lying motionless in the midst of strangely formed instruments, some of which had been smashed by the explosion.

The occupant of the next room had not been disturbed by the frightful shock that had nearly caused the old house to collapse. Partly out of anxiety for him, and partly to seek help for the dying man, the rescuers knocked on his door; he did not open it and they called out without obtaining any response. Common people do not usually exhibit great patience, so they had begun to break the door down with an axe when it finally turned on its hinges and revealed a face in which nothing human remained. Terrible scars streaked it in every direction, scarcely leaving anything intact but the eyes and mouth.

This being—for no one dared give him the name of man—went into the room where his neighbor as lying, and at the sight of him uttered a cry that resembled the sinister call of a hyena. He went to the dying man, revived him, bathed his face with fresh water and leaned over him to make certain of his awakening.

When the other, having emerged from unconsciousness, got to his feet and suddenly found himself face to face with the individual who had brought him back to life, he turned his head away, put his hands together and cried: "My God, have pity on me! Do not bring your just anger down on me! Do not deliver me to the eternity of Hell!"

"You're still alive, Bertel Granh," said the hideous unknown. "It's not face to face with Satan that you find yourself, but face to face with Ole Matthiesen. Pull yourself together! In exchange for a frivolous amour, you have given me genius—and soon, I hope, a glory without rival. I forgive you everything, including the hideous scars inflicted by the pistol-shot that I fired at my head to keep the promise I had sworn to you. Someone lifted me up, dying, as I lifted you up just now, and saved my life as I am saving yours, and since then, a sublime obsession has preoccupied me and cause me to renounce, joyfully, all the ridiculous passions of human beings. I shall be the benefactor of the entire universe. Statues of me will be erected; the face of the world will be renewed, and it is Ole

Matthiesen who will work the miracle. The work is complete! The light will not be long delayed in shining."

All this was said rapidly in Latin. Ole then turned toward the people the explosion had attracted.

"We thank you, Masters," he said to them in Swedish. Your care is not longer necessary. I have rediscovered one of my old friends in the man you have come to rescue, and if he needs help, he will obtain the most active and prompt assistance from me. As you see, though, he is standing up, recovered from the shock caused by the explosion that alarmed you."

Everyone withdrew. Ole and Bertel remained alone. Ole silently paraded his gaze over the broken objects that lay in the loft. They were apparatus used in chemistry and instruments used in physics. The explosion had been caused by a flask of hydrogen gas that had suddenly ignited.

Matthiessen remained plunged in a mute and bleak reverie for some time. Finally, he broke the silence.

"Listen to me, Bertel!" he said. "Because of you I attempted suicide. If you're still alive, it is me to whom you owe your life!"

"Yes, Ole—and I ask your forgiveness on my knees. I would like to be able to prove my gratitude, even at the price of my own existence."

"Well, you can."

"How?"

"By making once again the pact that we made before in Copenhagen."

"Stierna is free, Ole," Bertel interjected, with a sight. "You can marry her."

"Stierna!" said Mathiessen, violently. "Stierna! Is it really a matter of a woman? Tell me why, Bertel Granh, you have trampled underfoot that insensate passion that drove you to stake your life against that of a friend? You say nothing? I know why! It's for love of science and thirst for glory."

"Yes, I admit it."

"An idea—a great idea—is preoccupying you."

"Yes! Like the one you mentioned to me just now, it will regenerate the universe and make the name of the man who realizes it eternal."

"Do you know, Bertel, the thought that has occurred to me in the presence of all this debris of scientific instruments? It's that we're pursuing the same idea. A secret and accursed voice is murmuring in my ear that, once having been rivals in love, we are now rivals in glory. If that's the case, Bertel, one of us has to die!"

"You're right," Bertel replied, unhesitatingly. "Listen to me. Haven't you groaned sometimes, on thinking about the long nights that desolate Denmark? Haven't you thought that the man who could create a second sun with take a place second only to God in the admiration and gratitude of men?"

"That's your idea?" jeered Matthiesen, shrugging his shoulders. "I feel reassured—it's ridiculous and impossible, that's all."

"Impossible!" cried Bertel, picking up two jars that the explosion had spared. "One of these two vessels, each of which terminates in a narrow tube, contains oxygen, the other hydrogen. The two flames, combining in combustion, only give a bluish light, but let me bring in a refractory body—this piece of chalk, for instance—and watch!"

Immediately, a resplendent light sprang forth, at which the eye could not look directly, even furtively. Dazzled, Ole turned his head away. Bertel was exultant.

"You see, my second sun already appears to you to be more than a hollow dream! But this is only a rough and imperfect work. The light does not reproduce itself; the gases are exhausted ; the refractory body loses its properties. It requires a man versed in science to watch over the apparatus incessantly, to prevent an explosion. I shall create a sun that will be, in approximate proportion, as bright and as durable as God's sun. Listen closely, Ole.

"The solar fluid behaves like the electrical fluid. It produces the phenomena of light and heat when it strikes objects and finds any obstacle whatsoever in its rapid movement.

62

Thus, the sun is an opaque body which surrounds an atmosphere of luminous electricity.

"Starting from this principle, I have discovered that bodies become phosphorescent by virtue of the effect of heat and electrical discharges. I recognized, too, that bodies non-conductive of electrical fluid retain that phosphorescence longer than others.

"Given that—mark me well, Ole! This time, follow my operation with all the attention of which you are capable, for a prodigy will become manifest. I place a morsel of carbon, a refractory body, in the middle of this glass globe. I attach to that carbon two platinum wires, which are connected to the poles of a dry Voltaic pile.

"Take note: these metal wires are secured to the mysterious columns of the pile—columns enclosed in a cylinder of sulphur and made up of alternate leaves of zinc, silver and paper.

"I obtain a vacuum in the globe with the aid of a pneumatic pump. On your knees, Ole—here is a sun!"[10]

Ole could not suppress a cry of admiration. It was a sun, a true sun.

"You see," Bertel continued, "that I am approaching the completion of my work. It's no more than a matter of applying my sublime discovery on a vast scale. This is the means of ensuring that execution.

---

[10] What Berthoud has in mind is a carbon arc lamp, although his description is faulty, partly because his theory of solar light-production is mistaken. The principle of the carbon arc lamp had been demonstrated by Humphry Davy in the first decade of the century, but all attempts to produce a viable version of any sustained electrical light-source had been frustrated before Berthoud wrote this story. It was not until the 1870s that the first viable carbon arc lamp—the so-called "Yablochkov candle"—was developed, and not until 1878 that Joseph Swan patented the first electric light-bulb with a carbon filament.

"I shall construct, in sheets of copper, a balloon 500feet in diameter. The balloon will be filled with hydrogen gas, purified with extreme care, and purged, as far as possible, of all foreign bodies.

"Beneath the balloon I shall attach an apparatus similar—in with gigantic proportions—to the one you see, in which a small sun with shine. A veritable sun, moreover, like the Sun in the sky, since it is similarly composed of an opaque body and an envelope of luminous electricity.

"The Voltaic piles will be alimented easily; the Earth is nothing but a vast reservoir of electricity. Do not two eternal magnetic currents pass from one pole to the other? And has not our great Oersted demonstrated that magnetism is nothing other than electricity in one of its transformations?[11]

"My balloon has nothing to fear from external agents, since it is constructed of solid metal, rendered unalterable and indestructible by a chemical preparation that is easy to compose. I shall coat it with this preparation, which will protect it against the slightest oxidation.

"The hydrogen will not be able to escape from the interior, because the envelope that keeps it prisoner remains impenetrable from the inside as from the outside, even for the most subtle gas.

"Finally, a metal cable, which will also serve as a conductor to the galvanic piles, will suffice to hold my apparatus anchored in the atmosphere.

"You see, Ole, these theories are certain. I have created a sun! Soon, there will be no more nights for Denmark. Liberated henceforth from obscurity, Denmark will have almost

---

[11] Hans Christian Oersted (177-1851) discovered that electric currents create magnetic fields in 1820. This does not seem entirely consistent with the internal chronology of the story; the old man is narrating his tale in Spa 15 years before the story's publication—i.e., no later than 1847—and seems to be referring to events that took place at least 30 years previously, probably more.

nothing to fear from the rigors of winter. What do you say, Ole?"

"I say that your invention seems beautiful, great and useful to me, and that it will astonish Europe—but that it's nothing compared with mine."

"What's yours, then?" Bertel demanded, feeling jealousy bite into his heart as he saw the serenity with which Ole had listened to him.

"It will distress you, for my discovery will render yours almost useless."

"Speak."

"I've found a means of living without eating."

"Without eating?"

"Yes, I've discovered that nourishment is a prejudice."

"And with what are you going to replace alimentation?"

"With nothing. For a long time I've been meditating on this problem. Finally, I tried not to eat, that's all—and I succeeded. As the Greek philosopher did to prove movement, I walk. For 12 days already nothing has approached my lips. I feel a little corporeal weakness, it's true, but in compensation, my intelligence has never been more brilliant and richer! Freed from physical shackles, the soul acts in all its powerful liberty."

"But your idea is extravagant, Ole! You'll die of starvation."

"I haven't eaten for 12 days, and I'm doing admirably."

"It's an insane idea."

"No more insane than your sun."

"But my sun exists, and I've given you proof of it."

"And have I give you none? I, who am speaking, thinking, reasoning and acting, liberated from the inconvenience of nourishment for 12 days? Farewell, Bertel."

"No," cried the latter. "No, I won't let you complete an insane suicide, Ole. I won't leave you until I've made sure that you're taking some nourishment."

Ole took out a dagger. "Do you recognize this weapon?" he asked, with a sinister smile. I held it in my hand the night when you came to find me in my room on Madame Magnusson's house. You want to destroy my glory now, as you wanted to destroy my life then. If you take a step, I'll strike you. I'll kill you."

As he said this, the unfortunate madman left Bertel, went back into his loft, locked himself in and barricaded his door from the inside, with the aid of some enormous wooden beams.

For two days Bertel heard the noise of Ole's voice and footsteps through the wall that separated them. When that time had elapsed, he heard nothing more. Full of alarm, he had warned a magistrate of his anxieties. The door was broken down and Ole Matthiesen was found dead on his paltry bed. A manuscript was lying at his feet, entitled: *On the Prejudice of Nourishment*.

When Bertel went back to his cell, he fell on to the pallet that served him as a bed, devoid of strength. A frightful doubt had gripped his heart, his thought, his entire being.

In the presence of Ole's insane conviction, and the obstinate perseverance with which the unfortunate had believed in his absurd theory until his final death-throes, Bertel wondered whether he too might not be pursuing a lie, a demented Utopia. That doubt—and what torture is more rightful than doubt, Monsieur?—squeezed him in its execrable claws, choked him and ended up disturbing his reason.

His torment was horrible.

Suddenly, he threw himself furiously once again into the culpable dream to which he had immolated his duty, his conscience, his happiness, his entire existence. He clung to it; he wanted to sacrifice everything to it, to the last faculty of his life, the last thought of his soul. A moment later, he cursed his mad obsession, and, laughing bitterly, he repeated: "Insane! Insane!"

In that struggle, that doubt, that fever, he actually felt his mental strength weaken and his reason lose its lucidity. Inconsequential words escaped his lips involuntarily: truncated, aborted, incomplete, incoherent ideas were passing through his brain and filling it with tumult and disorder.

The peril was deadly and immense. If he did not put an end, by a prompt and energetic resolution, to that redoubtable crisis, his life and intelligence would succumb! Then, Monsieur, by a superhuman effort, Bertel desperately trampled his ideas of science and glory underfoot. He swore, by the salvation of his soul and on Ole's corpse, to renounce them forever, to turn his head every time the demon evoked them before him! But those ideas, more obstinate than ever, pursued him, harassed him, surrounded him with an infernal circle, and whirled around him, repeating:

"The second sun! The second sun!"

In the hope of feeing himself from that torture, Bethel departed in all haste for Copenhagen. There, he knew, he would find a celestial creature, the one who had already protected him against remorse! He wanted to renounce his prideful errors at her feet, to ask for a forgiveness that he would obtain, and shelter from despair and madness beneath the wings of an angel...

Alas, Stierna was dead. She had died praying to God for Bertel.

Since then, Monsieur, many years have gone by without Bertel having found a moment of peace and rest. Hunted by a horde of invisible demons, he still marches on without stopping, like Ahasuerus. To his right and his left stand two equally fatal ideas: the memory of Stierna, full of remorse; and the crazy conviction that the creation of a second sun was a great, wise, sublime work! In vain, Monsieur, since the day when he renounced that ridiculous folly, has he refused to open a book of physics; in vain has he carefully avoided contact with the scientists he has met on his travels; everywhere a voice repeats to him:

You could have created a second sun!

And that voice is right, Monsieur—at least, I think so. Do we not live in a century in which physics is progressing with great strides and working miracles? Electricity and its study have opened up a new world. With the aid of electricity, Monsieur Becquerel,[12] that illustrious scientist, has created veritable precious stones. I have seen little sapphires that have emerged from his laboratories; even for the most expert and experienced lapidary, they do not differ and any respect from the precious stones that nature produces. Monsieur Jacobi[13] has made veritable statues by means of electricity, which bear the imprint of the most delicate work with a precision imposs-ible for a skillful sculptor. Finally, Monsieur, Bertel's sun it-self, while the Danish professor rejected it as an absurd dream, was invented by Humphry Davy and perfected by Faraday. Those two celebrated physicists have used means very similar to Bertel's methods, and arrived at the same results.

As for the copper balloon, it has been imagined and proven possible by one of the most skillful physicists of our time, Monsieur Prechtel,[14] the director of the Polytechnic Institute of Vienna. That scientist has even drawn up plans for the balloon's construction; in order to realize it, it would be necessary to expend the cost of a frigate.

---

[12] The reference is to Antoine César Becquerel (1788-1878), the grandfather of the more famous Henri. Initially a mineral-ogist, his investigation of the application of electricity to chemical analysis and synthesis, following in the footsteps of Humphry Davy, allowed him to produce tiny precious stones in 1823.

[13] Moritz von Jacobi (1801-1874) invented electrotyping, or "galvanoplastic sculpture," in 1838; the technique was rapidly adapted for relief printing, which remains its primary applica-tion.

[14] Johann Joseph Prechtel (1778-1854) made numerous contri-butions to electrical physics and technology in the 1820s and 1830s, but the idea of making balloons from copper sheets had first been proposed before the end of the 18th century and several experimental models were constructed in France in the 1840s, although none proved practicable.

If Stierna's lover had not been discouraged, you see—if he had repelled his doubts, if he had not given in to fear, if he had had an unbreakable faith in himself, and if, finally, Ole's madness had not disturbed him—given the time, the patience and the will, he would certainly have immortalized his name and created a second sun.

The stranger, who had let his head fall into his hands and was holding it hidden therein, finally raised it again, displaying features more deeply scored, more downcast and more livid than ever.

"Bertel, such as he is," he said, in a sepulchral voice, "accepts his discomfiture with resignation, in expiation of his treason in regard to Stierna. If his sin was great, its punishment is terrible!"

As he finished these words, he got to his feet, turning away to hide the tears that were running from his lifeless eyes over his sunbronzed cheeks, and hurriedly walked away.

The French journalist searched for him in vain that evening during the 7 p.m. walk, at the ball, in the gaming halls, and the theater—in sum, everywhere. He did not find the unknown anywhere; no one could give him any information about him.

The next morning, it transpired that the old man had left the waters of Spa, not only without telling anyone, but also leaving all his luggage and a considerable sum of money behind in the room that he had occupied in the inn where he had been staying.

René de Pont-Jest: *Mimer's Head*
(1863)

Every population has its mania, or rather its monomania; that is an incontestable psychological fact. Does the mental aberration in question originate from the climate, customs, language and environments in which it lives, or is it innate within instinct, as certain phrenologists, especially Gall, would like to suppose, in assigning a particular protuberance to every folly? Does it develop in accordance with natural law or by virtue of circumstances? We have no idea, and we are too respectful of our readers' peace of mind to launch into the discussion into which that question might lead us. In our opinion, however, the internal word, the self, is always attached to the external world by threads that our incomplete perceptions truly do not permit us to grasp, and mental transformations inevitably have a material cause.

We shall therefore content ourselves with saying, along with many others, as many others will say after us, that every nation has its eccentricity. The English have the mania of spleen and voyages; the French that of loquacity and revolutions; the Spanish that of cigarettes and nobility; the Italians that of idleness and music; the Turks that of the harem and bestiality. The Russians like to pass everywhere for princes; the Chinese call us barbarians, taking their tea without sugar and crushing the feet of their women; The Indians want to be crushed under the wheels of the Juggernaut and drown themselves in the Ganges with the statue of Durga; the Madagascans generate little scars along the entire length of the facial angle; the members of Buddhist sects don't eat meat; the New Caledonians eat their peers. We would never finish if we were prepared to believe travelers' tales and wanted to continue in this vein, so let us get on to our story now.

One cold and foggy winter morning in 18**, Frankfurt-am-Main woke up ready to pay its tribute to the folly of the moment: bibliomania—an eccentricity of the collecting genre, certainly the strangest of monomanias, for what has not been collected since the day when humans first experienced that imperious need to possess, even what they could not enjoy? Some collect paintings when they no longer have any room in their galleries, others books—especially foreign books—but do not read the authors of their homeland. We know people who collect buttons, postage-stamps, theater posters, envelopes, pieces of rope with which people have hanged themselves and instruments of torture. One eccentric from Brussels, who died a short while ago, had a superb collection of crows' eyes, which he showed off with pride. We do not know what use his heirs made of it.

In brief, on the aforementioned morning, Frankfurt, bibliomaniac and bibliophile—it is necessary not to confuse the two: a bibliomaniac is a worthy imitator of the Englishman who bought in London, in 1812, at the sale of the Duke of Roxburghe's library,[15] a 1471 edition of Boccaccio for 2260 pounds sterling; a bibliophile is a man who loves books for what they contain rather than their rarity—Frankfurt, bibliomaniac and bibliophile, as we were saying, headed for the old Jewish quarter. The sale was about to commence of the library of Octavius, a savant doctor who was reputed to possess the most curious books, but all of whose science had not outlived him for a second, because he had not written it down on Earth or in Heaven.

Octavius' house was the most original and most somber dwelling that one could wish to see; the house of a true scien-

---

[15] John Ker, the third Duke of Roxburghe, became an avid book collector after finding a copy of the legendary first edition of Boccaccio's *Decameron* in Italy; he paid 100 guineas for it, but it fetched a much higher price when his collection was sold after his death in 1804 by the book-dealer George Nicol.

tist or sorcerer, and cold and damp as a tomb. It is necessary to go to Germany to find houses like that today. There were little low doors that opened on to long corridors, ill-lit at intervals by small windows trellised by spiders' webs, then large rooms with low sculpted ceilings, which only received daylight via tiny lead-framed windows. Everywhere, in the largest room as well as the smallest coverts, there were books, instruments of physics and chemistry and manuscripts, all beneath a layer of dust, as if the wrath and ashes of Vesuvius had passed that way.

The crowd that precipitated itself into the house when the doors opened was the heteroclitic and heterogeneous mass that one encounters in all assemblies in which passion brings men together: bibliomaniacs, bibliophiles, bibliographers, bibliotaphs,[16] lovers of good books, fine books, illustrated editions, fine bindings, fanatic collectors of rare books, cherished books, books annotated by famous men, bizarre books: in sum, idlers who were not buying anything and imbeciles who were buying everything.

What was being sold? We would need a whole volume just to provide a mere glimpse. After those works of general literature, philology, theology, jurisprudence, medicine, philosophy, pedagogy, science, geography, history and fine arts that everyone possesses or knows something about, came incunabula on which people swooped: xylographic impressions, among others *Ars Moriendi sive de tentationibus morientium* by Jean Sporer,[17] map-painter, a majestic in-folio of very

---

[16] A bibliotaph is a man who locks his book collection away, as if entombing it.

[17] Pont-Jest gives the first few words of the title in French—they translate into English as "The Art of Dying"—but the book is obviously printed in Latin so I have given the actual title. The text in question was not published (and certainly not written) by Jean Sporer, but the reference to Sporer as a "map-painter" strongly suggests that Pont-Jest cobbled this list of exotica together with the aid of the *Bulletin du Bibliophile*, a

promising appearance; a Mainz Bible of 42 lines;[18] a 1560 *Catholicon*; a 1517 *Theuerdank*; first editions of Jean Faust, or rather Jean Fust, and Peter Schoeffer; two copies of a Mainz Psalter; a Durandus *Rationale* in 60 leaves, with two initial letters printed in red and blue; a 1462 Bible in semi-Gothic characters; Cicero's *Offices* by Fust alone, and the 1467; a *Secunda secundae* of St. Thomas, by Peter Schoeffer alone, in his turn. Then a thousand other typographic masterpieces by John Schoeffer, Peter's son, Mentelin and Eggestein, and by those illustrious descendants of Gutenberg who emigrated to Italy following the troubles that overtook them in Mainz in 1462 and 1463; the *Lactantius* printed in 1465 at the convent of Subiaco, near Rome, by Conrad Sweynheim and Arnold Pannartz, who stayed in the monastery for some time before going to set up shop in the holy city; *Pliny the Elder*, Joannes de Spire, Venice 1460; *Tacitus*, Vendelin de Spire, Rome, circa 1468; *Horace*, Zarottus, Milan, circa 1470; *Quintillian*, Campani, also 1470, etc. etc. Then bindings by Derosne, Padeloup, Lervis, Roger Payne, old Dutch bindings in white vellum, others in morocco and Russian leather; and finally, manuscripts without end, in all languages and of all epochs: Egyptian manuscripts written on royal papyrus with inks of different colors and rolled up 3000 years before; Indian manuscripts from the library of some *madrassah*, a school on the banks of the Kaveri, on leaves of the talipot palm, cut into strips, on which the characters had been inscribed with a stiletto; Greek and Latin palimpsest manuscripts; red-tinted manuscripts written with gold and silver ink; Slavic manuscripts, Cyrillic and Hieronymian, *libelli* or wax tablets; manuscripts of the Carlovingian period, lavishly gilded in the Byzantine

---

mid-century Parisian periodical, where that reference appears in an 1843 issue.

[18] The Great Bible of Mainz is famous as a manuscript version contemporary with the first printed ones, so this reference is odd—but the Mainz Psalter, cited a few lines further on, was indeed one of the first books produced by the new technology.

style; 10th century manuscripts, in which a Byzantine influence was revealed once again in the shiny backgrounds; eleventh-century manuscripts with browned gilding and graceful arabesques lightly traced with a graver; Persian manuscripts garnished with emeralds and pearls; in sum, richnesses of every sort, fought over by madmen and amateurs. Alongside all that rolled, twisted and grimaced flasks, alembics and crucibles still full of strange substances, the sight of which made one think of poisons, the elixir of life and the philosopher's stone.

A young man of about 25 was leaning on the sill of one of the windows in the large room where the sale of all these marvels was talking place, paying very little attention to what was going on around him. His large blue eyes, half-closed, were raised toward the ceiling; those who did not know him might have thought that he was following some dream of love in the empty space. He had long hair, neatly combed back. His entire person had a distinction and an extreme elegance; his feet were a trifle long and narrow, his hands pale and slender, his figure well-formed. His mouth, although perfectly-shaped, had something sad about the contraction of the lips. His physiognomy, in conclusion, expressed a mixture of youth, reflection, insouciance and melancholy.

Franz von Heberghem was not, however, one of the century's unfortunates, as common parlance puts it. He had just come into possession of a considerable fortune, which his father had left him 15 years before; his comrades at the university liked him; his former teachers had the greatest regard for him; his mistress, if he had had one, would certainly not have been deceived very frequently; his tailor dressed him well; his friends did not borrow too much money from him. All these satisfactions, however, did not seem to make him happy; everywhere, in the public squares, taverns, theatres, fencing-schools—places where he was rarely seen—he was found dreaming, absorbed in thoughts that he did not communicate to anyone.

He was far from being in love; the beautiful Marguerite Heven, his cousin—who had blonde hair and blue eyes, like all Marguerites—darted her softest glances and most dazzling smiles at him in vain. He was not ambitious for honors and titles; at least, he had refused various positions from some prince of a country that has almost as many princes as subjects. His great misfortune was a strange indecision of the mind and an insatiable thirst for knowledge. Nothing attracted or pleased him, if it was not science. His mother, while pregnant with him, must have been struck by the beauty of some Neapolitan youth lying in the sun; he was a veritable child of Campania.

To play a game, or to discuss anything but a philosophical issue, was beyond his strength. He spent the greater part of his day smoking, lying on one of the divans in his library, all of whose books he devoured but without any order, attaching himself to all theories, all sciences. He contrived to shift himself of his own accord, from time to time, for some good deed, but he had to be extracted from his home by force for any pleasurable pursuit.

"Oh my God," he sometimes said, in a fit of misanthropy and idleness, "What wouldn't I give to have a friend who would think for me! I'd no longer have to do anything but dream."

One evening, when he had gone to visit one of his old university friends, who was a writer, he had found him in a moment of idleness and had said something that summed him up perfectly.

"There really are days when one is good for nothing, when one doubts everything," his former fellow student said to him, rising from his armchair and taking his arm.

"Oh yes, there are years like that," he replied, letting himself fall on a settee and closing his eyes in order to follow one of his aerial chimeras in a more tranquil manner.

Franz had, therefore, come to the Octavius sale without any purpose, without any desire to buy anything. The crowd had found him wandering along a street and had dragged him along without him having put up a struggle. It was simpler and less tiring for him to go where everyone else was going.

The vociferations of the hawkers, the arguments, and the bidders' cries of joy and despair had not woken him up. He had watched, as indifferent as the destiny that was his god, the battle of two amateurs impassioned by a 1549 in-18 Greek New Testament printed by Robert Estienne, with two defects, and had, so to speak, fallen asleep standing up on the spot where the crowd had left him and we have introduced him to the reader.

Suddenly, he was wrenched out of his semi-slumber.

"This is yours, Monsieur le Baron," said a short, thin and bony old man, presenting him with a small and venerable volume covered in dust, which seemed to be bound in parchment. "These people must know very little about it, or have very little money. Twenty florins for the *Colloquia* of Erasmus,[19] printed by Simon de Collines, the husband of Henri Estienne's widow! Twenty florins! Oh, if I were rich, you wouldn't have got it at such a low price. Anyway, it's yours."

"Mine! Why?" Franz demanded, understanding nothing of what the bibliomaniac in rags was saying.

"Yours, of course—a windfall!" the old man replied, putting the book into his hand after having darted one last regretful glance at it. "Twenty florins! No one covered your bid; they saw that you were determined."

"What bid? I haven't opened my mouth."

"Oh, Monsieur le Baron is joking. The bookseller Hartmann went as far as 12 florins, but you went to 20 in a single leap."

---

[19] Pont-Jest gives this title in French as *Collques d'Erasme*; as it has obviously been printed in France, it is possible that it is a French translation, but editions produced during the early days of printing would have retained the original Latin. It was one of the key texts of humanism, produced by the great pioneer of that philosophical stance, Desiderius Erasmus (1466-1536).

"Me!"

"You!"

"Me!" Franz repeated, in a whisper, wondering whether he was the victim of a dream or a joke. He was certain that he had not pronounced a word for more than an hour.

"Ask these gentlemen," the little old man went on, amazed by the young man's hesitation. He took the crowd for his witness, extending his arm toward it.

The public was too intent on the continuing sale to take part in this singular argument, which had flared up a few paces away. Several spectators, however, turned round to affirm that they had not seen or heard anything. One always finds witnesses for any cause in crowds. If a wolf steals a lamb, there will be several people ready to affirm that it was the lamb that had attacked the wolf.

"Have I really bought a book?" Franz wondered, passing his hand over his forehead. "After all, it's quite possible, although I strongly doubt it."

His turn of mind, his love of the marvelous and his laziness ordered him to believe it immediately. To seek the truth in what had just happened would have been laborious.

"Go on, then," he said to his interlocutor, "give me the *Colloquia*, and take the money from me."

And, taking the book, he put 22 florins in the old man's hand—which is to say, two more than the precious volume had sold for—then left the Octavius house at a slow pace, making the reflection that it was not prudent to stay at the sale any longer, for there was no reason why he shouldn't acquire further books, without being aware of it, ten times over.

Once outside the house, he put Erasmus into his pocket and continued the stroll that had been interrupted by the involuntary visit to the Octavius residence.

Never, until then, had Franz been subject to as many dreams and hallucinations as he experienced in the hours that followed. His dreams conducted him so far that he perceived, when the Sun was already very low over the horizon, that he had been following the Main for a long time, and that he was

77

no more than a short distance from the *schloss* of a relative who lived near Frankfurt—a relative he saw rarely, firstly because of the numerous society that he received and secondly because he was the father of the gracious Marguerite, the beautiful and naïve young woman who loved him—whom he avoided in order to run after science, that coquette who never unveils more than a fraction of her charms, in order never to satisfy all desire.

During the long walk he had, moreover, experienced a strange sensation: that little book by Erasmus had seemed to him have a weight disproportionate to its volume. He had been obliged to take it out of his pocket, as if it were made of lead, and carry it, sometimes in one hand and sometimes the other. That had ended up being so unbearable that 20 times over he had made the mechanical movement of throwing it away—but his fingers had seemed to clench around the parchment in which it was bound, unwilling to let go of it.

When Franz found himself outside the residence of his relative, the Margrave von Hersfeld, he thought about the long journey he would have to make to return home on foot, and took the chance of going in to ask for a place that the dinner that was about to be served. Everyone welcomed him with open arms; his beautiful cousin blushed with happiness when he bowed to her respectfully, and they sat down at table a few minutes after his arrival.

The Margrave's guests were only seven or eight in number. Franz was seated next to an old man who had known his grandfather quite well, and whom he had sometimes seen himself. He was an old German, a stubborn philosopher, who would debate until the cows came home, and who was, moreover, an irrepressible Swedenborgian. In consequence the Baron von Heberghem barely touched the food that was served to him. The old man rendered easily evident to him the apparition of the Lord to Swedenborg in a London tavern. During the second course, he was convinced that nothing was truer than the conversations of the Swedish apostle with the illustrious dead evoked by him.

When night fell, he climbed into the carriage that had been harnessed to take him home full of these ideas. He had not mentioned his book to anyone, and had even forgotten it himself during the meal, but as soon as he was alone, that sensation of weight became manifest again. He deposited the *Colloquia* in the seat of the carriage, and arrived home an hour after his departure, without having given it another thought.

He found a blazing fire in his study, prepared by his manservant, who had begun to get anxious about his unaccustomed absence. He pushed an armchair in front of the fireplace, into which he let himself fall as if he were harassed by fatigue, and then closed his eyes.

After perhaps half an hour of dozing, Franz remembered the morning's acquisition, and went to pick up the book, which he had set down on a sideboard as he came in. Remembering that Erasmus, in his *Colloquia*, had somewhat maltreated the pope and his monks, and being a Lutheran rather than anything else, he saw its reading as a means of passing the time according to his taste. It needed no more to decide him to leaf through a book, in spite of the late hour.

Having shaken and rubbed the covers of the Dutch philosopher's work, in order to get rid of the dust, he opened it and, leaning toward the fire—for the only lamp illuminating the room was on the mantelpiece—he set about scanning those pages of the *Colloquia* in which the author recalls the privations he endured in his youth as a result of the recklessness of the Bishop of Cambrai. But the fine and caustic mind of Erasmus did not have what it took to please our dreamer for long. He had been reading for scarcely half an hour when, settling back into his armchair, he placed his book, open and upside-down, on a little table that as within arm's each, and then allowed himself to be lulled yet again by his imagination.

At about midnight, Schmidt,[20] his manservant, came in to tell him that his customary bed-time had arrived.

The servant, although he was not yet 50, was already an old retainer of the Heberghem family. He had followed Franz's father over all the battlefields of Europe, and had been witness to a thousand follies on his master's part—follies which, even more than his wounds, had caused him to die before his son could get to know him. As for the Baroness, she had died giving birth to the Heberghem's sole heir. When Franz emerged from the hands of the tutor who whom the family council had entrusted his education, Schmidt had left with his young master for the university. There, he waited patiently, like a good and faithful German—which is to say, drinking beer and smoking interminable pipes—while the young Baron von Heberghem was sufficiently stuffed with philosophy, learned well enough how to sustain a thesis, parry a sword-thrust and became master of his fortune. He had paid little heed, during that time, to the young man's character and lifestyle; it as only when they returned to Frankfurt, to the Heberghems' town house, that he had noticed Franz's taciturnity and his love of reverie and solitude—sentiments that the silence and severity of the parental home were to augment rapidly.

In fact, that huge dwelling—princely but empty, with a façade blackened by time, pointed roofs terminating in rusty weathervanes, and long obscure and sonorous vaults—resembled a tomb. Franz only reached his apartment after having closed a heavy door behind him whose hinges screeched as they turned, having climbed up a broad carpeted stone stair-

---

[20] Pont-Jest gives this name as "Smith," but says explicitly, on several occasions, that the servant in question is German. I have therefore substituted the German form of the surname, just as I have substituted "Frankfurt" for his "Francfort," "Mainz" for his "Mayence," "von Heberghem" for his "d'Heberghem" and so on, in the interests of fidelity to local usage.

case, supporting himself on iron banisters that had once been gilded, on which his footsteps made no sound, and having traversed immense rooms ornamented with heavy velvet wall-hanging that choked the air and which only received, through gigantic stained-glass windows, a bizarre daylight full of sadness. It was necessary for him to open 20 brown-paneled doors, or have them opened for him, and pass in front of 20 ancestral portraits, which greeted him every morning and bade him goodnight every evening with same grave expressions or smiles on their lips. In order to get to his room he could have taken a little staircase that led directly to it, which was specifically dedicated to his use, but on the first day after his arrival in the house Schmidt had taken him through the large apartments; he had gone through them again the next day, then the day after, without taking any account of what he was experiencing in breathing their thick atmosphere, and once the habit was acquired, he went back every evening by the same route.

When Franz had sent his servant to have his apartment prepared, a few days after his return to Frankfurt, the worthy Schmidt had found the house so rich in wall-hangings and furniture of every sort that he had been content to take what seemed to be required at random, so Franz's bedroom, study and dining-room differed very little from the other parts of the house. His bed was one of those huge items of Medieval furniture with tall twisted columns, which one could only reach with the aid of steps, and around which fell heavy, exceedingly smooth tapestries representing historic characters in full size. His bookshelves were massive, made of old oak carved like Chinese ivory, with monsters and demons grimacing from every partition; his work-desk, similarly made of heavy black oak was sustained by satyrs' legs. An immense bronze inkwell, the work of some unknown Cellini, representing Marguerite at Faust's feet, occupied one of its corners.

In his dining-room stood a gigantic dresser with its back to panels covered in embossed leather wall-hangings, which proudly displayed the Heberghem coat of arms. At the large table that occupied its center, which had been designed to accommodate 20 diners, Franz was always alone.

He had had a few paintings hung along the walls, but if all these canvases were signed with illustrious names, by a bizarre choice, only offered to the eyes the gravest subjects favored by the Spanish school, the severe monks of Zurbaran[21] and the austere physiognomies reproduced so prolifically by Albrecht Dürer and his contemporaries. There was nothing young or cheerful in the apartment in which the young Baron von Heberghem lived.

If he stationed himself at the window of his study, his gaze was abruptly arrested by the impenetrable bushes in the grounds that extended behind the hotel. None of the multiple, joyful and lively sounds of the street reached him. Everything that surrounded him was like an unbreachable barrier raised by fatality between him and youth. Even the domestic servants had modeled themselves on the phlegmatic Schmidt; the service of the house was provided without a murmur; a bleak, lugubrious silence reigned in every part of the house; the dogs were reluctant to bark in their kennels, the horses lay down lazily in their straw without whinnying.

It is understandable with what ardor Franz, in his solitude, rummaged through the rich library that his father had left him. All philosophies, from antiquity to the present day, came together there. Without itemizing the Greek and Oriental philosophers, none was absent. Mingled there pell-mell were Swedenborg, with his mysticism and his angels; Descartes, with his vortices and his idealism; Montaigne and the entire Pyrrhonian school, with its skepticism and doubt; Bacon, with his sensualism; Locke, with his empiricism; Pascal, Nicole and Malebranche, with their mystical enthusiasm; Leibniz, with his monads and his rationalism; then all of that dogmatic, dreamy, aesthetic, skeptical, and especially eclectic Germany.

---

[21] The Spanish painter Francisco Zurbaran (1598-1664) specialized in monks, nuns and martyrs.

If Franz, reaching out his hand toward one of the shelves of his bookcase, chanced to want to escape from the phraseology of Kant, the exclusive self of Fichte, the absolute idealism of Scheling, the obscurity of Hegel, the epicureanism of Wieland, the German Voltaire, the theosophical mysticism of Jacques Boehm and his divine revelations, he could only find, to distract him from all those enthusiastic idealists and stubborn logicians, works scarcely calculated to remind him that he was scarcely 25 years old.

His grandfather, who had died only a few years before his father, had only compressed his dear philosophers to make a little space, between Goethe and Schiller, amid that ideal and several German literature which forms a transition between the literature of the Orient and that of the North, for a few Medieval poems, certain strange tales, such as the *Niebelungenlied*, the *Tales of the Monk of Saint-Gall*,[22] the *Story of Faust*[23] and a few novels by Ludwig Tieck—*Journey into the Blue Distance*,[24] for example—and all the books on chiromancy he had been able to find.

So Franz, driven by his nature to reverie and the love of the unknown, only breathing an atmosphere ten centuries old, in the midst of a heart-rending silence, lived like his silent companions, retreating within himself in confrontation with

---

[22] I have translated the French title that Pont-Jest gives to this work into English, although the Latin original, presumed to be by Notker the Stammerer, a monk at the Abbey of St Gall was titled *De Carolo Magno*; it is a collection of anecdotes about Charlemagne.

[23] Pont-Jest gives this title in French, with no indication as to whether it is the original *Faustbuch* or one of its many derivatives—perhaps Goethe's; again, it seemed best to render it in English, with a similar vagueness.

[24] Yet again, I have substituted the title of the English translation for Pont-Jest's French version although the book on the shelves must surely be the original, *Das Alte Buch: Oder Reise ins Blaue Hunein* (1834)

his ideas, his dreams, his hesitations, knowing nothing, so to speak, of the external world or of reality.

Nothing would have been easier for him than to shake off the ancient world that surrounded him, to populate his house with young and joyful friends; but, as we have said, his character was fundamentally melancholy and lacking in initiative. The young men of his rank in Frankfurt would have received him with open arms, but it would have required him at least to go in search of them. That was a step of which he was incapable, and those young men fled the young dotard who only wanted dreamers for friends and science for a mistress. So Franz lived alone, limiting his relationships to a few of his grandfather's friends, authentic old men, who gave scarcely any thought to his rejuvenation.

We left the Baron von Heberghem at the moment when his servant had told him that it was after midnight.

Franz tried to come back down to Earth on hearing his valet's voice. He rubbed his eyes, stretched his arms, yawned a couple of times and, releasing a sigh, got to his feet in order to go to bed, with the submissiveness and nonchalance of a child.

By chance, his eyes fell momentarily on the *Colloquia* that he had placed, as we have said, on a little table next to his armchair. The cover that had seemed to him to be made of parchment, which he had carefully dusted before opening the book, seemed to him to be covered with dust again. He put out his hand to make sure of the fact, and for a moment, could not make sense of what was before his eyes. He was not in doubt for long, though. The parchment of the cover, which he had seen as the most beautiful pale yellow, with no other marks than those produced by tiny natural asperities, was illustrated with strange letters.

He thought he was dreaming and, to the amazement of his servant, let himself fall back into his armchair without his gaze quitting the hieroglyphic characters before his eyes. Franz was more of a dreamer than a savant, but he immediately recognized that the letters did not belong to any European language, nor to Arabic or Sanskrit, with which he had some familiarity. For a good hour, he searched his memory, turning the books this way and that, examining the bizarre parchment from every angle, but none of the symbols it bore were familiar to him. For the most part, they were little straight lines, interlaced with one another, bearing some resemblance to cuneiform script.

Not succeeding in classifying these bizarre letters, he began to ask himself how he had not seen them earlier—or, rather, how they had suddenly appeared, for he was convinced that an hour earlier, the cover of the Erasmus had been quite bare. Curiosity and his natural inclination spurring him on, he launched himself forth into the realm of hypotheses. The little incident was doubly fortunate, in that he had not sought it out. He let his head fall into his hands and racked his brains trying to find the key to the enigma.

Suddenly, the heat of the fire—which was reddening his fingers, as white and slender as a young woman's—helped him glimpse the truth. Without paying any heed to the dolorously astonished gaze of Schmidt, who though he was mad, he held the cover of the Erasmus toward the flames. After a few seconds' delay, he uttered a cry of joy. When heated, the characters traced on the parchment stood out more clearly, the slightest strokes becoming evident. There was no more doubt; what had been written there had been done with the aid of a sympathetic ink, and it was in leaning toward the fire in order to read that, without intending to, he had drawn the characters out of oblivion.

"Eureka!" he cried, exactly like Archimedes, turning to his manservant, who was on the point of calling for help. "Yes, but what does it mean?"

Again, one by one, he considered the symbols that were grimacing on the parchment as if they were mocking the efforts of his intelligence.

"Come on, come on," he said, after a few moments of futile research. "Since Octavius is dead, Master Wolfram alone can extract me from this embarrassment; let's run to him. Schmidt—my coat and hat!"

"The Baron is going out?" asked the old servant, taking a step backwards, as if to strike a defensive stance.

"Yes—be quick!"

"But sir, it's after 1 a.m. and it's snowing heavily."

"I don't care—my coat and hat."

Schmidt obeyed, murmuring: "Oh, this will end badly, I know. Sir is always alone, and never amuses himself like other young people of his age. Day and night he works; he only likes books. For sure, misfortune has entered the house with this one. As if he hadn't got enough of them in his library, and as if the Bible weren't all that good Lutherans need to divert themselves."

While his domestic was muttering, Franz, without listening, had put on his coat and, with the *Colloquia* under his arm, had gone rapidly down the main staircase of the house, shouting: "You can go to bed, Schmidt; don't wait up for me—I might not be back until daylight."

"Divine bounty!" exclaimed poor Schmidt, on hearing these words and listening to the heavy door to the street close noisily behind his master. "Divine bounty! Until daylight! In such weather! And why? If he were at least to follow the example of his honored father, the Baron, who so often said to me: 'Go to bed, my good Schmidt; I'll be spending the night elsewhere.' But no, the poor young man! The prettiest girls in Frankfurt only know him by the color of his eyes."

The old German had pronounced these last words while respectfully lighting his pipe at the fireplace in Franz's bedroom, and he let himself fall in despair into the armchair that the latter had just quit.

Soon, a sonorous snoring replaced the energetic aspirations of the smoker, who had passed, without being aware of it, from one of his two favorite occupations to the other.

In the meantime, without worrying about the north wind that was whipping the snow into his face, Franz took the road to the old town at a run. If one of his rare friends had encountered him at such an hour, he would certainly have supposed that he had had a stroke of luck or had lost his mind, so strange was his gait.

The streets were deserted; on the thick layer of snow that carpeted them, his footsteps made no sound; the silence was gloomy. From time to time, in the distance, the echoes only sent back the cries of the night-watchmen, and brought back the silvery tinkle of the bells of a sleigh that went like a phantom along the road, on either side of which the large white houses of the new town loomed up, enveloped in their winter shrouds. Soon, the streets became narrower, more tortuous and darker, the sheets of snow thicker, smoother and less immaculate. The houses shrank, as if, doubting the strength of their old age, they wanted to support themselves on one another.

Franz was obliged to slow down. He was in the old town; the obscurity was such that he could no longer advance save, so to speak, by groping his way, and the same sensation of weight that he had already experienced in carrying the mysterious book for an entire afternoon, when he had been constrained to pass it from one hand to the other several times.

He eventually stopped in front of a little low door, abundantly studded with large iron nails—a door perfectly in harmony with the barred windows of the house it sealed. It was there that Master Wolfram dwelt, a scientist known throughout Germany and one of the old friends of the young Baron von Heberghem's philosopher grandfather.

If Franz had not known for a long time that Master Wolfram only devoted a few hours of the night to sleep, the flickering light that escaped through the two casements on the first floor of the house, and which designed peculiar shadows on the black façade opposite, would have told him that the old man was not yet asleep.

Baron von Heberghem lifted the iron door-knocker, whose sound reverberated in the silence of the night.

Slow and heavy footsteps son became audible on the steps of the stone staircase in the scientist's house, and the door opened.

"Why, it's you, dear child!" said the old man, utterly astonished, lifting up the lantern he held in his hand to the height of his nocturnal visitor's face.

"Myself, Master," Franz replied. "I have need of all your science."

"Come upstairs, then; all my science, as you are pleased to call it, is always at the service of my old friend's son."

"I feared that I might find you asleep."

"Oh, I sleep very little, my dear Franz; I count the hours, and I no longer have the time to waste a single one. Octavius was two years younger than me; his death reminded me that I need to make haste if I want to finish the work I've undertaken."

Master Wolfram was an old man of about 80, still robust although somewhat bowed down, whose profound wrinkles testified to an entire life of hard work. His little eyes, dark grey in color, shone in the midst of the numerous creases that surrounded them. Their gaze was direct, as penetrating as that of just men used to reading through the mask of the face to the depths of consciousness. His nose, severe in shape, had not been deformed by age and added, by virtue of its stark line, to the austerity of his expressive physiognomy—an austerity softened by a slightly large mouth, whose strong, smiling lips, often slightly parted, indicated the old man's generosity. Master Wolfram had devoted himself to study with love, but, as an honest man and a good citizen, without forsaking all his social duties on that account, without forgetting what he owed to himself and to others. The ambition to be useful, and not pride, had directed all his research. He was clad in a long brown robe that marked, along with his white hair, all the concern that the old man had for himself. He was, in a word, the personification of that travail in which there is a most admirable and most holy love of humankind.

Franz closed the door to the street and followed the scientist up to the first floor and into his study, a vast room cluttered with books, through which, not without difficulty, one picked a path in order to draw near the table on which he was writing.

A good fire was blazing in the hearth, but, in spite of its benevolent warmth, a cold and heavy atmosphere reigned in the room, vitiated by the miasmas escaping from all those old books, consulted every day. Only a scientist, by courtesy of his estate, could spend long hours there without danger.

But Franz had better things to do than wonder whether one respired an air exclusively composed of oxygen and nitrogen in Master Wolfram's home. As soon as he had entered, he had thrown off his coat and some to lean on the table, beside which his grandfather's old friend had reinstalled himself in his large leather armchair.

"Well, what is it, my son?" the old man asked, fixing is intelligent and benevolent gaze on Franz. "How do you come to be running through the streets in weather like this instead of being wrapped up warmly in your bed? How can I be of use to you?"

"Well, Master," the young man hastened to reply, handing his book to Wolfram, "by telling me what this is."

"Eh? My dear child, have you forgotten your time at university to the extent of no longer being able to read Erasmus?" The scientist had taken and opened the *Colloquia*. "An admirable edition," he added. "Very rare. Did you buy it at the sale of my learned friend Octavius' effects?"

"I didn't buy it," Franz replied. And he told the story of how the Erasmus had come into his hands, and the strange sensations he had experienced since it had been in his possession. Then, without paying any heed to his old friend's incredulous smile, he took the book from his hands, closed it, placed the cover before his eyes and showed him the mysterious characters.

"It's not Erasmus that interests me," he said, "it's this. On presenting this book, not by chance—for nothing happens by chance, in my opinion—to a flame, these characters you see appeared there. What do they mean? To what language do they belong?"

"Strange, in truth!" Master Wolfram replied, after a moment's silence. With a magnifying glass in his hand, he was examining, not the letters, to which he had devoted no more than a glance, but the parchment itself, in the places where it was not covered in writing. "Strange! I don't recognize the material of which this cover is made. It's neither goatskin nor sheepskin, of which the Geeks made use; nor is it pigskin, with the aid of which the Middle Ages have transmitted their marvelous church books to us. Ah! I think I have it. Look, these thin strips confused with one another, these little asperities that erasure hasn't completely removed, the multiform papillae, some rounded, others conical, have put me on the track. Moreover, I don't perceive on the inverse of the skin, any trace of the passage of hairs, which, in the animals I've just named, continue through the dermis as far as the follicles that nourish them and protect their roots. Light a lamp, if you please."

Never taking his eyes of the old man, Franz made haste to obey. He took a bronze lamp from the mantelpiece, lit it, and brought it to Master Wolfram, who had just delicately detached a fragment of the curious cover of the *Colloquia* with a penknife. Having steeped it momentarily in a chemical solution, he presented it to the flame.

The parchment, brightening close to the flame, twisted as if it were trying to get away. After a brief interval, it caught fire—or, rather, shriveled up, crackling.

"No more doubt," said the scientist. "In consideration of the manner in which that little piece of skin burned, and the particular odor it gave off, there's no more doubt. It's bizarre! What's inscribed there must be very precious, or it was written by a singular eccentric."

"Why?"

"Because it's written on human skin."

"On human skin?"

"Exactly. If the physiognomy of the parchment, the marks and asperities that I've just pointed out to you, had not been sufficient for me to recognize it, the color of the flame and the intolerable odor would have convinced me."

"Human skin!" Franz repeated, in amazement. "Is there any example of human skin being employed for such a purpose?"

"Askew,"[25] Wolfram replied, "the bibliomaniac English physician who succeeded in bringing together all the editions of various Greek writers, had one of his favorite authors rebound in that way, in order to possess a unique binding—but apart from the title of the book and the name of its author, nothing was written on the cover. It might well be that the membrane on which Joseph made sure that copies were made of the holy books that the high priest Eleazer sent to Ptolemy Philadelphius was made of human skin—but outside of those two cases, my dear Franz, our poor envelope seems to me to have been most frequently respected."

"And the characters?"

"Ah, the characters! Let's examine them together."

Bent over the cover of the Erasmus, like the old man, Franz began to study the letters on the fantastic parchment again. With each passing moment they were taking on a greater importance in his eyes. It was with a feverish anxiety that he waited for Master Wolfram's verdict. It seemed that his life—or, even more, his happiness—depended on what was written on that fragment of human skin.

"Of course!" the scientist said, after a few minutes. "My dear child, I have no need to search any longer; these letters are runic characters. If I hesitated momentarily in recognizing them, it's because they belong to the Scandinavian or Marcomanni[26] variety. As for explaining to you immediately what

---

[25] Anthony Askew (1699-1774)

[26] The so-called Marcomanni runic alphabet is actually an academic fiction cooked up by Carolingian scholars attempting to establish an equivalence between the runic and Latin

they mean, however, that's more difficult. I can see that these three letters"—he showed Franz three symbols placed separately at the head of the 12 or 15 lines traced on the parchment—"are the three first letters of the runic alphabet; they bear the names of three great Scandinavian deities: Freyr, Thor and Odin. Do they form here, by virtue of their combination, a word whose meaning escapes me, or are they there as an invocation of the three redoubtable gods? I can't be sure. For that which follows, familiar as I am with the interpretation of runes, the letters don't seem to me to be placed in a fashion to form any words—not ones known to me, at least. Perhaps the author of these singular lines did not think his secret sufficiently well-defended by sympathetic ink and, better to protect it from the uninitiated, he has written it down by giving to the letters of the alphabet of which he has made use a conventional value of his choice. The more I examine these different groups, the more I think that that's the case. Look, these two symbols"—he showed the young man two letters similar to the French B, only differing from one another by virtue of a dot placed in the inferior circle of one of them—"are, in runic words, two infrequently-employed consonants, the first corresponding to our B, the second to our P, but here I see them repeated continually. It's the same with this other letter, which is the same as the *djh* of the Indian Pali idiom, in the *Magadha* alphabet, and which corresponds to our K, from which it only differs in form, as you can see, by the suppression of the lower oblique branch. One encounters it quite rarely in the funeral and votive inscriptions that exist in great quantity in the Swedish province of Uppsala, but in these 15 lines it occurs more than 50 times. It's evident to me that it does not have its usual value-but what other letter is it replacing? I can't tell yet. It's only by feeling our way and calling hypotheses and probabili-

---

alphabets. It has nothing to do with the Marcomanni, a tribe that once lived in the Main valley but migrated to Bohemia during the days of the Roman Empire.

ties to our aid that we'll arrive at a literal translation of this singular manuscript."

Without saying a word, Franz listened to the old man, who also seemed to be gripped by an ardent desire to know what they had before their eyes.

Master Wolfram returned to the examination of the manuscript for several minutes, and then raised his head again.

"I think I'm definitely on the right path," he said. "I'd wager now that these three letters placed at the head of the page are an invocation of Freyr, Thor and Odin. If I'm not mistaken, that's a reference-point of extreme importance for our research. What comes next is perhaps only a prayer, or one of the supposedly magic formulae of which the priests made use, in the earliest historical epochs of Scandinavia, to interrogate destiny. We shall see—but tomorrow. To complete this translation I need more lucidity than one has at my age after a long day's work. I need a more considerable tension of the brain than I would be able to support at present. Come back tomorrow evening. I'll tell you then, my child, what is written here, or admit my ignorance."

In spite of his desires and his impatience, Franz dared not insist. After having thanked Wolfram and having promised to return at dusk the following evening, he left and went back to his house.

We have said that Schmidt had gone to sleep while waiting for his master. The impact of the knocker on the massive door to the street woke him up abruptly. When he opened it to the snow-covered young man it was with a maternal solicitude that he questioned him—but Franz, absorbed in his dreams, made no reply, and the fearful old servant followed his master to the threshold of his bedroom, whose door the latter closed behind him.

Schmidt heard him walking back and forth for half the night. The young Baron von Heberghem's imagination was struck by the sequence of strange incidents that had been logically strung together around him since the morning, and that idea drew him into the milieu of worlds of fantasy.

He remembered everything that had happened to him in a matter of hours: the purchase of a book that had had the effect of taking him out of the city, in the exact direction of the schloss of the relative that he avoided in order not to allow himself to be seduced by Marguerite's love; the intolerable weight of the little volume and the efforts he thought he had made to get rid of it; the bizarre coincidence that had sat him down next to a mystic philosopher who had taken him far from reality, and opposite the beautiful young woman who had offered him, on the contrary, all that the real world contains of joy and happiness; then the discovery of those mysterious characters on the parchment made of such a strange material; and finally, the visit he had just made to Master Wolfram, who had left him in confrontation with the unknown. He would have given ten years of his life to be 24 hours older.

Toward morning, Franz succumbed to fatigue, threw himself on to his bed and fell asleep.

His servant woke him up only a few moments before lunch-time. In his hand, he held a letter, and the *Colloquia* of Erasmus, which he had a strong desire to throw in the fire rather than taking it to his master.

"Give it to me, quickly," said the Baron to the old servant, snatching the book and the letter from his hands. He had guessed that the letter could not be anything other than Master Wolfram's reply. With a feverish hand he broke the seal and began to read avidly.

Dear child, the old man wrote, *I've been able to translate the runes on the cover of your Erasmus more rapidly than I expected. As I observed your impatience, I'm sending you the book and the translation without waiting for your visit this evening. As I had supposed after a brief examination, the runes are only a species of evocation and a magic formula. I hope that this only has the attraction of curiosity, for I firmly suppose that your brain is not in a poor enough state to believe in such follies.*

94

This is what the 15 lines so mysteriously traced signify, word for word:

Freyr, Thor, Odin!

You who have the intelligence and the courage, and who seek wisdom, go very far into the North, between the rivers Driva and Logen in Scandinavia. On the night of the summer solstice, when Hodur and Nott are the masters of the sky at the same time as Vali, climb the Nunsfjeld, and do not stop until you reach the summit. With a runic staff inscribed with the sacred formula in hand, you will stand it up, inclining it toward the pale star as it rises, in the lowest of the mysterious signs engraved in the granite, and, following its shadow to the place where it stops, you will lift up the rock, while invoking Vidar. Do not let yourself be seduced by the silver harps of Hogspolar, brave the Niks and the Valkyries; the spirit of the sage Mimer is there, confided to the Earth, under the guard of Moralfer, who will retreat before you.

Franz reread this strange invocation several times, striving to understand it; then, having got up, dressed rapidly and went out, without giving any more thought to the lunch that awaited him than to the supplicant expressions of Schmidt, who watched him in amazement.

"No more doubt about it—my poor young master is mad," said the old servant, taking his head in his hands, when he could no longer hear the young man's footfalls in the stairwell. "What are we going to do now?"

Twenty minutes later, Franz knocked at Master Wolfram's door.

"Ah! I was expecting you, my son," the old man said to Baron von Heberghem, while the latter took his place in the large armchair next to the fire. "Well, are you content with my translation? If, like your dear grandfather, you love the fantastic and the extraordinary, you must be satisfied—that's exactly what you've got."

"Listen, Master," said Franz, interrupting Wolfram. "You only remember me when I was very young; you don't know what has happened to my mind since I entered the phase that follows the 20th year. The indifference I had for everything toward the end of my adolescence—a sentiment that was perhaps not happiness but was at least calm—had soon been replaced, even before I left university, by a curiosity, a passionate desire for knowledge. When I returned to my father's house, especially, the quietude of my early youth gave way to fever and insomnia. This mysterious parchment has redoubled my thirst for the unknown. No, your translation doesn't satisfy me. However correct it is, it's obscure to me. I've come to ask you for a more complete explanation of these runes."

"Oh, my dear child," said Master Wolfram, drawing nearer to Franz, whom he examined for a few moments with his limpid and searching gaze, and taking him by the hand, "you really do have a fever—your skin is dry and hot. Take my advice and go home, without asking anything more. Have a horse saddled, gallop flat out along the bank of the Main until the evening, in company with joyful friends, or think about your beautiful cousin Marguerite Heven, whom, if what they say is true, you are killing with your indifference. You are certainly the grandson of my old friend the philosopher, the dreamer, your grandfather. For a head like yours, the tree of science only bears dangerous fruit. Avoid it; don't try to gather them; remember the parable of Scripture. Most of the time, we only harvest doubt in the arid fields of science, over whose soil we remain bent all our lives. You spoke of happiness, my son; ignorance, that's happiness! Do you think that a man who has tried to penetrate all the mysteries of nature can have a single day, a single hour or a single second of calm, unless his faith is strong, unbreakable and all-powerful?"

"But knowledge!"

"Knowledge! Doesn't every new step that he makes in knowledge show him his weakness, his ignorance, and prove the domination over him of everything that surround him? If a man interrogates his body, he fears death at every instant; if he raises his eyes to the Heavens, he sees how far away he is from God; if he lowers them to the Earth, he perceives his tomb at his feet. In the domain of science, he only overcomes one obstacle to find himself facing an unsurpassable one. If you only knew, Franz, the disappointments and frustrations that we laborers owe to that bitter fruit; if you only knew the despair into which those superb individuals have been dragged who have tried to cross the barriers that the Creator has imposed on our judgment; if you only knew the slow tortures in the midst of which those indefatigable seekers the world admires have succumbed—those insensate dreamers who are not content to interrogate the earth, that dust from which we emerged and to which we must return, but who also want to sound the incommensurable depths of infinite space with their human gaze! The love of science is the most frequent form of pride. Those whom you call great men know full well that they are only considered so by virtue of an inversion of the ordinary laws of physics. The further away they are viewed from, the larger they appear!"

"They know," Franz murmured, in a low voice.

Master Wolfram heard him. "They know! That's true—but they suffer in their pride if they are ordinary men, and in their love for humanity if God has put into their hearts that sacred love, for the first thing that science teaches them is the weakness of our perceptions. A scientist wishes to seek outside himself the miracles that are only in the man himself. Poor fool! He does not want to believe the falsifications that nature provides at every instant of the laws that he thinks he has discovered. What do we know about color? We are witness to facts and search in vain for causes. I can prove that by a thousand examples.

"Science offers no means of explaining the action of the moon on terrestrial objects by effects independent of its attraction and its light. In slow maladies, the cessation of life often coincides with the greatest possible distance of the Sun; it's almost always night, when that star is at our antipodes, that consumptives die. Why? To what causes can the changes of weather brought by the passage of the moon from one phase to another be attributed? Do you know why opium puts one to sleep? No more than Molière's physicians. What do you say about comets? And light—does it originate from particles belonging to the luminous body, which that body emits incessantly in all directions, as odorant bodies release the corpuscles that escape therefrom? Or is the fluid a subtle kind of matter that fills space, to which the luminous body imparts an agitation that is transmitted sequentially, as the vibrations of sonorous bodies are propagated through the medium of the air? Which of the two hypotheses, of Newton and Descartes, ought we to choose? Are we going toward the heavens or have we descended therefrom?

"We want to explain everything, even creation, and the person whom faith instructs to believe that God created light on the second day and the Sun on the fourth. Remove the Sun, however, and you're in darkness! To seek to know everything, to explain everything, leads to the absurd. The Hindus represent Brahma in the form of a serpent, supporting the world on his head. He is supported himself on a tortoise, but on what does the tortoise rest in its turn? They refrain from saying. All systems lead there, by dear child. The greatest geniuses have left their reason or their faith in these unfathomable precipices of mystery that surround us.

"Newton discovered the only one of the great laws of nature that it has been given to man to penetrate, and he ended up writing a ridiculous and futile commentary on *The Twelve Horns of the Animal of the Prophet Daniel*.[27] Descartes provided the explanation of the true law of reflection, and proceeded from error to error with his vortices. He, the great genius, supposed an absurdity: the identity of matter and space. Pascal, to escape doubt, threw himself into narrow religion and died at 39. Swedenborg began his life with useful discoveries and terminated it sadly in outré mysticism.

---

[27] Newton's *Observations on the Prophecies of Daniel and the Apocalypse of St. John* (1733) was published some years after his death, prejudicing his reputation in the eyes of some scientists.

"We're surrounded by even more material and palpable proofs of the poverty of our nature. Physicians have gone mad for having made mental alienation their constant study. Others have communicated to their children the respiratory maladies to which they devoted their exclusive attention, in the prideful hope of extracting Death's secret: an effect quite incomprehensible, if a strange hazard had not directed it. Bright, the English physician who devoted himself furiously to the study of diseases of the kidneys died of the cruelest of those diseases.[28] That's science, my child! Come on, come on! You're young and rich; thank God for those two benefits, enjoy life and love, instead of dying by virtue of anticipation before your hour has come.

"These lines that I've translated for you are rather bizarre, I admit, but at the end of the day, that's no reason to get so involved that you forget to eat or sleep. The fashion in which they came into your hands only seems supernatural by virtue of your imagination, overexcited by that ancient world of dreams into which you have drawn yourself, and the calm and rest to which you have condemned yourself—calm and rest dangerous at any age, but especially at yours, when he possesses a superabundance of strength and youth, which ought to be expended if one wants the equilibrium between those two enemy brothers, the physical and the mental, to be maintained."

"Perhaps I'll follow your advice, Master," said Franz, shaking his head, "but first give me the explanation I'm asking you for."

"Is it curiosity alone that drives you to ask?"

"Yes," the young man forced himself to reply, calmly. "You can certainly assume that I'm wise enough not to believe in evocations and the gods of Norse mythology."

---

[28] Richard Bright (1789-1858), who gave his name to a disease of the kidneys, actually died of heart disease.

"Oh, my child, on the contrary—I'd rather you were mad, but mad as one is at 20 years of age. All right! I'll satisfy you. Let's re-read the translation I sent you together."

Leaning toward Master Wolfram, to whom he had handed the letter, Baron von Heberghem prepared to listen to what the old man was about to say, without missing a syllable.

"Freyr, Thor, Odin," the scientist began. "Those three letters are, as I thought, an invocation placed at the head of our singular manuscript by the person who wrote it, to summon the protection of the three great Scandinavian deities. The custom of first putting oneself under the guard of a protective God before writing exists among many Asiatic peoples, and you know that the Scandinavians and the peoples of Asia emerged from the same cradle. The resemblance between Phoenician characters and runic characters is one of numerous proofs of that common origin. A Muslim never writes a letter without preceding it with an invocation of the prophet; a Hindu addresses himself to Vishnu, the protective god, his *Juvans Pater*, and willingly puts, at the head of the pages on which he is to write, the word *Aouan*, which is the one with which the Vedas commence.

"The three lines that follow—y*ou who have the intelligence and the courage, and who seek wisdom, go very far into the North*—have no need of explanation. First, the author wants someone to go to a country that he describes precisely enough for it not to be hard to find. The rivers Driva and Logen are two of the innumerable watercourses that emerge from the Skanderna mountains in Norway. Then it becomes less clear. *On the night of the summer solstice,* it says, *when Hodur and Nott are the masters of the sky at the same time as Vali*—which is today, Hodur and Nott being the divinities of the night and Vali that of the day, when it is day and night at the same time—a common phenomenon in the polar regions when, for several days, the Sun never quits the horizon. The peak of the Nunsfjeld is not close enough to the pole for the phenomenon to last for a long time, and it's for that reason that our magician designates as the night that must be chosen for the invocation that of the summer solstice—the epoch which, as you know, gives us the longest day of the year in our hemisphere.

"I continue. *With a runic staff inscribed with the sacred formula in hand.* This staff, on which the runic characters must be carved—probably the three words, or rather the three letters, placed at the head of this singular script—will play the role here that the staff always plays in magical ceremonies, from Aaron's rod to fairies' wands. *You will stand it up, inclining it toward the pale star as it rises, in the lowest of the mysterious signs engraved in the granite.* Which is to say that, after having placed the staff upright, with its foot in the lowest of the notches of runes carved on one of the slopes of the summit of the Nunsfjeld, the operator must point its other extremity at the Moon, as soon as it appears on the horizon.

"The Sun, which will still be illuminating the peaks of those desolate heights, will then project the shadow of the staff over the rocks, and it's where that shadow stops that one ought, *while invoking Vidar*—which is to say, employing considerable force, Vidar being the Hercules of Scandinavian mythology—doubtless to displace the rock, to find the spirit of Mimer. *Do not let yourself be seduced by the silver harps of Hogspolar, brave the Niks and the Valkyries* evidently means nothing other than: don't stop in towns, whatever pleasures you find there, and overcome all obstacles courageously."

The old man concluded: "That, dear child, is all that I can add to my translation."

"But what is the spirit of Mimer?" asked Franz, who had not taken his eyes of Master Wolfram throughout the time he was speaking.

"Oh, that's true—I forgot to give you that detail. Mimer, my son, has never been a man or a spirit. It was, according to Scandinavian legend, an embalmed head which possessed all knowledge, and which Odin, the first king of the fabulous times of the Aesir, consulted at awkward moments. One simple question addressed to the head, and its reply settled any matter. Does the author of these runes want to make it unders-

101

tood that the head of Mimer the sage is out there under the rocks of the peak of the Nunsfjeld, that it has conserved its singular power of knowing everything, and also that of speaking and giving advice? I don't know—it's quite possible. In any case, though, as I don't suppose that you have any more intention than I have of going to verify the fact, it would be silly of us to waste any more time on the story."

"You're right, Master, and I thank you," Franz replied, getting to his feet and shaking Wolfram's hand respectfully. "I'm very small by comparison with your science."

"Come on, come on, you silly boy! Put Erasmus and your cabalistic runes away in a corner of your library, and love Marguerite. Love—that's the science of youth. And sleep soundly, without seeking to know. Remember my advice, and when you have need of your old friend again, come back. You'll always be welcome."

Shortly after leaving the antiquarian scientist, Baron von Heberghem went into his house, much calmer, as if his decision was made. From that day on, he no longer set foot outside, shut up more than ever in his library, and broke off completely the exceedingly rare relationships that he had maintained in Frankfurt. Schmidt employed every possible means to find out what his young master was doing while he was alone for such long periods; he did not succeed. The Margrave von Hersfeld came knocking at his door, in vain. The sweet memory of Marguerite, a gracious phantom of the past, came knocking at his heart, in vain. Nothing could extract him from his studies and dreams.

More than five on this passed in that way.

"What's the date, Schmidt?" he asked his servant one day, as he sat down at table.

"The third of June, sir."

"The third of June?"

"Yes, sir."

"Already. I'll have time, though. Schmidt, get everything ready today that we'll need for a journey of several weeks. We're leaving for Stettin tomorrow morning."

"Where are we going, sir?" Schmidt asked, in terror.

"Norway, my brave Schmidt—Norway, the land of long winters and nights during which you can see the Sun."

The old servant went out and raised his arms to the heavens.

Franz set about reading Wolfram's translation of the runes attentively—a translation that he had never set aside—and transcribing for the thousandth time, for fear of forgetting them, all the explanations he had obtained from his old friend. Then he ran to shut himself up in his library, in order to dream once again of the power that he was about to possess, of the supreme science that he believed he had been summoned to snatch from oblivion.

He had been there, alone in the midst of his dreams, for several hours, and night had fallen, when Schmidt came in to hand him a letter. He opened it.

Franz, Marguerite wrote, *I hear that you're going to leave. Where are you going? To run after some chimera from which you hope to obtain happiness! I'm acting in violation of all social laws in writing to you—to you, who have forgotten for such a long time our joys and childish oaths—but I have a presentiment of misfortune, and if I cannot be your wife, I want to replace your mother. Stay, Franz—stay among us, I implore you! I have divined the torments and doubts of your soul. Stay! I pray constantly that you might remember, perhaps that you might love. It's not for my happiness that I beg you on my knees—who am I?—but for yours...for you, who are everything to me.*

Franz drew a piece of paper toward him.

Marguerite, he wrote, *in a feverish and hurried hand, I love you as before; I'm leaving, it's true, but I shall return soon, and as I wish to be, superior to other men. We shall be happy then. Since you love me, don't try to struggle against destiny.*

Proud man! He denied, in those few lines, that of which humans beings should be prouder than anything else—his free will.

Three days later he embarked at Stettin, with his servant, on the steamship that would put him ashore at Christiana after a crossing of 72 hours.

On June, 22 a little more than a fortnight after their departure from Frankfurt, Franz and his servant, accompanied by a guide, were climbing the Nunsfjeld. They had left the poor hamlet that suspended its wooden houses covered with birch-bark from the flank of the mountain at an early hour.

Although it was already 10 p.m., they could see almost as well as in the middle of the day. The Sun had not quit the horizon, along which its course extended. Its oblique whitened rays, drowned in mist, cut out huge shadows on the granite giant. The Nunsfjeld reached up proudly into the sky, dotted in the north by pale and vacillating stars. Its summit, covered in snow for eight months of the year, had now shed its winter shroud and presented nothing to the eyes but bare and brutal asperities.

The guide, a tall blond-haired Norwegian with harsh features—a true descendant of those men of Asia, the Aesir who had come from the east under the leadership of Odin—marched in the lead, his great iron-clad staff in his hand. Franz followed him with a firm step, plunging a calm gaze into the profound crevasses that the revolutions of nature had hollowed in the Nunsfjeld. Totally focused on the project he had undertaken, he marched without seeing the danger, thinking of nothing but the goal he wanted to reach. Schmidt came next, or, rather, trailed behind his master. Half crazed by terror, the old servant of the Heberghems sometimes crouched down on a rocky ledge in order not to give way to vertigo, but quickly resumed his course to rejoin those ahead of him when they had disappeared behind one of the thousand outcrops of the mountain.

They arrived thus at the summit of the mountain at about midnight. The most sublime of spectacles awaited them there. Beneath their feet, the precipices they had just crossed and the bare and brutal frocks, still sunlit, showed themselves in all their stark horror. Lower down, in a half-light full of poetry, immense forests of fir and oak extended, the monotony of which was broken periodically by *soelers*—little meadows of flowers and grass, seemingly suspended from the flanks of the mountain. Below that they made out the village, almost buried in the semi-darkness of the valley. Around them, somber colossi, loomed the peaks of the Skanderna mountains, with their eternal snows. Above their heads the desolate zones of the grey sky unfurled, with its tints of reddish yellow in the east. There was not the slightest breath of wind; the calm that surrounded them was so profound that they might have been able to hear the distant North Sea continuing its work of destruction in the fjords.

Franz did not pause to contemplate that marvelous landscape. Without wasting a instant resting on the platform that surmounted the mountain-peak—a platform on one of whose rocks Schmidt and the guide had collapsed with fatigue—he started making a tour of the summit of the Nunsfjeld.

After a few minutes of ardent, fitful and feverish research, he found what he was looking for. On a huge flat rock set against the peak, he saw three long gashes, corroded and pitted by time, but still reproducing with sufficient exactitude the three letters set at the head of the mysterious manuscript—letters that he had carved himself upon a birch-wood staff that he held in his hand. Hollowed out almost a foot deep in the granite, each of those symbols was more than a meter tall. Quieting the beating of his heart, Franz then turned his gaze westwards. At the extremity of the incommensurable horizon that it embraced, the light clouds were iridescent on their lowers borders. The Moon was about to rise.[29]

---

[29] Literary moons, unlike the real one, occasionally rise in the west.

"Schmidt!" he shouted, in a strident voice.

The old German shivered as this sound suddenly troubled the calm of the solitudes, and immediately rejoined his master.

"It's time," said the young man, when his servant was beside him. "You see that gash in the rock?"

"Yes," Schmidt murmured, in a hushed voice.

"Hold this staff upright, like this, in that horizontal cleft." He indicated the place described in the manuscript. "When the Moon appears, tilt the staff toward it, without taking the foot out of the hole."

"My dear master," said Schmidt, throwing himself on to his knees in front of Franz, "I'll do everything you ask of me, but is this Christian work that we're doing here?"

"Silence! Obey me. The pale star is about to emerge from oblivion."

"God protect me," said the poor servant, seizing the magic staff with a trembling hand and helping himself with his knees to hoist himself up to the mysterious symbol."

"Are you there?" Franz asked, after a moment.

"Yes."

"Pay attention! The Moon's about to appear."

The nocturnal disk was sketched on the horizon; a reddish segment extended skywards. The Sun continued in its course, reminiscent of an immense globe of fire. The shadow of the runic staff extended in zigzags over the asperities of the granite.

Soon the Moon showed in its entirety, red and bloody. Smith, feeling chilled by fear, tilted the tip of the runic staff toward it, recommending himself to divine clemency.

Franz reached the place where the shadow terminated in a single bound.

"Here, Schmidt—come here!" he shouted.

The old servant let himself slide down the declivity of the crag, collecting a few grazes. He found his master pale and wild-eyed, his hair in disorder, with his hand on the edge of an enormous boulder placed on the rim of a precipice, the sight of which induced vertigo. It was an irregular block with rounded corners, probably brought into that strange position by one the inexplicable prehistoric revolutions with the aid of which nature has turned almost all of Scandinavia upside-down.

"This is it—yes, this is definitely it," the young man murmured, in a low voice, as if he were afraid of being overheard. "The spirit of the sage, and all his science, is about to be mine." And he darted a boastful glance into space.

"Help me overturn this rock," he suddenly said, in a loud voice, to Schmidt.

"Oh, Master, Master! What do you want to do? It would need superhuman strength."

"Help me," Franz repeated, in a harsh and severe tone, which he was using for the first time on the poor servant who had cared for him since his childhood. "Combine your efforts with mine, and may Vidar protect me!"

Smith imitated his master, and bent down beneath the rock.

For a few moments, they made futile efforts—and for anyone able to see them, the strange spectacle would have been offered of two men struggling against nature, whose work of destruction had stopped before that mass. Suddenly, however, the rock quivered on its narrow based, oscillated momentarily as if it wanted to bury the pygmies who were attacking it, and, losing equilibrium, was precipitated down the mountain with a terrible noise, which awoke a thousand sonorous echoes.

They could hear it for a long time, breaking everything in its passage, drawing an avalanche in its wake of everything that in encountered on its route, uprooting trees, staving in *soelers*, then bounding into a torrent, where it sank with a thunderous rumble, after waking up the eagles sleeping in their eyries, which took flight, uttering their shrill and lugubrious screeches., and bears which fled their lairs howling.

Terrified, Schmidt collapsed on the ground. Franz pushed back his hair, which a cold sweat had stuck to his forehead. The guide, thinking the travelers he had led had just fallen victim to their curiosity, and that the entire mountain was crumbling, ran away uttering screams of terror.

A few moments later, a profound, harrowing silence replaced these multiple, horrible, indefinable noises. After having darted another prideful glance at the nature surrounding him, all of whose mysteries he was about to know—at the pale blue sky unfurled over his head and which, for him, would no longer have any secrets, and over the immense horizons that he was about to fathom to infinity—Franz recovered a fraction of his calmness and looked down at his feet.

In being displaced, the mass of granite, had uncovered a cavity that it had sealed for perhaps 2000 years. Without worrying about his servant, who was no longer showing any signs of life—what was one man to the person who was about to know everything?—he sat down, dangling his legs over the edge of the gaping hole, trying to see into its gloom.

There, involuntarily, the past suddenly appeared to him: the years of his childhood, with their insouciance, their naïve joys, passed before his eyes again; all his youth came back into his heart: the memory of that pure and devoted love, which he had refused in hastening his heartbeat to breaking-point. As if by means of a memory anterior to himself, he recalled his mother, whom he had never known; it seemed to him that a white form, with a smile on her lips and an aureole about her forehead, but with a broken, bleeding heart, was extending her arms to him.

He wondered then whether he was the plaything of a dream, if it was really him on this desolate peak, to which the genius of evil had transported him, as Christ had once been transported, in order to tempt him. And he stood up fearfully, to extract himself from that somber gulf, which seemed to be his tomb—but his foot collided with a sonorous object.

The Moon had risen into the sky; its tremulous rays showed him, at the bottom of the cavity into which he had gone breast-deep, an iron box corroded by rust. He remembered, and, chasing away the holy thoughts that had stopped him momentarily on the brink of the abyss, he reached out a hand.

On contact with the damp and icy metal, his fingers clenched around a closed ring on the lid of the box, with such force that he could not detach them. It was with fury, then, that he strove to draw the mysterious box toward him.

Schmidt, who had recovered his senses, had dragged himself to his master's side on his knees. "Oh, my dear Master," he said, in a faltering voice, "that's the work of the Devil—let's flee this place!"

Franz, who was not listening, did not hear. He dug his fingernails into the earth in order to extract his treasure therefrom.

It was a horrible hour, that hour of hard labor in the midst of the lugubrious silence, only broken by Schmidt's sobs, the curses of the seeker and the quivering of the air beneath the wings of the eagles that were multiplying the concentric circles of their flight around the mountain peak.

Franz finally succeeded in hoisting the box up to the platform. He made one last effort then, and hauled himself out of the hole. In the course of that final movement the box opened, and a mummified head rolled out of it, with sunken eyes, prominent cheekbones and cracked, partly open lips. It came to a stop at the feet of the young man, who had hurled himself in pursuit of it.

"What shall I know?" he demanded of the head, kneeling down.

"Everything!" it replied, in a strange voice that seemed to emerge from the bowels of the earth.

Schmidt, who was following what was happening in front of him with haggard eyes, screamed and fled. Franz, bruised breathless and exhausted, fell forwards, wrapping his arms around the head, as he might have done to a beloved woman, for fear that she might escape him.

Rising slowly into the sky, the Sun began its work of resurrection; the stars paled before the splendor of its rays. The clouds of mist extended over the valley were dissipating; red deer were belling in the forest; the tops of the fir-trees were shivering under the kisses of the breeze; the flowers of the *soelers* began to open their corollas; all the echoes of the mountain repeated the joyous murmurs of the nature that was waking up to the first fires of the day, and the ringing of the hamlet's church-bell, calling the faithful to prayer, rose up clear and sonorous toward the Heavens, repeating: *Fiat lux!*

We have passed over two years in a single bound, and we find Franz unrecognizable, even to those who had been his intimates. His cheeks are hollow; his complexion, once as fresh as a young woman's, is marbled and livid; his eyes are hollow and vitreous; his figure is bent; profound wrinkles are already furrowing his brow; his mouth is twisted into a bitter smile. Doubt has crept into the most secret recesses of his soul; pain has imprinted its cruel stigmata on his face; his youth has fled; at less than 30 years of age, he is already an old man.

And yet, he is knowledgeable! Science has lavished him with its most impenetrable secrets; his knowledge has astonished the entire world; his name is on everyone's lips, with admiration, but all forms of affection have deserted him—his oppressed heart no longer understands them. His proud and jealous mistress, science, has chased them all away.

One alone endured until the last moment: Marguerite only died of grief a few days ago, already aged, no longer the brilliant child of yesteryear. After these two years, during which she had given all her youth, all her soul and all her love, without receiving anything in return, she died without complaint, showing Franz the Heavens with her diaphanous and trembling hand.

He is on his deathbed in his turn, alone and isolated; he is holding Mimer's head between his thin fingers.

"But what is death?" he croaks, gathering the strength of the last breath that remains to him.

"Death, for the proud, is punishment, the end of folly and doubt," replied the head. "For those who have loved, it is the beginning of life in eternal love."

Franz uttered a scream, and expired.

When they came to take away the body, the gravediggers recoiled in fright. The cadaver was holding an embalmed head in its clenched hands, which could not be removed therefrom. They were obliged to seal it up with him in the tomb of the Heberghems.

Alphonse Daudet: *Wood'stown*
(1873)

It was a superb place to build a city. It was only a matter of clearing the banks of the river and felling a part of the forest—the immense virgin forest, rooted there since the birth of the world. Then, sheltered on all sides by wooded hills, the city would descend to the quays of a magnificent harbor, established near the mouth of the Red River, only four miles from the sea.

As soon as the government in Washington had granted the concession, woodcutters and carpenters set to work—but you never saw such a forest. Clinging to the soil with all its lianas and all its roots, when one felled it in one place it grew back in another, rejuvenating itself in its wounds, and every blow of the axe caused green buds to emerge. The streets and squares of the city, scarcely sketched out, were invaded by vegetation. The walls grew less rapidly than the trees, and crumbled as soon as they were built under the efforts of still-living roots.

To overcome that resistance, which blunted the blades of axes and hatchets, they were obliged to have recourse to fire. Day and night, thick smoke filled the dense thickets, while the tall trees above burned like candles. The forest still tried to fight back, hindering the fire with floods of sap and the airless coolness of its clustered leaves.

Finally, winter arrived. The snow came down like a second death upon the large areas full of blackened trunks and burnt roots. Henceforth, it was possible to build.

Soon, an immense city made entirely of wood, like Chicago, extended along the banks of the Red River, with its broad streets lined up and numbered, radiating around squares, with its bank, its markets, its churches, its schools, and an entire maritime apparatus of sheds, customs-houses, docks, bonded warehouses and boatyards. The city of wood—Wood'stown as it was called—was rapidly populated by new occupants. A feverish activity circulated in all its districts, but in the surrounding hills, overlooking the streets filled with crowds and the harbor cluttered with vessels, a dark and menacing semicircular mass was displayed. It was the forest, which was watching.

It watched the insolent city that had taken the place of three thousand gigantic trees on the river's edge. All of Wood'stown was made with its own life. The tall masts that swayed gown there in the harbor, those innumerable roofs descending toward one another, all the way to the last and most distant suburban hut—it had furnished everything, even the instruments of labor and the furniture, its services only measured by the length of its branches. What a terrible rancor it nurtured, therefore, against that city of plunderers!

For as long as winter lasted, no one noticed anything. The people of Wood'stown sometimes heard a dull creaking in their roofs and items of furniture. From time to time, a wall cracked, or a shop counter noisily split into two—but new wood is subject to such accidents, and no one attached any importance to them. At the approach of spring, however—a sudden, violent spring, so rich in sap that one sensed it underground like the running of springs—the ground began to stir, lifted up by invisible but active forces. In every house, the furniture and the partition walls became boated, and long swellings were seen in the floors, as if moles were passing through them. Doors and windows alike could no longer be closed.

"It's the humidity," said the inhabitants. "It will pass, in the summer heat."

Suddenly, the day after a great storm that had blown in from the sea, which brought the summer in its scorching lightning-bolts and warm rain, the waking city uttered a cry of amazement. The red roofs of public monuments, the bell-towers of churches and the floors of houses, all the way to wooden bed-frames, were sprinkled with a green tint, as thin as mildew and as light as lace. At closer range, it was a quantity of microscopic buds, or the unfurling of leaves already glimpsed. The bizarre abundance amused people without causing anxiety, but before dusk, clusters of greenery were blooming everywhere on the furniture and the walls. Branches were visibly growing; lightly retained in the hand, the increase in their size could be felt, and a fluttering as of wings.

The following day, all the apartments looked like greenhouses. Lianas followed the ramps of staircases. In the narrow streets, branches came together from one roof to the next, setting over the noisy city the shade of forest glades. That became worrying. While scientists met to deliberate upon this extraordinary case of vegetation, crowds gathered outside to see the various aspects of the miracle. Cries of surprise, and the astonished rumor of all those inactive people, gave a solemnity to the strange event.

Suddenly, someone shouted: "Look at the forest!"—and they perceived with terror that, in two days, the verdant semicircle had drawn much closer. The forest seemed to be descending toward the city. An entire advance guard of brambles and lianas reached as far as the first outlying houses.

Then Wood'stown began to comprehend and to be afraid. Evidently, the forest was coming to reclaim its place at the river's edge, and its trees, felled, dispersed and transformed, were liberating themselves in order to precede it. How could the invasion be resisted? With fire, there was a risk of burning the entire city—and what could axes do against that incessantly-renewed sap, those monstrous roots attacking the ground from below and those thousands of airborne seeds that were germinating explosively and causing a tree to grow wherever they fell?

Everyone set to work bravely, however, with scythes, harrows and axes, and there was an immense carnage of foliage. It was in vain, though. From one hour to the next, the confusion of virgin forests, in which the interlacing of lianas is combined with gigantic shoots, invaded the streets of Wood'stown. Already there was an irruption of insects and reptiles. There were nests in every corner, and huge fluttering flocks of birds, and masses of little chattering beaks. In one night the city's granaries were exhausted by all the newly-hatched broods. Then, like an irony amid all that disaster, butterflies of all sizes and all colors flew over the florid clusters and provident bees in search of safe shelters in the hollows of the trees that had sprouted so rapidly installed their honeycombs, as evidence of duration.

Vaguely, in the noisy surge of foliage, the dull blows of axes and hatchets could be heard. On the fourth day, however, all labor was recognized to be impossible. The grass had grown too high and too thick. Climbing lianas clung to the arms of the woodcutters, strangling their movements. Besides, the houses were becoming uninhabitable; the items of furniture, laden with foliage, had lost their shape. The ceilings collapsed, pieced by the lances of yuccas and the long spines of mahogany-trees—and instead of roofs, the immense domes of catalpas were displayed.

It was over. It was necessary to flee.

Through the network of plants and branches that was growing increasingly dense, the terrified people of Wood'stown raced to the river, carrying as much as they could of their wealth and precious objects. They had difficulty reaching the riverbank, though; there were no more quays—nothing but gigantic reeds. The boatyards, where timber was kept, had given way to forests of fir-trees, and in the harbor, where everything was in flower, the new ships looked like green islets. Fortunately, a few armored frigates were found there, on which the crowd took refuge, and from which they were able to see the old forest join victoriously with the new forest.

Little by little, the treetops became confused, and under the sunlit blue sky, the enormous mass of foliage extended along the riverbank to the distant horizon. There was no more trace of the city, neither roofs nor walls. From time to time, a muffled noise of collapse, the last echo of a ruin, or the axe-blow of an enraged woodcutter would resound in the depths of the foliage. Then there was no longer anything but the vibrant, rustling, buzzing silence, clouds of white butterflies spiraling over the deserted river, and downriver, toward the open sea, a fleeing ship, with three great green trees looming up amidst its sails, carrying away the last emigrants from what had been Wood'stown.

Camille Flammarion: *Love Among the Stars*
(1896)

"What up with you this morning?" I exclaimed, on seeing André arrive in my study, with a disconcerted and desolate
expression. His face was very pale, his eyes haggard his hair
unkempt and his step weary, as if he had come back from a
long-distance run. "You obviously haven't spent the night
stargazing, although the sky was as clear as I've seen it for a
long time."

"On the contrary—yes, I spent a long time observing the
sky last night; but I'm emerging from an unparalleled astonishment, and I certainly haven't slept a wink this morning.
I'm still flabbergasted. But what you mistake for terror was
only an agreeable and charming surprise, followed by a
boundless regret—a surprise so great that I haven't recovered
from it."

"Have you discovered a new star with a fantastic spectrum, a nebula of extravagant form, a comet with hectic
tresses? Is it only the insomnia that succeeds a vivid excite-
ment?"

"It's an adventure more extraordinary than any you could
imagine. I dreamed about Dora—yes, Dora, my deceased beloved."

"Oh, your imagination! What tricks it plays on you!
You've become the victim of hallucinations—you, whose
mind is so calm and ponderous. Don't trust yourself! I've already told you that. It's a dangerous slope. You're too much a
poet. I prefer mathematics—it's safer."

"I'm not arguing. Hallucination, dream, whatever you
like; but I'm still overwhelmed by what I've seen and heard—
and that's not unreasonable at all."

"Well, tell me your story. I don't doubt that it will be
very interesting."

117

My friend André was a young man of 25, an excellent observer of the sky, describing with great exactitude the planetary aspects of Mars, Jupiter or Saturn—to which his studies were preferentially devoted—but a trifle dreamy and mystical. A great and unforgettable distress had struck him, and since that time, which was still quite recent, he had been plunged into a constant melancholy.

He had fallen in love with a delightfully beautiful young woman, as dreamy as himself, ardent and passionate, whom he had suddenly lost after three months of adoration. And during the two years since the blow had struck him, he had thought of nothing but her, scarcely succeeding in forgetting her for a few moments in the scientific work that absorbed all his strength and energy.

Life without her was sad and colorless, and he had often wanted to die. He hoped to die soon, and in fact, his health, once so flourishing, was deteriorating insensibly. He believed in the survival of the soul and wondered incessantly where his beloved might be. Several times, he had told me that he thought he had sensed her presence nearby, and heard some kind of internal voice speaking to his soul. I had tried to deflect him away from these ideas, which seemed to me to be dangerous to his mental health, and I had believed that he was no longer thinking about them when he arrived that morning, so troubled and agitated by his vision.

He explained that at about 2 a.m., while he was examining through his telescope a region of the Milky Way very rich in stars, he had, so to speak, swept the beautiful constellation of Cygnus with his instrument, and had paused on the admirable double star Albireo, composed of two suns, one golden yellow and the other sapphire.

While he trained a very powerful ocular lens on the blue star, and was preparing to observe it with a spectroscope in order to make a special study of its curious light, he had experienced a sort of dazzling in his eye, which he had initially attributed to the bright glare of the star, and had also felt a

slight electric shock on his shoulder. He continued the observation nevertheless and fitted the spectroscope to the telescope. Either in consequence of the fatigue of the night's observation, however, or simply a to rest momentarily, he had sat
down in the large armchair in which, occasionally, after long
observations, we had the habit of stretching ourselves out and
going to sleep briefly.

The rays of moonlight entering through the cupola, forming a light streak of blue-tinted light, were caressing the apparatus, the globes and he maps. He tried to get up to carry out
his spectroscopic observation, but very close to him, he had
seen, with his naked eyes, the adored form of his beloved
standing in the moonlight, and had simultaneously felt nailed
to the armchair by a superior magnetic force.

I shall, however, leave it to André to tell the story, for
what follows is exactly what he told me.

Dora was standing there before me. Above her shone Albireo. My beloved was even more beautiful than before, idea-
lized and as if made translucent by a celestial clarity.

My first impression was amazement. I was not in the
least afraid, and yet I felt a glacial frisson run from my feet to
my head and I began to tremble. I remained sprawled in my
armchair, as if my body were made of lead. She didn't come
closer to me, and it seemed to me at first that I didn't want to
approach her.

She looked at me tenderly with her large azure eyes,
which always seemed to be opening on some new astonishment, and said to me eagerly: "Why haven't you come? I'm
waiting for you. We haven't yet known love!"

The tone of her voice was the same as before, and as
soon as I heard it, the apparition lost its strange character and
became—for want of a better word—natural.

At that mild reproach, that regret and that avowal, all our
hours of happiness reappeared before me, animatedly: our
passionate intoxications, our delightful ecstasies, our endless
kisses—and the very extravagance of our sensuality, all those

enchanting scenes suddenly resuscitated in my brain, went through me like a lightning-flash of radiant joy.

I couldn't help replying: "What! We haven't known love?"

"Certainly not," she replied. "We've only had its gross sensations."

"Oh, how exquisite!"

"Yes, for the Earth. But how different it is here!"

"Where's here?"

"In the system of Albireo's azure star."

And she told me that she lived there, in the midst of a sort of angelic population. While I listened, I seemed to be living that new life with her. It was no longer death; it was life. I found myself with her again, as before.

"Yes," she added, "what a difference there is between the love one knows here and that which we tasted on Earth!"

I confess that I experienced a disagreeable expression on hearing that confession.

"How do you know that?" I cried, piqued by a sudden bizarre resurgence of the thorn of jealousy.

"Foolish! Still foolish!" she replied, with her adorable smile. "Jealous of a dead woman!"

"But you're not dead, since you're talking to me about love, and claiming to experience joys unknown on Earth. No, I'm not jealous—but I still love you. Well, I'm capable of being reasonable. Explain yourself."

"On Earth, we only have five senses: sight, hearing, smell and touch each play a role in our sensations, although true love resides essentially in the attraction of souls toward one another. We only have five senses, or even four."

"How many more have you today, then?"

"Seventeen. And I repeat, I'm waiting for you. And of those 17, there's one that surpasses all others, worth as much as the rest put together, which on its own might be called the sense of love."

"Which is?"

"It's the electrical sense. In love, electricity plays a preponderant role, even in terrestrial organisms, which are so gross and obtuse. The human soul is a substantial entity, electrical in nature, which radiates far beyond our visible material body. That electricity emits invisible waves, which are very different from those of light."

"Yes, I know," I replied, my mathematical mind taking over. "Luminous waves are three ten-thousandths on a millimeter in length, while electrical waves are 30 centimeters."

"I didn't know that."

"I understand perfectly well what you're saying to me, therefore—that there's a radical difference between the magnitude of the vibrations that give birth to electrical or luminous effects."

"None of the five senses of the terrestrial body can perceive electrical waves. Among us, by contrast, it's the first of our 17 senses. It's much more important than sight itself. Why does one love? Why does one experience sympathies and antipathies? Why does one remain different? That's a mystery unknown to you, although it's very simple for us, who perceive it so directly by means of a special sense.

"The soul, which is an electrical substance, emits into its surroundings electrical waves invisible to you but perceptible to us. You might compare these waves to the sound waves that emanate from the vibrating string of a violin, a harp or a piano. If these sonorous waves encounter in their passage another string able to vibrate harmonically with the first, the second string will emit a sound without anyone having touched it. It's an experiment that you can make at any time.

"If two souls vibrate in unison; or sometimes, better still, in harmonic accord, their mutual waves, one encountering one another, associate and fuse, and the two beings are united with one another by a chain more solid than iron. It's not only their gazes that are knotted, it's their entire being. All that one might do to oppose that union would be wasted effort. It will be accomplished, if necessary, after death.

"If a cacophony results from the encounter of the vibrations, antipathy is the result, and the most beautiful reasoning can do nothing about it. That man is antipathetic to me; that woman gets on my nerves. Don't seek to correct the first impression; it will be wasted effort.

"Well, on Albireo, we see these vibrations of the soul, these etheric undulations, as you see by means of light; we perceive them by means of our electric sense, while they remain foreign to you. These electrical vibrations, which are like the very atmosphere of love, are unknown to you on Earth. You experience love much as the deaf experience music."

"Oh!" I said. "How ungrateful you are!"

"No my adored one, I remember everything. But remember that love is the intimate union of two beings. In terrestrial amours, there is no entire melting into one another. But here, where the electric sense is entirely developed, our etheric bodies are like two electric charges that annihilate one another in lightning. The combination is so intense that of two beings who embrace, only one remains—like oxygen and hydrogen, which, in combining, lose their individuality to form a drop of water, a limpid pearl that contains the entire rainbow and summarizes the universe."

"But what happens afterwards?"

"Well, afterwards, one can recover oneself! I don't know how it happens, but one is resuscitated."

"That's not impossible. Electricity can dissociate a drop of water and separate once again the oxygen and hydrogen whose union formed it."

"You know how to explain everything scientifically."

"So," I added, "one goes as far as losing consciousness of one's existence—really dying—and being reborn?"

"Do you understand now that our 17 senses, governed by the first among them, provide sensations compared with which the most vivid joys experienced on Earth are merely the coarse impressions of mollusks? And what light inundates us! What flowers! What perfumes! It's like a perpetual ecstasy. Of, if you came, if you were here!"

"Can't you take me?" I exclaimed, launching myself toward her.

"Come!"

I seized her in my arms, stuck my lips to hers, and suddenly saw, in the heart of a very soft and tender blue light, that Dora was bearing me away on immense wings. I was clinging to her body, lost in delight. Numerous beings, drifting like us in the atmosphere, had the form of dragonflies, with antennae, palps and aerial organs, which doubtless represented the new senses that she had mentioned to me.

I understood that I had been suddenly transported on to one of the planets of Albireo's azure sun. Cascades of blue water fell from the rocks and ran through an immense garden carpeted by brilliant flowers. Birds with bright plumage, seemingly luminous in themselves, filled their air with their songs.

"Let's go through this light," she said, "toward the evening horizon and descend into the palaces of night."

Having moved out of the illuminated hemisphere, we arrived in semi-darkness. All the rocks, all the vegetation and all the animals shone with a blue, green or roseate light, phosphorescent or fluorescent. The rocks undoubtedly possessed properties analogous to those of phosphates and sulfates of barytes, which store solar light received during the day and radiate it during the night. The flying creatures were similarly luminous, in the fashion of fireflies. Darkness, on this world, is never complete, firstly because of that curious phosphorescence of everybody, secondly because of Albireo's second, golden sun, the distant light of which is almost never absent, and also because of a ring analogous to that of Saturn, which, lit by these half-suns of different colors, is sometimes blue, sometimes yellow and sometimes green, and distributes the strangest gleams through the semi-darkness.

How small a thing is our poor and minuscule terrestrial world, which we imagine to be everything, by comparison with those ultra-terrestrial marvels!

My beautiful and beloved Dora carried me lovingly between her wings, and we descended toward the shores of a lake, beneath an immense arborescent foliage, the vast leaves of which extended like a cradle of verdure over a carpet of moss strewn with a thousand little flowers.

"This is where I live," she said. "Let's rest."

In my delight and ecstasy, I wanted to seize her in my arms and savor on her lips the exquisite happiness of being loved by her—but scarcely had she touched the ground than her terrestrial form was instantly transformed into another, similar to the beings that we had encountered flying in the atmosphere. She was no longer my Dora. She was, however, even more beautiful and more radiant, and compared with her, I felt like an earthworm.

"To love me still, to love me forever," she said, "it's sufficient to die! Quit the Earth. Here, you will be mine."

"Have I not quit the Earth, then?" I replied, astonished.

"No—look."

She touched my lightly on the forehead with the tip of an antenna and I felt a sharp electric shock. I opened my eyes and found myself alone, sitting in the large armchair. My beloved had disappeared.

I no longer have any doubt that she really is living on that star in Cygnus. She is calling me there and I shall soon recover her. I love her more than ever!

Such was André's story. That apparition had had such a powerful impact on him that, from that day onwards, his mind appeared to be wandering far from the Earth. His poor health declined rapidly, but he lived happily in his dream, with the desire, the obsession to see it realized.

I was not surprised when, a few months after the adventure that has just been reported, I was told of the sudden death of my dear comrade.

On a beautiful summer night, perhaps haunted by the same vision, he had stretched himself out in the same armchair, next to the great equatorial telescope, aimed at Albireo, and, in the morning, he was thought to have fallen asleep there—but his cadaver was completely cold.

To his right, a little bottle containing hydrocyanic acid—one drop of which is sufficient to dissolve the bonds attaching the soul to the body—had fallen on to the floor.

Charles Recolin: *The X-Ray*
(1896)

Doctor Cornelius Schwanthaler had not slept for a week. He had god reason. To have discovered an inoculable substance endowed with the astonishing power of making the eyes accessible to Roentgen rays—the famous rays then impassioning all Europe—was more than sufficient, it must be admitted, to trouble the nights of the only possessor of such a secret. So exclusive is the love of science, on occasion, that he had even completely forgotten the blonde fiancée who, a few days earlier, had accepted the homage of his heart. But might he be mistaken? Were the innumerable guinea-pigs into which he had injected the new serum really seeing the interior of objects and creatures, to the exclusion of their exterior forms? Might he not simply have impaired their brains, in trying to change their natural vision? The answer was doubtful—and Dr. Schwanthaler continued to observe his guinea-pigs tirelessly.

The little animals seemed singularly disconcerted. They could be seen turning in their cages, then suddenly launching themselves against the bars, which were made of wood, in the manner of flies when, unaware of the obstacle, they precipitate themselves into windows. The doctor transferred them to another cage made entirely of iron, and they remained tranquil; the experiment was in accordance with the theory.

Nevertheless, Dr. Schwanthaler knew that he would have to attempt a supreme trial. Its result was uncertain—but had he not consecrated his entire life to science? Ought he to hesitate to sacrifice his sight too, if necessary? Could he refuse, or leave the admirable opportunity to others?

To see inside everything, to penetrate to the very center of matter, to scrutinize the framework that sustains the human membrane and perhaps discover, in those depths, the secret of the soul and the prime movement of thought was a double dream of medicine and philosophy well worthy of some risk in order to make it a practical reality. What operation would he not be able to undertake on the day when his gaze, neglecting deceptive surfaces, would guide his infallible hand to a seat of disease invisible to anyone else? It was glory—and, to begin with, an assured revenge against his colleagues at the hospital, where his talents as a surgeon had recently been disputed, following an operation that had, it is true, left the patient alive, but which had failed completely.

Dr. Schwanthaler did not hesitate any longer. He filled a little syringe with the photographic serum, fitted the platinum needle, then went to the window to see whether the liquid had conserved the desired limpidity.

At that moment, Sunday bells resounded in the distance. There was a bright dawn that gradually enlivened the colors of the surroundings, where, bathed in pink light, frail bushes were swaying and all of nature was reawakening in spring. The perfume of nascent flowers rose up in light waves. Birds were singing amid the first leaves of the linden trees. Beyond the garden wall, a young girl was going to the well, rapidly and gracefully, with her pitcher on her hip.

Dr. Schwanthaler passed his hand over his forehead and reflected momentarily, deliberating. All things considered, he would only offer a demi-sacrifice. One eye would suffice for science. He would conserve the other to complete his vision.

He chose the left for his experiment. Bravely, he plunged the needle of the syringe into the cornea, as he had done with his guinea-pigs, and injected the serum. Then he lay down on his bed, having covered the injected eye with a kind of monocle whose glass he had coated with a platinum-based yellow substance impenetrable to the new rays.

The next day, a familiar knock on his door woke him up. The faithful Gertrude had brought him his breakfast: an excellent opportunity to carry out an initial trial. Rapidly, he unmasked the left eye and closed the right one.

Surprise! Instead of the old serving-woman whose red face and opulent flesh excited the hilarity of his pupils, he saw advancing toward him, with a comical waddle, a squat skeleton from which a few transparent viscera were suspended. The whole was covered by a sort of floating gauze, a trifle green-tinted, like the gelatinous envelope of a medusa but even more diaphanous, without any precise form, like a mist about to dissipate. As for the bones, he could distinguish them with perfect clarity. He even observed slight deformities, incorrect apophyses and misaligned ribs—and the heart, suspended in the middle of the carcass, like the clapper of a bell, seemed to be afflicted with a worrying hypertrophy. There was no more doubt: the experiment had succeeded!

He got dressed rapidly. It was the very day on which operations were carried out at the hospital. Oh, his colleagues would see! With his head held high, and the monocle covering his eyes, he went through the wards, while the interns nudged one another as he passed by, whispering: "Look! Dr. Schwanthaler's wearing a monocle, and a funny monocle at that!"

He went to the theater and arrived in the middle of a discussion. It concerned a poor devil who had been hit by four revolver-bullets during a brawl. Three had been extracted but the fourth remained undiscoverable. When Dr. Schwanthaler was seen, his opinion was solicited—purely out of deference, for it was known that, since his last operation, he was reluctant to undertake hazardous interventions.

To the great astonishment of the assembly, however, he advanced resolutely, removed his monocle, closed his right eye, seized a probe, inserted it without hesitation, and withdrew the bullet.

"There!" he said, simply, in the midst of a murmur of admiration.

Other patients were brought to him, and every time, after a rapid inspection, Dr. Schwanthaler identified the seat of the malady. He extirpated tumors, scraped bones, removed needles. Almost all the patients died, but the operations had been admirable.

"What insight! That Schwanthaler...it's so unexpected!" said the doctor's colleagues, amazed and jealous. In a single day, Cornelius Schwanthaler had surpassed all the surgical glories of the century.

Slightly fatigued, Dr. Schwathaler spent the afternoon lying on his divan, savoring the intoxication of his triumph. He received an angry letter from his fiancée reproaching him for his silence and summoning him to a rendezvous on the riverbank the following day—but he read it distractedly, almost bored. He loved her a great deal, however, his Marguerite, so gracious and so pretty, with her violet eyes, her peach-flower complexion and her figure as slender as a little. For the moment, though he was entirely possessed by scientific pride. Love paled beside the aurora of his renown, like the last star of the night in the rays of the rising Sun.

He was in a hurry to collect the first echoes of that renown. He recalled that there was a ball at the burgomeister's house. It was there, assuredly, that the news of his success at the hospital would first be hawked around. He resolved to attend. He detested social occasions and dancing, but he was a philosopher. He reflected that, in addition to the pleasure of being praised, he would be able to see the strange appearances offered to his Röntgenian eye by feminine coquetries and social vanities. He knew already what science would gain from his discovery; he would not be sorry to establish the profit that psychology would draw from it.

At the appointed hour, he put on his ceremonial frockcoat and headed for the burgomeister's house, repeating a line from a French poet: *Nothing true thereunder but the human skeleton.*[30]

When he made his entrance, the ball was in full swing. He was immediately surrounded, congratulated and ques-

---

[30] The line (*Rien de vrai là-dessous que le squelette humain*) is from "La Nuit d'août" by Alfred de Musset.

tioned. He allowed himself to be admired. Then, as a quadrille was forming up, dispersing the masculine groups, he hid himself in the bay of a window, closed his right eye, opened the left, and gazed.

The spectacle was certainly strange, and well worthy of the observations of a disciple of Schopenhauer. Black skeletons leaned over, bowing to one another, swaying, making graceful gestures, then suddenly gripping one another two by two, violently, as if they wanted to confuse their respective ribs—which were, however, maintained a short distance apart by the medusa-like envelopes that the doctor had remarked that morning in his old serving-woman, which were the flesh, the form and the beauty that had disappeared in the penetrating light of the implacable rays. Only jewelry and metals remained opaque, and it was only one bizarrerie more that all those osseous bodies bore diamonds and decorations suspended over the sternum, like votive offerings.

Suddenly, the doctor redoubled his attention. He had just perceived a furtive couple who had slipped behind the palm-trees in the gallery. Softly, slowly, through the transparent leaves, two jaws, two preposterous hollow noses and two skulls approached one another and stuck to one another for some time.

A kiss! the doctor thought, and his irony suddenly collapsed. He did not want to see any more. He left the ball, saddened.

He had to reason sternly with himself, tell himself repeatedly that science ought not to recoil before anything, that truth was the most important thing of all. "Yes, but love!"

He went to bed, slept badly, had nightmares, and woke up the next day with a violent headache.

He went out into the country. The freshness of a spring morning restored his serenity. After all, he still had one eye accessible to the lies of form; that was enough for love. It was simply a matter not taking off his obstructive monocle inappropriately and replacing it in good time. His vision would thus be divided into two parts: one for science, the other for life.

Reassured, the doctor opened his left eye, desirous of studying nature in its internal aspect. He was disappointed, though. The leafless, colorless trees, loomed up like the tentacles of an octopus. Sometimes, the small black skeletons of birds took off from the grey branches. That was the sole reality that arrested his gaze within the immense bare horizon.

He sat down on a mound on the river bank. His anxieties took hold of him again. In being a great scientist, one was no less a man.

Decidedly, he thought, *the truth isn't pretty. It is, however, thus that the Supreme Being sees everything.*

Around him, the morning was suave; everything was singing. There was an adorable concert of murmurs, a delightful harmony of colors and perfumes—and the flowers raised their corollas toward the pensive doctor, whispering to him: "Look how beautiful we are, Doctor. What do the names matter that we bear in herbals when dead, and the inert structures that we reveal to the microscope? God made us to give fragrance to humans, not to educate them." And the trees, in their turn, but more loudly, said: "Schwanthaler, Schwanthaler, make no mistake; we have been created to shelter nests and protect the fearful kisses of the amorous from indiscreet gazes." And the leaves lost in the sky quivered with anger, saying: "Schwanthaler, Schwanthaler, your science will bring you misfortune."

He raised his head again, as if to brave the universal malediction—and then, at a turning in the path, he perceived a frail skeleton that was advancing, its tibias bumping together, with a gross stomach wobbling in front of it, whose abnormal volume contrasted strangely with the slenderness of the bone structure.

Excellent! thought the doctor. *A new case, not yet studied, of gastric abnormality!*

Science had resumed it total grip on him.

Meanwhile, the frail skeleton was still advancing. When it was very close to the doctor, it stopped, and a youthful voice pronounced: "My dear Cornelius, are you so absorbed that you're unable to recognize your beloved? Oh, these scientists!"

Frightened, the doctor replaced his monocle and reopened his right eye. Malediction! His fiancée was standing before him.

It was too much. He lost his head and cried: "Never! Never!" Then he fled toward the town, gesticulating like a man possessed.

Gretchen stood there petrified.

Dr. Cornelius has gone mad, she thought. And she collapsed at the foot of a tree, her arms hanging down loosely, plunged into despair.

Having gone back into his laboratory, Dr. Schwanthaler took his head in his hands and shed abundant tears. "I didn't think of that!" he exclaimed. "What if I were never to see her otherwise again!" But he still had one eye. He opened it very wide to convince himself of its integrity.

Was it the emotional shock that had caused a slight infiltration of the phosphorescent serum from one or bit to the other? It seemed to him that he saw less clearly even with the reserved eye.

He looked at himself in a mirror. His flesh appeared to him less firm, his form less accentuated. Was he, too, going to assume the appearance of a mournful skeleton enclosed in a medusa? Horror! No longer to see, no longer to see himself, no longer to see in any other way!

Gripped by rage, the blasphemed against science. "Ecclesiastes was right!" he cried, tearing at his hair. "Whoever increases knowledge increases sorrow. God has retained the worst part for himself: the truth, which is sad. He has left us beauty, illusion and hope. And I have refused the role allotted to human beings, which was that of happiness."

Taking possession of an instrument, he tore out the accursed eye, and threw it out of the window.

And when the blonde Gretchen, all a-tremble, came in search of news of him, he explained to her that a horrible ophthalmia had obliged him to destroy his left eye.

"It was doomed," he told her.

When he offered to release her from her engagement, however, the gracious child put her arms around him and whispered to him: "But since it was doomed…and after all, you still have one…"

"And it's a good one," said the doctor, "for it sees beauty!"

Michel Corday: *The Mysterious Dajan-Phinn*
(1908)

It is 9 a.m. on a cool April morning, on the platform at the Gare de Lyon; scattered groups are awaiting the arrival of the express from Marseilles. All faces are turned toward the luminous access-route, amid a view encumbered by signals and motionless trains, watching for the first glimpse of the engine. If all the foreheads are orientated by the same gesture, however, how diverse are the thoughts that they conceal! What varied motives these seemingly-identical impatiences have!

Examine the little group of two ladies and three gentlemen who have advanced to the very edge of the platform. These five people have come to meet Doctor Bro, returned from Borneo after an absence of seven years. How disparate their sentiments are, though! To grasp them, it will be necessary to know the man who inspires them.

It would, it's true, require a fine mind to define Dr. Bro exactly. When he left for the Orient, at 45 years of age, his contemporaries had the most contradictory opinions of him: an unsound mind; a universal intelligence; an innocent; a charlatan; a semi-lunatic; a superman. His life had been hectic. As a naval physician, he had once traveled the world with an avid curiosity and a relentless ardor. He wanted to try everything, to know everything, to exercise himself in all the directions of human activity. Then, at about 30, during an extended stopover in Malaya, he had become enamored of a young orphan in the Dutch colony and had married her. Renouncing his naval career, he seemed to want to settle in Borneo, to devote himself to personal endeavors within the tranquility of the family. After two years, however, his wife had died giving birth to a little girl.

Bro threw himself violently into pure science. Having returned to France, he confided his little Suzanne to the care of a nurse, then to the protection of a boarding-school, and plunged himself entirely into his work. For more than two years he divided his time between his laboratories and research stations of marine physiology where attempts were being made to wrench the secret of organic origins from the oceans.

Finally, he published the results of his research on the living cell. Picking up the theory of spontaneous generation after Traube, Leduc and Raphael Dubois,[31] he claimed, with evidential support, to be able to create life. He displayed artificial vegetation made with his own hands. The manufacture and the experiments, the news of which expended beyond the scientific world to reach the crowd, were passionately contested.

By a singular hazard, his most redoubtable adversary was his best friend. This Bro, in whom brutal grief and the empery of science seemed to have dried up the wellsprings of affection, had remained faithful, throughout his turbulent life, to one adolescent friendship—but Ruchard, whom he had known during his student years, had followed a straight line. Now a famous professor, he defended orthodox theories with authority, from the height of State-approved chairs. Exasperated by

---

[31] Moritz Traube (1826-1894), Stéphane Leduc (1853-1939) & Raphael Dubois (1849-1929). If anyone doubts the force and scope of the scientific "orthodoxy" that set out to crush and annihilate the theory of spontaneous generation, they only have to consult the on-line biographies of these scientists and observe how their championship of the notion has either been expunged from the record of their careers or radically downplayed. We now know for sure, of course, that the theory is false, but in their day, the evidence was still weak enough to permit controversy, and there was no shame in their espousal. Modern readers of this story may find it advantageous to reassume an open mind temporarily, in spite of the certainty of hindsight.

the sight of his old companion compromising himself with pursuits that he deemed chimerical, he castigated him in private and pursued him in public. The contest was too unequal; Bro was vanquished. His doctrines were reduced to the rank of alchemical dreams and his experiments to the dimensions of puerile games.

Perhaps the defeat was all the more painful because it was inflicted by a friend. Nevertheless, he let nothing of that sort of that show. He did not fall out with the triumphant Ruchard. Shortly afterwards, however, he went into exile. His brother, the landscape-painter César Bro, had just got married. He entrusted Suzanne to the young household. As for himself, he applied for an obtained a post in the zoological gardens of Borneo.

It was thought, by those around him, that he was going to try to forget his disappointments in the country where he had got married, and where he had spent a few happy and peaceful years. For seven years, his letters—rare and brief—remained mute regarding his work, his leisure and his inner life. Detached from his relatives, indifferent to the questions that had impassioned him, in retreat from the world, he seemed to have accomplished a sort of moral suicide.

An event came into prospect, however, from which he could not disinterest himself: his daughter's marriage. If it had been a matter of some random fiancé, no doubt he would have left the matter to the clairvoyance of those he had placed in charge of Suzanne and given his consent, nothing more. But could he accept for a son-in-law, without protest, the son of Dr. Ruchard? Such was the man, in fact, to whom it would be necessary for him to give his daughter, according to the two young people in question—for they were in love with one another. Each appeared to the other as the living promise of honor.

Let no one see in this choice one of those fatal hazards which, in novels and plays, throw heroes destined to avoid one another together. There was nothing simpler and more logical than the circumstances of which the affinity was born. Professor Ruchard, although he had acted in the contest according to his scientific beliefs and in the interests of his friend, had experienced remorse over his excessively complete victory. He deemed himself partly responsible for the exile in which his old companion had buried himself alive. He had tried to repair the damage to the extent that was possible, and he had taken an interest and developed an attachment to the young girl who, without him, might perhaps have retained a father.

A widower himself, Ruchard found favor in the family in which the girl lived. That intimacy became greater still when Henri Ruchard, the professor's son, who was gifted with a considerable talent as a painter, took César Bro as a tutor. Thus the two young people were able, for years, to enjoy the benefits of one of those frank and healthy friendships in which temperaments and characters are revealed and tested, which ought to be the veritable school of marriage.

Warned by a letter from his brother—a small masterpiece of prudent diplomacy and emotional eloquence—Dr. Bro said that he might give his reply in two months' time. By the hundred-and-twentieth day, they were watching out for it with every mailboat from the Far East. Finally, a telegram came from Borneo: *Am returning*. Nothing else. And by means of a telegram dated the previous evening, from Marseilles, Bro had announced his return for that very morning.

One can now imagine the mental dispositions of the two young people and their family standing on the platform of the railway station.

The most excited, by far, is Suzanne Bro. She is going to see her father again. Oh, certainly, a father with whom she had hardly ever lived, whom she recalls in her schoolgirl memories, always feverish, quivering with the tension of thought, always about to leave. She does not hold that semi-abandonment against him. He must have suffered so much…having been left alone after two years of marriage, and then experienced so much unjust disappointment. Yes, unjust. Her knowledge of the great quarrel in which her father and Professor Ruchard were involved is somewhat confused, but she feels, and is sure, that her father was right. She has faith in him. And it is precisely because he was right that he was able to forgive his fortunate rival.

As for thinking that her father, in consequence of those old differences, might oppose his daughter's marriage, she refuses to believe it. Besides, will she not be able to vanquish him, to seduce him, if he makes any sign of resistance? One knows one's power. One is 20 years old. One is not too repulsive. And is there not a joy that must override and efface everything, for a father who has left an indecisive little girl to recover a fully-grown young woman, neat and blonde in the typical Dutch manner, with eyes of a blue so limpid that they seem to instill a desire to bow down before them?

One person who is not bringing so much forbearance or confidence to the station platform is young Henri Ruchard. He cares very little about the living cell, its opponents and defenders. It is sufficient to observe his energetic and harsh features, his face contracted with jealous passion, to divine that he would gladly have left in Malaya the restless fanatic on whom his happiness depends.

Professor Ruchard, by contrast, is standing tall, with his broad shoulders and his flourishing rosette, his handsome head serene and magnanimous. He is glad to have come to wait for his old friend to jump down from the train, effacing by that amicable step any possible rancor.

César Bro, slender and placid in appearance, is thinking sadly about the older brother from whom the vicissitudes of life have so often separated him and whose daughter has become almost as dear to him as his own children. The common memories of their childhood have, however, woven bonds between them that the imminent return causes to vibrate. And, with the instincts of a painter and the weakness of a man, he is apprehensive of the signs of age with which the last seven years have inflicted on both of them and which they will discover in one another's faces at the first glance...

His wife, a cheerful and tender individual, a little bit romantic, in the full glory of 30 years of age, is awaiting the traveler she hardly knows with the avid curiosity of an audience-member anticipating the denouement of a play. Not that she has the slightest doubt about the outcome of the adventure. She would like to see someone get in the way of the marriage of the two your people, whose idyll she has nurtured with so much benevolence! But who knows whether some unforeseen plot-twist might not emerge?

The train! Here comes the train!

Indeed, tall and dark, coiffed with a plume of white smoke, the engine surges forth amid the motionless trains that cramp the horizon. The black caterpillar of carriages undulates, seems to hesitate, even to draw away, but finally plunges into the station, drawing slowly level with the platform, and its doors open.

Gazes meet and search for one another. Hands wave. Muffled exclamations are heard, like moans of happiness. Already the most agile have leapt down to the ground. Some slip into the crowd, as if in a hurry to disappear and plunge into the city. Others are immediately seized, imprisoned by effusions.

Suzanne has discovered her father, leaning out of a window. "There he is!"

Everyone follows her.

Dr. Bro brandishes his traveling cap. An unforgettable vision! Beneath the overhanging brows, pitted by wrinkles and swollen with projections, in the hollow of blue-tinted and profound ridges, his mobile eyes have a phosphorescent yellow gleam. The abrupt nose displays the black holes of the nostrils. Sparse, indecisive hair, red, blond and white at the same time, frames the rictus of his mouth, curling over the jutting chin, climbing the thin cheeks, quivering alongside the faun's ears, and evaporating into down on the shapeless and tumultuous skull. And that chaotic, almost simian face, soiled with dust and carbon-grease, is resplendent with intelligence.

With a bound, elbowing people out of the way and bumping into suitcases, indifferent to collisions, Dr. Bro surges toward his relatives. A white scarf is around his neck. A discolored waterproof overcoat envelops his short figure. In the confusion and emption of the first contact he lavishes awkward kisses and nervous handshakes, stammering neutral words from tremulous lips.

Suddenly, he takes off, plunges into the crowd, and then reappears, holding the arm of a tall and handsome young man with an exceedingly pale complexion and an exceedingly brown beard. In a familiar manner, amicably clapping the unknown on the shoulder, he introduces him, in a voice clear, musical and a trifle vulgar, whose charm is surprising: "My laboratory assistant Dajan-Phinn, a very distinguished fellow, a native of Borneo, who wanted to come with me and continue to render me his assistance."

The stranger slowly takes off his hat. Heads and upper bodies incline. But this unexpected presence alarms and embarrasses the intimate little group, and that malaise increases in the family omnibus that carries everyone to César Bro's house, where a lunch is to celebrate the return of the absentee. The painter has been obliged to invite Dajan-Phinn, for the doctor has clearly expressed the intention of not being separated from his pupil.

In the racket of the rattling windows, everyone falls silent. No allusion to the past, or the imminent future. No effusiveness, no surges of affection. Nothing is exchanged but glances. Bro contents himself with scrutinizing faces.

The presence of the unknown is not sufficient on its own to explain the general mutism, but his appearance is fascinating. The gaze is fatally attracted by that extraordinary beauty, that nacreous complexion set within that coal-black beard, that face in which one searches in vain for an imperfection, in which nature has not committed any sin of color or design, in which every feature, taken in isolation, compels admiration and gives an impression of the ideal realized. In him, all is harmony, from his slender but solid build and his delicate joints to his careful and discreet bearing.

And yet the mind does not experience a complete satisfaction. What secretly irritates it is being unable to penetrate the mind that lives behind that admirable mask.

Does he feel lost, out of his element, transported to the other side of the world, among people he does not know, the swarming of the city? But on that face of triumphant beauty, which one would like to see animated by a flame as beautiful as itself, there is nothing to be seen but a slight astonishment, like the amazement of being alive…

César Bro lives in a villa near the Boulevard Pereire, a discrete house nestling in the depths of a garden. It is on the threshold of that pleasant swelling that the little company disembarks, still numbed by the long journey through the city.

After a rapid and summary refreshment, Dr. Bro launched forth on an exploration of the house, with which he was unfamiliar. Accompanied by the silent Dajan-Phinn and his brother, he bounded upstairs to the studio, which occupied the entire second floor. Running around, pausing and rummaging, he offered an appreciation of every canvas in precise terms, whose justice the painter was obliged to admit. Then he plunged down to the ground floor and sprawled on a sofa, head back, arms on the cushions and legs crossed, praised the painter for having combined the drawing-room and dining-room, took an interest in the Louis XV furniture, judged it authentic while pointing out a restored side-table, savored the old rose and pale blue wallpaper, gallantly declared that its flowery tints suited blondes and that his sister-in-law and daughter resembled, among these delicately-woven fabrics, golden bees at the heart of a corolla.

At that point, the painter's two children returned from their morning stroll; Bro took possession of them, set them on his knees, promised Chinese dolls to the three-year-old Lise and a Malay kris to the seven-year-old Claude, inspected their teeth, ears, palates, the inner surfaces of their eyelids and enumerated, very exactly, a few weaknesses of their complexion, prescribed a regime, assured himself of their knowledge and, as they were learning English with their governess, began to sing a minstrel refrain to them in a hearty voice.

Half an hour after his arrival, he knew the house, objects and people alike, as if he had always lived there.

At table, he was liveliness personified. Occupied in talking, he ate and drank whimsically. Sometimes, he forgot a dish on his plate, and then dispatched it in two or three mouthfuls in order to make up for lost time. Sometimes, he returned to a dish, not out of greed, but out of distraction, not realizing that he had already served himself once. He left all his glasses full, then emptied them one after the other, mixing the vintages and the colors. And above that incoherence and massacre his gestures fulgurated and his flavorsome speech sang.

Between the hors d'oeuvres and dessert, Bro re-lived his seven years in the Far East. He sculpted anecdotes, launched witticisms, mimed scenes, sketched locations. He was malicious, subtle, ingenious and profound. In accordance with an evident premeditation, however, he abstained from any allusion to his own work, to any scientific development, either by virtue of the skill of a conversationalist who fears boring his audience, or because he was firmly resolved to avoid any controversy with Ruchard, by awakening old questions that had been laid to rest.

He only interrupted himself to take Dajan-Phinn for his witness. The young stranger expressed himself in a very pure French. Doubtless unfamiliar with our language, however, he hesitated momentarily, with his mouth partly open, before speaking. Then, once released, his sentence would flow like a spring. Bro never took his eyes off him, encouraging him vocally and by gesture.

"Dajan-Phinn is a modest fellow," he declared. "He speaks six languages admirably: French, Dutch, German, English, Spanish and the Malay idiom most commonly used on his island. It's the embarrassment of choice that paralyzes him. Come on, don't be afraid. You're among friends."

At first, the young man abbreviated his replies, restricting them to the strictly necessary. Gradually, however, he gained in confidence, and when the meal was over, Dajan-Phinn had almost raised himself to the cordial tone that Bro's verve and good humor had given to the reunion. The doctor's gaiety seemed, in fact, to bode well. How could a man so full of zest be contemplating opposition to the wishes of his entire family?

Henri Ruchard, however, did not share this happy mental disposition. As everyone rose from the table to take coffee he isolated Suzanne Bro in a corner of the room. Her face radiant, she was already getting ready to rejoice with him with regard to the favorable omens, but he shook his head.

"I understand your confidence, but I don't share it. Now that our fate is about to be decided, I'm afraid; I'm not reassured…"

"Why?" she interjected, swiftly.

"Because your father manifests no bitterness, does it follow that he doesn't experience any? Do we know what he's thinking, de down?"

"But…"

"The proof that he's capable of hiding his true thoughts is that he has let none of them show for seven years. Certainly, the blow was hard: ten years of work, a whole assembly of doctrines; a whole set of experiments that would have revolutionized the world, all reduced to nothing, to less than nothing, by a few weeks of controversy. What a disappointment, what a blow! And yet, your father has never shown mine his resentment. By his exile, he seemed to abandon the contest—but has he renounced all hope of revenge?"

Many times already, before Dr. Bro's return, the two young people had broached this redoubtable question—but it seemed to be resolved by the very attitude of the traveler. That was what the young woman could not help opposing to her companion.

"Oh, come on! Does he present the appearance of someone who's been nursing a resentment, or who's considering causing us any difficulty? Look at him."

IIc obeyed. At the far end of the room, beside the fireplace, Dr. Bro, with his hand set familiarly on Dajan-Phinn's shoulder, was standing in front of Ruchard, who was sitting beside the lady of the house—and the animated cheerfulness of his old companion lit up the haughty and tranquil face of the professor with a smile.

The young man remained anxious, however. With his head bowed, he resumed: "Yes, perhaps you're right—but it doesn't matter. Why that long silence, then this abrupt return? There's something abnormal and mysterious about all this..." Then, suddenly revealing his true dread, he went on: "And look—this Dajan-Phinn. Do you find his presence natural? What is this tenebrous beauty, black and white like a domino, as multilingual as a hotel porter? We don't know where he comes from, or what he's come to do here. Have you noticed your father's insistence on praising him highly, on showing him off? Are you sure that he doesn't have plans for that dear pupil, that he isn't the fiancé he has in mind for you?"

This time, Suzanne burst out laughing. "What an idea! And what underhanded thoughts you're crediting to my poor Papa!"

Henri loosed a gesture of annoyance with himself. "Yes, I was wrong to tell you all that. But you mustn't hold it against me. If I'm anxious, it's out of dread. I'm so afraid of seeing some obstacle rise up between us, at the very moment when our fate seems settled. There are moments, you see, when I'm almost tempted to go find my father, and ask him not to talk to yours today, if he has any intention of doing so, so fearful am I of knowing, so preferable does doubt sometimes seem to certainty..."

Moved by this anguish and wanting to hide her own anxiety, she said, jokingly: "But I forbid you to do that. I feel so sure of the result." Then, suddenly becoming serious, she added: "Besides, it's too late. Look."

He turned round. Ruchard had risen to his feet and was leaning toward Dr. Bro's ear. The latter, acquiescing with a nod of the head, confided Dajan-Phinn to his sister-in-law. Laughing graciously, she invited him to sit next to her. The two men left the room.

They went up to the studio. Behind the imposing mass of the professor, who made the narrow oak-wood staircase creak, Bro climbed with an uneven and hurried gait—and he contrast between the two individuals was further increased in the bright crisp daylight that descended from the skylights. His solid clean-shaven face fully lit, his handsome plump white hands on the arms of his armchair, Ruchard seemed to be posing for his portrait. Incapable of keeping still, astride a chair one moment, throwing himself on a divan whose springs returned him to his feet the next, Bro tried hard to relight a stout cigar, which, moistened and reduced to pulp, fell apart.

In a voice habituated to the professorial chair, but humanized by benevolence, Richard opened fire.

"My dear friend, I'll get straight to the point. You know why I've brought you here. Our children are in love. I only have my son. You only have your daughter. We both want them to be happy. Let's marry them. Your brother has written as much to you, and I hope that I don't have to see in your delay in replying as an indication of opposition, and especially not the residue of old quarrels that once..."

Bro, who had stopped moving momentarily, bounded toward his friend and waved a peremptory hand in front of the professor's august lips.

"Shh! Shh! Let's not talk about that, let's say nothing about it. It's necessary not to confuse the issues. The happiness of our children has nothing to do with our laboratory disputes. I lost the game. I even think that I've been a rather good sport. But, after all, you beat me. That's understood. And it's not the moment to reopen the debate..."

"In that case...?" Ruchard began.

Bro was following his own train of thought, though. "Now, if I haven't replied to César's letter, it's because, as soon as I received it, I decided to return to France—but I'd undertaken a project that I absolutely had to finish before my departure. I was overwhelmed by work. In brief, I kept putting off from one day to the next the joy of bringing my reply myself..."

"So it's favorable?" the professor interjected.

Bro gripped his hands. "Can you doubt it, my dear friend? Such a project honors me and fulfils my desires…"

Ruchard got to his feet and breathed out expansively. "Mine too, believe me! And the proof is that your silence made me dread some snag. Without reproach, since you were decided, you might have spared the loving couple a two-month delay…"

A shadow of embarrassment passed over Dr. Bro's noble features. In an uncertain voice he said: "I couldn't…I didn't want to…in sum, I wanted to bring my reply in person."

"Let's not leave them in suspense any longer, then," said Ruchard, heading for the door. "As for the practical arrangements, in which we can't be uninvolved, I've discussed them with your brother. I know that he touched upon them in his letter. I hope that we're entirely in agreement in that respect too…"

"Perfectly, perfectly!" declared Bro, precipitating himself downstairs.

Professor Ruchard follow him ponderously. Had he exaggerated his anxieties during the months of waiting and incomprehensible silence? Had his son's impassioned disquiet gradually infected him? But his prompt and facile victory disconcerted him. It was the unease of deliverance, anguish in triumph, the state of mind of an assailant who believes a redoubt to be strongly guarded and finds it empty.

Henri Ruchard went swiftly through the garden in front of César Bro's house. It was May. New leaves were bursting forth on all sides: that Paris verdure which hastens to blossom as if it knew that it would die young in the July heat. But Suzanne Bro's fiancé seemed indifferent to the external world. Familiar with the house, he went straight up to the studio.

The pensive painter, one eye half-closed by the smoke of his cigarette, was sketching beside a box of charcoal. His wife was writing at a little table. They were alone.

While he shook hands with them, in a warm but slightly abrupt fashion, she said to him: "Have you seen Suzanne?"

Distractedly, he replied: "No, but I'm not displeased to find you alone first."

He seemed so worried that she became grave. "No trouble, I hope?"

"No trouble, strictly speaking, but the sort of dull irritation that you can prevent from bursting out, and can even dissipate." He let himself fall into a chair and twisted his hat in his hands. He attempted a meager smile, which contracted his energetic face, and went on: "You'll think me very demanding to complain since, in spite of our apprehensions, Monsieur Bro has granted me his daughter's hand without any difficulty and we're to be married in a month's time, but, sincerely, don't you think all the same that there's something abnormal about my situation? Why, we've been engaged for three weeks, and living under the same roof as my future wife is a young man endowed with all the qualities, handsome enough to turn heads in the street—in a word, perfect from every point of view! Me, I only come here as a visitor. He lives in complete intimacy with Mademoiselle Suzanne. Don't you find it natural that I take umbrage and want to see it ended?"

César Bro interrupted him in his tranquil voice, without ceasing his sketching. "I beg your pardon, my dear friend, but remember first of all how these things came about, and agree that they could hardly be arranged otherwise. It was natural on my part to offer hospitality to my brother for a sojourn that, he has told me, will not be prolonged beyond your marriage. Now, he has expressed to me his formal desire not to be separated from that young man. You know how forcefully and vehemently he has explained his reasons. The boy has never been to France; he is literally lost among us. My brother, who has brought him, has assumed responsibility for him, and does not want to abandon him. I could do no less than offer to accommodate both of them, since I have enough room. And take note that if my brother had refused, you would have lost out, for he would have taken his daughter away without letting go of his ward. All three of them would have been living together, instead of being disseminated among us."

As the young man, far from being convinced, became even sulkier, Madame Bro ventured in her turn: "Besides, aren't they living alongside one another in the most complete indifference? Monsieur Dajan-Phinn manifests and insensibility, a coldness, for everything touching matters of sentiment. Nothing seems to move him—the grace of a young woman no more than the extended arms of a little child. Have you ever caught a word or a gesture on his part to which you could take offense…?"

"That's all that's lacking" exclaimed the fiancé.

"As for Suzanne," she continued, "don't you know that for a woman in love, there is but one man in the world—the one she loves? The others don't exist. She doesn't notice them; she doesn't see them. It's the very sign of affection. Have you seen her pay the slightest attention to Monsieur Dajan-Phinn?"

"No, no," said Henri, swiftly. "And that's why I didn't want to complain in front of her. There would have been something indelicate about explaining my annoyance to her—but that doesn't prevent it from being well-founded. This cohabitation irritates me, wounds me. And whatever you say, there's a means of putting an end to it. Since this Dajan-Phinn is so intelligent, he'll assimilate our customs rapidly. There's no need for him to remain on the leash any longer, like an exotic animal that can't be set free. Let him live near his master, but not in the same house. And I beg you to say a few words to Monsieur Bro, since he thinks himself so far above these wretched details…if, however, it's out of disregard for consequences that he's inflicting this unpleasant ordeal on me…"

"What do you mean?" Madame Bro interjected, sharply.

Evidently embarrassed by the presence of the painter, Henri continued: "Nothing. I don't want to say anything about which I'm not certain. I might be wrong. Anyway, will you accept the commission?"

"I promise," she said.

He got up, relieved.

She escorted him as far as the door and there, lifting up the curtain while he set off down the stairs, she said: "How anxious you are, and what chimeras you conjure up. Can't you enjoy your engagement in peace?"

"It's exactly because I want it to be unshadowed, protected from any incident and any complication, that that I beg you to send away the overly handsome souvenir of Dr. Bro's voyage."

"The poor boy," she said. "He's no trouble though."

He raised his head and wagged his finger at her while going down the stairs. "Oh, I suspect you of having a little weakness for him."

Leaning toward him and laughing, she admitted: "That's true."

In her generosity, she felt drawn toward him by maternal instinct. He seemed to her as isolated as a lost child. Dr. Bro remained mute as to his protégé's origins, but she knew that he had no family and no ties. His admirable features retained the astonished mildness of early infancy, but they were gradually becoming charged with melancholy. On seeing him, one thought of a beautiful lily bowing on its stem—and the hesitation that marked the beginning of his speeches, which left his mouth partly open and his eyelids hesitant for a moment, added a further measure to his touching timidity.

Not that he was embarrassed in his movements, or ignorant of our customs. On the contrary, he possessed every finesse. In addition, he occasionally revealed a surprising erudition.

"So you know everything, Monsieur Dajan-Phinn!" Madame Bro sometimes exclaimed.

In fact, his culture was very extensive. No human knowledge seemed entirely strange to him. He was certainly a worthy pupil of Dr. Bro. Far from deriving vanity from his knowledge, he seemed confused by it. In order for him to give proof of it, one was obliged to press him and interrogate him, as one turns the pages of a dictionary to extract its science. In the

149

same way, being clever with his hands, capable of putting on paper a sketch, or even a water-color, of playing a piano pleasantly, he disdained his gifts. In brief, he had no passion for anything. He lacked the internal fire of enthusiasm.

Madame Bro attributed that lack of ardor and indolence to homesickness. She had tried to distract the young foreigner, but her attempts had scarcely been encouraging. In vain, she had put into his hands novels of which she was very fond. In vain, she had taken him to the theater. Books and plays nourished by love did not move him, did not draw him out of his melancholy. She was, in consequence, apprehensive about abandoning him to himself, as Henri Richard wished. Nevertheless, faithful to her promise, she explained the umbrageous fiancé's request to her brother-in-law that same evening.

At the first words, Dr. Bro manifested a wild gaiety. His eyes shining, he jeered; "Oh! The young man is jealous of Dajan-Phinn! Look at that! But it's perfect, perfect..."

"What?" queried Madame Bro, somewhat nonplussed.

He went on: "But that proves, quite simply, that he loves my daughter. Besides, it's of no importance whatsoever. An amorous fantasy. Don't insist, my dear friend, don't insist. I intend to keep Dajan-Phinn with me, you know, and nothing will separate me from him."

She dared not press the point. Her very duty as a hostess obliged her to be discreet. As her husband had remarked, the whole set-up would only last until the departure of the doctor and his protégé. Momentarily, she thought of having a word with Dajan-Phinn himself, but in case of success she would have arrived at an identical result: if the pupil left, the master would follow. She therefore renounced that vain and delicate step.

She was not very proud, therefore, when Henri Ruchard asked for news of her embassy two days later. Everything was conspiring to exasperate the suspicious young man. The professor and his son, who were bringing the engagement ring, had arrived a few minutes in advance of the agreed time. Suzanne had not come back. And—an aggravating circumstance—she had gone out in company with her father and the inseparable Dajan-Phinn.

Madame Bro received the two men in the Louis XV drawing-room. Sincerely affected, as a woman who, in her generosity, only wanted to see smiling faces around her, she allowed the admission of her failure and Suzanne's absence to be extracted from her by degrees.

Henri controlled himself, but his features contracted with anger. Through clenched teeth, he said: "That's all right. I'll have a word with Monsieur Bro myself."

Madame Bro made one last conciliatory effort. "Don't you fear poisoning everything? Remember that in a month, you'll be married, and you'll laugh at these petty nothings."

She turned to the professor in quest of his agreement, but he maintained a severe expression and sketched an evasive gesture. He certainly did not approve of his friend's behavior.

At that moment, Dr. Bro's loud voice became audible in the vestibule. He came in alone, extending his hands.

"Ah! Here's Henri, seething with impatience. His fiancée is behind me. She's…"

Henri cut in: "Pardon me—a word before she comes in. Madame Bro tells me that you've refused my request. Agree that it appears more legitimate than ever, on the day when you have gone out with your daughter and Dajan-Phinn…in such a way that someone in the street might be deceived and mistake that handsome young man for Mademoiselle Suzanne's fiancé!"

Dr. Bro, perched on his short legs with his hands in his pockets, swayed back and forth between his heels and his toes, jovially, and retorted: "What difference can that make to you, since she isn't deceived about it?"

Henri started. "I can see nothing in your inappropriate joke than your desire to push me aside, but I won't allow my-self to be deflected from my goal. Monsieur Bro, you know that I'm anxious and jealous, rightly or wrongly—and yet you have no hesitation, by actions like today's excursion, in provoking me further. Such conduct certainly has its reasons. I beg you to tell me what they are."

"And what if I don't want to?" Dr. Bro said, mockingly.

"Then I'll tell you what they are myself and you'll be forced to recognize that I've seen through them."

"I'm curious to hear them."

"You'll be satisfied," he young man declared, dryly. "From the first day, your attitude has seemed strange to us. I say *us* because my father shares my anxieties and suspicions. Your very consent, following your long silence, appeared to him too facile not to have any hidden motive. You forgot your former grievances against him too easily. As for me, the presence of this so-called laboratory assistant has always seemed shady. How can you explain it, if not by your desire to make your daughter love him? He's the fiancé of your choice! Thanks to his prodigious beauty, and his merits, of which you boast incessantly, and the continued intimacy that you maintain between him and Mademoiselle Suzanne, do you not count on him supplanting me? You would already have succeeded had she been less constant. And you would have succeeded, had I not seen through your ruse. Oh, it was a good plan. This way you would have evicted me while avoiding the annoyance of a direct refusal—and your vengeance would have been even more complete and more refined. You would precipitate me from a higher position, since, after having given me your daughter, you would have had her stolen away by a rival."

Dr. Bro's attitude was incomprehensible. He laughed, rubbed his hands, and seemed overwhelmed by jubilation.

"Ha ha! You've worked all that out by yourself! Or rather, you've done it together. My compliments. Well, my lad, you're on completely the wrong track…"

Disconcerted, Henri stammered: "But…if I'm mistaken…which I hope with all my heart…at least justify your conduct…"

Very gravely, the professor lent his support. "Yes, Bro, explain yourself. Explain to us why you have bought back that individual, why you keep him under your roof, and why you persist even when you know that your daughter's fiancé is suffering…"

Bro was no longer laughing. He walked toward to two men. His phosphorescent eyes were gleaming in the hollows of their blue-tinted orbits. His obstinate head swelled up. His entire face was grimacing with malice and intense satisfaction.

"Oh, you both want an explanation! Well, so be it—you shall have one. It wouldn't have been long delayed anyway. Since you offer me the opportunity, I'll take it. On one sole point you've seen clearly. Yes, it's true, I haven't forgotten the past. The defeat that you inflicted on me, Ruchard, is as sensible to me as on the first day. I lost my case thanks to your speech, but not without appeal. Except, as I told you, the happiness of our children has nothing to do with our quarrels. No, my lad, I haven't plotted to evict you. Beaten on the scientific battleground, it's on the scientific battleground that I wanted my revenge. But it had to be absolutely crushing. My adversaries had to be annihilated forever. Well, I have it, I have the means…"

He was excited. Uplifted, magnified by triumph, he was fearful to behold.

"Ha ha! You're jealous of Dajan-Phinn, angry Henri. And you share his dread, grave Richard! You see in my pupil a rival worthy of you, umbrageous fiancé. You do him the honor of hating him. You're afraid of him. Well, you've both fallen into the trap I set for you, which I've been preparing for you for seven years…and you've fallen into it even more deeply than I dared to hope. Oh, one can't make life! Oh, it's impossible for a man to create an organism! Oh, my plants were just puerile games! Well, know then that the odious Djann-Phinn emerged from my hands, that the detested rival is artificial, and that, to sum it all up in one word, Henri is jealous of an automaton!"

Dr. Bro wanted to annihilate his adversaries; he had succeeded. The painter's wife and the two Ruchards stood there, overwhelmed by amazement. The professor was tragic; one might have thought him a felled oak. He was, however, the first to speak, saying: "What? You claim that this Dajan-Phinn…"

But Suzanne came in then, animated by happiness. Suddenly confused by those petrified faces, she murmured: "What's the matter?"

The doctor, radiant, stroked her cheek and said: "Your fiancé will tell you that." Then, taking the arm of his friend Ruchard, he drew him toward the garden. On the threshold, he turned round and said, authoritatively: "Not a word to Dajan-Phinn, all right?"

Scarcely had he closed the door to the garden when Madame César Bro went upstairs to tell her husband the sensational news. The two young people remained alone.

"What's happening?" Suzanne said. "Tell me quickly."

Glossing rapidly over his own suspicions, Henri repeated the astonishing revelation. It was the young woman's turn to stand there astounded. Her fiancé had to repeat the doctor's last words to her. In her, however, admiration was soon mingled with surprise.

"I was sure that he would end up triumphant, that he'd never ceased being right. What a reply, and what a revenge!"

"You're certain, then, that this Dajan-Phinn emerged from his hands…?"

She cut him off, with a reproach in her limpid eyes: "Since he says so…"

"Oh, for my part," he protested, "I'm not in any doubt…"

Indeed, everything encouraged him, everything drove him to consider Dr. Bro's unexpected assertion as true. It reduced to nothing his jealous anxieties. It explained everything. The web of intrigue that he had thought woven against him, the rival by whom he believed himself threatened—all that disappeared.

But what about his father? Would the professor accept the miracle as easily? A champion of scientific orthodoxy, victor in the first round, utterly convinced of the justice and the grandeur of his cause, would he given in without a fight this time? If, on the contrary, he resisted, the contest between the two men would be resumed, more bitterly and violently than ever.

And as the young woman, slightly intoxicated with filial pride, tried to imagine the resonance of such a discovery, he gazed distractedly through the window, following the two scientists as they strolled around the garden.

Dressed casually in a yellow suit, coiffed with a shapeless straw hat baked by the sun, Bro was hanging on to his companion's ample frock-coat. From an inside pocket he had taken a thick portfolio, and he was parading an entire series of pieces of paper before his friend's eyes. From time to time, they paused. Bro's gestures became more pressing. The professor slowly passed his hand over his forehead, like a man seeing to dissipate the smoke of his dreams.

Dusk crept up on them in the garden. Henri was burning with the desire to know the result of that long conversation. So, as soon as he found himself alone again with his father in the street, he interrogated him with a word in which all his haste was concentrated:

"Well?"

"That man makes one dizzy," murmured the professor. "One loses one's footing. One is submerged beneath the flood of his words. Seven years, according to him, he's been keeping his secret! For more than a month he's been resisting the temptation to deliver it to us. Then he overflows, explodes."

"Finally, do you believe in this discovery?"

The professor, ordinarily sober in his gestures, waved his arms desperately. "I don't know any more...I don't know. It's necessary to believe everything, or believe nothing."

"What did he tell you?"

"He told me that he's been preparing his great work for seven years. He intended, in the case of success, to bring his Dajan-Phinn to France, to make him live among us, and, when we had taken well and truly taken the bait and believed in the reality of the individual, to reveal his nature to us. He had almost reached his goal, it appears, when our petition for marriage reached him. It was a trump card in his game. The period of engagement would bring us closely together, and put us in continual contact with his Dajan-Phinn. But he still wanted to be perfectly sure of his success, to be absolutely ready—hence his delay in replying to us, still according to him. Finally, he made the decision to take the boat. And once in France, the anxiety and irritation that the unknown inspired—and which Bro claims to have anticipated—would complete his ambition. Your jealousy was a homage to the perfection of his work…"

By the tone in which his father reported his friend's words, the young man sensed that her was hesitant, undecided. He persisted: "But after all, has he explained his method, furnished with technical details?"

Again, the tearful professor raised his hands toward the heavens. "Technical details! But to follow that man, it's necessary to forget everything one knows, to rid oneself of all one's convictions. One flounders in the unknown, the fantastic. Yes, he's explained his method to me. Yes, he's shown me photographs of his experiment at different stages. The only witnesses, moreover, for Bro claims to have acted alone, with no other auxiliary than a Hindu, a sort of semi-artist, semi-sorcerer, who only aided him from the plastic viewpoint. Oh, he has an answer for everything, naturally—but on what can one found a serious controversy when one advances on inconsistent ground, in an atmosphere as dark, beyond the solid ground and clear sight of science."

"So?"

"So, either we're confronted by the boldest trickery, and Bro is nothing but a poor madman unhinged by his past disappointments, or…he's telling the truth."

He pronounced the final words in a slightly ashamed voice, as if he blushed—he, the orthodox scientist, the famous professor—to admit the possibility of such a prodigy even momentarily.

"In the end, how can we know?" Henri queried.

"By studying Dajan-Phinn at close range now that we're aware of Bro's stupefying affirmation. By subjecting him to a rigorous close investigation that will end up revealing the truth to us.

Then, life in César Bro's house took a singular turn. With a common accord, the initiates had decided to keep the secret. Professor Ruchard had been particularly insistent that no news of the events should be spread outside. He dreaded, in the case that the investigation should turn out to his friend's disadvantage, the mockery of his colleagues. What! The grave Ruchard had been able to consent to examine such ridiculousness—and, in consequence, to take it seriously for a moment. What outbursts of laughter! And if, on the contrary, the implausible was true, would it not be better for the professor to be the first to announce his conversion, with considerable ceremony, before his colleagues could take possession of the question and constrain him to admit that he had been defeated.?

As for Dr. Bro, sure of his conclusive victory, indulgent to the last resistance of his old companion, he accepted with a good grace the examination demanded by Ruchard. He declared that, having waited for seven years, he could easily be patient for a few more days. Relatives and friends, touched by his faith, would become ardent disciples during this interval—and the news would break all the more violently upon the world for having been longer contained.

Even Dajan-Phinn—Dajan-Phinn especially—ought to remain in ignorance, for he knew nothing about his mysterious origin. Dr. Bro explained that very clearly. Before Dajan-Phinn became the object of discreet investigations, he had emphasized this point heavily.

"I've always hidden his origin and we all have an interest in maintaining the same discretion, To reveal his true nature to him would be to falsify his attitude, take away his ease and, if I dare use the expression, his naturalness. He would become my accomplice, he would hide his secret from you. While he believes himself to be similar to the common run of men, he acts as they do effortlessly, and does not suffer from being a prodigious exception. Oh, Dajan-Phinn, interrogated by you, will not fail to tell you that he lived until adolescence with two old people who brought him up on the outskirts of the city, near the gate, until the day when I took him to live in the zoological garden. He will describe to you very succinctly the surroundings of his childhood monotony: the hut, the nearby forest, the school to which he went every day. Why? Because, to give him the illusion of a normal life, I was obliged to create memories for him, as one furnishes a modern château with ancient objects to give it the appearance of age...."

And as those most inclined to believe the doctor could not repress signs of astonishment, he added: "What is there in that to surprise you? Have you not witnessed and admitted more extraordinary phenomena? Have you not seen, during a séance of hypnotism and suggestion, the operator leave stronger imprints in the consciousness of subjects, persuading them that a potato is a delicious fruit, that all the vowels are missing from a newspaper they're reading, or even constraining them to commit a theft or some other crime in the waking state? And he is acting on a fully-formed organism—a task more difficult than making an impression on an entirely new substance."

Fixing a few images in a brain was, was nothing for Dr. Bro. The most outstanding aspect of his work, in that order of ideas, was to have created in Dajan-Phinn a heredity of sorts, to have slipped instincts and knowledge into his skull as one injects sera under the skin. It was necessary to see Dr. Bro striving to make that comprehensible. As his listeners, with the exception of Ruchard, had been unable to follow him with regard to technical developments, he deployed an untiring patience in initiating them—adapting science for the usage of ordinary people, as he put it. He explained the cerebral localizations, pointed out the seat of each function in his head, struck himself on the cranium—everything but open it up to display the white substance and the grey matter—and, like a genial cook revealing a recipe, enumerated and measured out the notions and sentiments with which he had endowed Dajan-Phinn.

To model a character as one models a statue! To carry out an instruction, an education as one packs a trunk! To choose oneself the moral and physical qualities that ought to compose the idea being! So many exciting problems…but there was no time to linger over them. Dr. Bro carried everything away in the torrent of his loquacity.

Professor Ruchard was right: the man made one dizzy. On listening to him, one no longer knew whether one was living in a hallucination or reality. And he was always ready with a riposte, as Ruchard had also observed.

If one timidly expressed astonishment that a task s prodigiously complex had not required more time, he folded his arms beneath his chin and cried: "What! What! You admit without discussion, on the basis of a traveler's tale, that a fakir can make a seed grow, within half an hour, into a plant covered with flowers, but you won't admit that seven years have been enough for me to complete my work?"

Or, striking minds by means of analogy, he cried: "Living beings! But your industry has almost created them, and by the thousand. Do you think than an automobile is so very different from an animal? Add to it an organ of vision like a photographic apparatus, and an organ of audition like the telephone, which would alert it to dangers on the road, and react against them, and you would have an embryonic being capable of guiding itself and steering itself unaided."

Every time he launched into these fantastic comparisons, Professor Ruchard protested, shaking his head gravely.

"Yes, yes, I know," Bro anticipated. "The very principle of life is lacking, the energy inclusive in the seed, in the cell. The fact of having isolated and reconstituted that energy evidently constitutes the heart of my discovery.

Letting himself off the bridle briefly, he launched into vast considerations, affirmed that mineral, vegetable and animal matter each had a unique essence, represented as a con-

159

densation of forces, grabbed some random object, depicted it as an agglomeration of tiny worlds incessantly in vibration....

Then, having perceived a few signs of lassitude in his audience, he sketched some witty observations about Dajan-Phinn—a name that he had made up on a whim, for any trace of which one could search the world's records in vain. He imagined the automaton, alerted to his true origin, disconcerting an employee of the civil service with the unexpectedness of his replies, asserting that he had neither father nor mother and concluding with the prodigious affirmation that: "I was born at the age of 20."

Naturally, the young foreigner was never present during these conversations. As soon as he appeared, the subject was changed. Everyone did his best to dissimulate that abrupt leap and to adopt a cheerful tone—efforts more praiseworthy than successful. For, since Dr. Bro's revelation, the mere presence of Dajan-Phinn provoked an anxiety among all the participants that they could not suppress.

It must be agreed that their situation was quite unique. To live in the company of an individual whose origin is unknown, and unknowable! About whom one demands, on talking to him, listening to him and looking at him: "Is he a man or an automaton?" Certainly, he is human in appearance—but a scientist, a genius or a madman, has sprung forth and proclaimed; "He's an artificial being, emerged from my hand!" And from then on the mind doubts, alternately rebelling and submitting, and losing balance in those overly abrupt oscillations.

In the little group that was upset and impassioned by the enigma set before them, however, Dr. Bro immediately found two convinced partisans: his daughter, blindly rallied by filial faith; and his sister-in-law, seduced by the attraction of the marvelous. Nothing could any longer tear Madame Bro away from the conviction that she was playing hostess to an automaton. Into the ardent discussions that where whispered in corners in Dajan-Phinn's absence, she had even thrown a weighty argument, calculated to have an impact on the mind.

160

"Come on!" she said. "Is his absolute insensibility that a of human being? Have you ever seen him take any interest in the slightest adventure, imaginary or real, of which love might be the motive? Has he ever sat Lise or Claude on his knee? Have the funny little things they say, their mannerisms and caresses, which delight us and bring tears to our eyes, ever had a softening effect on him? The joy of Suzanne and Henri on seeing one another surprises him. Their impatience to be married is incomprehensible to him. Does he not lack what the doctor calls, in his scientific language, the affective faculties? And is not that imperfection in his work also the mark of its authenticity?"

Bro took on a contrite air. He confessed that, indeed, that was the weak point of his creation. He had, however, paid particular attention to those affective instincts so necessary to a human being, which are the sweetness of life. What cause had vitiated his cultures, caused the development of those faculties to be abortive? He did not know. Along with Dajan-Phinn's speech defect—the difficulty of release that delayed the beginning of each sentence on his lips—they were the two flaws in his work...

But such arguments were not sufficient to compel all conviction. Among the experts poring over Dajan-Phinn, two remained undecided: César Bro and Henri Ruchard.

Since his brother's shattering revelation, the painter had not ceased examining the young foreigner from the corner of his eye. And he found—but might it not be the effect of a kind of suggestion?—something artificial in the nacreous translucency of his complexion and the mineral gleam of his beard and hair, and an extra-natural perfection in the beauty of his lines and contours. At the same time though, as soon as he was inclined to believe, an instinct of prudence and pride rebelled within him and cried out to him to deny the miracle of science.

To that ancient horror of reason for everything unknown, Henri Ruchard was equally submissive, and it counterbalanced in him the impulse that, from the very first moment, had thrown him on to Dr. Bro's side, inclining him to the solution most favorable to his cause, the only one capable of putting a conclusive end to those wearying quarrels. In fact, if the artificial origin of Dajan-Phinn were to be proven and recognized, all controversy ceased. If, on the contrary, that origin were contested, the discussion remained open indefinitely.

Alas, Professor Ruchard did not appear to be close to giving in. In the little group, he represented the opposition, but a defiant, hostile opposition. In his dread of being duped and set up for mockery, he redoubled his gravity—and he set about studying Dajan-Phinn with concentrated but discreet attention: the attention reserved for a selected invalid to whom one does not wish to reveal his illness.

What about Dajan-Phinn? If he was insensitive, Dajan-Phinn was, at least, very intelligent, and it could not take him long to perceive that he had become the center of attention of the little society in which he lived. Once put on his guard, none of the signs of that metamorphosis could any longer escape him: neither the silence, nor the awkward transitions that marked his entrance; nor the hesitant hands and fugitive fingers that were extended toward him at moments of greeting; nor the gazes that lingered on his face: the ponderous gaze of Professor Ruchard; the sly and pensive gaze of César Bro; the limpid and marveling gaze of Suzanne Bro. He could not be unaware of the instinctive gesture with which Madame Bro sometimes drew her children away from him, as if she were pulling them out of the way of a moving machine. He could not fail to perceive the change of attitude on the part of Henri Ruchard, once somber and sulky, seemingly inclined to avoid him and even treat him with hostility, but who now interrogated him cordially about his childhood and youth. It was impossible not to notice the sudden solicitude of Professor Ruchard, who, indifferent at first, now sounded his chest and examined him minutely at the slightest sign of indisposition...

Evidently, Dajan-Phinn had to take note of all these symptoms and seek and explanation for them. For, if they did not cause him any emotion—given that nothing seemed to cause him any emotion—the mystery that he sensed around him had to appear to him as a problem of sorts, which his lucid mind would strive to solve.

Now, the solution offered itself. This period of intense but discreet inquisition had been going on for about a fortnight. The banns of the imminent marriage had been posted.

One afternoon, Dajan-Phinn went into the dining-room at an indolent pace in order to fetch a book that Madame Bro had forgotten. In the painter's house, the room in question was only separated from the drawing-room by a light curtain that was drawn during the day. Dajan-Phinn heard his name pronounced on the other side of that veil. He recognized Henri Ruchard's voice. He stood still and listened.

"...I told you that he would be our evil genius. You see, Suzanne, that my presentiments did not deceive me. Without him, this accursed quarrel would be dead. On the contrary, it's nourished by him—and now it's poisoned, in a state of acute crisis. What good does it do to hide it? My father's conclusions are injurious to yours. It's the most wounding denial, the most insulting suspicion. Oh, Suzanne, my dear Suzanne, will it be necessary for us to separate, so near to our union, to being together? And all for this adventure in dementia..."

"Please calm down," pronounced Suzanne's voice. "Don't demoralize me in my turn. We need all our composure. So, your father has made his decision, in a firm manner. There's no means of making him relent in his determination?"

"I've tried everything, but in vain. Nothing will deter him any longer from talking to your father imminently. His verdict is without appeal. Disconcerted momentarily by the prodigious assertion, he had gradually pulled himself together. Oh, I'm certain that he's undertaken the most scrupulous examination, with absolute probity. Be sure that if he had conserved the slightest doubt, he'd have admitted it frankly...but he no longer has any. For him, Dajan-Phinn is a mere mortal..."

"Then your father won't hesitate to accuse his old friend of lying?"

"I believe that objection has held him in check longer than the apparent proofs provided by your father—but he explains and excuses the trickery. For him, Dr. Bro's mind has been stricken, even disturbed, by the premature death of his wife, by excessive labor, and above all by his very defeat. And in consequence of that final shock, the idea developed within him of obtaining revenge at any cost, by means of this implausible but troubling fable.

"My father," Suzanne interjected, sharply, "will not admit the excuse of madness. He would consider that one more insult. But, all in all, is Monsieur Ruchard not struck by the singular signs that make Dajan-Phinn an exceptional being, beyond humanity?"

"You can be sure that I've struggled, that I've used every weapon at our disposal—I, who ask nothing more than to be convinced, who have so much interest in the miracle being real. That hesitation he displays at the beginning of every statement? It appears that it's quite common."

"The photographs that your father has seen?"

"He's sure, in the final analysis, that they're fake. One can express anything one wishes by means of photography—and Dr. Bro had as many models as he might desire among the anatomical specimens in the zoological gardens of Borneo."

"That excessively perfect beauty?"

"Why should it be the work of a man rather than that of nature?"

"That almost absolute insensibility?"

"Does one need to be an automaton to be heartless? How many human beings are ignorant of tenderness? No, for my father, Dajan-Phinn is a poor foundling, exceptionally endowed, like those little Alpine shepherds who are prodigious calculators, whom Dr. Bro must have discovered, cultivated and even subjected to suggestion. Come on—all these proofs are fragile, and break against reason. We can't avoid an explosion. Oh, one sometimes has to ask oneself whether people who attach themselves to nothing and are indifferent to everything might be better off. They don't have our anxieties..."

"Would you change places with them?" she asked, softly.

Stricken, he replied: "No, no. You're right—but I'm like one of those bad-tempered horses enraged by any hobble, you see. I blasphemed. Certainly, it would be insane to despair, since we love one another, since I have you close to me, sure and faithful, and since I only breathe for you. To love, to be loved...oh, that really is the secret of all effort, all energy, the motto of happiness, and the flower and perfume of life. Yes, we'll fight. Nothing will ever separate us."

"Have we not," she went on, "undergone many other ordeals already: the waiting, the uncertainty...the worst of evils, it's said, because it contains all of them."

"Dear Suzanne, I admire your smiling valor. Yes, for us the past answers for the future. There are already so many shared memories...that's a chain which nothing can break. You remember, last year, when we still didn't dare to admit anything to one another...taking little Lise for our confidant, who couldn't understand, and, leaning over that two-year-old child in her crib by turns, we told her...everything that we would have wished to say to one another..."

"Yes, that was the time when my uncle César, from whom you were taking lessons and who made you work on a portrait from a living model, exclaimed: 'That's odd—all your women resemble my niece Suzanne!'"

Thus they poured out the cordial of memories for one another in advance of the impending battle. They lowered their voices. Sometimes, even the slight murmur paused, and from the silence, the noise of a kiss emerged, as soft and gentle as that of a drop of water falling into a bowl. Then the tender litany rose up again, replete with murmured oaths, praises, reminiscences and plans, acts of grace and acts of retreat, words to lull, or to cajole, puerile words, words as old as humankind, but which always seem new to those who pronounce them and those who hear them, words akin to kisses which, like them, take on a new savor in passing over the lips...

165

Dajan-Phinn had heard everything: that he was or was not an automaton. No more shattering revelation had ever struck an understanding. To know that his origin was being discussed! To sense that he was on the frontiers of humanity! And, to the disarray into which such a dispute must have thrown his mind, was doubtless added the sadness of surprising that loving duo, of glimpsing the promised land in which he would never set foot.

That day, he was more silent than usual. The next day, he was hardly to be seen. He shut himself up in his room. During dinner, at which the Ruchards were guests, he remained concentrated within himself. A sort of anguish weighed over the table in any case. The professor maintained a grave and ominous expression. The two fiancés were apprehensive about their fate. Only Dr. Bro was dazzling. One might have thought that he had scented the coming conflict and was becoming intoxicated in advance in an atmosphere with a whiff of gunpowder.

After the meal, the guests spread out in the drawing-room, the door of which was open to the garden. The rain-soaked foliage was exhaling its green moist scent into the belated dusk of June. Dajan-Phinn wandered along the pathways. In common with the flowers that retained a certain phosphorescent gleam in the twilight, like a memory of day, his beauty was radiant and luminous. He stopped in front of Dr. Bro, who was camped on the steps of the perron, lighting his cigar.

The young man opened his mouth slightly, and his eyelids fluttered. Then he began, softly: "Doctor, why have you always hidden from me what you have said about me to those surrounding us? Tell me the truth. Am I truly a sort of machine forged by your hands, designed to astonish the world, to proclaim your merit?"

Bro threw away his match violently. "Everyone here will be my witness that I kept silent as much in your interest than in mine. And I would like to know who has permitted…"

Dajan-Phinn raised his arm to interrupt the doctor. After a brief hesitation, he said: "I alone committed an indiscretion.

No one said anything to me. I overheard...oh, my master! However it was done, I am what you have made of me. I owe you everything. But you have always been good to me. Don't leave me in ignorance..."

"It's precisely out of goodness that I left you there," Bro replied, rudely. "I wanted you to avoid the embarrassment, the shame, of feeling that you were on the margins of society, an exceptional being..."

Ruchard, who had been sitting in the drawing-room, had risen to his feet. The carpet muffled his footsteps. Bro did not hear them. The professor placed a hand on his shoulder.

"You don't have the right to torture a poor human creature to this extent, for the sole satisfaction of your insane pride!"

Beneath the sudden weight and the rude interjection, Bro started and turned round. He directed the disquieting fire of his of his yellow pupils at the professor. At the same timed, his features expressed absolute amazement. Had he, until the very last moment, nurtured the certainty of bring his adversary round?

Ruchard continued: "Bro, in the name of our old friendship, in the name of all that is sacred to you, in the name of our children, I beg you to admit the truth."

Bro straightened, rising up, so to speak, against his old companion. "What are you saying?"

Everyone—the two fiancés, César Bro and his wife—surrounded the two men. Dajan-Phinn had remained at the bottom of the steps, his face bright against the dark background of the garden.

"I'm saying," Ruchard went on, forcefully, "and I'm affirming, that Dajan-Phinn is a human being like all of us here: that your entire story is nothing but an elaborate hoax."

Bro folded his arms. The corners of his mouth were quivering. "Nothing can convince you, then—not the documents I have shown you, nor the proofs that I have put within your reach, nor the oath that I am ready to renew?"

167

Ruchard made a chopping gesture with his extended hand. "Nothing. And if you're acting in good faith, it's because you're the dupe of your own imagination."

"Not one word more!" howled Dr. Bro.

He was so terribly excited that Henri Ruchard drew nearer to his father. "Don't insist, I beg you."

"Come on, then!" Ruchard shouted. "It's necessary to be done with this once and for all, to nip this legendary impiety in the bud, to annihilate this execrable lie."

"Don't challenge me, Ruchard—don't push me too far!" Bro brandished his fist. He seemed to be suffering a paroxysm of exasperation. Saliva was running from his lips. His inflamed eyes were bulging from their orbits. Vainly, his daughter exhorted him to be calm, her gestures imploring.

The professor shrugged his shoulders. "Play-acting," he murmured.

Bro took a step back. He gathered himself together. He put his hands in the pocket of his capacious jacket. "That's it," he hissed. "You won't believe me?"

"No."

In a firmer voice, all the more frightening in consequence, Bro went on: "You believe me capable of a deception?"

"Yes."

"But you don't believe me capable of a crime?"

Ruchard did not hesitate. "No."

"But you admit," Bro continued, "that a sculptor has the right to smash his statue, that an inventor has the right to break up his machine?"

Ruchard made no reply, fearful of comprehension. There was, for all those watching, an interminable moment of absolute anguish.

Then, speaking and acting at the same time, Bro said: "Well, the proof that Dajan-Phinn is my work is that I am destroying him!"

Three gunshots punctuated this sentence. With a revolver withdrawn from his pocket, he had fired at Dajan-Phinn, standing at the bottom of the steps.

Amid the cries of horror and panic, Ruchard hurled himself upon his puny adversary, seized his wrist and disarmed him. Bro shouted full in his face: "Well, that's what you wanted! That's where it has led me, orthodox science! To destroy my masterpiece! Ha ha! Orthodox science!"

Dajan-Phinn suddenly collapsed, turning as he did so to fall face down. Aided by the servants brought running by the noise, Henri Ruchard and César Bro carried him to a settee in the drawing-room. Lamps were brought.

While the two women went up to calm the children woken up by the detonations, who were uttering screams of fright, the professor examined the wounded man. He shook his head. Dahjan-Phinn had received two bullets full in the chest. His condition seemed hopeless.

Indifferent to his victim, Dr. Bro strode back and forth in the drawing-room, filling it with his gestures and vocal outbursts. He declared that he was going to surrender to the law, that the instruction of his trial and the sensation at the assizes would compel the entire world to recognize the truth of his affirmations, the excellence of his doctrines and finally render him justice.

The professor, who was listening, left Dajan-Phinn momentarily. He drew his son and the painter into a corner of the room. It was, on the contrary, necessary to avoid the scandal of such a trial. Bro had evidently acted in a fit of madness. He, Ruchard, would do his utmost to prove it—and he would use his influence to cut short any pursuit. He begged the two men to aid him in this plan. They would pretend to acceded to the murderer's desire, but instead of accompanying him to the commissariat, they would take him to a nearby lunatic asylum kept by one of their mutual friends, where he would receive all the necessary case, and where the court would be able, the following day, to proceed with the customary inquiries.

A quarter of an hour later, Dr. Bro left the house with his two bodyguards, convinced that he would be turned over to the law and launching one final sarcasm and one final challenge at his adversary…

The hours went by, slowly, at Dajan-Phinn's bedside, in the drawing-room from which they had not dared to remove him. Madame Bro kept watch, while Professor Ruchard took a little rest in a neighboring room. The celebrated physician still offered no hope. The unfortunate victim would doubtless soon take the secret of his origin away with him forever.

Meanwhile, he had recovered consciousness—and as the good Madame Bro, wiped a tear from the corner of her eye with a fingertip, Dajan-Phinn murmured: "Don't cry. I don't regret disappearing. Yesterday, in this room, I heard your fiancés. I became conscious of my real misfortune, my true destiny. Whether or not I was born like other men, I would always have lacked the only faculty that makes life worth living, that reveals its charm and attraction…"

"And that is?"

"Love."

Jules Perrin & H. Lanos: *The World Above the World*
(1911)

I. In which we make the acquaintance of M. Goldfeller,
the Gem King

We had embarked on the special train at the station of Sommesous, and for 20 minutes we had been rolling along the line constructed with a view to linking the works to the Châlons-Troyes line.

It was a flat country, marshy and bare, the most wretched corner of Champagne. We were chatting without paying any attention to the landscape, whose sadness seemed infinite beneath a cloudy sky with rare clear patches; intermittent squalls twisted the already-leafless trees and spring, at its debut, was more sullen here than anywhere else.

"What's that?" exclaimed little Luneau of the *Informateur*, all of a sudden.

"That," said stout Blum of the *Young Herald*, with a clownish gravity, "is a reservoir."

Stupidly, simply for the pleasure of tooting my horn in the concert of surprise and buffoonery that united us all—my colleagues and I—I said: "It's the Tower of Babel."

I represented the news syndicate of the viticultural press. I was young—scarcely 25—not an idiot, but still irreflective, and I let myself get carried away by the need for irony and denigration that superiority maintains over ignorance. We jostled for position at the windows of the carriage to in order to contemplate the prodigious construction whose mass extended out of sight beyond the grey horizon.

Its immediate appearance was that of a cylinder several kilometers in diameter, with a height that I heard estimated at 1800 meters by Baroux, the engineer-director of the steelworks at Saint-Dié. On a masonry foundation about ten meters

171

high stood a mountain of steel, assembled, in a crazy multipli-cation of arches, cross-pieces, beams and metal joints, the suc-cession of which, regularly-repeated, discouraged the eye. A large fortified ditch isolated the base of the tower, whose mas-sive shadow darkened the countryside. In that endless plain, the spectacle was so colossal that we stopped joking in order to look at one another in amazement.

"It's as big as Paris."

"And it's higher."

The train increased its speed, which gradually became vertiginous, and the reason for that velocity became clear to us at the same time as the immense network of rails on which it was evident that we were in the process of making a tour of the base of the entire edifice.

"This," said Scordel, the Undersecretary of State for Finance, who was a former journalist and had been gallant enough to make the journey with us, "is one of Goldfeller's ideas; he's giving us the honor of a tour, externally."

Turning toward him, I said: "As you're in the govern-ment, can you tell us why Monsieur Goldfeller has been au-thorized to construct this *reservoir*, as Luneau calls it. Is the intention to build a new Eiffel Tower on a larger scale? What's the purpose of this…machine?"

Scordel adopted a prudent attitude, which contrasted with the good fellowship he usually professed in conveying official information to us. "But it's interesting as a project," he replied. "Nothing similar has yet been built as a metallic con-struction. Goldfeller is eccentric. Do you know him?"

He began to talk to his neighbors, thus avoiding any clearer response.

The explanations that Scordel did not want to give, Lu-neau—always well-informed—claimed to know. "Goldfeller is the savior of the Minister, Piérard. For several years work on the tower has taken up considerable manpower…no more unemployment…no one gives any more thought to the social question. Piérard governs as he wishes." He lowered his voiced. "It's said…it's said that Piérard himself received a huge bribe before granting authorization for the commencement of the works. At any rate, every time he's interrogated in the Chamber about the real purpose of the enterprise, he avoids explaining it clearly. It was only after a question from Gentilhomme—the député from Châlons—that the government decided to furnish vague explanations. Hence the invitation from Goldfeller, slightly forced, for this official visit. What are we going to see up there?"

He pointed a finger at the summit of the monstrous edifice, around which our course was continuing—beginning to decelerate, however, while our train described a curve through the network of rails criss-crossing the landscape. We went through several depots containing engines and wagons, a succession of buildings and hangars cluttered with trains and materials, finally emerging into the vast glazed hall of a station.

At the platform we got down from the train. Initially, there was a confused hubbub, due primarily to the joy of escaping the sight of the obsessive mass momentarily. There was a crowd there—an entire crowd gathered for the visit: the President of the Council himself, accompanied by the Minister of Public Works and delegations invited from all the great state bodies; military men, engineers and magistrates; personalities representing all the arts; curiosity-seekers, friends of anybody and everybody; and women, whose carefully-composed costumes were beginning to be powdered with dust while walking along the carpeted gangways garlanded with green plants and flowers by which we emerged from the station.

We saw a stone wall and, a few meters above our heads, the vertiginous rise of the metallic carcass that was lost to sight in the sky. Closer at hand, that iron trellis was confirmed in its boldness and lightness by the very enormity of the proportions of all those buttresses and superimposed beams. The dimensions were without analogy, the aspect formidable and mysterious, like a forest of needles sprung from a cube of steel that served as its base, a wintry forest devoid of foliage, the

173

color of rust, whose thick iron branches hid in their depths the secret of the man who was advancing to meet us.

"Goldfeller," murmured Luneau.

Of medium height, stiff and spry, with a hairless face and a gaze of steel, his hair thick and beginning to go grey, we saw him appear under the enormous arch of a doorway opening in the foot of the tower. An orchestra, which I had not seen, struck up the national anthem, and heads were spontaneously bared, while Goldfeller walked proudly toward the ministers.

Around me, people were whispering: "Goldfeller... Goldfeller... the gem king."

The name ran from mouth to mouth, whispered and murmured—then, as if acclaimed by an audience that had decided on flattery, a truly enthusiastic welcome was offered to the man by Piérard, the President of the Council.

"Government of the Republic...metallurgy...great interest...bonds of an old amity...personally happy...official consecration..."

Piérard's voice, which is weak, only brought us a few shreds of sentences, but that was sufficient to augur the highly flattering tone of the assembly. At any rate, Goldfeller seemed unmoved by it; he listening, nodding his head, with an air of approval rather than gratitude: *Good, Good, you're only saying what has to be said.* His dry voice, forceful and authoritative, rose up as soon as Piérard's had fallen silent, and he immediately set out to describe and explain his work.

"At an average speed of 100 kilometers an hour, M. President, you've just made a circuit of our works in 20 minutes, which implies a circumference of about 30 kilometers. That's a little more than the periphery of the fortifications of Paris. You can judge the base of the operation; I shall, if you will permit, take you to the culminating point of the construction-work.

Turning around, he retraced his steps; Piérard followed him like a docile subaltern. It seemed to me that the imperious voice of the man, who held his head high, those grey eyes, the greyish tint and the precocious wrinkles in that overbearing forehead, were not unknown to me. Where from?

People clustered around him, staring at him curiously, while he advanced, pointing at the elevator-room that was descending along the bare frame of the tower. Through the windows in the vast iron cage one perceived the luxurious installation, the Persian carpet with glossy reflections, the comfortable armchairs, the internal panels covered with paintings by masters.

An idea—an abrupt memory—suddenly occurred to me, which it was impossible for me to contain. I leaned toward Luneau. "Do you know who he resembles?" I said, in a low voice. "Cauchois—my math professor when I was at the Condorcet. It seems to me that I can still hear him calling me, dryly: 'Bayoud, to the board.'"

In crowds, one can speak in a low voice, counting on the preoccupation of the individuals who are the actors absorbed in those sorts of ceremony. The man had to be endowed with supernormal perceptive powers for a few words produced discreetly to reach his ears. He heard them and, continuing to advance with a firm stride, turned his grey-tinted and clean-shaven face toward me; the slightly hazy veil that had seemed to cover my eyes was snatched away, like the door of a lantern. I received full on, and from head to toe, the shock of fulgurant stare, under which I felt my legs grow weak. Then, indifferently, and with his eyes almost devoid of expression, Goldfeller stood aside, with an amicable gesture, to let the ministers and their retinue pass.

An electrical bell, an instant's delay, and the enormous elevator rose into the air, to the strains of a military march, played by a brass band installed on the platform above our heads.

Two other elevators had been sent down to bring the guests up to the summit of three works. While we jostled one another to get in, Luneau, always inclined to mock, with his meager head bobbing like an irritated cat's, whispered in my ear: "Whatever you say, Bayoud, Goldfeller or Cauchois, he's

175

not a cold-eyed type—someone, at any rate, that it's better not to have as an enemy."

Confusedly, that was also my opinion, but I tried not to think about the incident, only conserving a slight resentment and a tendency to consider everything in the ceremony in an ironic and ill-humored light.

We reached the summit, and found ourselves on a sort of round road a large suspended avenue, perfectly macadamized. Goldfeller's dry voice dominated all others, giving explanations:

"Our first platform," he was saying, "is at 500 meters, the second at 1250...."

A whole crowd was swarming around us, coming and going: the population of workers harnessed to the cyclopean task, some in work-clothes, tools in hand or on their shoulders, others idling momentarily, taking a momentary breather, getting in the way of the select visitors and considering us with the slightly satirical eyes of workers that one has just seen at work. All nations came together there: northern blonds, pale and plaid; brown loquacious Levantines; thick-lipped Africans whose teeth sparked in slightly cruel laughter; Chinese; Annamites with skirts tucked between their legs; and little Japanese shivering in their black lustrine blouses, inflated by the wind—which was free and violent at that height.

Above our heads, on the iron framework rising from the original foundation of the edifice, immense cranes were turning, causing metal beams and girders to rotate. As far as the eye could see the motors were panting and skips coughing as they were emptied. The blaring of sirens and prolonged whistle-blasts punctuated the maneuvers, but only the sonorous song of hammers riveting iron rose clearly above the rumble into which all the other noises of the colossal city made of an infinite number of construction-yards melted.

"What do you think of it?" whispered old Bourdon, the doyen of reporters, impressed although he had seen a great many things during 30 years of service.

I shrugged my shoulders amid the crowd of people were jostling to get to the head of the procession. "You see," I shouted to Bourdon, from a distance, "if whoever undertook this construction hasn't got a secret objective…he's a mere madman."

I struggled, stuck between two giants whose resistant inertia ended up annoying me. "Let me pass, then!" I exclaimed, looking at each of them in turn.

Two workmen, it seemed, properly clad in European dress—but they were bizarrely exotic. One had a short muzzle, slightly green-tinted skin and bovine eyes; the other a straw-colored complexion and the gaze of a tiger, which filtered between slitted eyelids, with a meat-porter's fists at the ends of his arms. They stood side silently, letting me pass n front of them, but they continued to follow me, without taking their eyes off me.

I succeeded in getting close to the hero of the celebration and the ministers. I arrived at the moment when Goldfeller was introducing Piérard to a white-haired old man bowed down by a frock-coat, as if he were unused to wearing one. The President of the Council shook his hand effusively.

"Where have you been?" Luneau asked. "You've missed the introductions. Our host is bringing out his collaborators: chemists and physicists who have manufactured producers never seen before; if you believe them, they're going to turn the world upside-down, and everything is being studied here that is necessary to ensure the happiness of humankind. The old man with the white hair is…what's he called, Buridan?"

The stout Buridan of the *Express-Globe*, who had gone around the world flat out several times, mopped his brow as he retorted: "Rassmuss."

"Rassmuss," scoffed Luneau. "That's fine name for a sorcerer, eh?"

"Don't mock," Buridan interjected, with the nasal accent of an "old boy" of Battery Place. "Why are you always mocking, Luneau?"

"But what is all this?" I said. "What's it for?"

Buridan advanced his shaven lip, circumspectly. "All I can tell you," he affirmed, "is that Goldfeller's a very powerful man."

"Do you know him well?"

"I met him two years ago in Winnipeg, last year in Bombay, and I interview him in the company of the starvelings of India, for my articles on world poverty—remember? I saw him strew money around everywhere without counting it."

"And where does it comes from, his fortune?"

"It's said that he's found out how to use Moissan's electric furnace[32] to good effect, and that he can manufacture precious stones as well as nature—that's why they call him the gem king."

"Pooh! Is he the one who found it? How do you know that he's not exploiting someone else's idea? Old Rassmuss, for example. The *bluff* king, at the most."

I was speaking loudly enough for the comment to raise a laugh. Looking around with a satisfied expression, I met the staring eyes of the two giants of a little while before, standing behind me. They too were smiling as they looked at me.

"What does it matter?" Buridan went on. "Here's a man who can make an idea fruitful that another might have left unproductive, and who's building a tower of iron, as the pharaohs rewarded themselves with the luxury of the pyramids and the sphinx; that makes work for the workman, raises the price of manpower and materials. Who's complaining? For the moment, it's resolved the social question."

"Hurrah for Goldfeller!"

"That's very true," said the director of the forges of Ancion, in the middle of a group. "At the present moment, unemployment no longer exists in the iron industry from one end of Europe to the other. All the available workmen have been

---

[32] The French chemist Henri Moissan (1852-1907) attempted to use an electric arc furnace to synthesize diamonds from the common form of carbon, but did not succeed.

drawn here, and the other countries of the world are furnishing their contingents, as you can see."

"But is there no danger for the future?" I remarked. "Vast as they are, these construction-works must come to an end. What then?"

What demon prompted me? What instinctive acrimony always drove me to search for possible flaws in an enterprise whose enormity alone was sufficient to win the enthusiastic unanimous consent of all the official visitors?

Goldfeller seemed not to have seen or heard anything, entirely absorbed by the concern of furnishing the ministers with the explanations they were rather timidly soliciting. In his wake, the procession advanced around the circular boulevard that overlooked, on one side, the vast rural extent, and on the other, that vast metallic forest, which, under the impulse of that man, was driving the accumulated effort of his rancor toward the sky. In its endless valleys and at the tips of its pro-digious bristles swarmed a host of workers, in obstinate masses and audacious clusters, whose activity seemed eternal. Except that, as we passed by, through the construction-sites, the men arranged themselves into compact ranks, shouldering their tools; in response to an overseer's whistle behind us, the work resumed.

At intervals, a brief pause immobilized the entire crowd. The dry voice of the "Gem King" was heard, replying to a few questions in curt sentences, discouraging replies and persis-tence.

"The level of this circular boulevard indicates the general plane of the work; within two months, these metallic valleys will be flattened under a uniform ground."

"How high do you intend to go?" asked Scordel.

"1900 meters—a round number."

II. Lost in the Tower

A great silence welcomed this declaration, made by Goldfeller without hesitation. People looked at him, and kept silent. I shrugged my shoulders again and said to Luneau: "It's madness—pure madness."

Goldfeller's grey eyes turned in my direction; his gaze brushed me. As I turned round to follow the direction of that imperious glance, I found myself face to face with my two gigantic neighbors of a little while before. They were following me everywhere, smiling, with placid expressions on their savage faces. Was there any reason to take umbrage, in that crowd in which everyone was scrambling avidly after the official personages?

In any case, an abrupt surge—a sort of crush—suddenly separated me from those strange companions. Everyone moved sideways and huddled against the balustrade bordering the boulevard above the void, because an obstacle was barring the route, forcing the procession to break ranks.

I heard Piérard asking: "What's that?"

Dryly, without stopping, in a slightly discontented tone, Goldfeller replied: "It's our future lighting system."

As they passed alongside the obstacle, people paused to examine it and took advantage of the pause to exchange reflections. Like everyone else, I lingered to take a look at the remarkable apparatus, extended like a beached cetacean for a length of a hundred meters.

Imagine a sort of monstrous iron seahorse, with its long tail and belly ringed and creased like an accordion, its head curved back, with its mouth wide open and excrescences of eyes in which one could imagine the future location of two immense lenses designed to spread afar the electric light channeled through that gigantic candelabra, all of whose rings seemed extensible, thanks to two sets of intersecting piston-rods. As it was, the entire apparatus was strange and disquieting in the inert sprawl, like a maleficent, supernatural, slumbering beast.

"Bizarre!"

"Curious!"

"That's new!"

"Yes—not banal, at any rate."

Everyone said his bit.

"Is that really a lantern?" I said, in my turn.

"But what do you think it is?" demanded the stout Buridan, laughing.

"How do I know? Admit that it's more reminiscent of an engine of war than a peaceful lighting apparatus."

Luneau started laughing. "What an imagination you have! Deep down, you've got something against Goldfeller."

"Me? What? To construct this beast with an iron carcass, with neither rhyme nor reason...unless it's to serve some maleficent purpose that none of us suspects."

"Oh!"

"You're insane, Bayoud."

"Remember that it's Piérard himself..."

"Eh? Exactly! What does that prove?"

Two years before Piérard, as Minister of Public Works, had signed the documents authorizing the works envisaged by M. Goldfeller, who threw millions into it recklessly. With money, one can buy anything one wants.

"Oh, if you're talking politics..."

Everyone laughed. They were mocking me. Generally, enthusiasm was stifling criticism. One person praised the audacity of the work that Goldfeller would leave to France after his death, under certain undetermined conditions. Others, determined to find some utility in it, ended up discovering some: the military governor of Paris would make it a work of national defense, a station for our dirigibles and aviators, and the director of the Observatoire talked about transporting his telescopes there.

They all went on, hurrying to rejoin the scattered procession. I ended up standing on my own next to the strange monster extended at my feet. Leaning forward, I examined the metallic carcass curiously.

The noise of a car rolling on rails made me lift my head. I saw before me one of those small wagons whose incessant comings and goings are utilized throughout construction-yards for transporting personnel and materials. This one, slowing

181

down as it passed in front of me, seemed to be inviting me to depart on a voyage of discovery through the exotic works. A sudden and deplorable idea crossed my mind; jumping into the little wagon, I let myself be drawn away into the unknown.

Was it waiting for me fatal decision? One would have been tempted to think so, in view of the vertiginous speed with which it set about taking me away. The diabolical vehicle's track used the gullies of the thousand iron workplaces open before it, following the intricacies of the roller-coaster system. I had got aboard at the summit of a curve and was immediately precipitated at top speed into a gulf, lost in the metallic web, where the song of hammers resonated terribly. In a few minutes, I had lost the official procession, on which I turned my back and, bounding from summit to summit to plunge back into abysses, after one descent steeper than the others, I ended up coming smoothly to rest on a sort of concrete platform at the foot of a granite wall.

Around the wall, the foliage of that metal forest billowed to infinity. Turning my head, I was seized by vertigo on observing that the platform on which I had landed was an interrupted section of the boulevard around the top of the tower. Below me was the countryside, and 1900 meters of empty space.

Mastering my terror and making a half-turn, my hands extended along the wall against which I had run aground, I moved away as rapidly as possible in the direction of the center of the tower. I marched thus for more than a quarter of an hour and eventually understood that the foot of the wall next to which I was advancing, far from limiting the upper platform of the tower, turned back on itself in the direction of the circular boulevard, whose curve it interrupted. I risked raising my eyes; above me I perceived, to my surprise, tall trees still denuded of foliage, which were leaning over the wall against which I was supporting myself.

A garden! At that height, and unique in the entire extent of that metal immensity! What did the garden signify? It must be very large, to judge by the extent of its boundary wall. Disorientated and confused, I scanned my surroundings with my surprised gaze. Some new perfidy of fate dictated that, exactly at that moment of uncertainty and surprise, I perceived a ladder thrown by a hazard of the works on to the boulevard—a ladder forgotten there by some workman, the mere sight of which suddenly brought my disorientated thoughts into focus. In a matter of seconds, I seized it, stood it up, and, leaping from rung to rung, reached to top of the wall, from which I could look into the garden at my ease.

Through the leafless branches I perceived a vast lawn, a pond and, in the distance, beyond further spinneys of trees, a residential house—whose style and size I did not have time to appreciate, because the sound of oars striking water immediately attracted my attention to the pond, where a boat appeared between clumps of reds. The bowed was propelled by a vigorous woman of mixed race, whose arms plied the oars with the skill and strength of a professional mariner. A young woman was sitting at the tiller.

Sitting on cushions that elevated her as if she were on a throne, wrapped in a light white fur, the apparition passed so rapidly before my eyes that I could scarcely make out the gold of her hair, the pallor and the smile on her face, and the graceful gesture of the pretty creature, who must have seen me and pointed me out to the woman. The boat disappeared behind a stand of willows. I heard the fading sound of a voice that seemed to me to be as precise as a musical instrument.

I did not have time to see or hear any more, however; a violent shock caught me by surprise, my ladder trembled under an unexpected weight, and I felt powerful hands grabbing me and covering my eyes. I was knocked down, dragged away I know knot where or how, and suddenly felt the ground shake beneath me. I began to descend at a vertiginous speed, into depths that seemed to me to be limitless. I could see nothing in the darkness into which I had been plunged, but I knew that I was not alone, for the Herculean hands that had grabbed me a little while before continued to hold me by the arms, in an irresistible grip.

After a minute or so, the platform slowed down and came smoothly to a stop. A door opened behind me; the light that sprang forth from it illuminated two terrible faces—the faces of the two giants who had followed me in the course of that stroll interrupted by a savage aggression. They shoved me again, forcing me to go into a rather large room, a sort of windowless waiting-room with grey wall-hangings, brightly lit by electric bulbs. The door closed again behind us.

Immediately, I ran forward, searching for a way out. Not finding any, I turned toward my two strange companions. A little while ago they had been laughing; now they were terrifyingly silent and ferociously serious.

"What's the meaning of this atrocious attack?" I demanded, violently. "I assume that you're acting on behalf of M. Goldfeller? What does he want with me? Is he thinking of taking me prisoner?"

I started laughing scornfully. The two colossi remained mute. That exasperated me. "I demand an answer. Remember that you're accomplices of this crime—I shall refer it to the law."

A kind of smile leveled the lips of the giant with the yellow face and uncovered his companion's gums, but neither of them said anything. I stamped my foot.

"Are you dumb?" I shouted, beside myself.

Their only response, both having consulted one another with their eyes, was to open their mouths and, with identical gestures, indicate the shapeless stumps of severed tongues. Under orders or incapacitated, the singular beings could not answer me. Ceasing my questions, I decided to wait, and went to sit down in a corner.

I affected a perfect tranquility. Deep down, the strangeness of the adventure and the eccentric character of the person who had ordered it, were beginning to make me vaguely anxious. Who was this Goldfeller? One of those semi-madmen unhinged by an unexpected fortune, capable of anything in their unbridled vanity? What could be expected of a man to whom the hazards of worldly existence had given control of slaves of the sort who had brought me here?

That anxiety lasted three hours.

Finally, the door opened. Goldfeller appeared. He favored my gaolers with a satisfied glance and sent them away with a gesture. Immediately, I advanced toward him, speaking loudly in a threatening manner.

"Monsieur," I said, forcefully, "All this is both odious and extravagant. Your conduct in my regard is criminal…"

He darted a cold sideways glance at me and set his silk hat on a table, while I continued talking, threatening him with reprisals, talking about making a complaint to the public prosecutor. With his eyes lowered, drumming on the tabletop with his fingertips, he let me vent my anger without seeming to pay any heed to it.

When I shut up, somewhat out of breath, he said, without any preamble: "You said something a little while ago that I didn't like. Afterwards, you committed an indiscretion in my home that might cost you dear."

"I don't have to account to anyone for my opinions," I affirmed. "As for my actions…"

The billionaire made a casual gesture. "I'm not asking you to account for them. I don't have time to waste. I simply forbid you to continue."

"You forbid me…?"

"Yes."

It was so clearly articulated, with such assurance, that I could find no response sat first. There was a pause of several seconds while I wondered whether the man of prodigious energy standing in front of me might simply be mad.

"Monsieur," I eventually said, "I don't suppose you intend keeping me prisoner here. Remember that I'll be leaving…"

A kind of smile stretched Goldfeller's tight lips. He shook his head, seemed to reflect momentarily, and, moving toward a corner of the room, opened a door hidden behind the

185

wall-hangings. At the same time, he gestured to me to go on ahead of him.

I went up two steps, and the door of the reception-room closed behind us. The darkness was complete, but almost immediately, a light came on above my head and I saw that we were in a sort of car with several seats, which began to move smoothly over rails, with a resonant sound.

Beyond the windows, the closely-set walls of the corridor along which we were gliding fled behind us without it being possible to distinguish anything. I sat down opposite Goldfeller, who, with his legs crossed and his face impassive, had lit a cigar and was drawing light perfumed puffs therefrom.

"Where are you taking me?" I asked, in a slightly softer tone..

With a gesture, he bade me wait—and after that, we remained silent.

III. Prisoner

While observing Goldfeller, I realized that he was guiding the progress of the car himself, reducing and increasing its speed with the aid of a commutator whose handle he was operating. Having rolled for about five minutes along that dark corridor of sorts, the horizon abruptly broadened out and lit up brightly. At the same time, the vehicle came to a halt.

I got to my feet in order to get out, but my companion gestured to me to sit down again.

We were in the middle of an immense open space, in the form of a rotunda, which reminded me of the Place de l'Opéra, with its electric candelabras, its bustling crowds, its glamorous shops and the perspective of wide streets radiating from it. A large population was circulating on the sidewalks, waiting on traffic-islands, hastening across the plaza and scattering into the adjacent streets; trolley-cars full of passengers were passing by, amid the abrupt sounds of bells and buzzers. At the junction of two streets, the tall façade of a theater advertized that evening's performance in luminous letters.

Where was I? We had not left the tower, and, on leaning to peer out of the small windows of our little carriage, I perceived nothing where the sky should have been but an inextricable metal trellis, within which air could doubtless circulate, but through which no external light penetrated. In spite of my bad humor, I could not help a start of surprise.

So, I thought, *the whole society of workers assembled here by the will of this man resides here, sleeps here, lives here, distracts itself here outside working hours; this shapeless colossus already hides an entire city within its flanks.*

On reflection, it was simple: in this marshy and desert land, far from any great center, it had been necessary to think about feeding, and even lodging, the laborers brought from afar, and the same thing had been done as in all sorts of works, where it was necessary to build canteens and dressing-rooms that were subsequently dismantled. Here, though, the proportions and the comfort were beyond all comparison.

I looked with even greater astonishment at the enigmatic man who resided over this phantasmagoria. A kind of satisfied smile strayed over his lips while he started the little car moving slowly again. It crossed the plaza and resumed its course rather rapidly along a brightly-lit street full of busy people. I watched the shop-fronts speed by, trying to read their signs: restaurants, bakeries, cafes, groceries and fashion emporia. That went on for a few minutes, and then, by virtue of a ramp with a balustrade, which rose gradually alongside us, I ended up seeing nothing but the legs of all the pedestrians. Eventually, the car plunged...can I say *underground?*...at any rate, into a long tunnel in which it became impossible for me to distinguish anything. Sometimes, beneath abrupt lighted vaults, at inappreciable distances, the interior life of the tower reappeared in clear patches dotted with distant shadows. Through blue-tinted bays I saw crowds agitating in abruptly-interrupted comings and goings, and I gradually became conscious of the

187

formidable power of the man who had been the determined organizer of this mysterious human ant-hive.

He remained impassive, his grey eyes staring into the void; one might have thought that he was dreaming. He let the vehicle bowl along at to speed, which must have crossed the entire breadth of the tower, for the journey lasted almost an hour.

At the end of it, letting go of his little handle, Goldfeller stood up.

I did likewise, assuming that we had arrived and that the Gem King, satisfied with having put on a display of his power, was about to set me at liberty.

Causing the car's glazed door to slide sideways, he ushered me out ahead of him, into a waiting-room, in which several gentlemen of correct appearance got up on our arrival to come forward and meet the billionaire, to whom they handed papers that he examined with a scrupulous gaze. His brow furrowed discontentedly, and he addressed one of the individuals deferentially awaiting his orders.

"Too many accidents," he said, in a curt tone. "These eight men are in hospital?"

An affirmative nod relied.

"Which one?"

"Hôpital Roux."

"Good. I'll drop in. You can go, gentlemen."

As he spoke he crossed the large room at a rapid pace. I followed him, assuming that the course would reach a liberating terminus and that the next door opened by my guide would set me free. We walked through darkness for several seconds and, to my great surprise, the ground shook once more beneath my feet, and I felt that we were rising up, lifted by an elevator toward the top of the tower.

Anger gripped me again. "Oh!" I exclaimed. "This joke is getting out of hand! Monsieur, if you've been trying to give me proof the extent of your power and your work, let me tell you that I'm convinced. Everything here, I agree, is enormous and surprising, and I shall certify that when the opportunity arises—but I want to go now."

A tranquil voice replied from the shadows. "But that's not what I want, Monsieur Bayoud."

"You're not intending of keeping me here against my will?"

"Yes, that's what I intend to do."

"As a prisoner?"

"As a prisoner."

I burst into nervous laughter and tried to make a joke of it. In our era, a kidnapping...the newspapers...the law...I said everything you might suppose, and had not stopped talking when I was seized by the arms.

"Neither the newspapers, nor the law, nor anyone else will be able to worry when you have, with the aid of a few letters, explained to those close to you that you have decided to go away for a indefinite period—a few months, perhaps a year..."

"But I won't write those letters, I said in a slightly tremulous voice.

The imperative voice hissed in the gloom: "You will write them."

The elevator rose up at a vertiginous speed, and abruptly sprang forth into the open air. We stopped in the midst of a tangle of iron beams and scaffolding, through which the wind was blowing violently. Night had fallen, but vivid electric light allowed me to see Goldfeller, his eyes sparkling. Still gripping my arm, he drew me on to a narrow iron walkway, which rang beneath our feet.

"Look," he said.

He pushed me, irresistibly. I perceived the blackness of the countryside, dotted with the pale and distant lights of a few villages scattered over the plain. No ramp or balcony had stopped out progress; we were leaning over nearly two thousand meters of empty space.

Instinctively, I closed my eyes, my heart distressed by vertigo and anguish, and threw myself backward.

"Let me go," I stammered.

He relaxed his grip. Turning my back on the abyss, I put my arms around a metal stanchion and looked behind me.

What a spectacle! Extraordinary in broad daylight, that forest of iron in the process of germination, in the glare of the thousands of electric bulbs that illuminated the expanse, became a dreamlike vision that blinded the eyes and terrified the ears with its roar.

In that white glare, one saw the little black shadows of men agitating as far as the eye could see and the wings and arms of machines turning in majestic gyrations, in a sort of apotheosis of that magical realm of human labor. The resounding groans of the metal, discharged without pause to be assembled and erected by machinery, rose up from the furnace-like glow toward the star-filled sky.

I was simultaneously terrified and gripped by admiration.

I turned unquiet eyes toward Goldfeller; his grey mask had taken on a lunar hue, and his eyes were animated by that fulgurant gleam which had impressed me from the outset.

"Well," he said, showing me the immense countryside sleeping at our feet, "What would happen if, this evening or tomorrow, someone were to discover your crushed body at the foot of the tower? Do you think that the plausible accident would hinder the progress of my work?"

I struck a dignified pose in order to reply: "It's your prerogative to commit a crime, Monsieur…"

"Yes," he interjected, sharply, "my prerogative…do you understand? I want my work to be above all criticism, justified or otherwise. Yours has annoyed me, made me impatient. I've decided to cut it short."

There was a brief silence. Then he went on: "I wanted to show you that I'm not a man like any other, Monsieur Bayoud. Unlimited wealth gives unlimited power, and I have many means to compel silence; the simplest is to keep you here—so I shall keep you, as a prisoner or at liberty, as you choose. Will you consent no sign the few letters that I mentioned a little while ago? They'll be put into the post in Paris and will serve to explain your absence to those who might be anxious about you."

I hesitated briefly, but eventually replied in a firm tone: "I refuse to write those letters."

The Gem King smiled calmly. "So be it," he said. "You choose prison. Reassure yourself; it will be at the top of our installation. You'll have time to reflect. Would you like to follow me?"

To remain in that sheer location, with the void in front of me and the uncertainty of interrupted construction-projects behind me, where it would be easy to break my neck at every step...there was no need to think about it. I walked behind Goldfeller to the elevator, which took us back into the depths of the tower.

IV. The Evil Geniuses

From the height of an immense balcony, from which we could follow the flight of an avenue quivering with recently-planted bushes, we looked out over the city.

We were smoking cigars; dinner had been delicious and we were talking uninhibitedly. Dr. Hartwig linked arms with me and murmured, as if in response to a professional thought: "1908 meters! The height of the Schwansee, in the Swiss mountains, where I was once installed in a sanitarium, where life was very sad..." He smiled at Goldfeller, who was smoking silently alongside us, and added: "And the table was inferior to yours, Master."

The billionaire shrugged his shoulders and turned to look back into the dining-room that we had just quit. "Speaking of that," he said, in his imperious voice, "where are you, Rassmuss, with your pills?"

There was a sound of hurried footsteps, and a slightly confused murmur; the bald head of the old chemist appeared in the still-bright June twilight, which caused his eyes, habituated to the artificial light of his laboratory, to blink.

"Excellency," he replied, in a hoarse voice, "the trials are finished and the formula is ready: oxygen, nitrogen, carbon, phosphorus calcium...a little gelatin to agglutinate the mixture."

I nodded my head, trying to make a joke. "My word, "I proclaimed, "I'm re-living that creole-style turbot and those delicious slices of duck, with their slight taste of lemon and paprika..."

"It's necessary, in any case, to proceed with prudent trials," Hartwig objected. "Imagine..."

He launched into a story to which Goldfeller listened placidly, surrounded by the general staff of scientists and energetic men among whom I had been living for months—for the Gem King was right; I had ended up yielding to the tedium of continued reclusion.

The first days of my captivity in the tower had passed under the close surveillance of one of the two giants who had brutally separated me from the procession of visitors to bring me into the depths of that strange prison. The man with the yellow skin, whose teeth shone cruelly behind his mauve lips, had ended up exasperating me and also frightening me, by his silence and the tiger-like gaze with which he watched my gestures while serving my meals. The little iron room where I had endured those hours of anguish, in intimate association with the colossus, whose severed tongue guaranteed his discretion, had eventually stifled within me any other idea but getting out of it, escaping those staring eyes, in which I divined the order to strangle me at the first sign of revolt.

I had, therefore, given in, signed several letters in which I had informed my friends of my departure for a rather long voyage, whose purpose I concealed. In exchange for my submission, I became free to come and go within the entire extent of the interior city. From that day on, I had shared the existence of those who were seconding, in his mysterious work, the bizarre individual whose prisoner I was.

Those men I had learned to know, to the extent that could be deduced from the external appearances they cared to manifest; as to their real personalities, perhaps their real names, who could tell? Goldfeller, doubtless—who, I rapidly came to suspect, had snatched them one by one, in the course of his global peregrinations, from one or other of those disgraces or catastrophes in which human determination and dignity founder once and for all. In return, they gave him the faithful attachment of bought slaves, or animals saved from drowning, and my miseries, my resentment toward their master, immediately crumbled before their silent respect for him.

They were, in consequence, as many spies dogging my footsteps. Nevertheless, in their company, I visited their laboratories, their libraries, their studies and their experiments, and assisted them in the installation of marvelous apparatus, whose purpose only ceased to seem inexplicable to me on the day when, liberated from that semi-captivity, I had been authorized to leave the interior of the tower to enjoy the open air once again, at the summit of the finally-completed edifice.

Imagine my surprise on then discovering that, in a matter of a few months, an entire city had been installed in the immense space that I had left in the state of a metallic construction-yard. In the streets and plazas there were the same crowds of workers, less active now at the culmination of their labor, circulating in rather leisurely groups, contemplating their work and living at ease in comfortable houses, furnished with all that an improved science had been able to anticipate to satisfy the demanding needs of modern humankind. The steelworkers had been succeeded by masons, plumbers, carpenters, locksmiths, painters, gardeners and the various tradesmen whose successive efforts had ended up making that city the marvel of comfort and delight that the man who was the soul of the enterprise had wanted to create.

From the depths of darkness, the dwellings, shops, the houses of business and pleasure were transported, definitive and splendid, into the full light of the Sun, refreshed by the pure wind, shaded by the gardens and parks sprung forth, as if by a miracle, under the restless effort of the millions of arms of that population of workmen. It seemed that all those men, whose work was almost concluded, happy with the result, could not resign themselves to let go of it, and were dallying there lethargically, with a vague desire to spend the rest of their transformed lives there, with the tacit consent of the man who had brought them here.

I had spent rapid days thus, wonderstruck, whose story would scarcely be more than a repetition of those that will follow, in which the details will be found of an assembly of unprecedented facts, crowned by the craziest and most coldly intelligent of the catastrophes that have devastated the world.

If I had ended up, little by little, by fathoming the mystery of the depths of my immense aerial prison, by contrast, I had not yet obtained from my companions the slightest revelation that might clarify for me the enigmatic personality of the man they addressed by turns, according to the habits of their private language and national servitude, as Excellency, Master, Your Honor, etc.

Goldfeller continued to appear to me as a mysterious and terrible man, pursuing a secret goal with an energy that was master of secondary energies no less audacious. Who was he? What did he want? I was able to suspect, without certainty. Apparently sharing our life, it seemed to me that the man must live apart, in the house whose discovery had cost me my liberty. The pretty creature I had glimpsed momentarily from the height of the wall I had scaled haunted my memory and my imagination, but I had never dared risk going in search of the place where she lived, perhaps a prisoner like me, amid the host of buildings, houses and gardens that had made the tower into a suspended city. I had no specific clue that would permit me to rediscover the garden where the pretty blonde fairy draped in white fur had appeared to me.

I could not help imagining that the young woman was the cause of the gigantic enterprise completed by Goldfeller; it pleased me playfully to associate that tiny image with the mass of an edifice whose shadow plunged the countryside into darkness for several leagues around. But beyond that, I was reduced to conjectures; thus, in his person as in his plans, the

Gem King remained for me the mysterious, impassive and closed individual that he was at that very moment, when he was listening to Hartwig tell him his story about concentrated nourishment.

The doctor fell silent. Passing his hand over his broad tanned forehead, Goldfeller murmured in a preoccupied manner: "Our provisions are undoubtedly enormous, but Rassmuss's pills might become indispensable."

"Bah! Are you afraid of a siege?" The physician laughed.

Goldfeller turned toward the dining-room. "What is it, Glubb?" he demanded of a kind of red-headed with a jockey's build, who was coming toward us, cap in hand.

"They're not satisfied," Glubb replied, in English, with a snigger that revealed his discolored teeth and creased his hideously bright eyes—those of a cockney street-urchin.

"Who? Who?"

A rapid discussion in English told us that after grumbling for a long time, the local peasants, whose hostility had increased incessantly, were about to pass from words to action. They intended to mount an armed attack on the workers engaged in the daily work of unscrewing the leather hoses of the pumps that brought our daily provisions of water.

In spite of my apparent submission, I could not suppress a sort of snigger.

"Ha ha!" I said. "It had to happen. Your work casts a shadow over the fields, hides the sun, devours the water from the wells and rivers. The other day, your trials of artificial rain drowned the peasants' meager harvests, and your dynamite explosions excavating new wells killed children who were coming back from school in Montepreux. Now, here's the revolt—you didn't anticipate that. The voice of the people—there's nothing like it to tame wealth, even science…"

A thunderous glance from Goldfeller interrupted me. He seemed transfigured, from impassive, his attitude had turned aggressive; his thin and supple figure stiffened, as if it had snapped into shape.

"Stupidity," he cried, in a thunderous voice, "is devoid of strength against determined intelligence. Popular revolts are as old as the world; they're not untamable. Do you think that the Pharaohs who built the Pyramids allowed themselves to be stopped by the squeals of an imbecile rabble? Come and see how these idiots are made to see reason."

He left the room swiftly. We followed him silently, all equally surprised by the sudden violence of his speech, usually more coldly imperious.

By means of rapidly-rolling walkways we transported ourselves from one end of the city to the others, through vast avenues planted with trees, to the doors of a building formed like an ancient temple, on the fronton of which was inscribed, in letters of bronze, the word *Government*. The temple I had seen constructed a short while before, with a magical rapidity, but the word defining its purpose had only just been added, in accordance with a recent order.

Goldfeller climbed the steps of the temple briskly. An armored door opened in front of us and we went into a bare room, at the center of which a sort of iron balustrade surrounded a basket, as in the Paris Bourse. We had to follow the Gem King into that cage, which limited the platform of an elevator that began to descend rapidly.

In scarcely five seconds, we found ourselves transported into an extraordinary place which, beneath the appearances of a simplicity specified at most by its enormous dimensions, was—as I soon found out—the centralized pandemonium of the audacious work of the men accompanying me.

Laboratory, study—what name should I give to that immense hall, in which, lined up for more than five hundred meters, there was a collection of inactive apparatus: screens, consoles of recording instruments or controls, telephone receivers, microphones…? I identify those whose purpose I could deduce, but had to content myself with gazing uncomprehendingly at the prodigious quantity of wheels, handles, buttons, tubes and speakers gaping like avid mouths that were aligned along the walls or distributed on tables of various heights, linked by elevators and colossal ladders that could be rolled effortlessly along polished rails. Above our heads, the iron arches of the ceiling were rounded into a vault, as high as that of a cathedral.

"Gentlemen," said Goldfeller, turning toward us, "now is the hour when our work will perhaps change its face. Let's show this imbecile multitude that we can, if necessary, defend ourselves. Attacked, it will be necessary for us to attack in our turn. Hernu!"

The man he had summoned was busy in the room, using rags to clean the handles, hand-grips and brass parts of innumerable items of apparatus installed around us; with his overalls, his little fitted jacket and his leather cap pulled down over his forehead, he looked like an electrician, and his accent, the purest suburban Parisian, confirmed that in the guttural tone in which he shouted: "M'sieur!"

At the same time, he turned toward us an intelligent and hideous face, lit up by two flame-filled eyes, but pitted by smallpox, and holed by two nostrils perched above a toothless mouth, which two halves of a moustache, pretentiously pointed, uncovered like an infected wound.

"A cloud-chaser to the west, and prepare a telescope. Glubb will help you. This, gentlemen will permit us to see clearly through the mists that have thickened around us since yesterday. Kositch, we're going to try your asphyxiating vapor."

Kositch smiled modestly. He was a Russian, a skillful chemical technician and one of the most agreeable of my companions in captivity—but I could not help noticing the slightly cruel quality of the smile that suddenly extended over his thick lips. And on the faces of those surrounding me I saw the same expression of expectation, simultaneously ferocious and delighted. In silence, they all seemed to be anticipating a promised, long-awaited moment, the charm of which would finally satiate the unhealthy instinct that their transformed attitude revealed to me. Goldfeller, for his part, had resumed his impassivity; standing to one side, watched by those con-

197

cerned and voracious faces, one might have thought him an animal-tamer whose voice had advertised the imminent arrival of a prey to his wild beasts.

Glubb's nasal voice cried: "Ready!"

The Gem King raised his hand. "Go!" he said.

A formidable detonation rang out, and almost immediately Goldfeller went to a telescope whose barrel, descending automatically along the metal wall of the hall, had come to settle at eye level.

"Good...lower...stop! Ah! Through the gap in the clouds we can see perfectly. The brutes! They imagine that we're afraid. Now, Hernu, aim tube 614 in the direction of the peasants. Point it at the very center of the groups. Tell me when you're ready and I'll turn the release-knob."

Around me, eyes shone. I was oppressed, emotional, vaguely terrified, no longer daring to say anything. To regain my composure, I moved to the telescope and put my eye to the lens. I saw, beneath us, the countryside, and groups of peasants gathering at the edge of the fortified ditch that surrounded the foot of the tower: men armed with scythes and pitchforks, a few with rifles, laughing, nodding their heads with an air of bravado, examining the stumps of the leather hoses they had cut. A few gendarmes, arrived from a nearby village, were listening to their complaints with slightly embarrassed expressions.

From the height from which we were contemplating the scene, all my sympathies were with the unfortunates, and I would have liked to be able to shout to them to flee, but I scarcely had time to think about it. I heard Hernu's guttural voice, the grating of a wheel, the hiss of vapor in an opened tube, and almost immediately, in the open, a mad stampede.

Swirls of light grey smoke permitted me to glimpse the disorderly gestures of hands clutching at throats, open mouths, eyes closing desperately, people tottering, hands blindly extended. The gendarmes, choking, rolled in the sticky mud that covered the ground, soaked by recent endeavors, for several kilometers around. In a few minutes, there was nothing left but two or three inert forms lying, dead or unconscious, on the edge of the armored ditch. The rest of the idlers were fleeing at top speed into the countryside, where gusts of pestilential vapor were still pursuing them.

V. Aeria

I was not alone in contemplating that scene. Taking turns, my companions had replaced me at the telescope, jostling for a better view. They were laughing, amusing themselves with the cruel spectacle.

"I hope that gas isn't lethal," I said to the Gem King, "and that those poor fellows…"

He did not take the trouble, or did not have the time, to answer me; already, a new concern was demanding his attention. An electric bell trilled a few meters away and Goldfeller, installed at the automated apparatus, was obliged to receive a dispatch, whose reading absorbed him briefly.

Then he came back toward us, and I heard him murmur, distractedly: "Bah! It's too late now! I'm master of the situation." Shaking his head energetically, he went on cheerfully: "For tonight, gentlemen, we can rest easy—but I have an idea that tomorrow won't pass without incident."

I did not yet understand the extent of the man's thinking, but I was disagreeably impressed and I dared not manifest the species of disgust that I had felt at the sight of the brutal attack I had witnessed. As for those surrounding me, the cruel face that I had just glimpsed beneath the mask of conventional benevolence that they had shown me previously inspired me with both fear and repulsion. These "outlaws" with anarchistic imaginations and professions, at the orders of a quasi-demented billionaire, these improved instruments of destruction…what might result from all that?

I felt a need to be alone.

When we had gone back up by means of the elevator to the interior of the building shaped like a temple, from which we had gained access to that disquieting laboratory of destruc-

199

tion, I took my leave of my companions and turned into the first street I came to in order to isolate myself.

I was positively choking; the suddenly-unleashed savagery of the masters of the tower disturbed and frightened me.

What did Goldfeller want? I wondered. What objective did he have in mind, and where was this madly murderous organization heading?

I wandered for some time through streets full of June moonlight, prey to these anxious thoughts, before going back to the apartment I occupied in the house where I was lodged with the Gem King's general staff.

The next day, during the communal lunch, I saw my companions again.

The meal was rather taciturn; our president, old Rassmuss—somber and preoccupied, as usual—scarcely exchanged a few words in English with his laboratory assistant Kandy, a tall thin Cinghalese with eyes of polished agate, whom I suspected of mixing a little magic with his experiments and whose knowledge of toxicology was frightening. As was my habit, I had sat down between Kositch and Hartwig, but those two, usually chatty, hardly opened their mouth. We were just finishing the last mouthful when the sound of horns blared forth outside.

"What's that?" I asked, running mechanically to the window, from which one could see the extent of the countryside, our house being constructed on the edge of the platform.

"It's the prefect of the *département*," Hartwig told me, "who's been sent to us to sort out yesterday's affair. Come and see the elevator arrive: the boss is waiting for the government delegation. It'll be interesting."

Everyone was going out; I followed the crowd, and we arrived in time to witness the arrival at the top of the tower of Monsieur Massicot, the prefect of the Marne, accompanied by his secretary-general and a departmental senator.

Each of the large service elevators arrived in a sort of glazed station in which it was easy to organize a reception. In front of the door, the two mutes, Siami-Si and Moldo, were holding back the crowd that was beginning to gather, but the order did not apply to us, and we arranged ourselves behind Goldfeller, who was busy exchanging compliments with the prefect. The latter seemed to be emotional, and lowered his voice to explain the purpose of his visit.

Then the Gem King said, in a loud voice: "Speak up, Monsieur le Préfet, speak freely. These gentlemen are my collaborators, and there is no one here who is not fully aware of what has brought you here."

"Well," the prefect replied, a trifle pale in a tone that he tried to make firmer, "perhaps you're aware of what happened yesterday in the Chamber?"

"I know that the Cabinet has been reduced to a minority, that the President of the Council has been accused of excessive…interest and complaisance in my regard, and that his successor will have the mission of ordering me to renounce my enterprise. It's a little late, perhaps, but for what am I being reproached?"

"Essentially, of disturbing the order of the State, by not releasing the three million workmen assembled here with a view to carrying out your works; additionally, of disrupting the economy of the surrounding region. You're taking possession of the water of rivers and wells; with the aid of special apparatus, you're attracting artificial rain that has drowned the crops, so…"

Goldfeller interrupted him brutally, saying in a loud voice: "Let's leave aside the accessory charge, which is, in fact, a matter of necessity. As for the first accusation, I'm not keeping anyone here by force, Monsieur le Préfet. Interrogate the people who are listening to us: are they pleased with the city they have created? Are they leading a life in conformity with their tastes here? Do they want to remain here?"

He turned toward the crowd at the station entrance, which was still growing. Cheers and shouts interrupted him.

"Yes! Yes!" cried thousands of voices. "Hurrah! Long live Goldfeller! Evviva! Hoch! Hoch! Bravo!"

In the face of these clamors, the Gem King could not retain a proud smile. He gazed silently at the prefect, who was biting his lip. The senator accompanying him came to the rescue.

"Monsieur," he said to Goldfeller, "this overreaches the agreement you made with Monsieur Piérard himself; you will understand that the government of the Republic cannot tolerate the establishment of a State within the State...above the State."

Without replying, Goldfeller turned to Siam-Si and ordered: "The service balloon." He went on: "Would you like, gentlemen to judge this State for yourselves, and take account of what our suspended city is?"

Having consulted one another with glances, the government's representatives silently followed the billionaire, who escorted them through the mocking crowd to a small platform, in front of which a balloon had just set its gondola—which accommodated everyone easily, while Goldfeller installed himself at the helm.

Without any jolt, the cigar-shaped tube of varnished silk lifted up us. The summit of the tower sank rapidly beneath us and we rose up vertically for about five hundred meters. There was a dry click and, like a gliding bird, the aeroscaph began to describe a large aerial circle above the immense aggregation of houses, green gardens and streets swarming with crowds in which one could distinguish quite clearly the gestures of minuscule pedestrians, attentively following the maneuvering of our light apparatus.

In the air of that calm summer day, the balloon stopped. With his hand on the steering-wheel, Goldfeller spoke.

"Here is the city! I've constructed it above your ancient and marshy cities with all the ingenuity of comfort: all of these houses, some of which are as tall as the skyscrapers of New York, while others don't exceed the proportions of Yorkshire cottages, have their public or private gardens, some under their very roofs, others around their little brick walls. Every quarter has its park, and all that verdure is watered regularly, either by

202

the artificial rain that we attract during the night or with the aid of the river that you can see shining in the sunlight, and which traverses the length of the city, alimented by the captures that we have made underground, and whose pumping channels and flow-pipes are carefully hidden in the mass of the tower. We have theaters, and even churches and temples for the various religions that are preoccupied with them. An easy life, free and pure air, all needs satisfied by a mysterious industry of which I am the master and the inventor—what more is needed to retain above your painful existence the thousands of individuals who have once tasted it? Henceforth, we demand but one thing: to be left in peace to enjoy that liberty above the world with which we are no longer preoccupied, in this open air city, to which I have given the name I made up for her: Aeria!"

The senator, M. Massicot, and his secretary-general looked at one another, nonplussed. At Goldfeller's last words, however, the prefect had begun to smile.

"Oh!" he said, staring fixedly at the Gem King. "You're sufficiently preoccupied with the despised old world to trade the produce of your diamond factory with it, and to exchange the gold of your transactions for the raw materials necessary to your existence."

Goldfeller remained silent momentarily. He put the gondola in motion again, which began to descend, then said, in a disdainful tone: "Certainly," he said, "and there you can see the esteem in which we hold you: your society is good for nothing but exploitation..."

Monsieur Massicot interrupted swiftly: "But it is possible for us to put an end to these transactions that allow you to live. We know your warehouse managers, your bankers..."

In his turn, Goldfeller cut into his interlocutor's speech; his grey eyes sparkled, and his voice took on the tone of hateful anger that had surprised me the day before. "It will be war, then," he said. "I will show you how we can defend ourselves."

Obedient to his guidance, the balloon descended with lightning rapidity. As we arrived at the height of the landing-platform, an unexpected gust of wind threw us back over an immense garden, a few meters from a small pavilion covered with a glazed dome, from which I heard faint music emerging. I turned my head sharply in that direction: a few feet from the pavilion, along the wall, I recognized the tall figure of Siam-Si, and, in the little building, I had time to glimpse a white form, an inclined neck and magnificent blonde tresses.

I immediately recognized the mysterious garden, and the feminine form whose face I could scarcely make out, but in which I rediscovered the features of the beautiful traveler on the pond, the sight of whom had earlier cost me my liberty.

I uttered an exclamation, the echo of which was lost in the tumult of the rapid maneuver thanks to which Goldfeller took us back up into the open air.

A smooth glide, and we entered a sort of bay, around which 20 balloons similar to ours were lined up.

"Here," said the Gem King, "is our fleet of dirigibles."

The secretary-general, a stout dark-haired man who had not said anything yet, began to laugh and murmured in a strong southern accent: "You don't count that among the number of your instruments of defense, do you? One rifle-bullet and *poof!* Eh?"

Goldfeller took a large-caliber revolver from a bag hanging in the gondola and held it out. He simply said: "Try."

Awkwardly, the other took the weapon, aimed it at one of the yellow envelopes lined up within range, and fired. The bullet was seen to ricochet from the fabric, which gave way slightly in response to the impact. A second shot had the same result, and all the other bullets in the gun.

Once again the prefect and the senator looked at one another without saying anything, and disembarked after Goldfeller on to the little pier running through the middle of the array of balloons.

Already the crowd was gathering around us.

Monsieur Massicot made one last effort, and took the Gem King to one side. "Monsieur," he said, "it's not a question of threats. All that we ask of you, for the moment, is to give a good welcome to the commission of inquiry appointed yesterday by the Chamber to…"

"No commission," Goldfeller interrupted. "My work is finished and I intend to enjoy it freely. Tell those who sent you what you have seen…and what you're about to see."

He had, with one bound, climbed back on to the pier. He pulled the cord of a flag that began to flutter in the air. To this agreed signal, a frightful roar replied. One might have thought that 20 monstrous mouths, opening beneath us in the depths of the tower, were inhaling air like so many vent-holes. Within a few seconds, the horizon was blackened by dark clouds; down below, in the fields, the trees began to bend beneath a storm-wind.

"This," said Goldfeller, "is an experiment and an advertisement."

"What is it, then?" murmured the bewildered senator.

"A cyclone. I dispose the weather at my will, thanks to apparatus whose construction is the secret of a few skilled men, whose talents I have been able to utilize. Your society made these men wretched outcasts, as it has made manual workers of all those that listen to us and whom I have undertaken to make free men and conquerors."

He indicated the crowd, and the shouts and acclamations heard a little while ago responded to his imperious gesture, even more enthusiastic, and mingled with gibes and cries of fury directed at the official envoys, whom it was necessary to escort back into the elevator-lobby by an indirect route. That explosion of howls was combined with the rage of the unleashed tempest, in the midst of which Goldfeller, raising his powerful voice again, shouted in a somewhat ironic tone as he took his leave of his visitors: "Farewell, gentlemen."

Turning toward me, he added: "Go with them, Bayoud. When you return, you can join me in my study in the governmental palace."

I rejoined the prefect, his secretary and the senator in the elevator. When the elevator began its descent they were pale and mute, seemingly overwhelmed by amazement and alarm.

For myself, I was as surprised as they were. Was Gold-feller setting me free? Alone, without any surveillance, he was depending on me to accompany the three frightened companions to the ground. Through the metallic cage, the apparatus of which effectuated the descent with a calculated slowness, they were considering the spectacle of a veritable typhoon, without saying a word.

Beneath the clamor of the storm-clouds and fulgurant lightning-flashes, the wind howled, sweeping everything in its passage, twisting and uprooting trees—which flew away like leaves—stripping the roofs off houses, sweeping away like flies the curiosity-seekers and people waiting assembled at the bottom of the tower. We saw a squadron of armored cavalry-men on maneuvers in the countryside lifted from the earth and the riders flying through the torment; with their red trousers one might have taken them for bloody leaves torn from virgin vines by the autumn wind.

When the elevator stopped the ground was strewn with debris of every sort, whirling and falling back furiously. The anguished cries of the victims of the mighty tempest were lost in the clamor of the unleashed elements.

Torn between horror and the astonishment of finding myself free, I did not know what to say, or to decide. Should I flee? Go back up? All that I had seen in the last 24 hours surpassed in intensity what I had been able to see during my forced sojourn in the tower, and was further surpassed by what I now suspected.

Curiosity proved the stronger. I said goodbye to the astounded prefect and his companions, and went back up to the city.

VI. The Unknown

There I found streets buzzing with a population ignobly amused by the surprise of events. Leaning over the balustrades of the boulevards, they were all following with amused eyes the various incidents of the catastrophe unleashed by Goldfeller's omnipotence.

"Depressed, the prefect."

"All right!"

I hastened to the governmental palace. The bestial Moldo was on guard at the elevator. He laughed at the sight of me, stood aside to let me pass, and steered the apparatus, which deposited me in the immense hall that the Gem King called his study. It was empty.

Alone in that singular place, I made a tour of it, initially inspecting things with a suspicious eye. I thought it might perhaps be sufficient to press one of those buttons, turn one of those wheels or pull one of those levers to unleash one of the catastrophes whose organization had been planned by the demons gathered in this place.

The childish curiosity that doomed Bluebeard's wife took hold of me. At ransom, I pressed a large ivory button set beside a large screen, and immediately saw, to my surprise, an image blacken, grow and come into focus on the square of white canvas extended before my eyes.

The image depicted a garden, an admirable pathway in a park bathed in sunlight, where the shadows of leaves stirred gently on the ground—for the screen was not limited to the photography of the invisible; it was cinematographic. After a few seconds, I saw appear before me at the corner of the path the white and marvelous form of a woman: the most admirable female form that I had ever contemplated in my life. I scarcely had time to recognize the young woman glimpsed on the pond, the musician of a short while before…the sound of footsteps made me turn my head: Goldfeller was behind me. To my great surprise, far from seeming irritated, I saw that he was smiling.

207

He began by pressing the button of the apparatus to make the image that had interested me disappear from the screen.

"Ah!" he said, thereafter, almost cheerfully. "You came back. You aren't afraid?"

I shook my head and replied: "No, I'm curious—that's all."

"Curious and even…indiscreet, still."

"Forgive me. It was by chance…a button touched by mistake."

He made a disdainful gesture. "No harm done. A week ago, that simple gesture might have cost you your life. Today…"

"Today," I challenged him, audaciously, "I'm satisfied: I know why you've constructed this tower. You're hiding a woman. The means are enormous, but the object certifies the immensity of the enterprise…"

He burst out laughing. The echoes rolled around the metallic vaults—but he suddenly stopped.

"In fact," he murmured, "there's a little truth in what you say. But I don't want you to retain that sentimentally clichéd image of me. Come."

A narrow strip of moving carpet hoisted us up to the top of the room; there, Goldfeller placed me in a sort of cage fitted into the wall that suddenly opened behind us. It was as if we were projected into the open air by the extensible uprights of a ladder at the end of which our feeble cage was trembling; then the uprights, turning on pivots, brought us smooth back to the wall of the tower, against which we leaned after being suspended above nearly two kilometers of empty space.

We set foot on the soil of a garden, in a host of greenery. Goldfeller maneuvered the strange apparatus to send it back again—after which, with an amiable gesture, he beckoned to me to walk beside him along a pathway strewn with white sand, both sides of which were lined with russet marble sphinxes, polished by time, devoured by decay and corroded by the Sun for centuries.

At the end of the tunnel of verdure residential buildings appeared, made of roseate brick and stone, with a vast perron and a porphyry balustrade. Framed by a set of French windows, I saw coming toward us the woman of whom my imagination had made the innocent genius of this strange place, a thousand times more beautiful than I had been able to glimpse or dream.

"Yella," said the Gem King, "here's someone who has only stayed with us in order to see you."

The delightful creature that I saw smiling before me appeared to me to be like the princess of an Arabian tale, whom the instruction of evil or protective genies has made prisoner in the depths of an enchanted palace, fortuitously discovered.

Pale and supple, with her precious golden hair, her eyes as blue and translucent as profound glaciers, she came to stand before us, greeted me with a regal smile and offered her forehead to Goldfeller, who kissed it.

I heard the young woman murmur: "Good evening, Father."

That charming and ethereal being was the daughter of the man of implacable will whose prisoner I had been, and in whom I was not long in discovering the most tender of fathers, most anxious for a health that he deemed precarious. Stroking his child's golden hair with his hardened fingers, that tamer of men stared at the frail Yella, and began to question her in an anxious voice.

"How do you feel, my child?"

She reassured him with a nod of the head and a distracted blink, directing all her curiosity at me, while I rediscovered on her father's forehead the slightly irritated furrowing in which there was more anger than sadness. One might have thought that concern for the gentle creature susceptible to suffering was mingled there with the willful determination of the Gem King.

Apart from that impatient irritation, however, Goldfeller, under the gentle influence of Yella, seemed a different man. He was almost cheerful, leading the conversation tactfully, warning me by means of interruptions that were swift without being abrupt of what it was necessary to avoid saying in the young woman's presence. I ended up understanding that Yella lived in Aeria with no suspicion of its history, without knowing anything of the imminent complications of the fabulous adventure above which she floated in a solitude that was perhaps necessary to her excessive sensitivity—but slightly burdensome, to judge by the eager welcome that she gave to a guest for an evening.

"Will Monsieur be dining with us?" She interrogated her father with a supplicant expression. Goldfeller left the reply to me, and, as might be imagined, I made haste to accept. For myself, the prospect of a few hours spent with that gracious young woman constituted a rare joy, after a year of exclusive contact with Rassmusses, Hartwigs and Kostiches. To substitute for the grating or ferocious voices of those demons the measure and musical voice of Yella, and to rise above that atmosphere of aggressive fever to respire the air of softness and peace that floated in the beautiful gardens—what a restful and refreshing dream!

Goldfeller seemed submissive to the influence himself and on hearing him thus, devoting himself at hazard to a slightly rambling conversation, seeing him walking under the trees beside a beautiful young woman who was his child, I was surprised to find the man that there is in the depths of every human beast made savage by pride, the spirit of wealth and domination.

A few meters beneath us Aeria was blazing and buzzing; its confused rumor came to expire at the foot of the immense park with which Goldfeller had surrounded this retreat. A few old domestics, smiling women of mixed race, looked after Yella, while Siam-Si or Moldo would be on watch outside the wall, silent watchdogs attentive to the noises of the external world.

After dinner, we went to the summer-house in the garden to make music. Yella sang; she accompanied herself on the harp, realizing, with her hair slightly ruffled and the floating silk of her dress, a delightfully young form within her old-fashioned appearance. At random, we deciphered all sorts of old tunes and modern music; it was an art in which I had some skill, which won me a great success with my companion. She made me promise to come back to help her read a recent publication full of difficulties. I promised everything that she wished, of course, questing in my turn in Goldfeller's eyes for the assent that would be indispensable to keeping that promise.

Seated on a divan, the Gem King smoked cigars without saying anything, gripped once again by his mysterious preoccupations. He nodded his head by way of polite acquiescence, letting the two of us pass through all the enthusiasms of the little improvised concert.

Abruptly, at about 10 p.m., he gave the signal for departure; hastening the separation and the farewells, he drew me into the depths of the garden along a round pathway, from the top of which the eye plunged into a deserted and silent street.

We were walking rapidly, when a heart-rending scream suddenly rang out; there was a noise of stamping feet and a concert of irritated voices, the soft and muffled sounds of blows silently exchanged by people fighting a short distance away from us. We were able to make out three men fighting one another furiously, trampling the body of a woman lying on the ground.

I wanted to shout, but Goldfeller grabbed me by the arm and squeezed, murmuring in an altered voice, in the imperious and brutal tone that I had not heard for several hours: "Silence!"

Meanwhile, two of the combatants seemed to be combining their efforts against the third, and the contest was cut short. We saw the wretches seize their adversary by the shoulders and legs and hoist him awkwardly on to the iron railings that bordered the wall encircling the city, from which they let him fall into the void. From that height, the noise of his fall was lost in the darkness. The two accomplices ran off and disappeared around the corner of the street, abandoning the woman lying in the roadway, unconscious or dead.

I looked at Goldfeller. He was pale but impassive, and ready to start walking again. In a low voice, I said to him: "Since you are the master here, will you let that crime go unpunished? By searching the woman's body, it's easy…"

He imposed silence on me with a gesture and said, simply: "I'll see to it."

He drew me away. I was obliged to follow him, so upset that I still do not know how I came to find myself alone in the middle of an avenue, from which I went home.

Such was the uncertainty and the incoherence of my sentiments with regard to that man that I suspected him momentarily of complicity in the murder I had just witnessed. His evasive tone, his preoccupied attitude and the pitiless rigor to which all his actions testified, all seemed at first to authorize me to mistake for an assassination ordered by him what I soon discovered to be a banal episode in the daily life of the new city.

If I note this stray fact, ultimately of no particular importance, here it is because it marked for me the point at which the situation we were in became complicated, and events began to hasten toward a terrible outcome, which Goldfeller's pride had not foreseen but with which he had already been secretly preoccupied for some time.

For as long as the work of construction had lasted, the masses of men in the tower had expended the active ardor of their energy in the fatigue of daily labor; to the few brawls inevitable in the life of such a human aggregation, the authority of the selected overseers had served as a sufficient brake, and the city's police had been scarcely more than construction-site security guards.

Since the work had been finished, however—since the cosmopolitan population of workmen had understood that, after having constructed a city, it would become permissible for them to live in it in idleness—things had no longer been the same. From that idleness a considerable peril had germinated, unforeseen by the Gem King. In a matter of days, brawls, attacks, scenes of murder, drunkenness and even greater scandals began to terrorize the inhabitants. A rather brutal police force, hastily organized and a trifle excessive in its measures, augmented the disorder instead of remedying it.

For myself, since my encounter with Yella, I scarcely paid any heed to the alarming rumors reported every morning by the few newspapers that had been founded, and it required a seemingly-trivial incident to attract my attention in that direction.

VII. The Festival of Gems

One morning, when I went out, as I did every day, like a good idler, to buy the newspaper in which I was accustomed to read the news, I found the kiosks closed and surrounded by crowds that were commenting malevolently on the first act of authority by the master of the city. Goldfeller had forbidden the sale of newspapers until further notice.

Without lending my ears any longer to the popular discontent, which seemed to me to be rumbling seriously, I hastened to join the billionaire, whom I found in his immense study in the governmental palace, surrounded by his general staff and in an attitude of deliberation.

Immediately, he barked at me: "Well, what are they saying?"

"They're saying," I said, "They're saying...that they're not content."

"We can see that perfectly well," said the Gem King. "Hernu, open the screens."

In response to a signal, Hernu, the technician, climbed a ladder and started running along an iron balcony mounted under the ceiling of the room, pushing buttons a intervals. In response to each gesture, a little luminous disk appeared in the immense roof, like a distant eye, whose gaze was reflected in images on an entire sequence of automatically-uncovered screens on the metallic wall in front of us. Imagine a sequence

213

of plaques on which we saw appear in succession, by means of instant cinematography, the simultaneous life of the entire city.

Goldfeller, Hartwig, old Rassmuss and his assistant Kandy, Kositch and myself went from one screen to the next, marveling with surprise, considering the movement of the crowds evoked before our eyes. We saw the passionate discussions of the crowds succeeded, within a few minutes, by frenzy: a fit of sudden anger, in which the disappointed idlers rushed the empty kiosks, overturned them, set them on fire, and then, tearing up everything they could disturb or break, began to drag through the streets the debris of lighting apparatus, chairs and benches, their open mouths signifying that revolutionary songs were accompanying these scenes of pillage.

"They'll destroy the city," Kositch murmured.

"But we must stop them," I said, running to Goldfeller. "You, Monsieur, stop them, speak to them."

Scornfully, he shrugged his shoulders, making no reply.

"Will you give me a free hand?" Kositch asked, coldly. "With a few of my little sulfurous bombs…"

Goldfeller uttered a cruel laugh. He looked at Kositch, thoughtfully.

The ancient voice of old Rassmuss suddenly piped up: "No unnecessary violence, Master. What's needed? To deflect the attention of these irritated children momentarily. Give me one hour—two at the most." He trotted over, murmured a few words in Goldfeller's ear.

He latter's face cleared. "Do it," he said.

Rassmuss had already disappeared through a door abruptly opened in the wall, followed by Goldfeller. We remained alone still following the progress on the screens of the spectacle of a mob that was growing by the minute. It was easy to see that nothing would stop those madmen in the fury of destruction, and that 1900 meters above the Earth, human folly remained the same.

An hour and a quarter after the Gem King and the old chemist had left, however, the symptoms of popular frenzy

214

appeared to be calming down. On the screens, we saw the moving masses slow their incoherent surge, pausing momentarily. A strange stupor seemed to paralyze the participants and the rare spectators who were watching them placidly from the doorways and windows of houses. Some yawned; others stretched themselves lazily; some sat down on the ground, others lay down, a few suddenly fell down as if stunned. Within a few minutes the streets were strewn with bodies succumbing to some kind of sudden fatigue.

"Well," said Goldfeller's voice behind us, "now that they're asleep, let's go home and discuss the means of procuring them a pleasant awakening."

Without giving us time to reflect, he led us away. Inside the elevator, before we left the palace, Rassmuss—who had followed us—gave each of us a partial mask designed to cover the mouth, nose and ears without impeding breathing. Equipped with that apparatus, we advanced into the streets.

What a strange spectacle the first few steps offered to our gaze! Lying on the sidewalks, in doorways, in the middle of the street and even on leaning on windowsills, the entire population was sound asleep; they were wherever the sudden lassitude had taken them by surprise, on the moving sidewalks, in the electric cars that had continued on their way, humming, until the order had been given to the central stations to cut off the current. In the public baths there were accidents, for the desire to sleep paralyzed the moments of swimmers in the pools, and more than one person drowned in a mere bath, without their being anyone awake who could rescue them.

Through the mouths of drains and orifices open at intervals in the middle of the public highways, the soporific vapor by means of which Rassmuss had put an entire city to sleep was still fuming.

It was after traversing this singular scene that we arrived at the house that served as our residence. It was an 18-story building with a garden terrace on top, from which one could see the whole city and, in the abyssal depths, the deserted countryside of Champagne at the foot of the tower. Magnificent sunlight illuminated the prodigious panorama above which, alone at that moment, we remained awake and conscious, but indecisive, still uncertain as to what the moment when the people sleeping before our eyes woke up again had in store for us.

"What do you intend to do now?" I asked Goldfeller. "The covetousness of these thousands of men that you have brought here, gorged with well-being and promises, will overflow if you leave them idle."

"It's necessary to occupy them," said Kositch. "The war…"

"What?" Dr. Hartwig put in. "Those down below are afraid. Since we've stood up to them so forcefully, they'll leave us in peace…"

The Gem King imposed silence with a gesture. "Perhaps, he said. "At any rate, our food-supplies have been cut off for a week, and my bankers inform me that my operations have been shackled on the steps of the Bourse, by order of the government. There's no cause for alarm, since our reserves are immense and our resources infinite."

"Well, in that case," Kositch resumed, excitedly, "what are you afraid of? The old world is attempting to starve us; let's show them that we're the stronger—let's crush them."

Goldfeller shook his head. "My strategy is to defend myself," he declared. "Defensiveness doubles our strength. In the meantime what are we going to do with this unoccupied rabble?"

"Let them sleep," Rassmuss proposed.

Surprised to find these violent men, whom I had thought so strong, irresolute, I raised my hand to ask to speak. Goldfeller gave me a sign to do so.

"Personally," I said, "I'm astonished that you haven't thought about this. You wanted to found a city, a world above the old world , but you've neglected an entire half of humankind. You've summoned thousands of workers to populate your city, but you can scarcely count a few hundred women among that number. Love, family, the bonds of tenderness and habit—that's what these unoccupied men lack."

I shall pass over the considerations I developed subsequently; I put into the task the ardor of the sentiment that was beginning to overwhelm me confusedly, to the point of bringing smiles to the faces of those men driven uniquely by ambition and the need to fight recklessly against a world that had rejected them all. Only Goldfeller listened to me attentively, and my reasoning did not seem at all contemptible to him.

"There's truth in what you say, Bayoud. We need women here. So be it! We shall have women."

In the bold brain of the Gem King, my simple words had planted the seeds of a plan whose extravagant audacity would have deterred anyone else. The preparations were made in secret and I only learned of its imminent execution 48 hours later, when the cataleptic sleep imposed by Rassmuss upon the entire city in revolt came to an end.

From the height of our terrace observatory I and my companions witnessed the slow reawakening of the sleeping streets. It was a comical spectacle at first; with lazy stretchings, yawns and stupefied gazes, all the men got to their feet, opening bewildered eyes and looking at one another interrogatively before exchanging their reflections and recovering their memories. At that moment, newspaper-sellers began to invade the streets at a run, shouting the titles of all the usual papers and those of Paris, which al announced in gigantic headlines the news that had impassioned public opinion since the day before.

"Get the *Réveil*, the *Jour*, the *Plein-Air*, the *Vérité*, the *Echo du Monde*…latest detail of the Festival of Gems…"

These newspapers were not being sold; they were distributed in profusion, and, at the same time, immense posters were plastered on every wall, informing the inhabitants of Aeria that the following evening, the city would be open to all women who cared to make the ascent. It was recommended that these voluntary visitors should be accorded the courteous and deferential welcome due to their sex; all of them would be admitted to visit the treasure of gems fabricated by the Gem King, who would make, in honor of the occasion, a distribution of diamonds, rubies and sapphires, which he knew the secret of making as perfectly as nature.

For two days, said the Paris newspapers, *luminous projections of a previously-unknown power playing upon the sidewalks and walls of houses have been announcing this fantastic news of M. Goldfeller; millions of printed prospectuses have been flying through the air, falling in clouds into all trembling hands. The reading of these mad promises has disturbed the minds of all women, and it's said that there are thousands of them already on their way, from every corner of France, to the tower that the Gem King seems to have made into the pandemonium of extravagance and perversity...*

It was true. In 48 hours, the news had run from telephone to telephone, from one end of France to the other, and the rough plan imagined by Goldfeller seemed to be succeeding beyond all expectations.

The sudden delight that exploded within the city at the announcement of these events was indescribable. In the blink of an eye, the crazed violence of two days previously was forgotten and everyone as occupied in preparations for the Festival of Gems. Directors briefed by Goldfeller supervised the work; in two days, everything was ready. It was to be a festival in which light would play the principal role; nothing comparable had ever blazed beneath the earthly night sky.

From what reserves of electricity did Goldfeller extract the current necessary to feed the prodigious Pharos that the tower of Aeria would become at 9 p.m.? I still don't know, the center of that metallic column having remained secret from me until the end, and his infinite resources always being for me as mysterious as they were amazing. I only knew the laboratory, the vast center in which all the simplified contacts of all the apparatus conceived by Goldfeller and his acolytes terminated. For two days, moreover, the Gem King was invisible to me; Rassmuss, Kandy, Kotisch and Dr. Hartwig disappeared too, and I had reason to suppose that in the core of that enormous metal tower, other collaborators that I was never to meet were, from then on, working on the accomplishment of the disastrous events of which the illumination of the Festival of Gems as to be the prelude.

That light was visible in Paris. In a few seconds, the metallic mass was garlanded, girdled and decked out with fire; ribbons of green and blue light began to blaze around the immense cylinder, which seemed to be enlaced by fiery serpents. At intervals, sprays of red sparks simulated monstrous hooks responsible for holding those necklaces of fire in place around the flanks of the tower. Thus, in the beautiful summer night, the edifice was like a beacon of joy whose supreme flame shone on high, in the form of a pyramid of light, which was nothing other than a prodigious mountain of gems of every color.

Yes, a mountain of gems. In the central plaza of Aeria, raised on a terrace planted with trees, so as to overlook the rural expanse, Goldfeller had transported his reserves of gems by the cartload, which we was ready to throw as fodder to feminine curiosity—and in the center of the precious heap was an electric lamp of unprecedented power, which projected its light through all those riches, making them sparkle with all their multiplied gleams.

Imagine the avid rush of a disorderly crowd, mad with greed, toward this beacon of splendor and opulence. The exodus had begun the previous evening; in tightly-packed ranks leaning over the outer balustrade that divided the limit of the city from the void, the inhabitants of Aeria saw troops of women of all ages and all conditions running through the fields. Old ones and young ones came, even little girls whose soft hair floated over their shoulders; there were poor women in rags who had come on foot, and timid seamstresses still clutching the embroidery frames they had not had time to abandon in order to run toward luxury and fortune; there were also elegant women in visiting hats, and society women in evening dresses, deposited by automobiles at the foot of the tower long before the hour fixed for entry.

The illumination of the city was the signal agreed for the admission of all to the elevators. The formal instruction was that only unaccompanied women should be admitted, and that gave rise to scenes, for there were husbands, fathers, brothers and anxious friends who, until the last moment, made supreme efforts to deflect from a dubious adventure the cherished individuals who were sacrificing them to the lure of easy riches.

The overexcitement of desire, however, and the intoxication of the light—everything, including the concurrent folly of uninhibited appetites, was to contribute to the success of the rough plan imagined by the Gem King.

The elevators, full to overflowing and garlanded with light, began to climb up toward the city. When they reached the superimposed platforms that constituted the height of the tower, loud fanfares saluted them as they passed, and when the women set foot on the soil of Aeria, orchestras hidden in the gardens and under the quincunxes of plazas greeted the crowds of visitors with voluptuous concerts.

The glare of the illumination was blinding. The facades of the houses, polychromatic in the play of little luminous bulbs, aligned ramps of fire as far as the eye could see. The fountains and public drinking-fountains in the parks, emitted fiery sprays and dazzling cascades, alternately blue, green, red and saffron, like molten gold. Above our heads, the silvery moon and the stars had lost their glamour in the overwhelmed heavens.

Then, in the tranquil air of the beautiful evening, long trails of odiferous vapors were seen to emerge from the ground, whose enervating action was not long in making itself felt. Numbed and intoxicated by these perfumes, in which the artistry of Rassmuss and Kandy was detectable, the women seemed to lose all hesitation and all memory; they breathed forgetfulness, as they had to do in order to drink the beverages dispensed in the depths of bars and the cafés of the city, transformed into buffets for the evening of folly. All these means were employed to prolong the kind of stupefied ecstasy in which they advanced through the city on fire, to the hypnotic center of that head of light.

In the largest plaza in Aeria, at the summit of a kind of labyrinthine garden, was the flamboyant pyramid of gems around which the members of the crowd crushed one another under the pressure of desire and curiosity. A simple luminous ribbon protected the treasure, a powerful electric wire in which, at a signal from the governmental palace, the current was suddenly cut off, thus delivering to the avidity of that overexcited population the mass of gems, which flowed through shaking hands.

In a matter of minutes, the streets were streaming with sapphires, rubies and fabulous stones radiating red fire in which Goldfeller had succeeded in imprisoning the crimson gleam of corundum in the glacial purity of diamond. Exposed throughout the evening to electrical rays, these stones were phosphorescent in the darkness and conserved their gleam long after the lights of that unprecedented festival were extinguished.

From the height of our terrace, we contemplated this spectacle, whose details were attenuated in a whole of quasi-fabulous grandeur. I saw the grey eyes of the Gem King gleaming with pride at the unison of that splendor, of which he was the master. As for his acolytes, the wild and violent expressions on their delighted faces, at the sight of scenes of greedy and bestial frenzy precipitated by so many unchained appetites, were indescribable. The drunken laughter that succeeded in spreading the contagion of its intoxication all around was the laughter of these silently contemplative maleficent geniuses.

As for me, I watched that bacchanal without saying anything, my eyes turned in the direction of the distant dwelling where I delighted myself by evoking the image of Yella. What was she doing? I blushed at the thought that she might be able to see what we were seeing; but, by virtue of studying the sea of phosphorescent light before our eyes, I ended up noting the relative obscurity of the quarter in which the Gem King's secret residence was situated, and I was pleased to interpret that as a mark of foresight on the part of that strange man. I imagined the frail and precarious child asleep at that moment, out of range of the orgy, and her beauty and charm appeared to me more perfect still.

VIII. Fulgurite

The next day, a stupefying calm—a kind of torpor—reigned over the entire city, while at the foot of the tower, an immense crowd was muttering in the surrounding countryside. A confused buzz rose up toward us, and the service elevators that were used for the routine provisioning of Aeria were almost taken by storm by those exasperated people who were demanding the return of the women abducted the night before and retained as prisoners, in defiance of all human rights.

It was necessary to send up the elevators in haste and, in order to disperse that crowd of malcontents, Goldfeller had recourse to the means that he had used to frighten the delegates of the government a month earlier. A frightful cyclone was unleashed, for several leagues around, sweeping everything away, sowing terror and death in its passage. Within a few hours, the vicinity of the tower had been cleared.

It was then that it was noticed that the usual trains bringing vita supplies were not arriving from Sommesous, and, on following the track that linked out mercantile station to the Châlons line, it was discovered that the rails had been cut. Taking reprisals, the government of the Republic had isolated Aeria, henceforth reduced to its own resources.

This news did not seem to surprise Goldfeller; it whipped up a ferocious joy in the lieutenants assembled around him.

"This time, it's war."

"Finally!"

"Finally…"

Kositch and Hartwig seemed intoxication with a delirium of destruction. Rassmuss and Kandy manifested the tranquil yawns of tigers. Hatred dilated the cruel hearts of those men, who all seemed to have been granted desires caressed for a long time. The general opinion was to enquire as soon as possible into attacking moves that might be made against the tower. To that end, two dirigibles were sent out as scouts.

Only one came back. The man aboard declared that, about 30 kilometers away, he had perceived the advance guard of a French army on the march; he and his companion had been attempting to advance, gliding over the troops, when an artillery shell had struck the first aeroscaphe. Its envelope had resisted the impact, but had caught fire in the explosion of the detonator with which the shell was loaded. Turning back, the aeronaut had immediately returned to his home base.

This news threw Goldfeller into a rage, which he only expressed by a gesture. Pressing a button within arm's reach, he rang a bell. It was Siam-Si who appeared. A few words pronounced in English were sufficient to convey to the master's orders to the Chinese. Less than an hour later, the inhabitants of Aeria were able to witness an extraordinary spectacle, of which I will try to give some idea.

You will remember the gigantic lantern in the form of a seahorse, the contemplation of which had cost me my liberty on the very day of the President of the Council's visit to the construction-works of the incomplete tower.

"Our lighting system," Goldfeller had replied, when interrogated on the subject by the minister.

Indeed, four monstrous specimens of this monument had raised their forms several weeks ago at Aeria's cardinal compass-points. In spite of the affirmations of the Gem King, however, I had never seen them illuminated, and until that evening their fantastic forms had remained black against the sky. One might have thought them four menacing and gigantic beasts crouching over the void, in the attitude of the arabesque gargoyles sculpted on the balustrades of Gothic cathedrals.

Scarcely had the Gem King given Siam-Si the orders I mentioned when a tremor agitated the four monsters, the formless and compact masses of which began progressively to metamorphose. The mass of shafts and levers on which they

223

rested dilated silently, advancing each curved and steel-helmeted head into empty space. At the same time, within the enormous glass globe that terminated it like a pale muzzle, a little star of light sparkled like a partly-opened eye.

Abruptly, with a single bound, in a definitive release of their mysterious organism, the four monsters launched themselves like living beings over the countryside, whose depths they seemed to be sounding with the undulations of saurians of prehistoric times. Almost immediately, an implacable light was projected into the distance by the fire-encircled globes of those quasi-living lanterns, which aimed and twisted in every direction. In the beams that they directed thus at one another, one could see that behind each of the globes, inside a little cage lodged on the head of the monster, a man was seated. To each of these beasts, a living an audacious intelligence had been assigned, for a still-mysterious labor of destruction and death.

Those at the foot of Aeria who were able to contemplate the descent of these four automatic reptiles, and who saw them writhing in the air, moving silently above the countryside, with their vaguely luminous muzzles and their metallic crests, which sheltered the technicians directing the maneuver, must have thought that they had gone back to the earliest ages of the Earth, to the epoch of great monstrous winged saurians...but of those living beneath the spectacle, how many are still alive?

For my part, lost in the crowd leaning over the balconies of Aeria, I followed with breathless emotion the unexpected twists and turns of the brief battle that took place before my eyes. After the somewhat contorted efforts of the first minute, the four monsters succeeded to a disquieting rigidity; combining in a spray the four rays of dazzling light that they were each projecting, they lit up the countryside for more than 20 leagues in the direction of Paris.

From the height at which we were it then became easy to perceive the scattered column of the army whose approach had been signaled by the aeronaut scout; its confused swarming masses could be seen in the implacable light of the four monstrous lanterns motionless in the shadows of the night.

About five minutes went by, during which the inhabitants of Aeria, impressed by the distant spectacle revealed to their eyes and variously informed as to the reasons for the battle in preparation, became unanimous in admitting the evidence.

"We're being attacked…"

"But why?"

"They'll be here tomorrow."

In the quarter where I was, it seemed to me that the prospect of a conflict overturned all suppositions. While it was no more than a matter of resisting the government and molesting its agents, the adventure had been able to seem singular, and even amusing. That was no longer the case, as soon as it was a question of declared war and resistance to organized force. However, the brutality of events put an end to the fluctuations of the nervous crowd, which was miraculously presented with the most terribly cruel of all spectacles of carnage.

Projecting into the distance the immense gaze of their flamboyant pupils, the quasi-living lanterns seemed to be both watching and waiting. Suddenly, the howling of invisible sirens cut through the air, and on that agreed signal, the four luminous monsters opened their globes of opaline glass like muzzles intending to breathe fire; on contact with the air the light caught fire, lighting up everything in its passage, inflaming instead of clarifying, instantly burning everything that it found in its path.

Beneath the ardor of those projections, the atmosphere caught fire within a radius of 20 leagues; entire villages burst into flames in the front of, behind and all around the army that had been asleep a few moments before, a day's march from Aeria.

In front of me an ardent furnace blazed, precisely limited by the straight lines of the spray of light projected by the lanterns. All the way to the most distant horizon, the Catalunian region of France, Brie and the Île de France, lit up and appeared as clearly as the lunar orb on an Oriental night. Against the golden background of the air on fire, a multitude of dots began to agitate, running back and forth; surprised in their sleep, the men and animals attempted to flee, but almost all of them caught fire in their turn, flaming like red sparks, finally falling and disappearing into the furnace.

The host of men and horses making up the army that was the target of the implacable light gave us the spectacle of a crackling brazier stirred by a poker; the caissons loaded with shells and gunpowder caused a series of explosions whose sound was audible to us and whose light stained with red the glided light of the unprecedented catastrophe.

Absorbed in the contemplation of the spectacle, I felt a hand slip under my arm. A nearby voice murmured: "Isn't it marvelous?"

It was Kositch.

The former Russian officer advanced his ruddy face closer to mine and extended his arm in the direction of the lanterns.

"Fulgurite," he explained, "is our finest invention. You see how simple it is. On contact with that mysterious current, the air simply catches fire and causes death as much by asphyxiation as combustion."

"To whom, then, has the maneuvering of those lanterns been entrusted?" I asked. "What savages…?"

Kotisch emitted a little laugh. "Tee hee! Savages, maybe—but for a first experiment, they haven't come out of it badly. You can imagine that resolute and cool-headed fellows were necessary for the task. Damn! An error in one line of the projection and the light might have reached us… Fortunately, the boss was alert, and would only have had to cut off the current. See how quickly it's completed."

Abruptly, darkness fell. Deeming the work of destruction sufficiently complete, the invisible dispenser of that murderous force had stopped its surge. A second or two after the extinction of the lanterns, one could see no more in the black extent of the region but a few clumps of trees and houses that were completing their consumption, and the moving patches of wretches who had been able to throw themselves outside the mortal projection by running at hazard into the darkness like errant torches, shaking off the flames that were finishing them off. The latter were uttering terrible screams, whose faint echo just about reached us, like the distant cries of nocturnal birds.

Meanwhile, Kositch drew me away. "Come on," he said. "Come to Goldfeller's study to witness the return of our four fulgurants."

By means of the moving walkways we arrived at the governmental palace, and went to the immense gallery from which the Gem King had directed the secret maneuver of the fulgurant lanterns.

In the latter, the anger of a short while before had given way to a furious delight. He only had Rassmuss beside him. The placid old man welcomed with a patriarchal smile the compliments his master lavished upon him regarding the results of the fulgurite, of which he was the inventor.

"Prodigious, eh?" said Goldfeller. "Rassmuss, you're the god of war. Five minutes of light and nothing more: an entire army annihilated, perhaps 40,000 or 50,000 men. Twenty square leagues of terrain charred and rendered desert. And all of that with one gesture, and in silence. Oh, that luminous and murderous silence—isn't there something magnificent and genuinely new about it?"

In the midst of that enthusiasm, supported by the warm admiration of Kotisch, the emotion that gripped me might have passed for mute evidence of complicity. In reality, my decision was made, and I was determined to get away as quickly as possible from the spectacle of all these horrors. I was approaching Goldfeller to ask him to grant me a private interview, when the access door to the communication elevator opened, giving passage to four fantastic apparitions.

They were the men whom Kositch had called the "fulgurants." They were dressed in costumes reminiscent of diving-suits, in asbestos fabric, and their heads were protected by glass helmets in the form of a raptor's beak, in which breathable air had been distributed to them throughout the dangerous maneuver of opening the lantern to contact with the atmosphere, which had rendered it fiery and deadly.

Aided by Goldfeller and Kositch, the four strange figures began to take off their helmets, which were firmly screwed down on their shoulders, and I saw the expected faces of the subaltern accomplices of the Gem King's general staff appear: Siam-Si, Moldo, Glubb and Hernu. All four were smiling at the compliments that were not spared, the first two with the silent laughter of brutes, the other two with the slightly grating laughter of street-urchins.

"We beat them, eh?" squawked Hernu, revealing his discolored teeth in a satisfied manner. Glubb clicked his finger-joints outside the incombustible gloves that he had just taken off and said, nasally: "Hollow! Hollow!"

No, I could not bear such odious contacts any longer. I drew nearer to Goldfeller. He came to meet me.

"Just the man," he said. "I need to talk to you. Wait there."

IX. The Secret of Aeria

Having accompanied Rassmuss, with whom he had had a conversation in low voices, to the far end of the room, Goldfeller came back, rubbing his hands, to place his hand on my shoulder in a familiar manner.

"The evening," he said, "there's a celebration. I'm taking you up—you've been invited."

Yella. It only required the evocation of that charming image to shake all my resolution. Wouldn't departure mean never seeing her again? Instinctively, the sacrifice seemed beyond my strength. Goldfeller led me away. I followed him.

By the same aerial route as before, we arrived in the garden. A slight, fine rain was falling, beneath which we hastened to reach the Gem King's house.

As we entered, an old black woman ran towards us precipitately and came to murmur a few words in Goldfeller's ear. He frowned. He signaled to me to wait, disappeared, and came back after a quarter of an hour.

"We're dining alone," he told me. "My daughter is ill."

It was not hard to see that his impassivity was feigned. During the meal we both remained silent, because I didn't dare interrogate the man I judged to be furious and fearful in the face of a difficulty that mastered his despotic will—and yet, I was prey to anxiety. Something soft and ender told me that this sudden illness brought me even closer to the charming and delicate creature imprisoned, like me, in Aeria. In the end, I was unable to suppress that curiosity.

When the dinner was over, we came to lean on the balcony of the musical pavilion, both of us smoking. From there, our eyes embraced the horizon previously lit up by the monstrous lanterns, and we could see the still-smoking embers of little clumps of trees set on fire by the fulgurite.

"Aren't you afraid," I murmured, "that the spectacle of these horrors, and all those the future has in store, might be more than a nature as delicate as that of your daughter can bear?"

That violent man had contained himself too long; those few words were sufficient to make him explode.

"Damn the nerves of these sensitive creatures!" he cried. "Is it my fault if they cut off our food supplies and armies attack us? In sum, I've done nothing but defend the integrity of my work, and Yella knows full well that she has the greatest interest in that."

I started abruptly at the idea that the person of whom he was speaking was mixed up in any way whatsoever with that work of folly and destruction. But Goldfeller continued: "What connects the sequence of human actions? From the day when a doctor in Lausanne, whom I had consulted about her, told me that Yella would die within a year in the valleys in which the greater part of humankind buries its life, the creation of this tower dated."

At the dull exclamation that escaped me, and the air of amazement with which I looked at him, Goldfeller started to laugh—the sardonic laughter with which he took care to emphasize the rare manifestations of a sensibility that he had mastered completely.

"Oh," he replied, swiftly, "Don't cast me too quickly in the role of a good family man who would turn the world upside-down to save the life of his child. No, it's not as simple as that. What, then? A caprice of nature determined that, in a development generally normal enough, the cellular development of arterial tissue slowed down in that child, with the result that, unless things change, the beating of her heart threatens to break the walls of the channels responsible for ensuring the circulation of the blood. There's no remedy for that save for circulatory regularization for which Dr. Leroux, feeling his way by virtue of ausculating the patient in various positions, gave the following prescription: to breathe the pure and light air that exists 1900 meters above sea level..."

"So that," I said, is the reason for Aeria's existence."

Goldfeller shrugged his shoulders disdainfully. "Pooh! There it is! For, in sum, you'll understand that it was impossible for me to admit for a single instant that, with the resources at my disposal, I was going to retreat in the face of nature and permit the daughter of the Gem King to be carried off by the most banal of the accidents of human life. In Switzerland, however, there is no lack of locations at the requisite altitude, where I could have built the palace in which I planned to install Yella. My effort would have been limited to that—but I dreamed of something better than that silent and solitary existence among the eternal snows. Instead of a house, to construct a city, no longer isolated above mountains where indolent ruminant-herders vegetate, but in the very heart of civilized activity; to endow this city with all the most recently-imagined refinements of luxury and comfort; to animate it with joy and audacity; to populate it with a busy host, which I would rule with all the ingenious energy that would ensure its existence and well-being, which I would defend against the temptations and attacks that always rise up from below against that which is lofty, proud and extraordinary. What a dream! Have I not realized it?"

His gesture embraced the enormous city that sparkled and hummed around us, in which the savage spectacle that had been offered to it a few hours before seemed to have augmented the bestial frenzy of enjoyment. Shouting, singing and laughter rose up toward us from all that population subjugated by gross instincts to the domination of the Gem King.

"At the price of what sacrifices, alas!" I murmured. "Can you suppose that the conflict you have undertaken will conclude according to your will?"

Goldfeller gripped my arm, and squeezed it hard, affirming through clenched teeth: "I shall annihilate them all, one after another. I..."

He interrupted himself abruptly, relaxed his grip and pointed northwards. "Look. What's that black mass, there, flying toward us?"

The rain had stopped, but the darkness was profound and at first I could not see anything. By dint of staring into the obscurity, I ended up perceiving a large patch that was curving around Aeria, fleeing eastwards under the pressure of the wind.

"A balloon," I murmured.

"Yes!" cried the billionaire. "A balloon, and a poor balloon at that, incapable of passing overhead or of fighting against the westerly wind that is forcing it off course. It's an attack. It's necessary to respond. Come."

He drew me away. Silently, I pointed at the dwelling where Yella was resting. He shrugged his shoulders, saying: "She's asleep. Besides, I'll attack from a distance; she won't hear anything from here."

I had to follow him. In a few minutes, his general staff was gathered in the machine-room and I watched a council of demons in which it was instantly resolved to send a flotilla of balloons to Paris, charged with peppering the city with a cloud of explosives.

Mute and distressed, I followed them through the city to the mooring-station where the little group of light cigar-shaped dirigibles was bobbing in the wind.

A long howl of sirens pierced the profound darkness, and with a common bound, the four fulgurant lanterns took flight beneath us in order to light and guide the course of the dirigibles. Four luminous projections extended over the countryside, increasing in intensity by the second, without their concentrated radiation revealing the mysterious flight they were responsible for guiding.

"The darkness will protect us," Goldfeller said, returning to the governmental palace. "No, it's no more than a simple matter of hours."

Indeed, there was nothing to do but wait. As the night was fairly well advanced, in spite of the anxious state I was in, I took my leave of the Gem King in order to go to bed.

I had been sleeping for less than an hour when I was awakened with a start by the noise of a formidable explosion. A blazing glare lit up my room, and almost immediately, the crash of a further detonation shook everything around me, while clamors of distress and pain rose up from the streets and houses in the vicinity.

X. War! War!

In the blink of an eye I was on my feet. I went down into the street and immediately deduced what had just happened on seeing the forms of three balloons fleeing into the darkness. the last of them dropped a black mass from the bottom of its gondola, which caught fire at a height of a few meters and landed in the center of a square, causing one last explosion. Paris was returning the explosive bombs that Aeria had dispatched against it, by identical means.

Without paying any heed to the clamors of the idlers who thought the city entirely destroyed, I ran to the governmental palace. As I ran around the circular boulevard next to the dirigibles' mooring-station, Kositch suddenly appeared running beside me. He seemed excited, and initially addressed by raising his arms to the sky with an expression of furious rage.

"Many victims?" I asked.

He shrugged his shoulders scornfully. "Bah! It would be little enough if it were limited to a few anonymous individuals. The worst thing is that one of their damned projectiles has broken one of the fulgurant lanterns, interrupting the current of air supplying the man responsible for maneuvering it—it's Moldo, and he must be dead by now. We're in the process of trying to recover the apparatus. Come and see."

With the aid of hastily-installed mobile cranes, a hundred men under the supervision of Hartwig were maneuvering to hoist over the balustrade the enormous dead weight of the injured apparatus. Electric searchlights illuminated the work, which lasted nearly two hours. I followed its vicissitudes by Kositch's side. Eventually, I expressed my surprise at not seeing Goldfeller with us.

"We were in the laboratory when the bombs began to burst," he replied. "It appears that a bell, whose origin I don't know, has summoned him to a point at which the bombardment has produced particularly dangerous results. I haven't seen him since then."

A name sprang to me lips, which I almost cried out in the suddenness of my terror: *Yella!*

I imagined the residence of Goldfeller's daughter ablaze, destroyed by bombs, and I launched myself forth. But where should I go? The laboratory was empty and the mysterious dwelling of the Gem King was as inaccessible from the street to me as to everyone else. I was forced to wait, to stay in the place to which he was bound to run as soon as he could. Mad with anguish, I watched the final maneuvers of the apparatus that finally succeeded in bringing the twisted debris of the gigantic lantern to rest on the ground.

Already, Kositch was carefully opening the door of the cockpit in which Moldo was enclosed. Rigidly immobile in his strange diver's costume, the fulgurant appeared in the depths of his little cage. The lenses in his pointed helmet were shining like staring eyes, and both his hands were clutching the wheel of the transmission mechanism that he used to direct the light of his apparatus.

"He's alive!" cried Hartwig, joyfully. "In order to have maintained his equilibrium during all the maneuvers that have just shaken the lantern, he must still be alive."

In a doubtful tone, I murmured: "But he isn't moving."

"Perhaps he's just fainted," Hartwig retorted, swiftly. "We need to get him out of the apparatus."

On his orders, a few men hurled themselves forward, and immediately proclaimed that Moldo was dead. The damaged controls of the lantern were crushing him against the back of the cage and maintaining him in the attitude of a living man. When it became possible to free him, his body collapsed. The visor of the helmet was unscrewed, and his face appeared, black and swollen.

There was a frisson of amazement in the crowd that surrounded us. A profound silence fell. Then whispers began to run around, and voices were raised. Obviously, the confidence of these people, gorged with pleasures to the point of exhaustion, had been dented by these unexpected events. Besides, Moldo was not the only victim of the bombs launched by the enemy balloons; on all sides, the extent of the damage was becoming manifest. Houses were burning; automobile ambulances could be seen passing by every few seconds, their warning bells causing the murmuring and disconcerted crowd to clear a path for them.

Goldfeller's lieutenants understood that it was necessary to react against the discouragement that seemed to be increasing around them. People knew them, and knew about their mysterious connection to the Master of Aeria. Already, the murmurs, becoming more focused as covert allusions, were threatening to turn into personal invective. Kositch, having given the order to take away Moldo's body, boldly turned to the people surrounding him.

"All this," he shouted, "has already been dearly avenged. At this moment, our balloons are burning Paris…"

A well-known voice interrupted him: that of Goldfeller, for whom everyone stood aside. The appearance of his imperious face brought silence again. Without pausing for discussion with the crowd, which he dominated with his sovereign will, the Gem King called out: "Kositch, Hartwig—and you too, Bayoud—come with me. We're going to take the necessary measures to make it impossible for this dirty trick to be repeated."

He did not spare a glance for Moldo's cadaver, extended at his feet: that mute brute who had served him like a dog for years now had no more value in his eyes than the debris of scrap iron against which he was lying.

At a rapid pace he led us into the glazed hall that served as an office for the commandant of the dirigibles' mooring-station. That officer, a subaltern aide of little importance, greeted us obsequiously, enquiring about the fate of the little fleet that had departed a few hours before, and whose return he had expected sooner.

"They're not coming back," Goldfeller declared, in a firm tone. "The wireless telegraphy station has transmitted an order to the squadron leaders to pursue the enemy balloons and bring them back over Aeria, by encircling them. The rest is up to us, and we're going to work, gentlemen."

"What are you going to do?"

He looked at me coldly and replied: "Poison the air above the city and drive the enemy dirigibles into that suffocating atmosphere, where their pilots will be asphyxiated, which will make them as many phantom balloons destined to be lost in space. The enemy fleet will be entirely destroyed."

The tone of implacable resolution in which he said this, and the triumphant expressions with which his lieutenants welcomed the expectation of further massacres, brought to a climax the impression of horror and disgust that had been increasing within me for two days. I had lowered my head; I raised it again to state at the Gem King, and my gaze must have expressed my thoughts clearly.

To my great surprise, Goldfeller did not even have a scornful smile for what he must have regarded as pusillanimity. He bowed his heads and simply murmured: "You'll be leaving—but keep quiet."

Feverishly, he went to take Kostich's arm, and walked for a few minutes with the officer, to whom he set about giving orders and explanations; Hartwig took his turn, and then the commandant of the aerostat-port. When he had finished, Goldfeller returned to me. "Come with me," he said. "We need to talk."

Such calm frightened me momentarily. In the cold insanity that was driving him to extremes of cruelty in order to ensure the triumph of his domination, what might it cost me to have dared to censure the conduct of a man jealous above all else of his authority? We had leapt into a car that was waiting in front of the door of the hall we had just left, and at first we moved in silence. I remembered my first voyage in the interior of the tower, through that subterranean city, by the side of the mute Goldfeller, smoking his cigar. To tell the truth, he had been more impassive then, and the wrinkles on his forehead had not manifested the anxious creases of today.

Abruptly, he began to speak. "Bayoud," he began, effortfully. "I need you."

The surprised gaze that I directed at him made his laugh and flattered his self-respect.

"Come on," he continued, with a sigh. "You're an intelligent child, but a child. Perhaps, in time, you'll understand that a soul that aspires to command the world must rise above the contingencies of sensitivity. Personally, it's for not having foreseen…"

He fell silent, frowning in irritation. The car was moving rapidly, and its speed was more favorable to thought than speech. I dared not interrogate the terrible and worried man, but I was already less afraid of him, and on seeing him pensive I almost felt sorry for him. The work of death in which he persisted appeared precarious and petty by comparison with the soft and radiant splendor of a summer sky in which the clouds were beginning to space themselves out, uncovering an infinity of worlds already paling in the light of dawn. At the idea of imminent liberty, the youth for which Goldfeller had reproached me a little while before had lifted my heart with joyous hopes that he no longer had, and I discovered him sad at the summit of his grim power.

Meanwhile, we had arrived at the governmental palace> A compact crowd obstructed it to begin with. At the sight of us, violent rumors broke out and a group of citizens, evidently having made preparations in advance, came toward Goldfeller. One of them began to speak on behalf of them all, demanding the free circulation of the elevators, which had been send down to the mid-way point of the tower a week before.

"You want to leave the city?" asked the Gem King.

The attitude of the delegates answered for everyone. There was a momentary silence. Suddenly, the eyes of the Master of Aeria flashed.

"What if I ask you for 24 hours to ensure general security?" he said. "What if I guarantee that this time tomorrow, the city that you have helped me to build will be conclusively protected from any kind of attack?"

He saw that they were hesitant, already reconquered, and then spoke ardently, with such assurance of tone that within a few minutes, the almost-menacing men had become cowardly and lustful slaves. The crowd opened before us, and we went into the governmental palace.

On entering his study, Goldfeller threw his hat on to a table. Parading his steely gaze around him, he spotted Hernu motionless in a corner. The latter was looking at him, his cigarette stuck between his lips, with the sly expression that the workmen of the Parisian faubourgs maintain, for no reason.

"What are you doing there?" the billionaire shouted, violently. "Get moving, to wherever I've commanded to you go!"

With a constrained smile that uncovered his discolored teeth, Hernu replied simply: "I'm waiting for M. Rassmuss, who's ordered me to help him carry something."

Rassmuss's head immediately appeared in the gap in a doorway. The old man exchanged a mysterious sign with Goldfeller, and a gesture instructed the technician to follow him.

XI. The Murder

Alone with me, the Gem King began by turning down the dimmer-switches of the laps that illuminated the immense room. When the darkness was complete, I felt him take me by the hand to lead me toward a corner where, suddenly, in the half-light of a night-light, I perceived a form lying on a bed.

It was Yella. In the middle of a narrow room, the door of which her father had just opened in front of me, the young woman was sleeping, so peacefully and profoundly that I thought she might be dead. I almost uttered a scream.

"Shh!" said Goldfeller. "No power in the world can wake her up before 48 hours, but above all, no one must suspect her presence here. She will only leave here to quit this tower, and it's to you that I confide her from now on. Do you accept?"

He could not mistake the emotion that I could not suppress on hearing these words. With a gesture, he contained the protests that he suspected I was about to make and, closing the door again, continued in the midst of the darkness that surrounded us once again: "You're at the impulsive age when the emotions still act directly upon a man's heart. That child shares your apprehensions and your scruples, and I'm counting on you to take her away from our troubles and violence. Later…"

In the gloom, it seemed to me that his voice was trembling slightly; it became hard and imperious to add: "Do I need to tell you what reprisals you would incur if you do not scrupulously carry out the mission that I've decided to entrust to you? What you know about me is sufficient to assure you of it. For the moment, stay here until I return, and if anything unusual should happen, press the button you see shining there beside you. The contact will activate a siren whose noise will

238

warn me. When I return, I'll explain to you how I expect you to get out of here."

I understood from his voice that he was drawing away; I heard the noise of a door clicking shut. I remained alone in the vast dark room.

I had been there for a quarter of an hour, scarcely daring to move in order not to lose sight of the faintly-phosphorescent button that Goldfeller had pointed out to me, when a muffled sound nearby made my prick up my ears anxiously.

I had no time to listen; a few paces away from me a door opened. By the light of a small portable electric lamp that he lifted into the air in order to get his bearings, I perceived old Rassmuss. Setting his lamp on the ground, he bent down, and the same muffled sound was repeated. I saw then that the old man, using all his strength to stiffen his arms—still robust in spite of his great age—was shoving in front of him a sort of flat trunk that must have been very heavy. He crossed the entire hall in this manner, stopped to catch his breath, and took a little key from his pocket, which he introduced into a lock whose catch he activated. A low door turned on its hinges, revealing a dark corridor into which the old man passed, still pushing his burden.

The door swung to behind him, and was about to close when a rapid shadow passed before my eyes. I saw it gliding noiselessly in the wake of light that the old scientist' lantern left behind, slipping through the gap in the doorway through which Rassmusss had just disappeared—which abruptly closed again, with a dry click.

Immediately, I seemed to perceive muffled plaints, a noise of trampling, and then of a fall. Then there was a long silence.

After a few minutes, I saw the door behind which I suspected that a struggle had just take place re-open. A man appeared, bent over a heavy burden that he was maintaining with both hands on his back. A little miner's lamp, attached to his forehead, was lighting his unsteady march beneath the weight that was crushing him. He crossed the hall slowly and went out.

Darkness had fallen again and I tried to pierce its thickness that kind of clairvoyance that comes to eyes adapted o obscurity. A slender thread of light streaking the ground eventually attracted my attention. Feeing my way, I advanced toward it. Wedging open the door through which I had seen Rassmuss disappear was a small portable lamp, which continued to illuminate the ground on which it had fallen. To pick it up, pull the partly open door toward me and direct the luminous beam into the dark corridor was the work of a moment.

I could not retain an exclamation on perceiving a body extended in front of me. I saw white hair, soaked in blood. It was Rassmuss, lying on the ground, his neck pierced by a knife with a horn hilt.

Although I had become accustomed to a few singularities in that monstrous city, it seemed to me that the event might seem unusual to Goldfeller, and I immediately carried out the procedure that he had indicated to me. Overhead, the roar of the siren that would warn him rose up, and while I waited for him to arrive I tried to render assistance of the old chemist, whom I had pulled out of the corridor. He was still breathing, faintly, but in that darkness, with the sole aid of a pocket torch, my resources were scarcely extensive, and I had not been able to do anything much when the lights in the hall suddenly brightened again and Goldfeller appeared in front of me.

"Who did this?"

Already leaning over the old man, he addressed the question to him as much as to me, but neither of us could answer him. In the blink of an eye he had brought water, and bathed the frightful wound that was bloodying Rassmuss's neck. The latter opened his eyes slightly.

"What happened?" Goldfeller asked.

The old man's lips trembled. In a single breath, he articulated: "Hernu…diamonds…money…"

A hiccup strangled that exceedingly feeble voice. Rassmuss's head became heavier in the hands that were supporting it, and his lips exhaled a profound sigh. The old chemist had just died.

Goldfeller leapt to his feet. Moldo's death had left him impassive, but the loss of an auxiliary like this one touched him more; there must have been rage and despair in his clear eyes. He pulled himself together rapidly, though, and seemed to be reflecting profoundly. Suddenly, he raised his head.

"This is an unexpected event that will delay your departure," he said. "The strong-box stolen by Hernu contains a fortune in English banknotes and a collection of diamonds whose beauty is unique: all that constituted the treasure of Yella's journey. I need to catch up with that wretch…"

A sound of a bell interrupted him. His gaze brightened. "I suspected as much!" he cried, in a triumphant one. "The imbecile! He knows full well that he can't escape me. Look…"

With his finger, he showed me a vast console divided by vertical grooves in which the buttons were located that activate and stopped all the numbered service elevators. One of the buttons began to rise slowly. Goldfeller dived forward to grip it and, with a violent effort, pushed it all the way down. Then, with a dry click, he released the immobilization switch.

"Number 213," he said, gripping my arm. "The embarkation cage is only a few steps away, in Government Plaza. You're going to help me to get hold of that brute and get back what he has stolen. As for his punishment, I'll see to that later."

The Gem King hastened out of the governmental palace. "We have him," he said. "He'll persist, out of pride in his trade, in trying to maneuver the apparatus that he released without Rassmuss noticing. He'll lose time, and we'll trap him *on the job*, as they say."

It was daylight outside—a delightful morning after the previous day's rain. To my great surprise, Government Plaza was almost deserted. I remarked on this to Goldfeller. He was about to reply when he was interrupted by the clamor of one of the service loudhailers that issued official proclamations on

241

the street-corners. Reminiscent of giant phonographs, they functioned automatically every five minutes, playing the same role in Aeria as town criers in rural areas.

This is what the resounding voice of the apparatus said:

"The inhabitants of Aeria are warned that they must go before 8 a.m. to the central elevators, which will take them down to the bunkers of the old city, where they will have to stay for a time no longer than two days. This respite is rendered necessary by the poisoning of the upper layers of the atmosphere, which will permit the annihilation of crews of the enemy dirigibles; the balloons, impossible to steer, will then be scattered at hazard by aerial currents. Before 8 a.m.!"

7:30 chimed on the immense clock that ornamented the fronton of the governmental lace.

"Hurry up!" said Goldfeller. "The orders have been given. In exactly 30 minutes, it will become dangerous to remain in the streets."

We only had to cross the plaza to reach the embarkation-point of the elevator by means of which Hernu thought he could ensure his escape after the murder of Rassmuss and the theft of his precious strong-box. To his great surprise, Goldfeller found the little station full of people anxiously occupied in following the gestures of a man who, crouching down on the ground, was attempting the impossible to discover the cause of the inexplicable arrest of the apparatus.

Without a word, the Gem King went on to the platform of the immense elevator; he perceived in a corner the strong-box stolen by Hernu, lifted it up without apparent effort, and came to hand it over the balustrade to me. I staggered under its weight, almost letting the precious burden fall to the ground.

At the sight of the Master of Aeria, a profound silence had followed the hubbub of conversations, and it was that silence, more than anything else, that attracted the attention of the man leaning over the ground and absorbed in his research. He raised his head. I recognized the unwholesome face and arrogant moustache of Hernu.

He leapt to his feet with a single movement and advanced toward Goldfeller. "You're going to give me the strong-box," he grated, "or else..."

"The strong-box isn't yours," the Gem King replied, calmly. "It's mine, and I'm taking it back—for you have stolen it from me, after having murdered the man who was in charge of it. For that murder, you will be punished."

The technician shrugged his shoulders; he turned toward the people who were watching the scene without saying anything, and with a mocking gesture, pointed at Goldfeller.

"Punished!" he jeered. "Punished! You think so? For having killed that old poisoner Rassmuss. Patience! That's nothing. It's the beginning of the end. We've had enough, you hear. While it was a matter of having a laugh, of striking out at others, it was all right—but the moment we started suffering in our turn and getting shot at, there's nothing to be done. Go on, be off! You can see that we want to hop it—it's a matter of getting the elevator moving, and double quick!"

"The only elevators working are those leading to the old interior city," Goldfeller said, calmly. "I advise you to take them as quickly as possible if you don't want to be asphyxiated by the gas that's about to be released above the city."

Hernu's eyes sparkled with sudden rage. He appealed to the crowd, on which Goldfeller's declaration seemed to have made a strong impression. "You heard what he said. Help me, friends. We can force him to let us leave from here."

"Yes...yes..."

Already, they were all running forward. The Gem King took a revolver from his pocket, with which he had been fidgeting for several minutes, and aimed it at the menacing crowd. The gesture interrupted their surge.

"I'll kill the first man who takes another step," he declared, calmly. "As for you, you blackguard, I could repay your insolence and your crime with a single bullet, but, I repeat, you will be punished. I want an exemplary, lawful, public punishment, and I'll catch up with you.

Lost in the crowd, into the midst of which he had prudently slipped, Hernu shouted: "Yes, villain, we'll catch up with you. I know every corner of this accursed tower; I know where the diamonds are, and the reserves of gold; I know the workings of all the elevators and all the machines. We'll begin to make use of them and…"

A powerful voice interrupted him. It was that of one of the service phonographs repeating the monotonous warning that had been resounding every five minutes at every crossroads in Aeria:

"…Before 8 a.m…!"

XII. The Flight

Scarcely a quarter of an hour remained, and the instinct of self-preservation was the stronger. The hostile crowd dispersed rapidly in the direction of the central elevators, dragging Hernu along, who peppered us with threats and bravado from afar.

Goldfeller put his evolver back in his pocket; a satisfied smiled relaxed his taut lips. "Let's get back inside quickly," he said.

He helped me to transport the treasure that he had just recovered back to the governmental palace. When the heavy bronze door had closed behind us, I paused momentarily to get my breath back; at the same time I looked at the Gem King and shook my head.

"You were mistaken," I said, "not to smash the skull of that rogue Hernu. Single-handedly, he'll bring together all the malcontents, and you'll have as many enemies inside as outside.

He interrupted me dryly. "I have infinite resources and innumerable auxiliaries at my disposal. If necessary, I'll imprison that imbecile mob until the day of triumph."

"What if there's a rebellion—if the auxiliaries on whom you're relying follow Hernu's example and turn against you?"

Goldfeller stopped me with his gaze and the slow gesture with which he took my hand. In a profound voice, he said: "I've never retreated, Bayoud, when it's a matter of imposing my will. I'll destroy everything, if necessary, rather than give in!"

A few moments later, we had returned to the huge study. Goldfeller's first action was to go and open the door of the little redoubt in which Yella was sleeping lethargically. He contemplated that radiant blonde and white image momentarily. She was the weak point of his exceptional nature; conscious of the dangers that threatened her, Goldfeller remained a man who wanted to protect his daughter, and, when the moment came to separate himself from her, when another might have wept, he reflected.

"Come on," he said, abruptly. "Let's get a move on."

He leaned over the young woman, took her in his arms, and then, in a voice that had suddenly changed, said: "Pick up that lantern and follow me."

The journey through the semi-darkness seemed to me to be a long one. The little lantern provided a poor light. Goldfeller walked slowly.

"It's here," he murmured, finally.

He had stopped in front of a door that sealed the exit from the corridor, and which doubtless opened by means of simple pressure on a spring that was known to him.

Abruptly, the narrow corridor broadened out to the proportions of a highway illuminated as far as the eye could see by electric street-lights. A few paces away, a magnificent limousine seemed to be awaiting its passengers.

The Gem King made a sign to me to open the door of the car, into which he immediately climbed in order to deposit Yella on a sofa.

"Now," he said, leaping to the ground, "let's go fetch the strong-box."

The second journey was quicker than the first. Everything was ready for the departure, and Goldfeller gave the signal himself.

"Allow yourself to travel without lights until the slope of the ground levels off. Then go at top speed for 20 kilometers; the objective of your journey is an elevator into which you can take your car, whose weight will be sufficient to activate the mechanism. Don't get out of the car before someone comes to open the door for you. The woman who will present herself is Yella's nurse; she will act, as you will, according to the instructions contained in this letter. Goodbye."

He held out a piece of paper, which I slipped into my pocket. I wanted to take his hand and I stammered some vague words into which, in spite of everything, I would have liked to inject a little tenderness. The supernatural individual pushed me on to the seat of the car, which was set in motion, gliding over the slope that drew it away. Goldfeller was already out of sight; I was never to see him again.

We went down a ramp that must have described a helical curve, in such a manner as to bring us at a gentle slope to a tunnel beneath ground level. A quarter of an hour sufficed to reach the elevator. I sensed that we were rising up to the level of a vast garage, whose door opened immediately.

I saw a thin and severe woman, dressed like a governess, with grey hair above a forehead streaked with wrinkles. Having greeted me without a word, the woman climbed into the car and leaned anxiously over Yella. I heard her murmur: "She's asleep."

As for me, jumping to the ground, I went out of the garage. I saw a spacious courtyard, a small flower-garden and a little house with green shutters at the top of a short flight of steps.

"Where are we?" I asked, mechanically.

With a gesture, the woman showed me the nearby bell-tower of a church and said, simply: "Troyes."

So close to Aeria! Within the radius of the fulgurite! Had the Gem King had brought us out into a besieged village only to expose us to the blows of his defense? I scarcely had time to evoke that terrible idea when I remembered the letter that I was to pen at the end of my journey.

It had been written by Goldfeller and signed by him. It contained these simple words:

Take Yella into the white room and wait for her to wake up. Leave immediately thereafter. M. Bayoud will drive the car to the Swiss frontier. There, I confide my daughter to her nurse, Sophie Moor.

The woman who was listening to me had already taken the younger woman in her arms and, carrying her like a child, headed toward the house, whose steps she climbed. I followed her.

On the first floor, in a white-painted room whose only furniture was an immense bed, the woman set down her burden. She straightened Yella's arms, covered her with a light sheet, turned toward me and said, simply: "I'm Sophie Moor. Do you want me to show you to your room?"

A few moments later I was installed in my turn. The windows of the large room that was assigned to me overlooked the countryside, and I immediately perceived the enormous mass of Aeria on the horizon.

It made a strange impression on me to see the monumental prison from which I had so unexpectedly escaped, gilded by the morning sun. Leaning on my window-sill, I began thinking about the extraordinary adventure that I had been living for months, and about the singular man whose pride, from the height of that mass, had tried to dominate the world. Eventually, the lassitude of that night of fatigue and emotion overcame me; I threw myself on the bed and slept profoundly.

I awoke slowly, almost painfully.

The sound of voices was rising from a nearby side-street. I eventually contrived to distinguish one word amid the buzz whose frequent repetition struck me: "Balloons...the balloons..."

The memory immediately returned, clear and obsessive, of the preparations that had preceded my departure from Aeria: the fleet of dirigibles was about to pass over the city.

Through one of the windows in my room it was easy for me to follow the movements of about 50 cigar-shaped balloons that were advancing in an uneven line to the west of the tower.

The little suburban street where the house that served me as a refuge was located was filled by an attentive crowd, and I heard the reflections and suppositions of the idlers rising toward me.

"This time, they've got the upper hand."

"One of them's moving ahead of the others."

"Watch for a moment—you'll see the bomb fall."

"They're going to bomb that pig-iron tower!"

I gazed at the accursed tower, in the pure light of the mid-day sun. It rose up like a monstrous black crag with a summit bristling with domes, roofs and bell-towers. The imagination of illustrators had dreamed of such giant mountains crowned with fortresses. Above this one the air was vibrating as above a torch, and I shivered as I thought of the poisoned wind that the monster was vomiting into the sky. I alone could understand the mute battle that was about to be engaged between the detested city and the aeroscaphs that were advancing above it.

At what moment would the murderous emanations begin to act upon the crews steering the balloons? That, no one has ever known, but it is permissible for me to presume, according to what I had heard Goldfeller say himself, that the intoxication was progressive, going from stupor to sleep, to end in death. At any rate, when the aerostats passed over the center of Aeria, it seemed that the vibration of the air became more energetic, as if the currents of deleterious vapor had increased their intensity. At the same time, there was a momentary pause in the progress of the dirigibles, a suspension—and, abruptly, all of them began to drift in the wind that as blowing from the east and, curving around, they began to retrace their route. There were even a few of them that bumped into one another and went on together, stuck to one another, to the astonishment of those who were watching the scene without understanding its mystery.

Two hours later, the scattered, soulless fleet passed over Paris and traversed western France to vanish, with its dead pilots, over the Atlantic Ocean, where the first cyclone arriving from the Antilles would complete its destruction.

XIII. The End of a World

How long those hours of waiting seemed to me! I scarcely dared to go outside, to show myself in the streets, for fear of awakening a curiosity that, given the entire region's exasperation with Goldfeller, might have been fatal to his daughter and myself.

I spent my time leaning out of my window, contemplating the tower from which all life seemed absent. Sophie Moor served me, exchanging a few laconic words. Who was that woman? One of the numerous creatures that Goldfeller had been able to attach to his fortune, but especially passionate in her attachment to Yella; she seemed very firm, avoiding any allusion to the drama that was being played out in Aeria. That evening, however, as I was walking in the garden surrounding the house, smoking a cigarette, she came to me and silently pointed a finger at the tower, whose black form rose into the sky, illuminated by moonlight.

"They haven't switched on the lights this evening," she said.

I nodded my head, pensively. Undoubtedly, I thought, Goldfeller did not consider the atmosphere sufficiently purified to permit the inhabitants to go back up into the pen air. Unless....

The general state of mind within Aeria did not seem to me to be at all reassuring for its masters. The revolt of a subaltern as important as Hernu seemed to me to be pregnant with threats for the future, and already I could anticipate some of what would happen. But the end—the apotheosis provided by Goldfeller for that terrible dream—no, I could never have foreseen the horror of it, in spite of everything I knew about that indomitable character.

Yella was to sleep for another 24 hours, and I hoped to have the time to leave, after her awakening, at dawn on the third day. The previous evening, I began to check the automobile, and filled it with gasoline—in short, used my time as best I could while waiting to depart. I was busy running oil into one of the pumps when Sophie Moor came into the garage and, without saying anything, handed me a printed sheet, a special supplement to the *Journal de l'Aube*, which was being sold in the streets of Troyes.

This is what I read in the latest news:

This morning, an aircraft in the form of a parachute landed on the roof of one of the outermost houses in Provius. Eight individuals were aboard the apparatus and, to the questions of those who found them, more dead than alive, they admitted that they had escaped by that means from the Goldfeller tower, thanks to a riot that had broken out in the bunkers where the population had been enclosed by order of the dangerous monomaniac who, for several weeks, has sown terror and ruin through our countryside.

In the first revolutionary movement that had caused the riot in question, the crowd had rushed up the stairways toward the balloons moored to the aerial stations, in order to pile into them; when the moorings were cut, those who were able to penetrate into the gondolas fled at hazard under a hail of projectiles launched at them by Goldfeller's maleficent gang.

Still trembling at the dangers they had run, these unfortunates affirmed that the inhabitants of the tower, weary of so many horrors, were absolutely determined to impose peace on the Gem King, who, aided by an entire staff of monsters, persists in destroying everything within the radius of his frightful empire.

This, combined with the sage measures that the Ministry of War is preparing to take for the complete isolation of the tower, permits us to hope for a prompt end to the nightmare.

Following a few rather confused interviews with the eight escapees, which indicated that the stores where the aircraft were kept had been opened by the rebels thanks to a sort of overseer whose name they did not know, but in whom I believed that I recognized Hernu. The man in question had, it appeared, been shot with a revolver by the Gem King, who had succeeded in escaping himself from the rage of the rioters and had disappeared into the secret coverts of the interior of the tower.

"Do you think," asked Sophie Moor, when I had finished reading, "that *he* will get out of this alive?"

I replied without hesitation that I believed so, Goldfeller having surely provided for himself the means of escape that he had provided or his daughter. The old woman nodded her head and murmured, as if to herself: "He's such an extraordinary man!"

Shortly after midnight, as I was dozing fully dressed on my bed, a knock on my door woke me up. I ran to open it, and found myself in the presence of Yella's nurse.

"She's awake—come quickly."

The effect of the narcotic had not lasted as long as Goldfeller had thought. Propped up on one elbow, the young woman was looking around her in surprise. She recognized her nurse and reached out to her.

Pausing on the threshold of the white room, I gazed at Yella. How beautiful she was, still pale with sleep, at the limit of life, this side of the angels, but beyond human creatures! She saw me, smiled, and beckoned me to approach.

"Where is my father?" she asked. "Why are we here?"

I told her about the attack on Aeria by the balloons, and gave her a succinct and softened account of the events that had constrained Goldfeller to send her away. As I spoke, I saw her grow paler still, then blush and begin to tremble. I hastened to conclude and, in order to convince her, gave her the letter that her father had handed to me as I left.

She read it and sighed profoundly; then immediately put her hand to her breast.

"I'm choking," she murmured, painfully.

Scarcely reawakened to life in the depths of the earth, she was suffocating, that frail creature made for high altitudes. Sophie more raised supplicant eyes toward me.

"Let's go," I said.

"Yes," said the old woman, forcefully, "let's go. Monsieur will take us as far as Switzerland, and we'll return to Falkenstein, my dear. We'll wait for your father there."

Yella smiled sadly. Then she held out her hand to me. "You'll stay with us, won't you?" she asked, in an imploring tone that excited me delightfully.

I bowed, and stammered that I was at her disposal. Such a plea seemed the culmination of a strange joy to which I dared not abandon myself entirely, so little did the ravishing creature before me seem fitted to lead a human life.

It only remained to quit he house.

As I was about to give the signal for departure, we heard a bell ringing on the ground floor.

"What's that?" I asked.

"It's my father" cried Yella.

She made as if to run downstairs. From Sophie Moor's anxiously prudent glance, I understood that she feared some mysterious complication whose revelation it was important to spare the young woman.

I stopped her with a gesture.

"It's the garage bell, isn't it?" I said, affecting a tranquil assurance. "It's not your father, Mademoiselle, for he'd already be in the room. Perhaps he's sending us a message. I'll go down and see."

Leaving the old nurse with the Gem King's daughter, I went down to run to the garage, whose double doors I opened wide. What I had said to Yella was to calm her; I understood that it was necessary, to begin with, to remove the automobile that was to carry us away and send down the platform to allow the elevator free play. All that took some time, and it required all of Sophie Moor's ingenious cleverness to prevent Yella from running to the window, from which she would have been able to contemplate the frightful spectacle that offered itself to my eyes as soon as the new vehicle had surged from the well at the bottom of which its journey had concluded.

On the front seat off the green-painted limousine that came on o the platform to replace the one I had take our I perceived Siam-Si, his eyes staring and his hands clenched on the steering-wheel. Inside, sprawled on the cushions, his temple pierced by a black hole and his face streaming blood, was Kandy, the young and unfortunate Kandy, whose open mouth still seemed to be smiling.

I had to make a violent effort not to cry out. Turning my head toward Siam-Si, I sought distraction in the direction of the mute. His eyes wide and staring, his arms stiffened in a strangely attentive pose, the Chinese still did not budge. I reached out to help him to get out and took his hand, still warm but inert—which, coming away from the steering-wheel, fell limply on to the seat. The movement was sufficient to make him lose equilibrium, and the man—*who was no more than a cadaver*—collapsed like a mass on the linoleum of the front seat.

In the stupor into which this spectacle plunged me, I nevertheless retained the consciousness necessary to reply to Yella's voice, which was calling out to me impatiently.

"News of my father, Monsieur Bayoud?"

"Yes, yes," I stammered. "At least, I hope so. Be patient a little longer, I beg you; the automobile isn't here yet."

Before anything else, I wanted to gain the time to make Siam-Si disappear. As I made every effort to pull him from the seat—and you know how heavy a dead body is!—I strove to find an explanation for the explanation of this arrival of two cadavers. Had the two men discovered the escape-route reserved by Goldfeller for his daughter and himself? Had there been a fight between them, and had the Gem King been able to kill one and wound the other grievously enough for him only to expire at the end of his journey?

The truth, simpler and more terrible, suddenly appeared to me. On the mute Chinese's right arm, attached by a sturdy pin, I perceived two letters that I made haste to grab. On the envelopes, I recognized inscriptions in Goldfeller's handwriting. One was for his daughter; the other was addressed to me. I opened it.

Do you know human nature better than I do, my child? What you anticipated has happened. After the brutes, the monsters of the elite, who all owe their lives to me, rebelled against me. I am playing my final game, alone against all of them, defending for as long as possible the passage that would lead the blackguards to the light and toward my daughter...the villains that I will tame again. Be patient for another quarter of an hour; send the platform back down and if you don't see me arrive, flee. Even if Yella is still asleep, flee at top speed, as if you were being pursued. This letter is for you; the other will provide you with a pretext; give it to Yella. May it not be my last farewell to my child.

It required the weight of two men and the hand of only one to maneuver the automobile charged with bringing you here. There's no shortage of cadavers here; I've thrown one into the car. The other, charged with driving it, ought to die on reaching you, if the cordial I have given him to drink acts within the time anticipated by Rassmuss. As for those besieging me, they have no suspicion of the fate I have reserved for them. You ought to be able to see it from a long way along the route that you're to follow. I...

What incident had forced him to cut the letter short, in spite of his abominable presence of mind? Perhaps he alone could say. Shoving Siam-Si's corpse into the car, on top of Kandy's, I closed the blinds to hide them from view. Pulling the limousine outside, I activated the platform, and ran in haste to the house, where Yella was getting ready to come down, in spite of her nurse's efforts to retain her.

The letter from her father calmed her impatience. She opened it, scanned it with a happy expression, and read it to us.

"My dear child, be tranquil. All is going well and I might be able to join you soon. In any case, and whatever happens, don't worrying about me. If I can't leave with you, as I still hope to do, I'll join you later. One last time, though, I wanted to write to you, to give you, before our future reunion, one last sign of affection and benediction. I embrace you, my beloved daughter, with all my heart."

Yella lowered her head; a tear ran down her cheek and fell on to the piece of paper that she held in her trembling hand. She murmured: "Never has he written to me in such a tender manner. Dear, dear Father…he must be in danger. Oh! Something tells me that I shall never see him again."

"Let's go," I said. "We must obey the orders that M. Goldfeller has given us himself. We're leaving."

Guided by her nurse, Yella came down to the car and, a few minutes later, we emerged from the town on the Dijon road.

It was getting dark; the sky was slightly cloudy but clear and milky, infinitely soft. From time to time, behind us, lightning flashes lit up the landscape and it seemed to me that they were increasing in number, intensity and duration. Anxious, fearful of a storm and wanting to take stock of the state of the sky myself, I stopped and got out.

A terrifying and grandiose spectacle nailed me to the spot. The tower of Aeria, standing out squarely against the sky for almost all of its height, dominated the countryside like a block of fire. Streaked with lightning in every direction, it loomed up in the darkness like prodigious carbuncle whose radiation, increasing by the second, was fixed in place as it passed from blue to red. Soon, the entire mass was ablaze, the cube of metal reddened to the translucency of a colossal ruby, radiating an unbearable heat as far as our position. At the same time, its summit was flaming like a torch; on top of that mountain of red-hot metal, Aeria had just caught fire.

Overwhelmed, I could not tear my eyes away from the spectacle. I felt a hand touch my arm. Yella was interrogating me with her gaze, demanding to know the cause of the frightful phenomenon. I pulled my arm away desperately, as a sign of ignorance.

And yet, I suspected the cause without being able to suggest it. I recalled Goldfeller's last words. "I've never retreated, Bayoud, when it's a matter of imposing my will. *I'll destroy everything, if necessary, rather than give in!*"

What revolts, what scenes of carnage, had marked the final moments of Aeria? No one knows, but it was evident, to me, that the final conflagration was the supreme effort of prideful power of Goldfeller's death-throes. Did not that succession of lightning-bolts preceding the flameless fire denounce a formidable concentration of all the dynamic currents accumulated in the tower? Electricity, the source of the Gem-King's power, had been chosen by him as a final resource to destroy at a stroke, by fire, the million human beings in revolt against his authority; it must at that moment be incinerating and stifling the inhabitants of Aeria imprisoned within the tower.

A cry from Yella snatched me out of my reflections—a cry of horror, anguish ad agony.

"Oh!"

Her extended finger was pointing at the incandescent block, which, yielding to the devouring fire, was tottering on its base. Whoever saw that experienced a unique moment in human life. Abruptly, with its plume of flames crowning the blazing city, the colossal monument seemed to slide over the sky, collapsed in on itself, flattened, and disappeared from the horizon in an apocalyptic light.

We could no longer see anything but the disencumbered sky, still plink with the flamboyance of the star-like entity that had just collapsed into the countryside.

At the same time, beside me, Yella collapsed, without uttering a cry.

I supported her with one arm, leaning over her anxiously. So pale when she was alive, now that she was dead, her cheeks were animated by the colors of life.

Beside me, Sophie Moor sobbed without shedding any tears.

The proud dream of the father, as it crumbled, had borne away the faint breath of the woman who had been its unwitting soul.

.

André Mas: *Drymea, World of Virgins*
(1923)

I. The Awakening

During the North African War, in 1935, at the battle of Gersons Pans, Hertha Helgar was captured in her hospital post, along with the wounded men in her care.

She was then 23 years old. Her magnificent stature combined grace and strength. Pale and very beautiful, beneath her abundant blonde hair her clear eyes seemed to reflect, by turns, the various skies that she admired on the vast Earth. She laughed rarely and said very little, but there was intelligence resident behind her honest forehead; when she wished it, her smile was full of sweetness. In Kartha, her homeland, she volunteered for service, believing it to be her duty, although she knew what her life was worth.

The indomitable virgin refused herself to the bestial desire of Arnabasse, the enemy general. In an unpublished atrocity, he had her sealed in an enormous shell of the so-called telescopic type, captured by his troops. There was no limit to the projectile's range if one multiplied the charges. In spite of the pleas of his officers and soldiers, Arnabasse ordered that the shell be fired. In an incandescent explosion, the sky swallowed his victim.

But Hertha survived. In a ring on her finger she carried a liberating poison. She thought she would anticipate inevitable death, but she was spared. Her inert body, devoid of heartbeat and breath, but in which the spark of life subsisted nevertheless, advanced through eternal space, the empire of night and silence, year after year, toward a goal that surpassed our dreams...

Hertha opened her eyes. A young and gentle face welcomed her first gaze. A small brown hand lifted a silvery vessel to her lips, full of a red liquid. Hertha drank. A more ardent life colored her cheeks and increased her heartbeat. She propped herself up on the large cushions and expressed her gratitude.

Youth was exultant in her body now; a sea breeze brought the greeting of the open sea. The triumphant summer around her unfolded in florid expanses. The magnificent calm of the sunset stained everything red. Before her eyes, the blue sea filled the horizon and the golden sun was sinking toward the slow waves to her right. The great peace of dusk was about to envelop the world.

Everything imposed itself on Hertha at once. In front of her was a young woman, attentive and smiling. She had a tanned complexion, under and enormous mass of dark hair, covered by a light veil retained by a silver sun. A tunic decorated with embroidered butterflies undulated over her supple body, tightened about her waist by a girdle that was silvery, like her sandals. Hertha realized that beneath a tunic with blue-tinted flowers, she was naked.

Rapid thoughts passed through her mind. *I must have fallen in the Pacific...some island...someone has been caring for me...for how many days, or perhaps months...?*

The young woman placed her hand on her breast several times, repeating: "Greena."

Hertha understood: it was her name.

Then the little hand touched her arm benevolently. "Nevea! Nevea!"A childlike gaiety filled the stranger's black eyes.

Hertha pronounced a few words, evocative of various nations. Greena smiled, offering an opaque reply.

Hertha turned toward the sea—and suddenly, out of that calm mass, she saw a strange star rise: a silver sun.[33]

---

[33] The author adds a footnote: "These strange systems of several associated suns are not exceptions in the sky. Our astronomers know of hundreds of them, associating red with white,

It continued to lick the waves briefly, and then they slowly fell away beneath its ascent, while the motionless Hertha felt her universe falling apart around her. Somewhere in space, an immeasurable distance away, an Earth that was hers was whirling, while she was breathing here, beneath the ironic splendor of two suns. Her knees trembled, and a wave of anguish overwhelmed her.

Soon, however, straightening up, she stared intrepidly, as if it were her destiny itself, at the silver sun rising into the sky. How long ago had the North African War been laid to rest in the dust of dead centuries? Hertha knew what titanic distances separated the stars; even light takes years to cross them. She was alive again, simultaneously isolated by the double immensity of time and space, as much a stranger to this as-yet-mysterious world as to the Earth from which she came.

Then Yesterday loomed up before her: but a yesterday centuries old. All those she loved had passed through the gates of Death during her long voyage. The eternal exile would end with her life, and only with her life. Terrestrial society might have been annihilated, leaving her, on her awakening, as the sole inhabitant of the globe; that would have been preferable. Even dead things have their memories and evoke pity. Our existence leaves a little of itself behind there.

With her face in her hands, Hertha wept silently. Also silent, Greena remained beside her. When Hertha opened her fingers, though, she saw an immense pity in the friendly stranger's eyes. The latter's slender fingers wiped away her tears, awkwardly but gently.

They're unfamiliar with tears, thought the daughter of Earth.

Greena's hand was placed on hers. A gesture encompassed the sky, the sea, the flowering bushes. "Drymea, Drymea," pronounced her voice. "Drymea nyrril Nevea."

---

orange with blue, yellow with azure, white with violet, according to the stars that comprise them. Sometimes the two stars are of the same hue: blue, pink, golden…"

That's the name of their world, and it's welcoming me, Hertha thought.

The entire sea was shining like a mass of silver extended beneath the darkened sky. The white sun, a satellite of the golden sun, weaker and more distant, permitted a lunar crescent to tender its faint light. Another white disk rose over the waves.

Greena took hold of Hertha's wrist then, and led her away along the flowery pathways. Hertha was a head taller than she was.

Then there was a marble wall, a metal door, luminous corridors and large bays. Draperies were parted. The enormous room into which Greena and the daughter of Earth entered was completely white. A cheerful rumor emanated from a group of women wearing ample, brilliantly decorated garments, with golden suns in their dark hair.

Hertha found that she was at the foot of a flight of steps leading up to a white marble couch. The cushions on which a woman was enthroned, amid the gleam of golden and silver suns, were also white.

The White Queen, Hertha thought—for she was clad from head to toe in the immaculate hue, without a single ornament. Suns were enlaced upon her forehead. For a moment, the brunette queen contemplated the pale stranger, while Greena made a slight indicative gesture and whispered to Hertha: "Nacrysa."

Queen Nacrysa seemed to be tall and beautiful, in the splendor of her prime. Her face radiated authority, but her eyes were capable of softening. Thus Hertha saw them, seated at her feet. The Queen stared at her face for some time. Everything was mingled in her gaze: pity, interest, curiosity, reflection. The blonde virgin sensed that she was in the hands of a powerful sovereign, but she was not afraid. For Nacrysa, the weight of whose power oppressed thought, recalled something of the best of Earth.

Two young women approached and fixed a veil with a silver sun on Hertha's hair. The queen seemed to give an order. An enormous metal door slid aside in the wall. Nacrysa's people went in like a wave. For hours, Hertha watch the strange humanity pass by at her feet. "Nevea. Nevea." The murmur ran from everyone's lips. Eventually, before the Queen, they covered their eyes momentarily with their hands: a gesture of respect.

An immense attention was fixed upon Hertha: women with serene faces, which seemed unfamiliar with everything that creases, hollows out and erodes the faces of our world—passion, fatigue, anxiety, grief; virgins[34] with cheerful, insouciant smiles; girls with large eyes filled with the joy of a new curiosity. Abundant dark hair helmeted their tanned faces; tunics in pastel shades mingled; sandals incessantly trod the thick carpet. Black-eyed people, they passed by in thousands, and tens of thousands.

Sometimes, Hertha turned toward the Queen, with a mute interrogation. The sovereign's gaze seemed to say: "Don't be afraid. My people are satisfied with the sight of you, stranger." Then, finally, the ranks thinned out, and the doors closed again.

There were at least two hundred thousand of them, Hertha thought, *but are the men of this land not curious...or...*—the rapid thought made her shiver—*am I in the hands of an illimitable despot with an immense harem?*

She looked at the Queen. It scarcely seemed, given the authority written in her face, that she could sense anything above her head but the heavens.

Nacrysa gave an order. Greena then led Hertha through the palace. They emerged on to a gigantic terrace. There was a garden, a clear basin, polychromatic statues. At one extremity,

---

[34] A noted in the introduction, there is an evident problem in describing the young women of Drymea as "virgins," because the term carries implicit sexual connotations that will soon be revealed to be unwarranted here. There is, however, no easily-available alternative translation for the text's *vierges*, and I have therefore retained it.

the gaze plunged over a city and its harbor, where floating gardens, ships with large sails and cargo barges were lined up in hundreds, and then the vast sea, extending for leagues. The Royal Park around the Palace and the terraces of large edifices were directly below Hertha's viewpoint; there was no higher one than that of the birds.

The blue horizon followed, more distant than the city, extending as far as gentle hills.

"Nirvanir," said Greena.

Nirvanir, city with a thousand gardens, you are so beautiful that there is only one attitude before you: gratitude to the God that permitted your birth. Beautiful, the location between the enormous sea and the blue hills beneath the sky, darkened or clear, depending on the suns; beautiful, the vast river unrolling its mirror between your marble quays; beautiful, the rose color of luminous edifices on the crown of the thousand gardens; beautiful also, your women, of spring and autumn, because for them as for your flowers, there is no winter on Drymea. And you extend placidly, far from the cruelties that torment our world.

Gazing at Nirvanir, Hertha thought that her immense voyage would not be in vain. She brought to Drymea the wherewithal to pay her debt, for a mutual confidence had arisen between her and the other humankind. She arrived with flame in hand, but not to destroy. Her own relatives would have instructed her to serve without weakness, honoring their memory by useful action, not sterile regret. Know, desire, dare and keep silent, ordered antique wisdom.

The enigma of this world posed itself to Hertha. Who, apart from the Queen, reigned in Nirvanir? What truth was behind those smiling veils?

In a summer-house on the terrace Hertha found all her worldly wealth: her watch, pen, check-book, slicing knife, a pocket Gospel—a gift from her sister Mary, her sister of the other Earth!—and a Memorandum, of the point that humankind had reach on her departure, facts and figures, carried in

263

her jacket pocket: a possible protection against a shell-burst. That summary of her world seemed marvelous here.

Then Greena took Hertha down into the Palace. There were statues and paintings along the walls. Another enormous room, where the portraits of Queens were displayed—60 of them, pale and endiademed, with unique power in their faces. The features of Nacrysa were repeated therein. Then, in another room, the books of Drymea, the thousand designs, with brief hieroglyphic characters, in which its science and beauty are contained. Page after page passed before Hertha's eyes. Countries, women, animals, work and play, joys and duties; everything that this world might know was proven for Hertha in its written memory.

Nothing permitted the belief that there had ever been kings, warriors, priests or savants. The vague idea grew, acquired substance, and became fixed. On Drymea, man, with all that he brought of good and evil, cruelty and inconstancy, anxiety and effort, remained an unknown. Although, on Earth, two sexes are opposed, there the Virgin Mary—the being so marvelous to us that a third of our humankind has set her on the altar[35]—reigned supreme.

---

[35] The author adds a footnote: "For millions of years, on our Earth, creatures were ignorant of sex and reproduced by budding or the division of their bodies. Presently, still, various insects manifest several parthenogenetic generations between sexualized ones. An evolution of the Drymean sort has nothing absurd of impossible about it. It is rational, and everything that is rational is real, here or elsewhere. Our readers are familiar with the classic works of Delage on experimental parthenogenesis."

Yves Delage (1854-1920) and Jacques Loeb carried out a series of experiments with sea-urchin eggs in the first few years of the 20th century, summarized and contextualized in Delage's *La Parthénogénèse naturelle et experimentale* (1913). Although now recognized as a key exercise in what would subsequently be called "cloning," the endeavor was regarded

Hertha was silent for some time. Everything is possible, everything is probable, in the infinity of worlds. Then she looked at Greena's smile and wondered: *Are they happy? They're different. They're ignorant of amour, but not of maternity. For myself, I shall be obliged to grow old here, without ever smiling at my child. But I bring another light and I shall not live in vain.*

Speech, the emblem and sign of Humankind, resonated on Greena's lips, naming one object, then another. She laughed and clapped her hand in a child-like manner when Hertha repeated words after her, and soon anticipated her thought by the interrogation of gesture. The small notebook seemed marvelous to her.

When Hertha went to sleep, the little Drymean, ignorant of sleep on her doubly sunlit world, remained leaning over her, listening to her breath—and the virgins of the silver sun, anxious for once, watched over the resurrection of the pale stranger.

In the warm hours, when the golden sun rose, Hertha awoke. The new life opened its unexpected doors. On Earth, old Helgar, Hertha's father, governed the State of Liberty with a strong hand. Herrer, Hertha's brother-in-law presided in Kartha, the new nation of North Africa. And the blonde virgin had gladly accepted the burden of a multiple power, a power that was not to be an end for her, but a means. An Instrument of the State, she was familiar with responsibility, fatigue, the pain of others, the power of evil, and the science of life that only informed dead lives. She had lived in 20 capitals, and she knew a great deal—especially that she did not know everything. She had few friends, but good ones. She had lived doubly; it is not the duration of life that counts, but what the days weave.

---

as little more than a curiosity at the time, and Delage became better known for his investigation of the Turin Shroud, whose authenticity he supported.

In the midst of her memories, Greena called: "Nevea." At the tender name, she found a welcoming group of virgins of the silver sun, and they left together. Outside the Royal Park, the countryside of Nirvanir was flourishing. Fresh water interrupted their footsteps in the shade. Quite simply, Hertha's companions lifted up their tunics. The daughter of Earth was struck by their healthy beauty. The afflictions of our human-kind had never oppressed Drymea. Consumption, alcohol, hopeless work, limitless poverty, haggard uncertainty: all of that subsists in what we, intrepid in our pride, call our civiliza-tion. That still does not exist, although we believe that we pos-sess it.

They swam marvelously. Greena was astonished to see Nevea remain immobile beneath her veils. An anxiety seemed to appear in her eyes. She was already imagining an ignorance or fear on the stranger's part. With a smile, the tall daughter of the North, in order to reassure her, untied her garment and plunged into the slow waters of the river. Floating gardens and colored boats passed by. The golden sun rose into the sky. But old Eros was not there to lie in wait for the insouciant Dry-means, who feared no gaze.

Only Hertha knew that the hunter existed, elsewhere. The law of Drymea did not know it. Her beauty was reflected in the eyes of Eden.

II. Princess Nyve

Five long months went by. Hertha's life, which she in-itially organized herself, was full of continual labor. Every golden morning, she went into the Royal Park with Greena, whose gaiety and good will she loved. They bathed in the broad watercourses that ran down to the sea. In the summer-house on the terrace, by order of the Queen, impatient to hear the pale stranger tell the story of her previous existence, skilled sketch-artists and expert teachers awaited her. Hertha specified and corrected drawings and suggestions, sketching herself all that she judged it worthwhile to communicate regarding her life. She wisely hid the darker side of the Earth and the opposite sexes. No other humans had ever come to Drymea. It was impossible for her to identify the stellar system in which it was located—not a star close to Earth, at any rate.[36]

In their turn, landscapes with one sun, female types, animals, cities and machines appeared before the curious eyes of the Drymeans. The Palace "books" were placed at her disposal. Capricious words were fixed in her brain. The enormous branch of our civilization constituted by books and newspapers does not exist on Drymea. Drawings with short captions, indefinitely multiplied, supplanted it from the outset, and they have not sought anything better.

Hertha was beginning to speak the language of Nirvanir correctly when the Queen sent for her one golden morning. Alone in a room in the Palace she questioned her.

"Stranger, does this realm please you?"

Hertha replied, without lying, for she knew that there was only one sex on Drymea, ignorant of not only of the miseries of our women but of desire and sensuality, the great trap of mortals: "I have never seen its like on the world where I was born."

The Queen gazed at her attentively. "You're telling the truth, I know that. Explain further. I'm curious to know more. You've already learned a great deal about our world. My people have named you Nevea—Purity—and that is what I shall call you. Your mind must be as pure as your face. The Goddess who protects this realm has saved you for our benefit."

If Nacrysa had been familiar with snow she would have named Hertha after that, but it was unknown on Drymea.

"I thought," the Queen continued, "that you came from one of the globes that follow us around the suns, which the

---

[36] The author adds a footnote: "None of those presents the characteristics of a gold/silver double system."

sages believe to be inhabited, but your world has only one sun. Where do you come from, then?"

Nacrysa knew nothing of stellar distances; she listened to Hertha talk about multitudes of stars. She believed her; her face relaxed in the presence of this daughter of another world, perhaps a friend. Her eyes became soft, when she saw that she was understood; Nevea received a favorable welcome.

Sometimes, Nacrysa gazed at her city and, further away, her realm. Sixty Queens had already preceded her. Then, a proud authority reappeared in her face. Hertha knew that Nirvanir had three times of surface area of France and that the subjects of the dark-haired queen were counted in tens of millions; Nacryra undoubtedly believed that her realm would last until the end of time. No atrocious war or howling mob had ever been manifest on Drymea.

The Queen questioned her for a long time and seemed satisfied. Every morning, Nacrysa wanted to see her. Sometimes, she had her bought down to the white room and, surrounded by advisors and artists, she asked for details of terrestrial inventions. Without the Memorandum, and the accumulation of facts and knowledge that it represented, and without her direct knowledge of the part of it to which she had been exposed, Hertha could not have satisfied the Queen. More than once, Helgar's daughter saw the wall that limited her mind. Above all, Nacrysa was concerned with practical results: transportation, machines, cultivation. Unconscious of them, she paid no heed to the blonde virgin's difficulties and fatigue.

Finally, though, Hertha satisfied her. The Queen showed her manifest favor; she liked to keep her close at hand, among her favorites and dignitaries. Often, in the white room, near the Queen, with the gentle Greena by her side, Hertha was haunted by the idea of a voyage not in space but in time. This Queen in a tunic, the florid bays of the high palace and the warm sun suggested to her a world long lost. But it was sufficient to look at Nacrysa's magnificent face, in which no cruelty or sensuality ever appeared, to feel that she was a long way from the Earth's past.

The Queen read something in her eyes; she summoned her and spoke to her softly. On one of the early days she said to her: "Daughter of another world, I feel sorry for you, but I feel sorrier for your mother." And the white sovereign showed Hertha a quasi-maternal sentiment, for her heart knew pity. She invited her to royal festivals, ceremonies in honor of the Goddess of the realm. The ornament, the flowers, the young women of the silver sun—the golden sun was the emblem of mothers—offered a lovely spectacle, although Hertha understood nothing of the age-old rites.

If it had not been for the memory of her family, her happiness would have been complete. Her blood ran smoothly in her vigorous body, her life unfolded, free of care in a beautiful setting, in the midst of the benevolence of all and the affection of a few. She did her best to be of service.

One golden morning, Nacrysa came into Hertha's room. Joy animated her beautiful features.

"Nevea, my daughter, Princess Nyve, is coming to see you. I've been testing you for months; I'm satisfied with you. I want you to be her companion. Your responsibility will be heavy, for she is my heir. Be attentive to her. Promise me that if her caprice demands astonishing things that you are able to accomplish, you will warn me first. She's coming back from her annual voyage through the realm."

As she finished speaking, Princess Nyve came in, clad in white with a silver diadem. She was not yet 16, and if her mother personified beauty, Nyve was charm. Grace and the enjoyment of the springtime of life radiated around her; she still love everything. Her soul was innocent of the pride of power. Her sapphire eyes, very rare in Nirvanir, settled on Hertha with infinite softness.

Lord, she thought, *what Prince Charming would merit this fairy princess?*

On Drymea, however, Prince Charmings have never existed. Nyve certainly had no suspicion of Nevea's initial reflection in her regard. She said to her, politely: "Are you free, pale stranger? When will you be able to come to my palace, in the Summer Land? As soon as possible, for I have a thousand things to ask you—you who know everything."

"I will go with you," Hertha replied.

Nyve smiled. "Make your preparations quickly, Nevea; bring what you need to my ship. I'm very glad, for I've heard much talk about you and you please me marvelously, Nevea, who are as wise as you are beautiful."

The dark-haired Queen looked at Hertha silently. The tall blonde virgin was a head taller than Nacrysa, and Nyve only reached her shoulder. Nacrysa made a sign: "May your strength protect my daughter! I know your soul. We Queens can penetrate hearts. I have confidence in you, for I have looked into your eyes at length!"

Hertha made her farewells according to ritual. Nyve's ship, the *Dragonfly*, elegant and white—the royal color—with a raised deck in the bow, received the two young women. Hertha begged the Princess to bring Greena. Smiling, Nyve said: "Nevea, I wish you would ask me ten times as much, for I would be glad to grant it to you."

As soon as they were aboard, the *Dragonfly* set off, like a dream. Two women in grey tunics comprised her entire crew. Hertha now knew that they were wearing the costume of "the age of harvest"—that in which one leaves temporal life for art, science or the care of others.

Nyve and Hertha found themselves side by side on the deck, and to be sure, total stranger as she was to our humankind, the daughter of other suns was a thousand times closer to her companion than a slave-driver of our world. In Nyve's mind, there was none of the enormous and confused tumult of Earth. On could not, however, compare her to a joyful and rich child, for the latter is only happy by virtue of being ignorant. The princess had already traveled through her future realm, seen and felt a part of its life. Her rank, her power and her responsibility were clearly manifest to her eyes. Heavy certainties filled her gentle soul. She had been educated on the subjects of Drymea, the Goddess and her duty; no anxiety troubled her.

After a long silence in which she had gazed at her, smiling, she said to Hertha: "You're thinking about your past, Nevea. While the edifices of Nirvanir of the thousand gardens are passing before your eyes, you're saying to yourself: How happy I would be if those I loved were here! I feel very sorry for you; I can't do anything to help you, princess as I am. Your world shines far away, I believe?"

"Thank the Goddess of Nirvanir for not having been born there, Princess Nyve. But you read my heart—I was thinking about my family."

"Tell me about them!" said Nyve. "I know that will console you, although I have not suffered. It's good to have a listener when one is afflicted!"

To please her, Hertha described her life, truly, but nevertheless altered—for she knew full well that it is necessary to guard one's words, and even one's thoughts, and that their pernicious power extends further than one knows. They appeared, her relative and friends on Earth, in affectionate words.

"Your mother was a queen," Nyve concluded, "since she governed a state, and you tell me that your sister reigned in Kartha, where you lived. You are, therefore, a Princess, like me. You should be one again here, in all justice, and you shall be my equal, my fellow princess from the stars!"

Ships moved aside before the *Dragonfly*, at the sight of the royal colors. The daughters of Nirvanir said to one another: "There's the Princess, and Nevea, the pale stranger." They offered ritual greetings, and Nyve smiled.

"I've heard," she continued, "How you were picked up from the waves, out to sea off the northern coast. Those who opened your iron box found you cold and pale, like a dead woman. They took you to the nearest house of rest; people care for the sick and injured there, as the rules dictate. The Queen ordered the sages to study everything that you had with you. They spared no effort to wake you up. The Goddess permitted it, by her favor! For you have no suspicion, Nevea with the golden hair, of everything you have already done for Nirvanir. The sages, the builders and the workmistresses have studied your replies and your drawings. You have been extensively interrogated, for Queen Nacrysa's first priority is the good of Nirvanir. All that you have revealed to us has been transmitted throughout the realm. You still have more to tell us.

"It is true, since you have told us, that you travel through the air, descended beneath the waves, and that your speech traverses your entire world. You know the secrets of the heavens and the depths of the world. Why, then, have you come here?"

"Because evil people wanted me dead," said Hertha, "And entombed me alive in the machine that brought me to Drymea."

And, to redirect the ideas of the Princess with the soft eyes, she rapidly began to talk about the brighter aspects of her life. She concluded: "Out there, we have more power over inert matter than our own hearts. I have bitter knowledge, sad experience—but I ought not to regret anything, for it might serve you better!"

Toward the end of the morning, the landscape became harsh and sterile. The murmur of the sea increased to the right, and a wall barred the *Dragonfly*'s route. A door slid aside in front of its prow; there was the cool obscurity of a bushy wood, then the profound horizon, around the lake they had just entered. In the background the princess's palace rose up, reflected in the calm water. A flowery mass separate the inlet from the sea. The edifice presented a sequence of columns sustaining arcades; bays opened beneath their protection. Between polychromatic statues a stairway with large steps descended from the palace to the clear water, and there were bright flowers everywhere, scarcely interrupted by white marble paths. In the Drymean fashion, the terrace was also ornamented by an aerial garden.

"You shall meet my companions," Nyve said. "Helya, the wiser of the two, and Venja, as giddy as she is pretty—but her heart is very soft."

They appeared; by now, Hertha could easily distinguish these strange faces. Although they were favorites, they were not forgetful of Nyve's rank, and their greeting showed it. Helya gave orders for Hertha's room to be prepared. Venja and Green went off to pick flowers.

"Are you glad to be here?" the Princess asked. "I can do nothing about your past, but a great future remains to us. On the far side of that life, you will see your family again. Here, except for my favorites and the two women who have been with my since childhood, I am alone. I'm only resting from my duty, for you know that I shall return to traveling throughout Nirvanir, as is the custom.

"Don't be astonished, Nevea, to find me so quickly favorable. Before meeting you, I knew you well. Since your awakening, everyone has tried to fathom your heart. You lived in the shadow of the Queen and my mother has experience and wisdom. I can repeat what she said about you: 'There is in Nevea an invincible strength, and I want you to have the amity of this virgin with the golden hair. I have read the stranger's worth in her eyes!'" And, very softly, the little Princess added: "I would not have needed the Queen's advice. Friend with the profound eyes, I would like you to love me."

III. In the Summer Land

The silver sun has risen 20 times since Hertha's arrival in the palace. Handed down from mother to daughter, it belongs to the princess heir, along with 50 edifices, in order that she might learn to reign. On a marble tablet, the names can be read of those whose young joy has enlivened these places, who wore the crown and then disappeared from the world.

The palace was built by a quasi-mythical Queen for a daughter charmed by the ardent climate of the South. "Summer Land" is an inexact translation for, on Drymea, whose axis is almost vertical—like that of Jupiter in our own system—there is nothing resembling our seasons. From year to year, the only changes are those of the winds and the silver sun, in its slow course through the sky, which takes more than a century.

The life of the palace's inhabitants was one of placid happiness. From her room, with walls painted with familiar scenes, Hertha could see the sea or the flowers, as she wished. By virtue of taste and reason, her life remained sober; besides, Drymea knew nothing of stimulants, or even the flesh of animals.

Nyve took care at first to carry out her duties—the care of her possessions—while Hertha was asleep. Every golden morning, she and her companions came to find her. They plunged into the cool lake. Hertha found herself a young barbarian among the gently daughters of Nirvanir, tender children docile to every caprice. She surpassed them in strength, often in skill and always is determination. Nyve loved seeing Nevea extend herself freely in their games. There was so little to fear on Drymea that she gave no thought to any eventual protection. But the old anxiety subsisted in Hertha, and her knife rested in her belt. Her calm energy anticipated some peril, according to the law of our race, which has always known fear.

They lay down afterwards among the flowers, beneath the slow rise of the golden sun; the Drymeans were content to mask themselves with their long loose tresses. The veiled Hertha talked. Nyve's *why*s were often as naïve and terrible as those of children; she never tired of listening to Hertha, who often had to admit her ignorance, or that of her humankind. The important difference between Earth and Drymea on which she remained silent—the sexes—did not help to clarify her descriptions.

In her turn, she occasionally interrogated Nyve regarding her edifices. Responsible at 16, with no one but the Queen above her—and what limit had Nacrsya's authority?

If the Queen rules Nirvanir, the Queen is ruled by custom, the daughter of years and of the proof of good and evil, protected from the arbitrariness of individual will. Everyone, high and low, has her duty, and no one can or would think of avoiding it. From the Realm to the inhabitants of an edifice, beneath a power absolute in appearance, a host of more or less powerful organizations is regulated and administered outside of dead letters or leaden bureaucracy. The centuries have polished all the mechanisms—and the power of Nacrysa the Prudent is no dismal despotism.

Every day, however, questionnaires arrived for Hertha, blank pages with brief signs. Drymean writing, entirely ideographic, requires a long apprenticeship before being fluently employed; admittedly, it is understood in all the realms, even though the languages differ.

It was the difficulty of answering that gave Hertha the idea of decomposing the language of Nirvanir into a few dozen sounds, with the help of Greena, the most literate of her companions; it seemed marvelous to all of them. How had they not thought of it before?

On the 23rd day, the unusually bright morning gave rise to the desire for an excursion to the coast, above the palace. All the young women departed, in the fresh wind, over the soft fine sand, the Drymeans as tender and joyful little girls, devoid of suspicion or mistrust, around the tall virgin, daughter of a tumultuous world.

They arrived at a near-island projecting into the waves; it was terminated by a beach, scarcely uncovered by the tide. Nyve's eyes had quickly discovered blue or emerald seashells, and they went on to the sand. Hertha followed them. When they were on the beach, the little princess forgot her dignity, to go into the glaucous water. Suddenly, Hertha saw her totter. Nyve's gaze remained fixed, her hands clenched in fear.

Ten meters in front of her a huge grey mass loomed up out of the waves: then a dull and greased skin shone, and two yellow eyes, staring and ferocious, settled on her fright.

"The terror of the sea!" Nyve murmured. Then the daughter of Earth rose up in front of her; she seized the wrist of the royal child and cried: "Save yourself! I'll take care of it!"

Nyve obeyed.

Clenching her teeth, Hertha pulled the knife from her belt. In the blink of a eye, Nyve was out of reach. At least the Princess with the soft eyes would live.

Then, all the ferocity of the rude Earth rose up again in Hertha's soul. It was necessary not to die, but to vanquish. With eyes of steel and an expression in which every line signified: "Fight!" she looked at her knife: the terrible instrument of throat-cutters; six inches of thick sharp blade, double-edged, with a metal guard to protect the hand.

She waited, weapon in hand, to strike—if necessary—upwards. The monster was in no hurry. It hauled itself aloft, ponderously, on two massive fins. From its somber maw to its bifurcated tail it measured 12 feet. It drew nearer, sure of victory. With a rapid glance, Hertha examined the ground. An unexpected pebble might cost her life. The beast seemed to be heavy as well as strong, and that was her one chance of salvation. To the attack!

While the monster considered her, stupidly and slowly, Hertha strode forward. Out of range of the gaping jaws, her armed fist struck at the ferocious eye. With one bound, she avoided the riposte. The beast pivoted, howling. Then the mortal contest began.

Hertha observed that the monster was trying to drive her into the water, where it would triumph. She avoided its charge, and found herself on solid ground again. The creature reared up in front of her, but, inconvenienced by its wound, it was wounded twice more, without result.

Plowing through the sand, howling, it attacked again. She avoided it, counting on its loss of blood. Once gripped by those terrible jaws, it would all be over for her. It was necessary to wait, and only attack with a sure thrust.

Suddenly, the powerful creature stopped. It perceived the virgins in the distance; that prey seemed more tempting than the ungraspable creature with the painful sting. Roaring, the monster advanced straight toward them, but Hertha bounded on to its slippery back. She held on with her knees and left arm; her knife drove into the dense throat all the way to the hilt. All her strength went into her arm, and she felt the dark flesh opening wide beneath the blade.

A gush of blood sprang forth. She let go and threw herself backwards. The wounded beast reared up, almost upright, while muted howls emerged from its throat. It fell back.

Hertha waited, wanting to strike the other eye. As she drew nearer, on the alert, the heavy mass collapsed, and she felt that she was safe. Standing up, she put her bloody knife back into her belt. In the sea breeze, her tunic flapped like a flag; her loose hair undulated around her. The joy of triumph swelled her breast.

An incarnation of victory, uplifted by the battle and giant strength, she went back to the palace with a firm stride, with Nyve breathless in her arms. The princess's heart was beating next to hers, and the child with the soft eyes murmured: "You saved me, Nevea. You risked your life for mine; it belongs to you."

The Queen soon arrived. How tenderly she took Nyve to her heart! What a soft gleam shone on the face that knew how to command! The Drymeans do not kiss as we do; their foreheads touch, or their eyes meet. Nacrysa looked at Nyve for a moment longer, her heart too heavy for her to speak. Then she turned to Hertha. "I cannot reward you as you deserve! What strength and courage you have, Nevea!"

"Queen," Hertha replied, "I had to save Nyve; you had entrusted her to me."

"Your eyes did not deceive me," said the Queen, very softly, "but Nevea, you have surpassed my expectations."

After this alarm, the peaceful days resumed. It is human to become attached to those that one has saved from harm or death, and Hertha perceived that in herself. She understood, in Nyve's soft eyes, that she could set aside her mask without fear—the mask that it is necessary to wear on Earth against everyone. She would be able to love her forever. Summer would come, the Queen would emerge within the princess, the years would pass, and Hertha would be able to serve her.

"Twenty-seven realms form the central continent of Drymea," Greena told her. "Many sea-girt places remain in the great wilderness of the Realm of the Sands, which are uninhabited, with neither water nor plants, but arid mountains and sun-burned plains."

"Don't forget," Helya added, "The ten realms of Lisfer in the East, a country of rocks and woods. Its inhabitant work metals, dig in the ground and trade across the deep ocean with Tremelha, the last realm of the continent. Already, Tremelha is many days' journey away. She we see it?"

"And do you know your world's poles?" Hertha asked.

They all replied: "It's the Ocean. No one goes beyond the misty isles of the North. Of what lies beyond the Southern Sands, we know nothing. Drymea is so large! It's better to discover one's happiness than desert oceans."

O Christopher Columbus! thought the Terrestrial woman—but she smiled and kept silent.

The realms were evoked, with their sonorous or harmonious names, their immense rivers, their vibrant capitals in the plains, sentinels of the river-banks, their multiple populations, from Rovenar in the North to Manharvar in the South: two million souls, in total.

"Two hundred years ago," Nyve said, "the Terror of the Sea was unknown on our shores. No one before you has vanquished the monster. Where do these creatures come from, which want to do harm to us, the innocent?"

"I can answer that," said Hertha. "What seems rare to you is the rule on our terrible world. Life multiplies there so rapidly that only pitiless destruction can balance it. Nature on our Earth, 'red in tooth and claw,' destroys an immense surplus of existences in every generation, which can find no place in life. The contest between beings and death is constant on the Earth. Here, I understand, it is not the same. Life increases more gradually, death does not scythe it down as rapidly. In your humankind, two hordes do not hurl themselves after the same booty. Ferocious beasts do not hunt defenseless flocks. The rule of our Earth is a war of all against all. Governments, sure that the hosts of the living will respond to their call, ignore the suffering and death of peoples. There will always be survivors, our despots think. But it seems to me that on Drymea, everything looks around with eyes that are open to life. The highest value, among you, is humanity, the greatest wealth, a healthy mind in a healthy body. Your law, signed by the name of the Goddess, rules and commands your Queens. But does not the advent of new existences depend on you? Your nature has determined that since the origin of Drymea and its humankind. So, respect life as a gift of your Goddess, not as wealth that belongs to you."

She did not add: *On Earth, tyrants and generals sacrifice human material judged inexhaustible at their leisure. They say, with a smile, in confrontation with a field covered with the dead: a few nights will repair all that. The universal struggle, daughter of life without measure, prepares a humankind hardened to all massacres, and especially to carrying them out. And women suffer; that is their lot!*

Ought one, however, to judge the Earth as innocent as Drymea? The latter planet without winter, created beneath its suns, went its own way, vaster and better endowed. But Hertha knew that its evolution, even in a spiritual sense, was not ours. She had run aground, alive, in a world that she should never have reached even beyond death. Somewhere, everything would become clear. But where?

IV. Through the Realm

The silver sun had just risen. Nyve, her hands folded around her knees, was sitting on one of the marble steps with Hertha beside her. The placid hour moved on in its transparent flight. Then, Nyve abruptly raised her brunette head and her soft eyes.

"Nevea, you who are never mistaken, answer me without evasion. Now, I like you best of all my companions. That is not only for your strange beauty, nor your invincible strength, which saved me, nor for your boundless knowledge, not for all the marvels you have brought us. Why is it?"

Hertha replied: "The answer is to be found in our hearts, Nyve. There are spiritual laws, like the laws governing matter, on my world as here. Souls of the same realm recognize one another quickly."

"It is visible in your eyes that you cannot be mistaken or wrong," said Nyve, "but they're full of mysterious depths— and sometimes, also, so terrible that I'd be afraid if they were not Nevea's. But I know that I can rest in peace upon your heart and reveal all my thoughts to you. For you cannot feel the pain and joy of others, as we do." She was making allusion to the psychic or collective sense of the Drymeans, which Hertha was beginning to discover.

The daughter of Earth reviewed the past. Already, in Kartha, women overwhelmed by pain as well as soldiers with black hearts, hardened by 20 years of mercenary war, had said to her: "In you we trust!" The president of Kartha, the ascetic Herrer, a man who knew no forgiveness, also put his trust in her words and thoughts. Few people possess the rare gift of inspiring faith in others, and deservedly so. Hertha was worthy of it. "In truth," Nyve murmured, "it would be pleasant to abandon myself to your rule, for you are only able to want good. I sense more in you than you know yourself. In Nirvanir we're skilled in divining the souls of others. A little more every day, my realm is yours, Nevea, because you love me a little more."

"Nyve," said Hertha, smiling as she looked at her, "it is written: the words of sages are worth no more that the three little words that a child who loves will say to me."

Oriah was shining in the silvery sky, and Nynfa was rising over the vast sea. Nyve took a sparkling necklace from her belt and passed it around Hertha's neck.

"It's my birthday today, a realm-wide celebration. Accept this unnecessary gift to your beauty, to please me!"

Helgar's daughter looked into her Princess's soft eyes, full of the tranquil innocence that knows nothing of evil; then she thought that she herself, whose rude race tamed men and the waves, had brought from her previous life, and from the black wine of books, a powerful, monstrous, inhuman and glacial science. Her name, Hertha, recalled the old Earth-Mother of the tribes of old. She shivered at the terrible heritage that was dormant in her blood. Her former friends had also inherited it: Marre-le-Rouge, the somber Helen Ers, even the pure and handsome Hersen who was known as Helmeted Love. That was the law of our Earth!

"Nyve," she said, "you make me think of what we call the Garden of Eden, when the first of the women of Earth knew nothing of unhappiness. Our race soon learned the merciless lesson. Yours is better, Nyve."

"But you," said the Drymean, "are better than your race and me. For one can see well when one loves, and I know more about you than you do, Nevea."

Days went by. They left the Summer Palace. According to the law of the realm, a princess has to spend half the year traveling through the State that she will inherit. She thus becomes familiar with women and places personally, not through others, and there is a human relationship between the future queen and her subjects; no high wall devoid of echoes is raised at birth between she who commands and they who obey. The Princess arrives, sees and departs according to her whim; ceremony is banned during the journey.

Hertha told Nyve a tale of Haroun-al-Raschid, altering it somewhat.

"All is not evil in your world," said Nyve. "Besides, it has given birth to its most beautiful flower in you, and I forgive it because of Nevea."

The Queen had awarded Hertha titles equal to the greatest in the realm, and the white costume of virgins of the royal blood, with the golden girdle and the silver sun.

Drymea has not yet invented railways. Its paved roads only know human footsteps—but a marvelous network of canals and rivers covers the entire central continent, incessantly furrowed by boats.

Nirvanir reappeared before the *Dragonfly*. Hertha's life continued, placidly, but her cold beauty became animated and radiant with a new glow; an idea and an affection has arisen within her life. She read it in the dark eyes of the Queen.

"Nevea," said Nacrysa, "it was a happy day when you came to Nirvanir. Firstly, you have saved Nyve's life. Then, in your works, my sages have found a thousand benefits. You have revealed to us marvelous secrets enclosed within the books of your world. You are certainly a messenger of the Goddess, and I thank her. Every year shall celebrated your coming. I know your merit, and congratulate you on your work!"

A grave joy filled Hertha's heart; she wanted to be such a dazzling presence in her adoptive realm as to be worthy of living there.

Then the Royal Palace and the city disappeared over the horizon. Again Hertha remembered her former life, indomitable and distended with pride, joyous in the glaucous waves or when she exerted her will, not wanting, in her pride, to be mistaken, to lower herself or to fear. But Nirvanir slowly took possession of her. Now, she almost feared her empire over the Princess with the soft eyes, for the innocent child abandoned herself blindly to her affection for her, forgetting that Nevea was not of her race. Hertha sensed powerful spiritual forces around her. Drymea, which knew no more of desire or sensuality than men knew of profound friendship. And Hertha suspected that she might break Nyve with a word—but she felt sure of herself when that tender head rested on her shoulder and her own eyes were mirrored in hers: Drymea's kiss.

All Drymean machines employ water, air and the suns. Fresh water circulates everywhere, like blood in a human body. It measures time, purifies edifices, imparts motion to public and domestic machinery. The music also makes primary use of wind and water; they go a long way in its melodious empire. The arts seem capable of unlimited development, every beautiful work expanding in a few years over the entire planet, whether it is a harmonious movement of the living or a new edifice.

One of the causes of the slower material progress on Drymea, Hertha thought, must be the pity people feel or one another. Everything is paid for in blood on Earth, the mastery of the waves or great edifices. One ends up calculating the average number of deaths for a construction of such a value; the human material enters into the calculation of depreciation. But here, the Queen feels pity for her people. Time and matter are expended to spare the living. Machines are made for human beings, not humans for machines, themselves slaves of the economic struggle to which we all submit even as we detest it—the law of Earth!

How is it, too, that one our world, antiquity was familiar with the wheel and flowing water, the Middle Ages with the canal, the wind, the beginnings of the force of matter in the service of humans, but that nothing was ever attempted to alleviate the pain of peoples? Here on Drymea, they know nothing of steam, explosives, railways, electricity...they are still in the era of St. Louis! And yet, their science supports their labor.

There was slavery on Earth, serfdom, economic exploitation in all its forms. The dominant sentiment of States was scorn for humankind and hated of the poor. What good did it do to lessen their pan? The living replaced the dead without the masters having to do anything. The just and the sage—who listened to them? But bloodlust dominated the heart of the male with strong arms, and the best responded to a call to arms with secret joy: the mark of the beast!

The Drymeans make use, most especially, of solar energy. Perhaps the relative imperfection of their machines forces them to replace roads by water. Travel has developed in a fashion incredible in our world, broken up into peevish nations. Different languages are no obstacle with the employment of ideographic characters and the fluvial company constituted by Drymeans approaching the age of retreat. The latter travel the entire continent in order that their eyes might see the greater part of their world before they die.

On the other hand, the young girls exchange one realm for another with disconcerting facility. There is no law to guide the circulation of living beings on Drymea but their pleasure.

For days, the *Dragonfly* advanced through plains cultivated like gardens or low hills covered with trees. Everywhere, the edifice-villages stood up, various in height, form and color in different provinces. If the press and the telegraph do not exist on Drymea, drawings reproduced without limit spread all over the planet, and Hertha aw her image everywhere. Everywhere, too, she found a singular mix of private and public property. The wealth of each individual was supported by the enormous wealth of all. That had accumulated for centuries, untroubled by wars and revolutions. The tendency of Drymeans to form groups must have commenced, originally, by virtue of the necessity of assisting mothers and children. Everyone, at some time in her life, would have need of everyone else—but in their living flesh, not according to dead books.

Above all, though, the effect of that sixth, psychic or collective, sense ensures that a Drymean enjoys another's joy, and feels a part of her pain. No one can ever isolate herself is solitary dolor; invisible ties link her to the souls that surround her. If, among us, the unit of society is the individual, on Drymea, it is the group; a more powerful life superimposes itself on the life of each individual, enough to raise her up, but not enough to oppress her. We might have a feeble image of that faculty in our times of crisis, momentarily. The profound instinct of Drymeans brings them to combine forces against any difficulty or pain suffered by one of them; they arrive effortlessly at loving one another, for everyone among them also suffers. The Queen senses the invisible bonds, and she could not resist the distress of her people, if it wished to overwhelm her with its power. Drymea of dreams!

In the edifices, elect sages mingle with the most highly-paced delegates; above them is the law of the realm, a heterodox mixture, by our lights, which nevertheless seems successful. The force of a unilateral heredity supplements education in the modeling of souls. So called precious metals were soon vulgarized by fortunate discoveries. The only money is valued as much for the beauty of its engraving as for its conventional value; it circulates, signed with the supreme seal of the Council of Queens, throughout Drymea. No great fortunes, initial wealth, land and mines being attached at the outset to edifices or provinces. Industry is scattered, as mobile as water. Only the Queen and the Princess possess vast domains and great wealth by inheritance; in their responsible hands immediate help can be promptly given in the case of a sudden disaster.

Hertha imagined the life of an ordinary young woman prior to maternity. Surrounded by her group, uninvolved in necessary work, she would devote at will to a preferred art, graceful sports, faithful friendships, inter-group relationships and other ideals unknown on Earth, resulting in that faculty of being all for one and one for all. Her placid career was free of the moral struggles and passions of our Earth. The best are worth less if the general level is superior. In the spiritual hierarchy of worlds, Earth and Drymea have nothing in common. The latter seemed to owe its durance to the lassitude of the Goddess, while the Earth rotated in a whirlpool of blasphemy and prayer, hatred and lust, theft and baseness, without anyone being able to foresee who, in the end, would win out.

As for Hertha, she savored the vast serenity of Nirvanir. Her pride was flattered, artists having multiplied her image; everyone in the large realm was familiar with it. The sages asked her advice, and the virgins with soft gazes came to her trustingly. Without even desiring it, she ruled, the harder tempering of her soul imposing itself on those who had not struggled.

She loved the pleasure-edifices, all columns, flowers and transparency, which framed the life of the Drymeans in their hours of rest. Outside the capital, the enormous crowding of our cities does not exist. The largest towns do not exceed 20,000 inhabitants; they can be understood and organized by human brains. By contrast, our giant States and vast cities surpass the possibilities of the direction and comprehension of leaders. In consequence, the instincts and the unconscious govern masses of men with a frightful wastage of suffering, and sometimes of blood. Nirvanir exceeds the population of France, but actually constitutes more a federation of petty States, under the rule of a prudent Queen, rather than an empire.

The Goddess of Nirvanir is represented as a veiled woman, the only image permitted in the rites. Gracious legends surround her: the creation of the world and the first Drymean, the Goddess's messengers bringing the first sciences. Around the Veiled Being stand certainties. The priestesses, visionary or inspired, from mother to daughter, know what we seek to know about death. "It opens a door to another world," said Nyve, "And we don't fear the Goddess, for she is better than us!" Hell and the fall do not exist in the theologies of Drymea. No one has ever killed, even an ignorant beast, except in self-defense.

One golden night, brief darkness appeared, before the silver dawn. The tranquil hours were about to begin. Half the year on Drymea is an endless day, the other is divided into periods of increasing and decreasing darkness. Oriah and Nynfa then reign in the skies. Hertha was able to raise her eyes toward the stars. Even the familiar constellations had disappeared. Nothing remained of the Earth.

The nights grew longer; she found herself at ease there—her companions less so, at first. The tranquil hours brought Drymean life to a standstill. The solar machines ceased to beat, all becoming immobile. The inhabitants waited for dawn on the terraces, in the moonlight. The temperature remained mild, travelers caught out paused without fear in open country.

During these nights, curious gazes, armed for the first time with knowledge, were raised toward the skies. Drymea's companion planets were revealed as worlds. Satellites displayed their seas and mountains.

"What do you know," Hertha asked, "about the profound heavens?"

Nyve smiled. "Very little, Nevea. Some think one thing, others something else. We can't know." The Princess added, with slight malice: "I understand that on your world, people study the stars, but little children die for want of care. You told me that. You did well to come here, my golden-haired friend!"

One morning, they came into a deserted lake, amid sterile plans. The inland sea advanced its lagoons. They had reached the borderlands of the realm, and in that bleak extent, a silent city slowly emerged.

"The city of dead Queens," said Nyve. "When a Queen dies, she comes here, dressed as she preferred, as an eternal inhabitant, to occupy and edifice built for her during her life. In its funereal hall, she rests on a bed, surrounded by those who pleased her in this existence. No one goes in there by the Sovereign or her daughter."

The edifices succeeded one another, differing in accordance with the times and the Queens. The most ancient presented massive forms with bare walls. In others, grace sought to soften power. Figures in relief recalled rites and legends unknown to Hertha.

In accordance with an ancient custom, the Queen comes to the city of the dead for one week every year. Her ship waits for her at the entrance. Alone with the Queens and before the Goddess, she comes into the City of Silence, and she thinks at her leisure of the day when neither crown not subjects can be of any use to her before the Justice of the other world—which demands a heavy count of a Queen, for she is Responsible.

Darkness descended on the city. The yacht, equipped with an auxiliary engine, continued on its way, and in the morning, Hertha woke up in the realm of Manharvar, confronted by the profoundly blue horizon of the inland sea.

"Drythea, the Queen of this realm, desires to see you," said Nyve. "All Drymea knows of your pale beauty and your golden hair."

There are pure and good individuals who are only able count as a benefit; to live with them and cherish them without reservation is only granted to a few of us. Nyve was that to Hertha; she erased in her the legacy of Cain; her soft eyes made her a better person, and she shivered at the thought of losing her princess's esteem. The latter took pleasure in spending all her days in the company of the daughter of Earth. Curious, Nyve had no idea of the obstacles that might separate humans here, but Hertha learned to comprehend those strange souls, and loved them too much not to forgive them a little indiscretion.

The edifices of Nirvanir disappeared, replaced by domes sprung from aerial perspectives or light constructions open to the cool wind. Painted boats with high prows came toward the *Dragonfly*, laden with curiosity-seekers. Their clothes, bright beneath their hair, so dark that it seemed blue-tinted, and the eyes shining in their bronzed faces, were different from those of Nirvanir. They greeted her in an impenetrable language.

At golden mid-day, they reached the capital. Then a heavily-decorated boat with six rowers came to meet them. In the bow, on a seat decked with purple fabrics, stood Queen Drythea. Her red clothing made her dark beauty stand out. She seemed to be no more than 25 years old. Taller than Nyve, she was nevertheless surpassed in height by the daughter of Helgar.

She invited them into her boat. After a few obligatory remarks to the Princess, Drythea said: "Nevea, I have been told of your marvelous destiny and everything that you have bought to gentle Nirvanir. Queen Nacrysa will permit you to come back here. I was very desirous of seeing you." Her words and voice resonated pleasantly, but her ardent eyes revealed the flame of her race. It is not in vain that a burning simmer reigns over Manharvar!

Drythea had them escorted to her Palace on the river; beds were ready to receive them, under arcades beside the transparent water facing the golden sun, attenuated by red veils.

I have lived long beneath vast porticoes/Which marine suns tinted with a thousand fires,[37] Hertha thought. She translated the lines for her companions.

"Have you seen anything as beautiful as my Palace on your world?" asked Drythea, with pride in her dark eyes.

Venice rose up before Hertha; she described the famous city to the queen with the ardent eyes—but months on Drymea had taught her to soften all speech, so she added: "That city, of which your palace reminds me, is regarded as a rare marvel; people visit it from everywhere in the world. All those who love beautiful works would praise your dwelling."

"I will show you the Water Palace, pale stranger, which my builders have just completed for my Nobles."

The royal boat took them under a vast gateway, a hundred meters further on. The walls were 20 feet high, painted in the brilliant colors that the daughters of Manharvar loved. Above them loomed caryatids whose arms supported the floral roof. Fresh air circulated between their superb figures. A vast basin with marble quays rolled the limpid water into the palace, with the iridescent caprices of clear fountains. On the edges were the statues of heraldic beasts.

A population of bathers was swimming in the basin or circulating beneath the whiteness of the marble. Hertha rediscovered something of the Earth in their features. They would have been excessive in any context—art, work or pleasure—impassioned by their affections, but perhaps familiar with anger or scorn. They were, however, beautiful and graceful.

Hertha was able to praise the Water Palace sincerely. The young women at play showed themselves to be as clever in the waves than their counterparts on Earth. A few steered

---

[37] The lines are from Charles Baudelaire's poem "La Vie antérieure" [The Anterior Life], in *Les Fleurs du mal* (1857).

capricious boats, always unstable; many contented themselves with enjoying the coolness and rest and closing their eye. As soon as they entered, the queen had given brief instructions, doubtless ordering that nothing in the scene should change

Soon, she asked: "Are the daughters of our world as beautiful as my nobles? For I cannot believe that all of them, out there, are like you."

To please her, Hertha evoked the women of Earth and their various beauties. The dark queen seemed alternately charmed and astonished. Her eyes never left Hertha, searching to see further than her words.

Nacrysa's first priority is utility, but Drythea's is beauty, Hertha thought. She replied: "In the countries of the North, from which my race came, the women resemble me: tall, pale, with blonde hair, and blue or clear eyes." She astonished the Queen by talking about ice, snow and harsh winters. But she saw in her ardent eyes that Drythea believed her.

When Hertha fell silent, the Queen murmured something in her own language. Nyve understood and replied: "The route is too long to go there."

"It was a long time ago that I left my Earth," said Hertha. "I cannot even recognize the sun that was mine; everything has changed out there. I no longer know anything of my world."

"You have doubtless seen many lands, many beauties," said Drythea. "You eyes must have learned to judge on your strange world, inhabited by more varied races than ours: black, red, yellow, white…"

"O Queen," said Hertha, "Most of all I have seen, as I gained experience, the suffering and misery of human beings. In order to be useful, I learned to care for others, to relieve pain, in the great service given to me by my sister, the Princess of Kartha, my realm. Much sadness reigns on the Earth. Now, in our country, everyone is always dressed when outside. Although the human form is regarded as the most beautiful of things and is reproduced a hundredfold by skillful artists, it is considered very shameful to be seen naked by strangers."

"Why?" asked the Queen, surprised.

Hertha judged it wise to keep silent, once more, about the opposite sexes, the hunter and the prey. She justified her words by the existence of various different civilizations and savages. In any case, so many things struck the Queen. She interrogated her until nightfall in the palace to which they returned. Drawings were mingled with speech in order to depict the natural and artificial beauty of our Earth and its varied mores. Drythea seemed to take great pleasure in the conversation, never taking her eyes off the stranger.

When the stars appeared, a celebration began on the river. Luminous boats danced on the waters; invisible musicians played; the edifices became unreal and profound in the imprecise light; perfumes rose up in the shadows. Nyve and her friends went back to the yacht, but Drythea wanted to keep Hertha on her boat. Stretched out, they went downriver, perfumed lamps burning overhead. The rowers took them to the middle of the river. Manharvar alternately emerged from and faded away into the darkness, colored flames rising up beneath the stars. The light revealed a statue supporting an arcade, and the moment was very sweet.

Suddenly, the Queen turned abruptly to Hertha and said: "Nevea, listen to me. I am Queen of Manharvar. I have everything in my hand, from the Inland Sea to the mountains of Noral. You have seen my beautiful Realm. Stay with me, pale stranger! You will be the most highly-placed, after my dignity. I will give you ten cities! I will surround you with the most beautiful of my subjects, and I will have a palace like mine built for you. Do you accept?"

Softly, Hertha replied: "It was scarcely a few hours ago, Queen, that you saw me for the first time. Am I worthy of your generosity? You do not know me."

"It is plain to see," replied the Queen with the ardent eyes, "That you were born in a world of ice. Do you think that I need a thousand years to love you? You do not know that

291

here, in Manharvar, our hearts are as hot as our suns. You know how we feel the pain and joy of others, and I can divine something in you. I have had your companions questioned by the cleverest of my women and you would not say that they do not know you. Do you think that I am blind? I have been able to read the heart of your princess, for she is of my race. Paradise, for Nyve, resides in your eyes. Would Nacrysa, the prudent Queen, have allowed you to become the mistress of her soul if you were not worthy of it?"

After a pause, Drythea continued: "I sense that your words are steel. The women of my realm are sometimes fickle and inconsistent, their winged words coming and going. But you! Fortunate is she who can put her head on your shoulder and rest in your golden hair, for your heart knows neither deception nor weakness. But listen! I will unite myself with you by the Cup, the Mantle and the Terrible Oath, before our shining Goddess. All Drymea trembles to break that irrevocable indissoluble bond. You can entrust yourself to me, Hertha!"

"Thank you for your judgment," Hertha said, "but since I awoke on Drymea, I have lived on the generosity of Nacrysa, and Nyve with the soft eyes has shared everything with me. Should I abandon her? You've said that she loves me."

"You speak well," said Drythea, animatedly. "You are as wise as you are beautiful. But will you compare the royal virgin, the pale silver sun, with me, a queen? Nacrysa's generosity will be rendered to you a hundredfold. In any realm on Drymea, a stranger would have been cared for and fed. What more has Nacrysa done? Think, then, that I am a queen and not a child. I can leave you my beautiful Manharvar! If ever a daughter is born to me, you will reign for years in her name. I will make your life more beautiful than your greatest desires. Stay!"

"I have saved Nyve's life," said Hertha. "I cannot stay. You say that my heart is faithful, my word firm. I have to return with Nyve to the Summer Land. How would you judge me in the depths of your heart if I abandoned someone who had confidence in me?"

Suddenly, the Queen exclaimed: "Nevea! I'm afraid! Don't you see…?"

Within a second, the tall Hertha had put a strong arm around the Queen. Her other hand fell to her girdle, and, pointing her weapon at the perfidious waters, she said: "Don't be afraid. With this weapon, of which I made use in Nirvanir, I can kill the Terror of the Sea at a hundred paces, if that is what you've seen!"

But the Red Queen smiled and said: "I've deceived you. There's nothing. You saved Nyve's life, but you would also have risked your life for me. You fear shame more than death. I've seen the terrible depths of your soul. Like a wall, you stand up between peril and others. I'm not surprised that you defeated the monster of the waves. You could break me I your embrace. You would stand firm against my rowers! And, your strength unleashed, with that unfamiliar weapon, could Manharvar resist you? But Nevea, I entrust myself to you!"

Hertha was seized by an impulse. She took her weapon from its sheath and held it out to Drythea. "Take it," she said. "I put myself in your hands. I want nothing from you but your word as a Queen."

The gesture was bold, but Hertha was learning to judge souls. The Red Queen exclaimed: "No one was ever able to flatter like you! Keep your weapon, Nevea." A softness appeared in her ardent eyes, and she leaned on her companion's shoulder.

Sincerely, Hertha said: "Queen of flame, how beautiful you are thus! How many, on my Earth, would be at your knees!"

"You accept!" cried Drythea, with real joy. "Yes, I merit that you should stay with me! Tomorrow I shall take you to the most beautiful of my charming cities, then to my palace under the sea, and my Azure Isle. I shall keep your white beauty at my leisure, and the golden dawn will rise for me in your eyes. You will rest your head in my warm hair and my tender arms will protect your…sleep." She, who did not sleep, had to search for the final word.

Hertha looked at her silently. The purity of the body and soul of the Queen with the ardent eyes was strange and perfect. In her passionate words, only Drymea spoke: the world that was ignorant of men and desire.

"Permit me," said Hertha, "to tell you a tale of my distant Orient. There was a wise Queen. One of her subjects was a commander on the borders. Thousands obeyed her. The Queen's favorites aroused her suspicions against the one who governed. It is necessary, they said, to bring her to your court and put her in chains in a dungeon, for she has become too powerful. The wise Queen ascertained the truth. She knew that her subject was loyal, brought her to her and heaped her with wealth and praise; then she sent her back to her province. Then the Queen said to the favorites: I have followed your advice. I have put her in chains, but chains stronger for a generous soul than any bonds!' Was that Queen not wise?"

Drythea smiled. "That Queen of your world trusted her subject—but she did well if the latter's soul was worth a high price. Invisible bonds!"

"Queen," said Hertha, "Look into your heart. Those invisible bonds, which you know to be powerful, the Princess with the soft eyes has woven around me."

Drythea laughed faintly. "How you have played me, Nevea—how you have caught me in the trap of my own words, of my royal word. I cannot reproach you, however, for being faithful. Why did you not come to Manharvar first!"

"I shall come back here soon," Hertha said, "to you—for grandeurs and the love of beauty are resident in you. I cannot display harshness to one who treats me gently You are deserving—you, not your crown!" She spoke gravely and calmly, her eyes on the ardent eyes, which softened.

"I no longer know how to say no to you," said the Queen, smiling.

V. Anxiety

The *Dragonfly* left Manharvar a few days later. Hertha reviewed the cities that she knew to be eternal, where generations of Drymeans were accumulating treasures of beauty and well-being without fear of devouring war and pitiless scourges that their efforts had tamed.

Aided by her companions, she succeeded in translating the language of Nirvanir into facile signs. Even Hertha scarcely suspected the enormous revolution that she was bringing. Nyve, however, said: "Where do your ideas come from?"

Communal life, a reef to some, puts the seal on the alliance of others. Hertha took care to educate herself in the manners and rites of Nirvanir. All her actions and all her words were beneficial for Nyve. When the later saw her clad and coiffed in the fashion of the virgins of the realm, she said to her, joyfully: "The more I see you resemble my race, the more I love you, for I forget then that you come from a sun so distant that I'm afraid to think about it. I shall end up forgetting completely, Nevea."

The little Drymean sensed the abyss between them, however, without being able to identify it precisely: the intellectual maturity of Hertha, who had come from a harsh world, tended toward strength and not toward generosity. Hertha had never been able to talk about the sinister side of the Earth. She knew that certain ideas are as toxic as poisons. What good would it do to bring back the dead past? Only the future of Drymea existed. Her pride was sufficient to keep her honest and pure.

One evening, under the stars, she talked about Drythea's offer. When Hertha came to the cup, the mantle and the oath, Nyve cried: "She was sincere! She would have bound herself to you forever, for there's an unknown secret in those ceremonies! And you would have forgotten Nyve! But what would that matter, if a royal crown circled your golden hair!"

Then Hertha saw that the Princess loved her for herself, and not selfishly, for she added: "There's still time to accept!"

"Would you suffer?" asked Hertha.

"Yes, a great deal," Nyve admitted. "But you would reign!"

The blonde virgin wondered whether she would have found a similar affection on Earth, for the love of a man is often that of a master. But she knew that Marre-le-Rouge had loved her for five years in silence and died some years after her disappearance from Earth, still faithful to her memory.

All she said was: "I prefer to remain with you. But you haven't spoken to me about these strange ceremonies. Why?"

"Listen," Nyve whispered. "Would you like...me, by the Veil, the Shadow and the Cup, to consecrate you as the mistress of my soul? It's possible—I know it is. Spiritual Forces are active of which I know nothing. I would be in your hands like a flower in the hands of a little girl. But you are Nevea. Would you like that?"

Hertha, rich in bitter experience, replied gently: "No. I only want you to be duty-bound to yourself, and I fear the Unknown. I'm right, believe me."

Astonished but docile, Nyve talked about Dythea then. The Red Queen had a sincere love of beautiful works, and fostered the arts. She had no lack of a generosity more physical than pensive. Her authority maintained justice among the various classes of her realm. Proud and enthusiastic, she was able to forgive, and sometimes bowed to wise advice. "Your world would have considered it beneficial," said Nyve. "It had terrible lacunae, you told me?"

What we call civilization, Hertha thought, *is based on a fundamental error. Our humankind only wanted material progress, paying no heed to moral progress. And only the former counted, in truth! Atrocious weapons humiliated our science. The Earth gloried in power and wealth, not in wisdom and not at all in generosity. The sages said so, eloquently, but who listened to them? Drymea judges its destiny differently.*

At daybreak, Nyve gazed at the golden sun, the fields of Nirvanir where life was awakening, and her sleeping friend. What was she dreaming? Nyve could not follow her there, but what did it matter? Happy years would pass in her company.

Hertha saw the capital again as a familiar place, but a heavy task awaited her there. By order of the Queen, she had to install herself in the Summer Land with Greena. The Princess would finish her journey alone. Scarcely arrived in the palace, Hertha found a house of science built on Nacrysa's desires, already filled with models and drawings. There, the most intelligent of the virgins of Nirvanir were to receive a new culture from Hertha.

The nights were decreasing then; every day, the silver sun rose earlier. In Nirvanir, there is only one stage of education for all girls, and then the most enthusiastic or most brilliant direct their studies into a preferred art or science. The group furnishes artists or specialists. There are inequalities of mind, but they are not abyssal. There is not an edifice-village through which new ideas and new faces do not pass every day, by road or water. War, oppression and the merciless struggle for existence do not force groups to isolate themselves from the world. The common hall always welcomes traveling guests. No Drymean has ever known isolation. Surrounded by her group, supporting her pain and joy in its stronger thought, her wealth in the more powerful fortune of the hive in which she lives, she will not experience illness without assistance, nor dark poverty. The group does not surpass human proportions. Its collective soul is invincible.

The multitude of personal problems that oppress us here is swept away at a stroke by the strength of all; groups rally round quickly if necessary. Living brains, rather than dead regulations, decide.

Hertha could not help thinking: *What an astonishing mixture: a monarchy superimposed on a semi-communist society, with an absolute spiritual belief—for there are no atheists on Drymea! Beneath that calm ocean of human beings, does the pain of life reign or not? No. That propensity of their collective mind yielded centuries ago. Heredity is invincible. The collective sensibility is in play. All for one and one for all! Generous beings, on Earth, have dreamed such dreams—but men with strong arms, the sons of past conflicts, do not feel that they need other men. Women have been prey for a hundred thousand years. Everyone has a life, even at the expense of others. Everything breaks those dreams: the couple ambitious for themselves and their children; amorous rivalry; bloodthirsty governments. I've named amour: that alone, the law of Earth, is sufficient to disturb it. These Drymeans do not know it, and their world is peaceful.*

Meanwhile, Hertha found her pupils. They were between 16 and 20 years old. At first, the strange distance between Hertha and themselves intimidated them—but the blonde virgin found them docile and trusting; she quickly made them love her. Teaching seemed to her to be have a humorous aspect. Queen Nacrysa did not want to heave the exceptional messenger from another world idle. Then she got a taste for it. From the dawn on the golden sun onwards, she gave lessons. In the hottest part of the day, people rest on Drymea. At sunset, she went out on to the shore, followed by those who wished. She was better than fair to all. The soul of the group formed around her. The stranger did not sense that, but she knew that the happiness of the others was aiding her own.

The Queen had made the new alphabet known throughout Nirvanir. All of Hertha's lessons were distributed throughout Drymea, in the old and new script. It was necessary to equip workers with versatile characters rather than unique symbols. Once the idea was born, it did not go to sleep again.

On Drymea, no Pasteur or Jenner had ever appeared, but the healthy life and preventive methods had let nothing persist but accidents, pain and sudden illnesses. Solely by her knowledge of anesthetics and the microscope, Hertha justified her advent. Instruments familiar to Hertha brought out the contrast between the double suns.

During the hot hours, she wrote brief treatises, in which she tried to condense in clear language the intellectual flower of our Earth. Then, in the golden evening, she read them to those who wanted to follow her. In the white dawn, she went to bed, the only person on Drymea who slept. Alone in her room, whose walls were painted with smiling faces, she examined her conscience, asking herself whether she had done well that day. There was none above her thought but God. It was up to her to separate the wheat from the tares. The responsibility seemed heavy. "You have made me, Lord, powerful and solitary..." Her influence over the gentle daughters of Nirvanir frightened her a little. Hertha alone knew the depth of the abyss that separated them. All the terrestrial demons were dormant within her; they might awaken, those which were not even suspected on Drymea.

While preparing the next day's tasks, Hertha told herself that she had not acted in vain. Raising a little higher the light that would no longer perish, she had spread the best of what we have through another world.

By the sea, on golden evenings, she thought about that strange life. She was the torch for these virgins in flower; she was opening to them a vast spiritual and material universe, hitherto unknown. She reigned by her own value. Her proud and honest soul was slightly flattered.

The daughters of Nirvanir conceived an exalted admiration for her. They believed, easily, that Hertha alone had discovered everything, done everything, invented everything, and refused to recognize her as the messenger of another humankind, heavy with pain and experience. Smiling, Helgar's daughter rectified their error. She talked to them about the best of our world, who alleviated suffering, saved others from death, soothed pain or enlightened minds—but of that truth, her pupils took no more than they wished: the messenger was a pure jewel of Earth; and Nyve, on her return was able to confirm that.

The Princess brought news. Queen Nacrysa judged it appropriate to give Hertha a share in the produce of new inventions derived from her knowledge. Neither the Queen nor Nyve calculated the terrible leverage that sudden wealth would put in Nevea's hands, for Drymca had no large-scale industry, the maker of power and manipulation.

Hertha knew it. In response to her desire, a magnificent jewel was sent to Drythea, as a memento. Then she ordered the best of ships from the yards of Nirvanir. The old call of the sea had awakened in her soul.

One golden evening, as she was speaking on the shore, a thoughtful little girl seven or eight years old appeared. Her thin and asymmetrical face was concealed by her dark hair, but her brown eyes were intensely keen. She wanted to approach. The young women smiled and said: "Go and play"— but Hertha sat her down next to her.

That evening, she was talking about the Woman who had said: "Suffer the little children to come unto me." But it was necessary to admit that she had been killed, and the virgins of Nirvanir said: "How was Nevea able to be good there? The wicked would have wanted you dead too. We can thank the Goddess that we were not born on Earth."

The little girl came back. She was grave and placid, huddling close to Hertha, and appeared to understand. Then, one day, she disappeared. Hertha missed her, but did not know her name.

She tried to get to know her pupils. Souls seemed to her more important than lessons. Everything goes smoothly when one knows how to handle those one is teaching—and she was able to do that.

There are two kinds of innocence: that of the ignorance below evil, and that of the science above. Hertha had read and understood a great deal during her Earthly life. She was equally familiar with the brilliance and the monstrousness of our world. Her knowledge extended from Eden to Gomorrah, but she thought about it as little as possible, knowing what beings dismal thoughts of evil attract.

Besides, she was rarely alone in the silver dawn. Nyve's slender arm parted the draperies, the little princess came to lie down beside her until she went to sleep, to talk about the thousand events of the day, sure that Nevea would be able to understand everything and clarify everything, like the Goddess herself. For the daughter of Earth had also learned how harsh, and sometime mortal, words can be. If she found fault, it was with a smile. Her eyes spoke sufficiently.

Then her ship arrived. She named it the *Seagull*, in the language of Nirvanir. It was a large vessel as light as a bird, with two masts and the Drymean system of sails that unfolded like a fan. Graceful, docile and unsinkable, combining terrestrial science with Drymean artistry, the *Seagull* moved over the waves. From that day on, all of Hertha's leisure time was spent at sea, accompanied by those who wanted to, with expert pilots.

The days went by. One night, as Hertha slipped into sleep, a scene from the past abruptly resurfaced. On Earth, in Kartha the superb, beside the enormous Atlantic, a woman dressed in ermine, with oblique eyes in a gilded face, confronted her. Her hair was like a black radiance. With a strange smile, she said:

"Poets have sung about Our Lady of Tears or Our Lady of Darkness—but their powerful sister, me, they have forgotten. Now, I am our Lady of Evil Desires, those which one dares not admit even to oneself: sins of the mind that do not descend into action and which are seven times worse than the others. I once reigned over accursed cities, over islands of strange amours. How many still worship me in their hearts! And by night, I whisper monstrous dreams!"

Then the Atlantic became blue, and the Inland Sea extended its azure isles. The phantom went on:

"Proud cold daughter, you reign here, worse than the despots of Asia or the Caesars of Rome. They only caused their bodies to be adored, but you have elevated your thought on to the altar, and you make the gentle daughters of Nirvanir kneel before it. Even when dead, you flatter yourself that they will still be enchained—and does not your heart covet the place of God, you who are an immortal Being? You have refused a crown, but out of pride. You want to encircle yourself with a more beautiful one, and of your own accord!

"Now, when you walk in the silver dawn with your pupils, you rejoice in knowing than their souls are in your hand, like a fledgling in a fowler's. And I have read your heart when Nyve with the soft eyes puts her head on your shoulder and gazes at you, smiling and attentive. You say to yourself: 'My thought is her thought, my law is her law, my will is hers. She would follow me, if I wished, beyond the good and evil of her world and mine! I hold that ignorant child Nyve of Nirvanir in my fingers, for Heaven or Hell.' You are queen of a black realm, like our all-father Satan. It's not bodies that you want but souls, and not for a time but for eternity."

Then Hertha, shivering, cried: "You're lying, for I have sounded my heart!"

"I wear an immaculate garment," the apparition jeered, "to show that externally, I am irreproachable! You resemble me. For you remain pure in your cold whiteness, not out of virtue, but out of pride—Pharisee, as the Christ I hate would have said. But don't think that you can mock me forever. One day, your thoughts will descend to action. Then, you will no longer belong to me. Your race will reawaken within you, horribly! You will be the queen of war, the sovereign of exterminations. You will pit one half of a world against another. You will set tortured cities on fire. Your dismal troops will follow the army of war-machines behind your Behemoth of steel, daughter of the Antichrist, smasher of the altars of the veiled Goddess. Terrible being who combines the strength of men with the cunning of women, you will mount the throne of Drymea on the bloody eve of great massacres. And you will not forget, in making yourself Queen, your Princess with the soft eyes, bewildered but submissive!"

"Never!" cried Hertha.

She looked the demon in the face.

Then, she was woken up. Nyve was leaning over her, anxiously. "What's wrong? You were speaking in an unfamiliar language, and there was pain in your thoughts. Tell them to me, and I will console you!"

Hertha told her a part of her dream, but not all, for speech is already redoubtable. Sometimes, singularly sharp dreams do not correspond to anything real, now or in the future. Do they come from the depths of conscience or beyond? Hertha wondered momentarily.

"The Queen has summoned you to her palace," Nyve said.

Three hours later, Hertha found Nacrysa alone on her terrace. She was meditating, her black eyes fixed on Nirvanir at her feet.

Hertha waited beside her. Then the Queen spoke, slowly: "Nevea, I wanted no one to be between us. I see you most highly-placed after us. But I'm anxious about you!

"I do not reproach you at all. You are irreproachable, loyal to me and the Realm, as best you can, devoted to Nyve until death. I would entrust my very life to you. Queens have ears and eyes everywhere, and I know that you rejected the magnificent offer of Drythea of Manharvar. She was sincere! The Red Queen always is. Yesterday, again, she asked me to send you to her. You have brought the disturbance of your world into my Realm. You are making the virgins of Nirvanir lose their heads! On listening to your words and deciphering the writing of your mind, as endless as the sea, before your pale beauty and your golden hair, they imagine something better than their calm happiness. They know that you have come from above, from the stars. Your pupils would believe in you, as in the Goddess, if that did not offend her!

"I have nothing for which to reproach you, personally. I suspect that a terrible knowledge also inhabits your thoughts, of which you have never said anything—but you know as much of the dark abyss as of the great light!

"You are innocent, Nevea! The disturbance comes with you, in spite of you. I want to talk to you about the Princess now—for her soul is in you; she is no more than a reflection of your thought. In your profound eyes, Nyve forgets the Realm! Now, she must reign. She once knew her Duty, and what this Realm that has seen 60 queens demanded of her, and will demand of her—but now her strength and her destiny are in you. You will be able to sustain her, Nevea the invincible—but be careful of what you might break! For Queens pass, and the Realm remains. You know that; you have said so to Nyve.

You have been, in that respect too, as clear as fine crystal, seeing her Duty better than she does herself.

"Nothing in the Princess's heart remains hidden from me, and I know that she has offer you the Veil, the Shadow and the Cup. She would belong to you forever, and Nirvanir, after me. But you refused! A Drymean would have accepted. You see other duties on our horizon. You dread not being perfect. The very excess of our virtues overwhelms me! You hold us in your hands. Your anxiety, spreading among us, has attained all of Drymea. It surpasses your life and your thought, daughter of a tumultuous sun. I look at you, and Anxiety with you. Can you banish from Nirvanir that which you brought with you, in spite of yourself? Be irreproachable one more time. I cannot oppose you because I love you too. Reflect. Judge!"

Hertha raised her head.

"You say, Queen that my words, and more especially my writings, have troubled many young hearts?"

"Yes," said Nacrysa. "Now that a month gives the virgins of Nirvanir that which formerly cost ten years of difficulty, they believe that the light burns solely in you. A thousand years of experience does not weigh as much as a line from your hand. Their heart is very light!"

"I have done wrong," said Hertha. "I did not want to disturb you. I have hidden much of the evil on my Earth. Our life, viewed from afar, seems enchanted. Drymea seems a world of monotonous happiness. I was favored on my planet, but the daughters of Nirvanir think that all my sisters out there are like me! I will do my best to combat the error. A new word will efface the old one!"

"You can do that," said Necrysa, satisfied. "Nothing seems to be impossible for you."

"Now," said Hertha, "order me to travel all over Drymea. Permit me to choose companions and pilots for my *Seagull*. I will travel the seas as far as distant Lisfer. I will come back, and I will have served during my journey. I can charge Nyve with a duty that will please her, and will teach her once again to make decisions and act. Could I think to harm her because I love her? Don't be hard on me, for I too will be sad. When I am back in Nirvanir after my long ocean voyage, I promise you, by the veiled Being that we all adore, not to see Nyve again if you think that it for the best. I can do no more, except die!"

"Nevea," said the Queen, "I would like you to be my daughter and Nyve's sister. We shall see one another again one day. May the Goddess protect you!"

She took Hertha in her arms, and their foreheads touched. The blonde woman returned to the Summer Palace. Then, mingling the bitter truth with the familiar language of Nirvanir, she revealed to the Drymeans what an abyss of evil they had been spared, and that a higher destiny awaited them in the vast universe—for Nevea's harsh and tumultuous world did not oppress them. Peace extended throughout Nirvanir, for "Nevea has written it."

Ten days later, Nyve saw the *Seagull* open her sails. Her blue eyes knew nothing of tears; her race did not weep—but she learned pain then. Sadness weighed upon those who stayed behind.

Standing at her command-post, however, dressed in somber leather, with a helmet, gaiters and a girdle around her waist, the mistress of her vessel after God, Hertha sensed the indomitable soul of the Vikings within her. There was blue sea between the Seagull and the quay. Then Hertha turned to smile at Nyve, with a gesture of farewell, and said in her heart. *I love you Nyve, and for you, also, I must leave!*

VI. Drythea, the Red Queen

The *Seagull* arrived in Manharvar a few days later.

"You've come back," said the dark Queen, when Hertha appeared before her eyes. "By our shining Goddess, I've been waiting for you. How long will you stay?"

"I obey and I serve," Hertha replied, "although I am here in my own realm."

"It rests upon the abyss."

"If my empire is narrow, it will bear me across the world that I must visit, on the orders of Queen Nacrysa."

"I shall remain on your ship," said Drythea. "My scarlet vessel will be able to retrieve me when you leave again."

And they sailed toward the Charming Cities. Human minds, eyes and hands had harmonized their works with the beauty of nature. The crowned will of queens had served the genius of artists and builders. Destructive war had never passed by. There lived the nobles of Manharvar. Crowned with roses before the blue bays, beneath the flowery ceilings, they forgot that there is a higher life and an inevitable death. They moved among the music and the perfumes, their dark hair ornamented with jewels, brightly clad, their eyes full of dark fire—and beauty crowned them. Hertha watched them from her post, upright in her strict costume.

Beside, her Drythea said, proudly: "Have you seen their like on your world? And what will rival my cities? What is your heart's desire, then, Nevea? Would you not be better off lying beside me among the flowers in this palace, while songs resonate for you, delivered from the capricious waves? You have done so much for Nacrysa that the Sages cannot reproach you for lingering among my Cities!"

Thus spoke the Red Queen, and any of us who had seen her leaning over the blonde virgin would have compared her to the Tempter. But more evil inhabits a single terrestrial heart than all Manharvar embraced!

Then, after a week's crossing, Drythea ordered a landfall on the Azure Isle. She took Hertha to the Palace Under the Sea that she had once mentioned to her. Soon, fish similar to flowers were moving above their heads. Crystalline columns sustained the transparent ceiling, Perfumed pools slumbered at their feet. The golden sun, shining through the waves, made the palace iridescent. The dark queen took pleasure in showing her companion the marvels of her realm's art. Then came the silver sun, inundating the palace with white light. The impression of a beautiful dream overwhelmed Hertha and, plunging into the warm water, she thought that she was swimming in the moonlight.

"Are you satisfied?" Drythea asked.

"You seem like an enchantress of our world," said Hertha, sincerely—and she spoke about enchanted beings, children of the mist, the woods and our dreams.

"I love your repose," said Drythea. "Motionless as a statue, I can gaze at you at my leisure, and your eyes cannot reveal your thoughts, of which I know nothing."

She was clad in a dark, starry garment. The whim seized her of ornamenting Hertha in her fashion, with heavy jewels and bright clothing of Manharvar. She loosened her abundant hair and led her to a tall silver mirror. "Look at yourself, Nevea. I want to add the final touch. Life is beautiful above all things." She placed a golden diadem on Hertha's forehead. "Only a crown befits your royal beauty!"

"My futile beauty," said Hertha, sadly. "Never will my child smile, for my world is not yours. The past still oppresses me, the future holds ordeals in store." Suffering marked her face.

Pity overtook the queen at these passionate swords. With a bound, she was beside Hertha, lying by her side. She placed her blonde head on her shoulder and said: "Nevea, Nevea, you can be sad. I am scarcely acquainted with pain, but I know sympathy. Your destiny is marvelously mingled with the pain of life. You have lost everything that you loved, and your daughter will never come!"

She spoke many other tender and consoling words, and was able to show her the luminous path of good that Nevea was following. "You seem to me dearer for not being inhuman, Nevea. Your knowledge, your wisdom and your strength are not worth as much as your soul, which was sincere for me."

"For the last time," Hertha said, "I will l think of myself. "Among my Earthly sisters, there are those who have more to bear! Hope and magnificent duty remain to me. I shall serve Drymea. Nevea will be wiser, by virtue of the suffering of she who was Hertha on Earth! Queen, I shall think of you tenderly, for I have sobbed in your arms and you have felt pity."

When Drythea's vessel appeared the next day, the Red Queen said to Hertha: "You must go, but you will remember me. I shall give you Flormal, the most beautiful of my Charming Cities, with the 2000 faces of its inhabitants. That's not enough. You shall choose from all of Maharvar the virgins with the beautiful eyes who please you the most; they will be charmed, for your law reigns gently. You will be a sovereign , having no one above you but the Council of Queens and the Goddess. A crown alone befits you.

"You should go to spend a few months in Flormal before your departure. The daughters of Nirvanir have lukewarm blood in their veins, but ours burns red! Everyone obeys me, all remain faithful to me—but you would reign by your profound eyes and your beauty alone. If you wished it! You would have them body and soul. Those who would be our subjects would take your slightest caprices for law. On their knees, they would present the golden cup to you. They would be the royal support for your pale beauty; they would place their foreheads on the hem of your tunic and your silver sandals would trample their hair. To your will, no one would dare say 'No!' You would inspire all the masterpieces, for you are wise, and your life would be nothing but one sole joy. You would wake up beneath a shower of roses, in perfumed waters. And it would not be by your orders, but in spite of you! For I know that Manharvar has embraced you, and we know how to love. Do you doubt that I am the first of those who would obey you? For I am thirsty for your eyes, which render me better."

"Drythea, Drythea," said Hertha, gravely and gently, "even if I had on my head the 37 crowns of Drymea, what use would that be to me if I lost myself? You are not of my race, beautiful queen, and you do not know its terrible heritage; you do not know what flames might set me ablaze! I dread absolute power; I dread its intoxication; I dread, above all, those foreheads bowed down beneath my sandals. I have already been obliged to choose my route on Drymea, not once but 20 times, between renunciation and damnation. As you have said to me, I dread black shame and I must direct the prow of my ship far from the Charming Cities. For I am a stranger, and believe me, Red Queen, I have reason to flee virgins with beautiful eyes who do not know how to say 'no' and the perfume of roses!"

Drythea gazed at her, smiling.

"I want you, however, to retain some of the sweetness of our encounter. You must go; that is your wish. Flormal is yours, unconditionally. Name a Regent! It will, however, be necessary for you to rest your golden hair on its fertile soil, O beautiful vagabond of the seas!"

Then they went on to the *Seagull*'s bridge. Hertha reflected. She raised her voice slightly to summon Greena, the virgin of the butterflies, the friend of her earliest days. She ran a tender hand through her hair. "Thank the Queen, Grena, and be loyal to her, for by her desire you shall be regent in Flormal, the Charming City that belongs to me. You will go with the Queen on her departure, Greena. Respect the Sages, and may generosity secure justice in your new power!"

"Now, Nevea," said Drythea, "depart, as you wish. After all, you have accepted from the Queen that which your friend offered you! My grandeur sometimes isolates me, but today, I bless it, because of you. You have not worn a crown, but you are my equal. In Manharvar my palace will always be yours."

The next day, the ship's paddle-wheel was driving it across the sea toward Oaryl, the realm of a thousand isles. Its capital, Rynea, loomed up before the prow, a sentinel of peace and prayer in that calm land. The realm is that of quietude between work and heaven. Its inhabitants feel the presence of the veiled Being more keenly than others. The queen also wears a priestess's mantle, and the invisible bonds are doubled for her.

Hertha thought about the weights of those lives that followed her. Vain curiosity did not attract her as much as the need to know, in order to be better able. The *Seagull* went

309

along the coasts, traversed arms of the sea, entered into gulfs, went up large rivers and anchored in cities on the shore of changing seas along the entire length of the central continent. A hundred cities appeared and dwindled in Hertha's eyes. Where her ship could not penetrate, flowery boats came to meet her. Faces passed by in multitudes, a thousand edifices charmed her. Multiple languages greeted her. Her name had preceded her everywhere. Everywhere in 20 realms, serving Drymea, she held conferences with the sages. She saw mountains and plains without end. In Normany of the Marbles, as autumn came to a close, the queen, clad in the spotted folds of her gilded garments, offered her hospitality for as long as she wished.

The Drymeans do not live longer than 50 of their years, which are a third longer than ours, and the birth of their children occurs at 24 or 35. Hertha resumed on land the costume of Nirvanir, and the gold star of her principality of Flormal shone in her hair. She greeted more than one Queen, and Princesses asked her for news of Nyve with the soft eyes. She saw those who honored Drymea by beauty or wealth. Then, Helgar's daughter discovered the full extent that her renown had attained. In a world without war and vast suffering, where the daily struggle does not crush humanity, her arrival opened a new era.

Confusion would soon have arisen in her mind, without the notes and letters she sent to Nacryra. All that seemed beautiful to her departed for the Summer Land with Nyve's courier, for Drymea, with its immense circulation of living beings, admits errant thought, oral or written, better than ours.

Tremelha, the last realm of the East, intermediate between the central continent and Lisfer, mingles the various beauties of the Drymeans. Its ports resonate to 20 languages. Queen Rheeve had just inherited the realm, and power weighed heavily on her 22 years. Her azure-hued vessel came to meet Hertha. With a blue fur on her supple body, the young queen with the handsome face pleased the blonde virgin. Rheeve spoke the language of Nirvanir fluently.

Before launching forth on to the great Ocean, it was necessary to examine the *Seagull* inch by inch, and to supply her with skillful pilots. Then Hertha wanted to let her crew rest. A month ran by in Rheeve's company. When they parted, the Blue Queen regretted losing Hertha and told her so, for the women of Drymea are frank. They have never learned to use cunning against strength.

The ocean opened up—not always clement, but they won the game. Lisfer expanded. Its daughters live at a higher altitude, with winds from four seas to sweep their continent. They know how to bring harvest forth from the soil; they quarry and carve rock, fell trees, dig mines and send forth convoys of boats in joyful activity.

The *Seagull* went up the great river Nerval, which penetrates further than Martelar, city of metals, the capital of the third realm. Enormous quarries open in the hillsides. The workers extract iron therefrom ingeniously, manipulating the heavy material with fire and water at their leisure. Smoke rises on the horizon and the sound of metal striking metal dominate all other noises.

If Hertha had thought she was in Essen or Pittsburgh she would have been rapidly undeceived. The spirit of the planet was still dominant, and put the instinct of the group and the pity of all for all above the great organization that frames iron with human dust. The powerful nature of Lisfer, however— lakes, rocks or woods—stamps its mark on the harder labors of its women, compared with the gentle plains of Nirvanir or the pleasant shores of Manharvar, and activity dominates its Queens with paler faces.

Lisfer of the ten realms! The *Seagull* went up your rivers, along your coasts, slept in your harbors. To the daughters of Nirvanir, your life appears harsher and more active, and yet labor does not forget beauty. The eyes of your young women are reflected in their eyes while they seek a mutual exchange of thoughts. Your rudely-wooded mountains loom over them. Your cascades expand in veils of foam in your rocky gullies. Your lakes extend on your windswept plateaux. But every-

311

where, there is benevolent brightness. Two lunar cycles of Oriah pass by every 74 days.

Although the Drymeans only have their pole star for a few months of the year, their navigators, following indications provided by the suns, have discovered the compass. Momentarily, Hertha wondered whether she ought to set a course southwestwards to reach the realm of Sands, but she did not feel that she had the right to risk other lives than her own for the sake of vague curiosity. For there was open sea between Lisfer and Nirvanir. Couriers traversed it continually during the endless day, but now the period of nights was beginning.

The *Seagull* set forth over the long billows. All day long the steel wheel whipped the sea, and during the brief night searchlights scanned the waves. The wheezing engine pushed eastwards. There was sometimes bad weather; the clouds might cover the suns and the winds whistle—but the *Seagull* advanced like an arrow. The young women raised eyes full of confidence toward their leader when unstable air darkened the horizon. Then, the waves became clement again, and when the brief stars appeared one evening, Nirvanir emerge slowly from the wave.

At the first port, Hertha sent warning to the queen; then, the following morning, the *Seagull* resumed her journey toward the capital. With her tall masts, the ship could not travel along the canals. Joy radiated from the faces of the daughters of Nirvanir. They had shown themselves gentle and docile throughout the voyage, but they had endured the dread and sadness of separation. Nevea showed herself to their eyes in every crisis; they turned their hearts and gazes toward her. Standing at her post, she inspired feelings of security, but in her absence, everything crumbled.

An obscure regret rose up in Hertha. That unity of ship and crew, which had made the vessel almost a living being beneath her hand, was about to break. She saw her companions, leaning on the rail, reciting the names of familiar horizons. For months, they joys and difficulties had been united. Doubtless they had been astonished that Nevea, dominating everything—humans and things alike—from her station, had wanted to go further, ever further. But now, finally, they were seeing Nirvanir again!

VII. The Return

A few hours later, the *Seagull* anchored in the royal port of Nirvanir, at the foot of the palace. Months of issuing commands, always obeyed, constant responsibility, and distant skies, had hardened Hertha's face, tightened her lips, deepened her eyes. Old Helgar, on seeing her standing there, tall and strong in her leather garments, would almost have acknowledged her as a son, without the abundant blonde hair that fell over her shoulders. On arriving in Nirvanir, however, she took care to put on the white costume of a daughter of the royal blood again, with the silver sun on her forehead and the jewels that Nyve had give her on days of celebration. The city seemed to her to be a welcoming homeland. She had left something of her life there.

Queen Nacrysa received her with visible pleasure. She spoke to her on the same terrace where she had once invoked anxiety.

"Nevea, I experience more joy in seeing you again than I would have thought. I have no more to fear from that torment that you wear around you. A new influence has arisen in the realm: Nyve, my daughter, who is everywhere called the Princess of the Little Girls. I don't know how she has found among the virgins or women of my realm those who support her work, but it's said that in travelling through Nirvanir she had caused to emerge from their hearts or skillful fingers harmonious drawings, enchanted tales and ingenious prudence for the joy and health of the smiling people of tomorrow. 'You should not be jealous, Mother,' she said to me, at the outset, 'if I reign over the children; I'm still very young.' I sensed her thought then, but like a benevolent star, not like the devouring suns. If she is the idol of little girls, she does not neglect her duty at all. She consults the sages and her actions are all that my heart can desire for the realm—and I am satisfied.

"I know what you part was in this; I've read all that you wrote to Nyve, and I know your heart. What I love is that you said to her: 'Consult the Queen and the best; their wisdom is polished by the experience of centuries, and mine is foreign.' You may see her again now. I've notified her of your arrival. She's waiting for you in the Summer Land. You may go."

The golden sun still reigned in the sky when the Seagull came in sight of the Summer Palace. Hertha quickly took her ship to the quay. Scarcely was she among the flowers of the park when she saw Nyve coming. She seemed more beautiful than before, and her face was radiant. Power in the service of generosity is a rare encounter. Hertha thought of a line by a Greek poet: *Equal to goddesses, save for immortality.*[38]

They looked at one another momentarily, their hands interlaced in the silence that is the homeland of souls. Around them, summer was triumphant. Then Hertha took the Princess in her arms and kissed her gently on the forehead, for the first time. The kiss was like a prayer, for it thanked God for having permitted her an amour.

When the stars appeared, they were still in conversation beside the calm lake. Hertha confessed that she had sometimes been afraid on the violent sea—not for herself, but for others. It had been necessary to smile as she gave her orders, though, for the daughters of Nivanir turned to her as if she had the tempest in her hand. As well as the bleak solitudes of the waves, there were the resplendent cities of Drymea. Hertha's memories appeared in Nyve's eyes and the golden dawn rose on her slumber. The heavy burden of those months abandoned her. Nyve stayed momentarily, leaning over the motionless Nevea, but her Duty drew her away.

When she came back, Hertha felt at home again in the Palace. Then, Nyve said: "How I regretted your departure! I often prayed to the Goddess for you. I was no dupe, but my

---

[38] The line is from Euripides' tragedy *The Trojan Women*.

mother said nothing to me about the true reason for your going away. You can admit it now. Why did you leave me, my friend, in spite of your own wishes, and mine?"

"You want the truth," said Hertha, smiling. "I left because I wanted time to efface the mark I had made on you. I want to love you, my Princess, and not myself in you. I feared my empire over your soul. Was I wrong? You are worth more than a charming reflection, Nyve. My words might seem to you to be full of foolish pride, but you must judge me as if I had passed the portals of death. You seem to think, daughter of this world, that I am a goddess without sin or stain. I'm only human, oppressed by my race. I refused the Veil, the Shadow and the Cup because I was afraid for you. I know how dangerous the Forces are with which you were playing; space does not exist for them, and on my Earth, I knew something about them. So, I did not want to become the mistress of your soul. To set you free, I put a world between us. I loved you more highly than you did yourself; I have returned you to yourself. Will you forgive me for the pain I caused you? Mine has been heavy too."

Nyve with the soft eyes smiled and asked: "What is that unfamiliar caress, when you placed you lips on my forehead? Nirvanir shall know it because of you."

"The gesture of the best friendship," said Hertha.

"And who taught you that?"

Hertha reviewed ages past. Her mother, who never complained, her sister Mary, the support of the little girl or the bright-faced adolescent, and her father, hard Helgar, mild for her. The dark Helen, her unique friend. Grief came back into her beautiful features, for, other than that, she had never loved.

"This is my response, if I forgive you," said Nyve, having listened to Hertha. She kissed her on the forehead, not without a hint of awkwardness. "Now I want to prove to you my Princess's knowledge, for I know how to command. I have learned that since your departure. I cannot call you my subject, when I see the star of Flormal on your forehead, but you can promise me obedience to one of my wishes." She rested her dark head lightly on Hertha's shoulder, in a familiar gesture.

"What do you want from me, Nyve, my Nyve!" Hertha exclaimed, slightly intoxicated by the joy of her return, the success of her voyage and the assurance of further triumphs. "Must I build you a palace under the sea? Shall we travel all over Drymea with the wings of a bird? Should we fathom the abyss of the waves? Conquer the realm of the Sands? Were you ask me, my Princess with the soft eyes, for Oriah or Nynfa, for voyages without end, I would be able to give them to you—because, for you, save for combating the black spirit of death, nothing seems impossible for me."

Nyve looked at her friend as a little girl of legend admires a marvelous fairy, but she replied, not without a certain malice: "It's much easier to do, and you'll have nothing to regret. The Queen won't reproach you for having said yes. You see, Nevea, and now, obey me if you love me!"

For once, the blonde virgin, descendant of a hard race, understood that it is sweet to yield when the heart alone commands. "I will obey!" she said.

"You will not leave without my accompanying you—for I tremble at your danger. At least, if misfortune arrives, we shall depart together for the land of the Goddess."

"What are you saying?" Hertha exclaimed. "I have only my life to lose. I am justified in having lived, now, for it was not in vain—but you support a realm."

"I believed so," said Nyve, "but I believe it less. You have upset the universe in which I was complacent. What is Nirvanir, what is Drymea, in the infinity that you described?"

"To think thus, you are equal to your position. You bear heavy responsibilities, but you must and you can be worthy of them. You will see, as it was written in my world, the stars 'snowing' in the skies. You know that."

"Nevea, who has revealed so much to me, and who speaks to me of eternity, I would like to hear about the sweetness of your world. It must exist. You have shown me its dark and cold side, its harsh power, its inhuman science that guided you, and that you did not guide, although it was yours—but nothing of its heart.

"You have told me about wealth, knowledge, the actions of your companions, but how strange they seem to me. Some were friends, faithful auxiliaries, but none was able to love you. Out there, however, you must have encountered gentle virgins. Does there ever exist among you, daughters of a powerful and icy world, profound gazes, caressing hands and words more caressing still? Tresses that mingle when one hears a sincere heart beating? You have never told me about such things. Nevea, Nevea, have you ever loved?"

Lord! Thought Hertha. *I have never loved. Nyve is right without knowing it, but in her ignorance, what is she asking me?*

"People also love on my world," she said, "but my life was submissive to cold reason. I had seen too many faces while too young. I set before my eyes a model that overstretched my will. Glacial intelligence ruled my heart. I loved the vast world, I served duty, and chose no one. I was two years older than you when I arrived in Kartha, where my sister reigned. I became a piece of the machine of State. Add ambition, work and pride. You cannot imagine the rigid mechanism that we constructed: hard and just, in which everyone turned her wheel. That realm, regarded as a model, we submitted to iron regulation. Implacable organization, precise efficiency, bleak equity. I judge Drymea better! Many lies deceive naïve hearts. The wicked mingle with the good on my cruel Earth. You know how unfortunates and innocent children were dying of poverty."

"I don't understand," said Nyve. "Your science, so great, your machines, so industrious—what purpose did that serve? Your land produced everything; you had tamed it. Why the poverty of humans amid the wealth of humankind?"

"We had not tamed our hearts. Power belonged to a few. They did not want to and could not produce anything except for those who were able to exchange with them. The most useless objects were fabricated for the rich who wanted them, but in famished countries, the wheat was stolen to sell to others. Nyve with the soft eyes, you cannot believe that—but it was so."

"You also spoke to me about the Goddess with the welcoming arms worshipped by your white race. She ordered you to love one another, to forgive one another's sins. Now, I only see queens or subjects obedient to those precepts. You have translated for us the book of your Goddess, which your sister of Earth gave to you. You do what she wishes—but what of the others?"

"Alas," said Hertha, "there were temples and priestesses in multitudes, but those who believed in the Goddess—for many refused to worship her—served her with their mouths, not their hearts. Rich people and queens, for a thousand years and more, spilled blood while justifying themselves in her name. In my childhood, in the Occident, innocent multitudes were sacrificed to the ambition of the few. Those who caused their deaths said to their people: *The Goddess is with us; she approves this murder!* Or they talked about right and justice, faces of the veiled Being. If some did not want to obey and shed the blood of others, the queens and the powerful had them tried by judges who always condemned them to death. Wickedness governed for years; goodness and sincerity were not the stronger. The mouth said yes, the heart said no."

Nyve shivered. "I understand that your world had expelled you because you were too good. But on death, will you go to your Goddess, and I to mine? Will we be separated for eternity?"

Hertha was momentarily amused. She became serious again in order to reply. "You worship the veiled Being, sincerely. But the Goddess with the welcoming arms said: 'In my Mother's house, there are many mansions.' Yours will receive me, if I merit it. Banish all anxiety, little Princess of dreams. In the Infinite reigns the Unique!"

In the clear warm night, Hertha wondered whether Prince Charming might not have given better answers than her to the Princess's questions—but it was as well that he had not come.

Would the child with the soft eyes have understood him? Son of a hard-hearted race, would he not have broken her?

VIII. Northwards

"You've told me tales of your world," said Nyve. "I know why you like to call me your Princess with the soft eyes; it reminds you of your childhood and your dreams: a thousand images of beauty, devotion and generosity, more brilliant than Earth and Drymea, for your soul has no limits."

"I do indeed, my Princess, put many ideas into those words. I think about your future grandeur. Beautiful Nirvanir will name you its queen, and I shall serve you beside your white throne."

Once again, they were as they had been on Nyve's birthday, before the already-distant departure into the realm. Gazing at pale Oriah, Nyve said: "I think that I might call you my distant and charming Princess, you who have taught me so much about the heavens and worlds, of yours and even of mine. Listen to my question. Do people in your world love as we do in Nirvanir? You must know that, Nevea, and yet, you never loved there—you would have told me, for you love me too much to deceive me. Even your dark Helen, your faithful friend, was not your beloved. No one was your beloved!"

No, Hertha thought, *not one.*

"But on Drymea, I am your Nyve with the soft eyes. I know that, for your soul shines brightly for me. You are my strength and my joy, you lift me higher by your gaze alone. I am not taking into consideration what you have done for Drymea, for Nirvanir, for me. I see only Nevea, who gives. You feel no difficulty or burden on my account, and do not excuse yourself the impossible. You would kill yourself for me! Compared with Nevea, I am weak and unarmed, but you bend to my smile, except when you want something better for me than I do. I can say, however, that I am not looking for anything in you, for then I would love you less. You sometimes call me daughter of Eden, the garden of innocence—but would your world have been able to love you like your Princess of the soft eyes, since it pleases you to name me thus?"

Hertha replied slowly: "There are few on Earth who know what you know. The majority are egotists. They love themselves in the beloved, not her. There is often a disturbing element of strength and tyranny, or personal pleasure, mingled in terrestrial amours. More than half of the inhabitants of my Earth, on my departure, knew domination rather than love. It is difficult for me to explain clearly a planet different in its souls—for you ought not to judge the others by me. Nyve, Drymea is worth more in terms of love than the Earth."

After that judgment, there was a silence.

In truth, Hertha thought, *Nyve has spoken to me as amour would have spoken to me on my world, But there is no abyss her between amour and amity. Among us, the amorous couple breaks friendship for others, and sometimes itself. Why are there frontiers between sentiments? The crushing crown on the head of old Eros has dazzled everyone. But I ought not to dream about the past. Here, friendship is lifelong, if desired. Are you right, little Princess? Would I have found a heart equal to yours on Earth? Since the Azure Isle, I have promised to forget. In my strange adventure, of which my youth never dreamed, I must act according to the law of Drymea, and Nyve will be the only amour of my life. Of the two of us, one will be happy according to the avowal of her race!*

Then, on the tenebrous sea, fires appeared: ships with two lights, red and green. Abruptly, a beam shot into the sky, and another; then the luminous beams fell back and began to search the shore. Momentarily, it passed over Hertha and Nyve.

"There are...ten," the blonde woman counted. "They are responding, gladly, to the call of the sea."

"My beloved," said Nyve, with a smile, "you have not had confidence in me. Come on—I understand your silence! You have built palaces under the sea to please me. You have launched your flying machines into the air—Aeracs, as you call them. You have not forgotten Flormal and its blue islands.

You have been working for us. Inert matter has been better educated to obey us. But I see your eyes fix upon the horizon. Your race still lives in your heart. You have not said anything, however, because you fear for me. Those ships, the best in Nirvanir, await your orders, along with your *Seagull*. The Queen consents to your departure—and mine! These days at sea will be my repose."

Hertha's heart swelled with tenderness. She kissed Nyve's forehead gently.

Ten days later, they were heading northwards. The Misty Isles received the fleet in their harbors with squat edifices, under the winds of three seas. They were dependencies of Rovenar, a continental realm. Wars and harsh scourges had not driven human migration, and their inhabitants were not numerous. Everyone was astonished to see the southern princess on the waves, solely for the sake of adventure.

The fresh and limitless sea, the foamy wakes, the long miles that the ships devoured; the pilots no longer knew the route. Hertha's companions searched her eyes. Her finger pointed northwards.

She had anticipated the cold and ice. No one aboard had suffered from the slow lowering of the temperature, but there had been no sign of snow. The air inflated the captain's breast, with rediscovered joy. The horizon was ringed by waves and the journey had extended for days while the lookouts wearied their sleepless eyes. Finally, one of them shouted: "Land!"

Gradually, a vast coast extended, which seemed to have emerged from the waters the day before. The horizon swallowed up florid steppes. The islets were dark with woods. A lazy river opened up. The ships sailed up it. The daughters of Nirvanir smiled at that land of which they had never dared to dream, sprung from the legendary, unlimited, sterile ocean.

After long miles, a cataract blocked the route. The vast majesty of inhuman, snowy mountains appeared. For the first time, Drymean eyes rested on summits blue-tinted by ice.

They anchored in the river, and for several days they explored the land around the cataract. Beneath the white sun, pink snows could be distinguished, and distant valleys filled with blue tints. When Oriah or Nynfa poured forth their cold light in the silver dusk, it became an entire landscape of dream and legend. On the Polar Continent, an eternal spring reigned as far as the foothills of the mountains.

A frozen lake reflected the distant landscape, leagues away. On the plateaux, Hertha felt the days of her childhood return. A little further, the North!

She said to Nyve: "You have done more than I hope, my Princess of dreams. Let me go on alone, to be alone out there before the sky and the mountains. That lake will receive the Aerac I brought on my *Seagull*. There's nothing to fear: I shall go straight ahead!"

"You may go," Nyve conceded. "It seems to me that in the mountains of this terrible land, the arm of another would be a welcome support—but your motives are always good. Come back quickly."

A few minutes later, Hertha left. The flowery steppes flew by, the lake became enormous. A transparent mirror of water, it reflected a bleak solitude. Hertha knew once again the absence of living individuals. An immensity of plateaux and an infinite extent of brutal stone surrounded her, mounting toward the North. No greenery; just ricks and dormant waters. Solitary peaks bristled. She left the Aerac moored to the bank, and went on.

After a long march, a marine horizon, masked until then, was suddenly revealed: a frightful and monotonous landscape; bare walls plunging steeply into the silent waves. And when the silver dusk came, beneath the cold moons, Hertha could have believed herself to be on another planet. Beneath the motionless sky a dead world surrounded her. The mountains loomed over her, pitilessly. She had the impression, in a silence so overwhelming that she thought she could hear it, of a hostile, crushing, dark omnipotence. Thus might be imagined the great infinity of space is which all life is erased, in which the Stars die!

For two days she remained in that silent land. Alone, she was able to meditate on others and herself, review her past, contemplate the future. Twenty times over she was haunted by Invisible Presences, so close that she sometimes felt a frisson, as if someone were looking over her shoulder. Voices whispered in her heart: *This continent sprang from the waves during our long voyage. Nothing exists here yet but plants and us, free spirits. Hertha, in driving the prows of your ships northwards, you have gained a thousand years for Drymea. A vigorous race will be launched on this soil when you reign here! In these mountains metals lie dormant that Drymea does not know, but which exist! Hertha, you have not lived in vain. Accept this proof as a necessary step.*

She bowed her proud head, but she also saw the proud summit that it was necessary for her to reach. She accepted all the burdens. Tempered and pure, like steel, she drove her Aerac upwards into the sky. A part of the Continent was reflected in her eyes, an emerald ocean with broad rivers, a rising mass of somber plateaux The mountains in the continent's center were dazzling in the golden sunlight; the distant sea was like a blue ribbon.

Then she steered toward her goal, landed on the waves, and was received as if she had brought back its very soul. For a long moment Nyve looked at Hertha, calm and silent in the serenity rising up in her clear eyes. "Nevea," she said, "you have seen your Goddess up there in the mountains. I know your gaze, which I have mingled so many times with mine, and you have seen more than we can."

"Her throne is not of this world, and no one can see her face to face—but perhaps I have heard her counsel, in the Solitude."

While exploring the Continent, Hertha convinced herself that, thanks to the southern currents, the two suns, and the very slight inclination of Drymea's axis, the temperature was similar to that of our temperate regions, save for the mountains. Its surface represented several million square miles, lakes mingling with the steppes, and a warm arm of the sea penetrating as far as the plateaux.

I shall rediscover the cold landscapes of my childhood higher up, Hertha thought, but if my body is young, my mind is a thousand years old. I have, in truth, passed through death. It would be easy for me to await the other awakening, when the hour will sound that only comes once to everyone.

IX. The Years Pass

Drymea has orbited the golden sun, gently balanced in the double light, nine times since Hertha's arrival. Her work has spread through the 37 realms, and continues, extending ever further. To millions of souls she has brought joy and beauty. But what of Hertha?

Hertha is leaning, this golden evening, on the terrace of her palace. Built in black granite, it overlooks the Blue River of the pole. All that she can see is hers. Everything that lives, works and thinks, from one end of the polar continent to the other, is obedient to her law. Although her subjects know her name, they usually call her the Helmeted Queen—for, always clad in somber leather, beneath the great white cloak that undulates around her, the queen with the pale face travels her continent at a rapid pace, by land or water, in a low helmet with a narrow circle of gold. The blonde virgin has risen as high as a mortal can.

The discovery of the new Continent has resounded through the 37 realms. The greatest power that exists on Drymea, the Council of Queens, which brings together those of the pale north and the bronzed south, has awarded Hertha the sovereignty of the unknown realm, by right of discovery. Queen Nacrysa proposed it, Drythea and Rheeve offered their support. The Council approved. This time, Hertha accepted the burden of command and the golden crown—for it was not a matter of enjoying the labor of generations, but of being the captain of a human conquest.

In the port of Nyverel—Nyve's city, the capital—at the foot of the palace, a large vessel gleams, with scarlet sails and hull. The queen with the ardent eyes, beside the blonde queen, thinks: *In its somber beauty, Nyverel rivals Nirvanir or Manharvar.*

"Nevea," she says, "day by day and month by month, your cities grow. Every realm sends you its subjects. In truth, they are living in a beautiful tale, under your law. Your knowledge and your power serve their happiness. I still cannot hope to understand them, but what are your thoughts?"

"Before coming to this harmonious world," Hertha says, "I acquired a bitter knowledge. Nevertheless, it gives me the love of those who depend on me. I always rise to raise them up. I pray for success."

"Yes," Drythea replies, "They say, even in Lisfer: in the polar realm, Queen Nevea can lie down in the most bitter solitude! She opens her eyes to find a devoted court in her safekeeping. But I also see you, motionless or launched in rapid movement, thinking, seeking and working for our realm. Your beauty charmed me once, the your will, your vast intelligence. Now, I'm astonished by your generosity, which is all-inclusive. It seems that for years, a vast horizon has been growing before your eyes."

The Red Queen, whom Nevea has made better, continues: "And yet I know what terrible depths there are in your soul. Your strength is immense; you have limited your power but in a crisis, your people turn to you, who can do anything. On our organization you superimpose the endless possibilities of your science. You unite everything into a whole, which is you. Your fleets sail for Lisfer, your great aircraft display their hulls in every realm. Your captains have discovered the pole of the thousand lakes, on the far side of Drymea. On isles once unknown your flag flies. Everywhere, eyes watch out for you. And you encircle the world with such a network, at your orders, that the 16 auditors of Nyverel have fingers in every land. A tempest may form in Lisfer, a volcano erupt at the south pole, a cliff collapse in the realm of Sands, and the 16 are aware of it in Nyverel—and they inform Drymea! You have saved many lives at sea, Nevea, now that our ships are bolder. Colossus of power, Nevea, your three realms—Flormal and the Ocean Isles, the Sands of Kartha and this one—encircle us!"

"You said to me once, Drythea: I will leave you my beautiful Manharvar. Do you think that my three realms are not enough to crush me? Fortunately, your daughter has been born—for I am responsible for the good that I do not do and the evil, if any, that I cannot help doing. Crowns are heavy, to judge by these."

"Responsible to whom?" said Drythea. "Your people love you and you are the equal of the queens. Above your head there is nothing but the veiled Goddess—who is indulgent."

"We differ, then," said Hertha, smiling. "You have seen the Temple that I have built, in honor of the One, Being with the welcoming arms or Veiled Goddess. When I a judged, I will not be as tranquil as you, for I know that I am the daughter of a redoubtable world."

"I know that, Nevea. If you wished, your unleashed force could crush Drymea. I'm not afraid, my friend, for you would defend me from yourself. But I know that south of Nyverel, there is a weakness before which your strength bends. Although there are moments in the Council of Queens when you, who see two worlds, could overturn Drymea with your hand, I know that during the months when you read your duty in the eyes of your Princess, for a third of the year, Nyve is queen in Nyverel."

The Red Queen went on: After all, "you're right. The Princess with the soft eyes is the best of us. You charm her still, but she remains herself, no longer a reflection of your thought."

That evening, according to her custom when she was resident in Nyverel, the queen received the young women who had reached their 16th year. For a week, they are welcomed by her in the virgins' palace. From all over the realm, they are able to know her, and their queen is no bleak abstraction for their young eyes.

The short night was about to begin. Sleep, after the day's work, was imminent for Hertha. The visit of the virgins of her State would not disturb her.

They appeared, their garments embroidered with flowers or birds undulating over their supple bodies. They surrounded the queen and took their places at her feet, on cushions. On Hertha's orders, cups of perfumed beverages were brought, sparkling with jewels. They interrogated her gently. They had no fear under that profound gaze, which contemplated two worlds.

Suddenly, the Red Queen reappeared. "Nevea," she said, "someone is suffering in your Palace of Virgins. I sensed it when I got back to my ship."

"Yes," the young women admitted, "one of us is not here. In spite of her pain and ours, she did not wish to come, for Mynia does not dare appear before your eyes."

The great queen stood up. "Thank you, Drythea, for alerting me. One of you take me to Mynia. Renhea, would you like to take these young women to the dining hall."

"Child," said the queen, when she found herself before a small melancholy form, half-hidden among the flowers of a reception room, "I had to come to you, for you do not dare to come to the Queen. Come, tell me your name."

In that thin, asymmetrical face, devoured by dark hair, there was nothing beautiful but the large gleaming eyes, full of an intense life.

I've seen them before, Hertha thought.

After the feast, she interrogated her on the terrace of Nyverel, from which she liked to look at the suns, the stars and the sea.

"I've seen you before, Mynia, but when? I have read it in your eyes."

"Do you remember, Queen, the little girl who came on to the shore in the Summer Land, before your departure? You seemed to me so wise and so beautiful. Everyone was talking about you. I was little then, and no longer had a mother, but you were able to take notice of me. I couldn't understand all the light in your words, but it gave me such great joy to listen to you, go be near to you! Then you left us."

Her words flew into the darkness. Hertha listened, silently. "You wanted to come to my realm to see the Nevea of yesteryear again, as queen?"

"But I did not dare," sighed the child, "for back then, you were close to me, and here, your triple crown frightens me more than the others. For no one, I know, fears your eyes."

"Do you trust me, Mynia, and can you obey me—now that you know that Nevea has not been forgotten by the queen?"

"I will obey you until death," said Mynia.

"Death does not belong to queens, and you are wrong to say that, Mynia, but I know your intentions are good. Will you tell me your dreams and desires, known only to the Goddess? I can understand a great deal, for I have known suffering. I can forgive more and perhaps clarify more than a Drymean, for I have a double experience."

In the bilunar night, the soft voice whispered, becoming bolder and louder. The Helmeted Queen listened, smiling or gravely. Suddenly, she said: "Mynia, let me review times gone by."

A summer evening in her 20th year, during a voyage to France, her mother's homeland, on the terraces of Versailles, following a day that had soothed her hear. The intoxicating music of a celebrated orchestra; eminent men seen at the home of Tertius, her half-brother, the ambassador of Liberty, who made a fuss of her. That morning had brought her a book from Kartha, *Tales of the North*, a collection she had assembled for schools, with graceful illustrations. Flattering comments had accompanied it. The evening brought lively intellectual pleasures among selected friends. Now, in a beautiful setting, Hertha was listening to the evocative words of the novelist Tarol, and people were crowding around here. Very beautiful, rich, and the stepsister of two heads of State, and also well-educated, it was felt that she might dignify a life, and, once her heart as given, remain a faithful friend through good and bad times. In the middle of an eloquent sentence, a sickly little girl came forward and handed Hertha a bouquet of common flowers. But the latter looked at her almost with hostility. It was necessary for her to fall out of her enchanted world to think that the poor exist. The child was sent away, with alms.

That entire scene reappeared before the queen who was Hertha. *Lord,* she thought, *how harsh I was that day. Overburdened with happiness, I did not want to be distracted from it by giving a crumb to another. I could have changed that child's life at a stroke. I had the power to do so! The sin remains. The immense future lies before me, and the lesson will serve me.*

Then she turned back to Mynia. "I was thinking of long ago, before I came to Drymea. Would you like to stay with me? Would you dare? Do you think that I would choose a sterile life for you? You could do something for the benefit of our sisters. The silver sun is rising. Go into the halls of rest, with your companions. I will come soon."

Thus Hertha rediscovered the thoughtful and ugly child, Mynia of Nirvanir.

X. An Act of God, By My Hand

One year, the Helmeted Queen went to the Council of Queens. She left power, during her absence, to the princess heir—because, for two years, Mynia, adopted by the queen, had worn the light diadem of daughters of the royal blood. Happiness and a new life had rendered her pleasant to the eye. She had not forgotten the groups of Nirvanir or the pole that had looked after her as a child, nor her companions. Her affection for Hertha approached adoration, but she did not lose sight of the realm in her clear eyes. She learned to reign, and the younger soul of the queen lived again in her.

Hertha found Nyve and her daughter in Nirvanir; the line of the queens of Nirvanir was continuing. Then, her yacht carried her through Armela toward the profound monuments of Harya, the capital of the central realm and the seat of the Cuncill. It was held during the period of endless days. Even distant Lisfer delegated two crown-bearers to the supreme power of Drymea.

When Hertha arrived, royal ships were already swaying in the transparent canals. Some lifted up swan-like prows, some were elongated like gondolas, and some were decorated with variegated flowers. Drythea deployed a red canopy supported by brightly-colored statues.

"What news is there of your emerald land? Have those of my subjects who have come under your law any regret for my fiery skies?"

"The flight of my machines sets Nyverel and Manharvar only a few days apart. I can only reign over a free people, for them and not for me. Whoever desires may quite my realm immediately. I learned those lessons in lands of silence and solitude, Drythea."

The Red Queen smiled. "Your ideas are beautiful and you believe in others. My daughter does not follow them all. Next year, though, I shall send her to you. Whoever has not yet seen your eyes has not yet lived!"

All the queens knew Hertha. She belonged to Drymean history. As Drythea had said, the world of the two suns sometimes rested in her hand. She took no vanity from her enormous invincible force; it was at the service of other realms.

The Council lasted a fortnight, and the queen with the golden hair left content, having not been useless, followed by the affection of all.

When the nights began, the mistress of the Great Observatory came to Nyverel from the lands of silence, and she told Queen Nevea that her orders had been carried out. A unique sun had been found in the constellation of the Golden Bird, among the closest stars; it corresponded to the queen's indications in color, spectrum and the number of its satellites. It would be visible that very evening. For the optical progress of Drymea had been prodigious, since the day when certain minds had applied themselves to it, initially guided by our science.

When the golden sun set, Hertha, Mynia and Nyve were in the observatory. In the black sky the stars stood out. Then, one of them was slowly magnified as the immense apparatus increased its power—and Hertha recognized her own sun. Another dawn was breaking out there! How many trillion leagues away? Without leaving her position, she asked the question. The response was clear, as her companions gazed at the star where Nevea had been born.

"How far away from us it shines!" said Nyve. "And yet, it seems less strange to me because of you. It is rising in your eyes, Nevea!"

"How the centuries must have embellished your world, Mother," said Mynia, smiling. "But you seem pensive."

Hertha was thoughtful. The route that she had taken from Earth to Drymea she could retrace. On her orders, her three realms could launch a projectile at stellar velocity toward the distant sun. The days and the years would pass over her sleeping body, in the care of vigilant machines. In the outskirts of our system, her thoughts would become lucid again, in order that she might steer toward the Earth. Then she would reappear on the old planet, returned from another world. She was still in the prime of life. The most marvelous of dreams.

But centuries had gone by! That Earth revisited would no longer be her Earth. The races would have changed, and the lands too. Everything gone: languages, cities, memories. Who would reign there now? A stranger, she would find an Earth a thousand times less fraternal than great Drymea. Then again, it would be necessary to tell the story of her voyage. Men with avid hands would try to lead their race to the harmonious world of the two suns. The first arrivals could do no harm, but their sons? They would look at the Drymeans and think about their beauty. Desire might kill them. Would the women of Earth have pity on them? And what effect would that pity have?

Hertha knew the history of her race, and saw an ominous prophecy in the past. No fusion would be possible between the two races. One day, Drymea would rise up as one, with the force of its masses united, body and soul. They had the science of murder in their hands—a few sages, at least, Nyve and Mynia, would have bequeathed it to their descendants. And Drymea would sacrifice, in an infernal war, ten, 20 or 30 million of its inhabitants, in order to be victorious. Now, that might happen, if Hertha returned to Earth—solely because of her, and her egotism. Duty and affection bound her to the world of virgins.

You must stay, her thought commanded. *There are no limits upon souls. You will recover those for whom you weep— beyond the gates!*

She gazed at the attentive Nyve and Mynia. For once, she concealed her thoughts from them, in order not to sadden them.

"I was thinking about my voyage," she said. "It was not in vain, since I found you two at the end of my journey. I have served Drymea. Look at the sun that as mine at your leisure. It is no longer mine now. I am like you, my beloved, a daughter of the two suns. One single heart is worth more than a distant star!"

Three years passed thus. Herttha saw Drythea's daughter beside her, an ardent little creature, red and sometimes so ender that the tall blonde queen could not help smiling. Terrestrial force was in the hands of a better race.

On the morning of a calm night, Hertha felt a sharp pain in her heart, and knew that she was dying. She had suspected it for days. Azrael does not arrive late. She could not deceive death.

As was customary, she brought together the Sages. The auditors informed Queen Nyve—for she had been wearing the crown for several months—and Drythea. Looking back on her life, Hertha knew that the most frightful thing is to have lived in vain, to have left empty a vast frame that one might have filled with thought and action. She bequeathed an achievement to justify her power. Her existence seemed full of enormous happiness. On Earth, her limits would soon have become manifest; on Drymea, things were different. Her duty had been to accept her destiny, for she had acted as the instrument of a higher wisdom.

She did not have to write her last will and testament. Her power had put her thoughts into action. Mynia knew the rest.

The next day, she felt weaker, and pain gnawed at her like a sly beast. She had wanted to die on her feet, but the middle of the day lay her down in her bed, pallid, and the Drymeans understood. They displayed the stars in her high window.

Then Nyve of Nirvanir arrived.

"Thus I would like to die," said Hertha, "before the distant suns. Don't grieve too much. A little time, and we shall see one another again."

In the shadows, she seemed to see the faces of yesteryear mingling with those that surrounded her. The latter could no longer understand her, for in the hour of her death she reverted to the old language of Earth to say: "I have had my destiny. Have I done my duty? An act of God, by my hand…."

Then she regained consciousness, and smiled at Nyve and Mynia, taking hold of their hands.

"When Drythea comes, tell her always to be good. Nacrysa has preceded me. Embrace me for the departure, Nyve— you remember! My beloved…"

As they leaned over the Queen, they saw her eyes become troubled in gazing at the star that they call the Eye of the Gazelle and we call Sirius. Her hands became heavy in theirs.

Thus died, on the 15th day of the Month of Breezes in the Drymean year 5397, Nevea the Helmeted Queen, who had been, on Earth, Hertha Helgar.

Conclusion.
The Final Farewell

Three months later, the High Priestess of Nyverel presented herself to Queen Nyve, bowed, and said: "Queen, my seers have seen Queen Nevea, and she desires your presence."

A few hours later, the enormous temple closed its door on them. The darkness was profound. The priestesses ignited golden vases from which an odorous, flameless smoke rose up. Motionless and silent, Nyve, the Queen with the soft eyes, felt her head spin.

The priestesses were speaking ritual words a thousand years old. Confused images whirled before Nyve's eyes. Long minutes went by. Then a white cloud appeared; it became clearer and its forms became precise enough for Nyve to see Nevea's face beyond a luminous veil—and her smile was full of serenity.

Then a voice became audible in the shadows. The apparition spoke, through a mouth of flesh.

"My Nyve with the soft eyes, my merits and faults have been weighed by infallible Justice. Entry to the eternal Realms has been granted to me. I shall quit Drymea forever—but my prayers have obtained one great favor. Revested in the veil of flesh, I shall live again on Oriah, your second satellite.

"Its inhabitants are voluptuous and harsh, enslaved by their passions. The shadow of their thought would terrify your virgins. Some of them, however, might become better. Through years of struggle, poverty and persecution, I will try to bring light, for I have been permitted to undergo a proof, there, where anything is possible!

"I see your thought, Nyve. We know the secrets of Heaven, and I would be able to prevent Nevea's suffering, up there—but you do not know that the daughters of Nirvanir, under pain of being subject to every outrage, might reign by terror over a corrupt people. I have bequeathed terrible weapons to you and Mynia. A virgin of 16, within the immense war machine that you could build, could scythe down ten million heavily-muscled living individuals in a minute. But blood calls to blood. The contagion of evil poisons the souls of those who reign on Oriah. My destinies must be completed.

"By virtue of a spiritual law unknown on Drymea, I have undertaken in my proof the weight of your sins, for your entire life. They are not very heavy, my Nyve with the soft eyes.

"You are now thinking: *why is Nevea forgetting her beloved daughter?* Mynia has no need of it. She is already worthy of endless recompense, and my burden had been limited.

"When the inevitable hour comes for you, Queen of Nirvanir, the hour when no human will be able to help you, I will have preceded you into death once more, and you will find me welcoming you at the threshold of its gates.

"Then, we shall depart toward a new sun. Mynia will be able to join us there, soon for us but later for her, for time is not the same for spirits as for those living in flesh. The veiled Goddess, the Being with the welcoming arms, will allow me to recover those for whom I weep.

"Do not grieve for my destiny on Oriah. You are hearing me here for the last time; I must depart for my proof. It will be lighter for me because of you, for your soft eyes will console me on Drymea, which is better than the Earth, for love is better here."

Silence fell again, and Nevea vanished into the shadows.

SF & FANTASY

Guy d'Armen. *Doc Ardan: The City of Gold and Lepers*
G.-J. Arnaud. *The Ice Company*
Cyprien Bérard. *The Vampire Lord Ruthwen*
Aloysius Bertrand. *Gaspard de la Nuit*
Richard Bessière. *The Gardens of the Apocalypse*
Félix Bodin. *The Novel of the Future*
André Caroff. *The Terror of Madame Atomos*
Didier de Chousy. *Ignis*
Captain Danrit. *Undersea Odyssey*
C. I. Defontenay. *Star (Psi Cassiopeia)*
Charles Derennes. *The People of the Pole*
Georges Dodds (anthologist). *The Missing Link*
Harry Dickson. *The Heir of Dracula*
Jules Dornay. *Lord Ruthven Begins*
Sâr Dubnotal *vs. Jack the Ripper*
Alexandre Dumas. *The Return of Lord Ruthven*
J.-C. Dunyach. *The Night Orchid; The Thieves of Silence*
Henri Duvernois. *The Man Who Found Himself*
Achille Eyraud. *Voyage to Venus*
Henri Falk. *The Age of Lead*
Paul Féval. *Anne of the Isles; Knightshade; Revenants; Vampire City;
The Vampire Countess; The Wandering Jew's Daughter*
Paul Féval, *fils. Felifax, the Tiger-Man*
Charles de Fieux. *Lamékis*
Arnould Galopin. *Doctor Omega*
G.L. Gick. *Harry Dickson and the Werewolf of Rutherford Grange*
Nathalie Henneberg. *The Green Gods*
V. Hugo, P. Foucher & P. Meurice. *The Hunchback of Notre-Dame*
Michel Jeury. *Chronolysis*
Octave Joncquel & Theo Varlet. *The Martian Epic*
Gérard Klein. *The Mote in Time's Eye*
Jean de La Hire. *Enter the Nyctalope; The Nyctalope on Mars; The
Nyctalope vs. Lucifer*
André Laurie. *Spiridon*
Gabriel de Lautrec. *The Vengeance of the Oval Portrait*
Georges Le Faure & Henri de Graffigny. *The Extraordinary Adventures of a Russian Scientist Across the Solar System* (2 vols.)
Gustave Le Rouge. *The Vampires of Mars*

Jules Lermina. *Mysteryville; Panic in Paris; To-Ho and the Gold Destroyers; The Secret of Zippelius*
Jean-Marc & Randy Lofficier. *Edgar Allan Poe on Mars; The Katrina Protocol; Pacifica; Robonocchio; Tales of the Shadowmen 1-7*
Xavier Mauméjean. *The League of Heroes*
John-Antoine Nau. *Enemy Force*
Marie Nizet. *Captain Vampire*
C. Nodier, A. Beraud & Toussaint-Merle. *Frankenstein*
Henri de Parville. *An Inhabitant of the Planet Mars*
J. Polidori, C. Nodier, E. Scribe. *Lord Ruthven the Vampire*
P.-A. Ponson du Terrail. *The Vampire and the Devil's Son*
Maurice Renard. *The Blue Peril; Doctor Lerne; The Doctored Man; A Man Among the Microbes; The Master of Light*
Albert Robida. *The Adventures of Saturnin Farandoul; The Clock of the Centuries; Chalet in the Sky*
J.-H. Rosny Aîné. *Helgvor of the Blue River; The Givreuse Enigma; The Mysterious Force; The Navigators of Space; Vamireh; The World of the Variants; The Young Vampire*
Han Ryner. *The Superhumans*
Brian Stableford. *The New Faust at the Tragicomique;The Empire of the Necromancers (The Shadow of Frankenstein; Frankenstein and the Vampire Countess; Frankenstein in London); Sherlock Holmes & The Vampires of Eternity; The Stones of Camelot; The Wayward Muse.* (anthologist) *The Germans on Venus; News from the Moon; The Supreme Progress; The World Above the World*
Jacques Spitz. *The Eye of Purgatory*
Kurt Steiner. *Ortog*
Eugène Thébault. *Radio-Terror*
Villiers de l'Isle-Adam. *The Scaffold; The Vampire Soul*
Philippe Ward. *Artahe*
Philippe Ward & Sylvie Miller. *The Song of Montségur*

MYSTERIES & THRILLERS

M. Allain & P. Souvestre. *The Daughter of Fantômas*
A. Anicet-Bourgeois, Lucien Dabril. *Rocambole*
A. Bisson & G. Livet. *Nick Carter vs. Fantômas*
V. Darlay & H. de Gorsse. *Lupin vs. Holmes: The Stage Play*
Paul Féval. *Gentlemen of the Night; John Devil; The Black Coats ('Salem Street; The Invisible Weapon; The Parisian Jungle; The Companions of the Treasure; Heart of Steel; The Cadet Gang)*

Emile Gaboriau. *Monsieur Lecoq*
Steve Leadley. *Sherlock Holmes: The Circle of Blood*
Maurice Leblanc. *Arsène Lupin vs. Countess Cagliostro; Lupin vs.
Holmes (The Blonde Phantom; The Hollow Needle)*
Gaston Leroux. *Chéri-Bibi; The Phantom of the Opera; Rouletabille
& the Mystery of the Yellow Room*
William Patrick Maynard. *The Terror of Fu Manchu*
Frank J. Morlock. *Sherlock Holmes: The Grand Horizontals*
P. de Wattyne & Y. Walter. *Sherlock Holmes vs. Fantômas*
David White. *Fantômas in America*

SCREENPLAYS

Mike Baron. *The Iron Triangle*
Emma Bull & Will Shetterly. *Nightspeeder; War for the Oaks*
Gerry Conway & Roy Thomas. *Doc Dynamo*
Steve Englehart. *Majorca*
James Hudnall. *The Devastator*
Jean-Marc & Randy Lofficier. *Royal Flush*
J.-M. & R. Lofficier & Marc Agapit. *Despair*
Andrew Paquette. *Peripheral Vision*
R. Thomas, J. Hendler & L. Sprague de Camp. *Rivers of Time*

NON-FICTION

Stephen R. Bissette. *Blur 1-5; Green Mountain Cinema 1; Teen An-
gels & New Mutants*
Win Scott Eckert. *Crossovers* (2 vols.)
Jean-Marc & Randy Lofficier. *Shadowmen* (2 vols.)
Randy Lofficier. *Over Here*

ART BOOKS

Jean-Pierre Normand. *Science Fiction Illustrations*
Raven Okeefe. *Raven's L'il Critters*
Randy Lofficier & Raven OKeefe. *If Your Possum Go Daylight...*
Daniele Serra. *Illusions*

HEXAGON COMICS

Franco Frescura & Luciano Bernasconi. *Wampus*
Franco Frescura & Giorgio Trevisan. *CLASH*
L. Bernasconi, J.-M. Lofficier & Juan Roncagliolo Berger. *Phenix*
Claude Legrand, J.-M. Lofficier & L. Bernasconi. *Kabur*
Franco Oneta. *Zembla*
L. Buffolente, Lofficier & J.-J. Dzialowski. *Strangers: Homicron*
Danilo Grossi. *Strangers: Jaydee*
Claude Legrand & Luciano Bernasconi. *Strangers: Starlock*

www.ingramcontent.com/pod-product-compliance
Lightning Source LLC
Chambersburg PA
CBHW060420030726
47495CB00003B/658